CW01645598

# Go Home Birdie Brown

Laura Blake is a Birmingham-based writer of English and Jamaican descent. She has a master's degree in Literary Studies from Aberystwyth University.

Her short fiction has been shortlisted for the Floella Benjamin Writing Prize, the Leicester Writes Short Story Competition, the London Independent Story Prize and the George Floyd Short Story Competition. Birdie Brown first appeared in a short story entitled 'Home Is Not Here', which was shortlisted for the 4th Estate and Guardian 4thWrite Prize.

*Go Home Birdie Brown* is Laura's debut novel.

# Go Home Birdie Brown

Laura Blake

HarperCollins*Publishers*

HarperCollins*Publishers* Ltd
1 London Bridge Street
London SE1 9GF

www.harpercollins.co.uk

HarperCollins*Publishers*
Macken House, 39/40 Mayor Street Upper
Dublin 1, D01 C9W8, Ireland

First published by HarperCollins*Publishers* Ltd 2026
1

Copyright © Laura Blake 2026

Epigraph from 'The Death of Joy Gardner' by Benjamin Zephaniah, reproduced with the kind permission of Bloodaxe Books.

Laura Blake asserts the moral right to be identified as the author of this work.

A catalogue record for this book is available from the British Library.

ISBN: 978-0-00-877586-5 (HB)

This novel is entirely a work of fiction. The names, characters and incidents portrayed in it are the work of the author's imagination. Any resemblance to actual persons, living or dead, events or localities is entirely coincidental.

Set in Sabon LT Std by HarperCollins*Publishers* India

Printed and bound in the UK using 100%
Renewable Electricity at CPI Group (UK) Ltd

All rights reserved. No part of this publication may be reproduced, stored in a retrieval system, or transmitted, in any form or by any means, electronic, mechanical, photocopying, recording or otherwise, without the prior written permission of the publishers.

Without limiting the exclusive rights of any author, contributor or the publisher of this publication, any unauthorised use of this publication to train generative artificial intelligence (AI) technologies is expressly prohibited. HarperCollins also exercise their rights under Article 4(3) of the Digital Single Market Directive 2019/790 and expressly reserve this publication from the text and data mining exception.

FSC
www.fsc.org
MIX
Paper | Supporting responsible forestry
FSC® C013604

*For my grandparents*

She's illegal, so deport her
Said the Empire that brought her.

– 'The Death of Joy Gardner',
Benjamin Zephaniah

# One

## *2016*

Birdie Brown sat on a metal bench and stared at the clock on the wall, paying little mind to the sweat pooling into her elasticated waistband, the ache in her tired legs or the numbness of her backside. The second hand swept around the face of the clock, another minute to add to the sixty-seven she had already spent waiting, one minute for every year of her life. The letter had warned that lateness would not be tolerated, so she'd made sure to arrive ten minutes early, out of breath from hot-footing it from the bus stop. But in the end, she had rushed for nothing.

'Take a ticket and get in line,' the security guard at the door told her.

'I have an appointment,' she said, fishing the letter out of her handbag. 'I'm a little early—'

'Take a ticket. Get in line.'

She put the letter back in her handbag and took a pink paper ticket from a dispenser. Then she joined a queue that filed into a waiting room and found an empty spot along a bench. Then she waited. The letter had said nothing about waiting.

To: Ms Bridget L. Brown,

NOTICE OF UNLAWFUL IMMIGRATION

You are a person with no leave to enter or remain in the United Kingdom. You have not given any reasons as to why you should be granted leave to remain. Therefore, you are liable for removal to Jamaica.

Please report to your local Immigration Reporting Office (Solihull) on 24th August 2016, at 11 a.m. Failure to do so could result in your immediate removal from the UK.

It was some kind of mistake. Had to be. The letter had been sent to the wrong Bridget Brown, perhaps. Or maybe she was a victim of identity theft, and some unscrupulous so-and-so was gadding about using her name to shirk accountability for their misdeeds. Either way, it wasn't *her* they were after. She had called up the number at the top of the letter to tell them so, but the person at the other end of the telephone had invited her to hold her questions until her appointment, reiterating the importance of her attendance.

'You don't understand, I'm trying to tell you you've made a mistake—'

'Ma'am, I am afraid I cannot discuss the details of your case. This number is for enquiries only.'

'I *am* enquiring,' she'd said hotly, wondering why, in this day and age, people had to make things so complicated. 'I'm *enquiring* as to why I've been sent this letter.'

'Please refer to your letter for your appointment date and time. Will that be all today? If you need another department I can transfer you—'

'Will another department be able to answer my questions?'

There was a slight pause, then the voice said, 'Thank you for calling UK Visas and Immigration,' and hung up.

'Well thank you too,' Birdie said to the dial tone. She supposed that an entity as large as the British government had its own way of doing things, however backwards, so she'd better just attend the appointment like they wanted her to. And she reckoned it'd be easier to get things cleared up in a face-to-face interview, too.

Only there was no interview. Just waiting.

The waiting room had not been designed with the comfort of its temporary inhabitants in mind. Fluorescent lights cast a sickly pallor over the dirty-white walls. At one end was a long counter, where dim figures moved and stretched and yawned behind a thick sheet of glass, and at the other end was the door, where she had been herded through a metal detector by the sour-faced security guard who had been overly thorough in checking her handbag. He'd reminded her of the nightclub bouncers of her youth, the ones with strict instructions to limit the number of black patrons they granted entry to lest the establishment obtained a *reputation*.

She wiggled on the bench, trying to coax a little feeling back into her bottom. In an effort to make a good first impression, she was wearing her best skirt, a floral-patterned blouse from Marks & Spencer (purchased at a charity shop for only £2) and the good pair of shoes she wore to funerals. They were rubbing her bunions. She was wedged between a woman bickering with her chaperone in hushed Mandarin, and a pale, twitchy man with dark rings around his eyes. She could smell aftershave, and body odour, and Chinese food; the woman had retrieved a stuffed Tupperware container from a carrier bag with a defiant air, despite the remonstrations of her chaperone.

Birdie admired her foresight. All she had to sustain herself was a fluffy breath mint stuck to the bottom of her handbag. She made a mental note to tell – well, whoever it was she was here to see – that they really ought to install a coffee machine in the waiting room. And comfier seats, while they were at it.

'*Ticket number eighty-three to window three, please. Ticket number eighty-three*—'

The young man to her left exhaled and vacated the bench.

Birdie's ticket was number one hundred and thirteen.

'Come on, Dad.' A pretty young woman, with white and purple braids that fell to her waist, was heading towards the now vacant space, gently leading an older man by his elbow. Birdie crossed her legs in order to make more room, her knees groaning in protest, and the woman smiled gratefully.

'*Ticket number ninety-one to window one, please. Ticket number ninety-one*—'

Birdie sighed. She was definitely going to miss the lunchtime special bingo session. She couldn't text her friend Nancy and ask that one of the Bingo Babs buy her books for the mid-afternoon madness session either, because her phone had been confiscated by the security guard. There was nothing to do but wait for her number to be called and wonder what everyone else in the room had done to warrant their removal from the country. You heard about it all the time – people outstaying their visas and tourists taking advantage of the NHS and foreigners taking up hospital beds and prison cells. The country was at breaking point, apparently. The papers had been full of it all summer long, culminating in a vote that was supposedly going to take back control of the country's borders.

But Birdie wasn't like *those* people. She wasn't an illegal immigrant, out to fleece the British taxpayer for all she could. She'd been born a citizen of the British Empire and she'd had to waste an entire morning to remind the government that she was one of their own.

*'Ticket number one hundred to window seven, please. Ticket number one hundred—'*

Beside her, the woman was remonstrating quietly with her father. She repeated that he had to sit tight, that they could leave as soon as he'd been seen. He didn't understand. Why couldn't he just go home?

'I told you, Dad. We just need to wait here until we're called.'

'You tell them that I've had enough. Does your mother know about this? I warned you – you can't just treat a person this way and expect them to go along with it—'

The woman touched him gently on the arm. 'I know, Dad.'

Birdie shifted uncomfortably. It couldn't be helped, but she felt as though she were eavesdropping on a private conversation. She reached into her handbag for a distraction and pulled out a notebook. She could get started on her Christmas list. Though it was only August, she liked to plan ahead – her pension would only stretch so far and she had five grandchildren to spoil.

'For God's sake, Dad!'

With a sudden, garbled grunt, the old man shoved his daughter and she ricocheted into Birdie's shoulder. Birdie dropped her notebook, her pen skittering across the floor and out of view, and the woman let go of the bulging cardboard folder that had been resting in her lap. Sheets of paper fluttered through the air like confetti.

'I'm so sorry,' the woman gasped. She sank to her knees and handed Birdie her notebook (the pen vanished forever) and then began to gather up the papers.

'Do you need help?'

'No, it's fine. I can manage.'

Birdie watched awkwardly as the woman swept the papers into a haphazard pile and reclaimed her seat on the bench, her shoulders stooping forward.

'He's – he gets confused,' she muttered beneath her breath, so quietly that Birdie struggled to hear. 'He doesn't understand what's happening . . .'

She closed her eyes for a second, then shook her head and set to work putting the sheets of paper back in order, her braids falling across her face. Birdie wanted to say that she understood, but in her experience, words didn't mean very much.

'Oh.' A loose sheet of paper was resting against Birdie's too-tight shoe. 'You missed one.'

Birdie bent at the waist, her soft stomach digging into her waistband and her fingers grasping for an official-looking letter typed on thick, white paper. The words jumped off the page.

I can confirm that John Myland emigrated to the United Kingdom from Barbados in 1967 and was enrolled at St Chad's Primary School until he graduated in 1971.

'What's this?'

The woman glanced up. 'It's a letter from his old school. Part of his evidence.'

'Evidence?'

'You know – the proof that he's been here since childhood.'

A terrible sense of foreboding prickled down Birdie's back.

'I've got bank statements, national insurance payments, school records—' the woman took the piece of paper from Birdie's hand and slotted it back in the folder. 'Although his secondary school doesn't exist anymore – it was bulldozed and paved over in the nineties. But that shouldn't matter. At least, I hope it won't—'

'I don't understand,' Birdie said slowly. 'Why do you need to prove he's been here since childhood?'

'Because if I can't they'll deport him.'

'Why? What did he do?'

The woman stiffened.

'Do? He hasn't *done* anything. Look at him. He's not a *criminal*.'

John Myland was fiddling with his wedding ring and staring at a spot on the ceiling, his face placid, his earlier outburst forgotten.

'He moved here in the sixties with his uncle – *legally*, he had a passport and everything – but they're saying he's an illegal immigrant. They want to send him back.'

'But why? Why would they say that?'

'I don't know.'

The woman tapped on the folder with a fingernail that had been chewed to the quick.

'But that's what all this is for. Proof he's been here since he was eight. Proof he didn't sneak in on the back of a boat. Hopefully it's enough to convince that lot.' She jerked her head angrily towards the counter. 'Though anyone with an ounce of sense would take one look at him and realise that he's not well and just let him be . . .'

The prickly feeling reached Birdie's stomach.

'But that's not – surely – *I* moved here in the fifties—'

The woman's face immediately creased with sympathy. 'Is this your first appointment?'

'Yes. But I'm just here to tell them they made a mistake.' She fished in her handbag for the letter and smoothed it out on her knee. 'They sent me this, but they've got the wrong person—'

'My dad got the same letter,' the young woman said quietly.

'But I haven't done anything wrong,' Birdie insisted. She waited for the woman to agree with her.

'Do you have anyone with you?' she asked instead. 'A friend, or a family member?'

Birdie didn't. She hadn't told anyone about the letter, not even her daughter. Why worry her? She had thought that it would all be sorted by lunchtime. A clerical error, an apology. A story to tell the girls at bingo.

'You should always have someone with you. In case you get detained.'

'*Detained*?'

The room pitched sideways. Fear crashed over her like waves colliding with the side of a cliff.

'*Ticket number one hundred and thirteen, to window number four, please. Ticket number—*'

'That's you,' the woman said softly. Birdie looked down at the crumpled ticket in her lap.

'Do you want to give me the number of someone I could call, just in case—'

'No.' She swallowed. 'That won't be necessary. It's a mistake, that's all.'

'Alright,' the woman said. 'If you say so. Good luck.'

Birdie stood up and walked towards the counter, her handbag clutched tightly in her hand like a talisman, her underarms wet with sweat.

*The letter was not meant for you*, she told herself.

The letter that said she was not what she knew herself to be.

*This is all just a mistake.*

*You belong here.*

*This is your home.*

But it hadn't always been.

# Two

## *1948*

One hot and humid day in May, HMT *Empire Windrush* sat in the shallows of Kingston's port. Her boarding passengers – pioneers, all 492 of them – made their way up the gangplank and jostled for space on the deck, their dreams of a better life packed carefully into suitcases and stowed in the belly of the ship.

England was calling!

She was a battered old cruise liner, the *Windrush*, once put to work by Nazi soldiers and then commandeered by the British as a prize of war. Did her passengers care for the history that swayed gently beneath their feet, or the stories riveted into her steel hull? Not likely. Their own stories were unfolding before them. Hats and damp handkerchiefs were waving furiously at full mast. The port was crowded with well-wishers and those who felt they were watching an opportunity slip through their fingers and over the horizon.

*If it wasn't for my old mudda . . .*

*Next time I'm getting a ticket and no one's going to talk me out of it . . .*

*They say the streets of England are paved with gold. Can you imagine?*

Precious Brown, a young woman of twenty-five, *couldn't* imagine. She didn't care about no raatid boat.

The baby was coming. The baby was coming *now*.

Pain coursed through her body, despite the ineffectual hushing from her aunt, Lucille, who laid a cool cloth across her forehead and offered up her fingers to be tightly squeezed. It was six weeks too soon, she sobbed desperately. Six weeks!

'It might not live, more's the pity,' Auntie Luce stated, shifting her bulk in the too-small hospital chair. 'You were early, and no one thought you would live either.'

She paused and helped herself to a handful of ice chips.

'Of course, your brudda was late. And that killed your mudda. So maybe early's not a bad thing, eh?'

Lucille was a thick, heavyset woman who liked to dole out her opinions as though they were candied yams. With hair greying at her temples and lines criss-crossing her forehead, she moved slowly and sweatily in her old age, giving the impression of a fat mouse wading through molasses. She had hands as wide as spades and a look so unforgiving she could make a full-grown man's pecker shrivel where he stood. Mrs D. Barry – Auntie Luce to all who knew her, blood relation or not – was the closest thing Precious had to a mother, and she had arrived in her niece's life shortly after her own mother had departed it.

She'd been four years old – much too young, they said, to remember the day that God admitted her good mother to heaven, but if anyone had asked, Precious would have told them she could recall it in shocking detail. The sounds and smells that Death brought with it. The emptiness it left behind, and the woman who came to fill the space.

Lucille, her father's older half-sister, had appeared like a whirlwind, arriving at a house struck down by sudden grief.

'I left as soon as I got the telegram. Poor Amaretta.'

'You're here for nine night, I suppose,' Precious's father said, his voice stripped of emotion. Precious peered curiously around his legs and surveyed the stranger. The house was full of them, and she supposed this one too would say how sorry she was but then falter when asked if she knew where her mother had gone.

Auntie Luce snorted heavily, like an affronted bull.

'And the rest.'

'The rest?'

She shook her head, the hat crammed on top of her hair wobbling like a rum custard.

'Aubrey Gladstone, how you gwine raise *two* babies now Amaretta's gone, God rest her soul? I've given up my house in Bog Walk. I've come to live with you.'

He was not in the right mind to argue. Dazed, he handed over his newborn son and stood back to let her cross the threshold.

'Got a lickle rum?' she asked, marching straight into the kitchen, past a collection of women preparing a funeral feast. 'I can't abide a fussy baby.'

Whether the rum was for her or for the baby, she did not say.

'Jeezam, he's heavy,' she said to no one in particular, deftly unscrewing a jar of guava preserves one-handed and sniffing the contents. 'This is one big baby. He's ugly, too. None of the Silvera in him – he's all Gladstone.'

Precious, who had followed Auntie Luce into the kitchen, was watching from a dim corner. Every shutter in the house had been closed, as though to seal up all its grief inside and leave it to stew, like the soup that simmered on the stove. There had been sad songs and delicious food and the baby had cried, which was to be expected, and her father had cried too, which was not, and her mother had gone away and no one seemed to remember that Precious was still there, that she had been left behind.

'But ugly babies need love too,' Auntie Luce continued. She turned her head and locked eyes with Precious, half-hidden in the space beside the pantry, as though Luce had known she was there all along.

'And so does she. That girl needs a mudda now that hers is dead.'

So *that's* where her mother had gone. Precious knew what death was – she'd watched fishmongers in the market plunge their hands into writhing buckets of eels then come down on their slimy heads with a cleaver; she had seen the mean old lane cat bat a dead mouse between its paws then surrender the broken body to the flies for them to lay their eggs in – and somewhere, deep inside her heart, she understood the finality of it. Her mother wasn't coming back. But instead of crying, as Aubrey had done, a high-pitched wail that had brought the women of the lane running from their beds, their bare feet slapping on the ground like rain and leaving dusty footprints all up the veranda steps that no one had yet thought to sweep away, Precious only nodded. Auntie Luce opened her free arm and Precious went to her, inhaling the scent of stale rose water and sweat and newly made babies. Peter gurgled and Auntie Luce held them both against her breast. This was a new sensation. Amaretta's arms had always been bony and frail, but Luce's grip was as weighty as an anchor.

*I'm not going anywhere*, the embrace seemed to say.

Lucille was a widow (*in between husbands,* she liked to say, though to her disappointment the prospects were slim in Portmore) with no children of her own, so as far as she was concerned it was her duty to take on the Gladstones. She quickly established herself as the centre of their neighbourhood, and on the lane not a single decision was made, not a marriage entered into or a baby named, without Auntie Luce first passing her judgement, whether her advice had been sought or not.

She raised the children properly, to be seen and not heard, never dreaming of sparing the rod or spoiling the child. But she loved them too, which is why she found herself sat in a dutty hospital room, of all the dyam places.

Not that she hadn't bellyached about it, of course. Going all the way to the hospital just to have a baby? What was the world coming to? She'd delivered plenty of Bog Walk babies in her time, in bedrooms and on kitchen floors and once, in a backyard (the mother had been picking green beans for dinner when her water broke), but never in a *hospital*. It seemed so unnatural.

'Any chance of a cup of coffee?' Luce hopefully asked a passing nurse. 'Or anything to eat?'

She was starving. She had just got the water boiling for coffee that morning when a timid knock at the back screen door had alerted her attention to her niece's unexpected predicament.

'What d'you want?' she asked testily of the small boy standing nervously on the veranda.

'It's Precious, Auntie Luce,' he replied, standing well clear of her enormous hands.

'She said the baby's coming and she needs you to find Winston and take her to hospital and . . . and I forgot the rest,' he added guiltily, inching backwards out of reach.

'Baby's not due for another six weeks,' she remonstrated, narrowing her eyes. The boy, wisely, said nothing. You didn't argue with Auntie Luce. She sighed.

'Tell her I'm coming. And *that*,' she lunged forward and swiped him around the ear, 'is for forgetting the rest.'

With one sad last look at the gleaming silver coffee pot, she put on her raffia hat and took up her handbag and waddled down the lane. She found her niece on all fours in the kitchen, a dish towel clamped between her teeth and sweat pouring from her brow.

'You sure the baby's coming?' Auntie Luce asked suspiciously. 'Might just be gas.'

The dish towel muffled the worst of the expletives.

'And what's this about going to the *hospital*? This is a *baby*, not a broken neck.'

Precious spat out the dish towel. 'They might be able to stop the baby from coming . . . it's too soon . . .'

'Where's your husband?'

Precious didn't know. She had sent a message down to the docks, where Winston worked, but word had come back that he was not there. She didn't know what else to do, she panted.

'That's what you get for marrying a wastrel,' Auntie Luce chided, huffing as she helped her niece to her feet. 'Where are your shoes? Kingston Royal is filthy. You and the baby are both likely to get ringworm or diphtheria or God knows what else. This a foo-fool's game, if you ask me.'

She left a scribbled note for her nephew-in-law, telling him to get his batty to Kingston Royal because the baby was coming and what's so important for you to miss a day's work, hmm, don't you have a wife and child to support and *hush up, I'm coming* – then walked Precious to the bus stop at the end of the lane, a bunch of newspapers wadded under her arm.

'It's alright,' Auntie Luce told the other waiting passengers, patting Precious's belly. 'She's just in labour.'

The bus arrived (*late! As usual*) and Auntie Luce clucked at two young men until they relinquished the front seat. She would not let Precious sit until she had laid out a generous pile of newspapers for her to sit on (*what if you give birth right here? You don't know who's had their dutty backside all over this seat*) and then leaned forward to tap the driver on the shoulder.

'I've got a gyal here having a baby. You don't need to stop at *every* stop.'

At the hospital, Precious's hopes for medical intervention were quickly dashed. The nurse at the front desk took one look at her and asked if she had a name picked out yet.

Luce had yet to make the case for naming the baby after herself, if it was a girl. She thought she'd have more time, six weeks in which to drop hints and launch subtle petitions or else begin stitching the name Lucille into the baby gowns she'd made over the winter and pretend as though it were a done deal. That had worked with *three* other babies. But now she would have to work quickly. Winston wouldn't like it, but then, Winston wasn't there.

'Just like that man to miss the birth of his first baby,' Luce began, sneaking another handful of ice chips. 'You'd think, after all the trouble you had—'

She didn't get to finish her thought, as hasty footsteps in the corridor heralded the arrival of Precious's husband of almost three years. He fell into the room, breathless and bewildered, and scrambled to his wife's side.

'I came as soon as I heard,' he proclaimed, kissing Precious's damp brow. 'What's the doctor said?'

'Never mind what the doctor's said. Where . . . the hell . . . you been?' Precious growled, gripping the rough cotton sheet in her fists.

'At work,' Winston replied sheepishly. 'Where d'you think?'

'No you ain't,' Auntie Luce piped up. 'Your wife sent word down to the dock and they said you didn't show up today.'

'It's that ship, isn't it?' Precious panted. 'You *had* to go see that ship.'

'I had no idea the baby would come so soon. Six weeks early, Precious!'

'So you admit it?'

Winston looked from Precious to Luce and back again, like a naughty puppy accused of getting into the larder.

'It's – it's a big day!' he began. 'It's going to go down in history—'

'*You're* going to go down in history, Winston Brown, if you don't shut your mouth and fetch your wife some more ice chips.' Auntie Luce proffered the empty cup towards him. 'We've run out.'

Winston, sensing an opportunity to get back in his wife's good graces – or perhaps wishing to escape a lashing from Auntie Luce's tongue – rushed out the room as quickly as he had entered it.

Auntie Luce narrowed her eyes at his departing figure. 'Cho. As if he thinks some rasshole ship is more important than his own baby. *Emigrating to England* – ha! They'll soon come home, mark my words.'

Precious responded with another howl of pain. Luce reached into her handbag and pulled out a rolling pin.

'Here. You squeeze this. Where's that man with the ice?' Her jowls shook. 'Honestly, Precious, I *told* you not to marry him. If I'd have known you were planning on going to a night-club that night I *never* would have let you go—'

* * *

Precious Gladstone met Winston Brown in a smoky dance hall in Kingston. The club was tightly packed, with long queues forming for watered down rum and overpriced cigarettes. No one complained though. It was a time for *celebration*.

The war in Europe was finally over.

As children of the Empire, England's fight had been their fight, too. Although far removed from the frontlines of battle, the people of Jamaica had done their bit to help send Hitler packing: they grew food to feed armies and mined bauxite to build bombers. They had welcomed American service men to the newly created naval bases with open arms and sent some ten thousand of their own boys to fight for King and Mother Country. They had marched off, their buttons gleaming and their heads full of heroics. For most of them it was their first time leaving the country of their birth. Not all of them came back.

'But Precious, please.'

Janice Goodby had been pleading with her friend for the best part of an hour, to no avail.

'There's a party at Sam's for the American service men – they'll all be leaving the island now the war's done.'

'I don't care.'

'But they'll be looking for some fun tonight.' Janice waggled her eyebrows suggestively. 'And I'll have a better chance if you're with me.'

Janice had realised early on that she could be jealous of her friend's beauty, or she could use it to her advantage. Having Precious, a serious, slim-waisted young woman, with high cheekbones and a heart-shaped face, at her side improved her chances considerably. Boys fell over themselves to get Precious's attention, and when they failed, they typically turned to Janice for consolation.

'Please, sis—'

Precious rolled over onto her front and buried her face in her pillow. Why couldn't she be left alone with her grief? She'd courted Errol King for almost two years. She'd been sure that once he returned from the war they would have been married, but now . . .

The bedsprings groaned as Janice flopped down beside her.

'Moping's not going to bring him back, Presh.'

'I know that.'

'So get out of bed.'

'There's probably a handsome GI looking for a gyal with killer legs right this second. Go and have some fun, for goodness' sake,' Luce hollered from the hallway, a basket of freshly ironed laundry balanced on her hip. She paused, waiting for a response that didn't come, then continued heavily down the corridor with a sigh as loud as a hurricane.

'Please,' Janice pleaded again. Precious didn't move. 'Come out or I'll tell Auntie Luce what you said about her new hat making her look like a warthog in a wig—'

Precious sat up. 'I have nuttin' to wear.'

'What about your new dress?' Janice indicated a neat pile of soft, sea-green material draped carefully across a rattan chair. She held it up against her body. 'This is *real* pretty. Make me one next?'

'It's not finished. I still need to sew in the sleeve.'

Janice put a hand on her hip. 'Just pin it and *we go*. World War Three'll be declared before you move your batty.'

'Fine. But I'm not after a man, Janice—'

'All the more for me. Make a move!'

Luce ordered Peter to give the girls a ride into the capital and they followed the thrum of the music into Kingston's most popular nightclub. Precious lost Janice almost immediately to a trio of identical service men, all with blue eyes and dazzlingly white smiles, who fell over themselves to buy the girls a drink. She detangled herself from an unwilling embrace – *aww, shucks baby, where are you going? Come back, baby* – and skirted around the dance floor, a glass of rum held tightly in her hand, feeling as though she were stood on the edge of a precipice and not a pockmarked hardwood floor. Everywhere she looked, she saw smiling faces; entwined couples kissing and grinding and spinning like tops. The last time she had been here, she had danced in Errol's arms. Two days later the army had shipped him overseas and now she would never see him again.

It was too much. She would finish her drink, make her excuses to Janice, and go back home to her bed . . . and then, through a gap between the dancers, she locked eyes with a sharply dressed man on the opposite side of the dance floor. His confident demeanour, his arms crossed in front of his chest, gave the impression he was taller than he actually was. He was standing alone, but he didn't look lonely. He looked completely at ease with the world.

She looked away, then glanced back at him half a minute later. He was still staring: his eyes moved down to her legs and then back up to her face and he smiled. He had a beautiful smile. She turned her chin but kept him in her periphery, checking to see if he was still looking at her. He was. She didn't care. He had broad shoulders, she noticed. She didn't *care*. He was moving towards her, roughly parting dancing couples like Moses parting the Red Sea.

'Hey gyal.' The man plunged his hands into his pockets and grinned. 'The name's Winston. Winston Brown.'

She tilted her chin haughtily. 'I wasn't asking.'

'P'raps not. But I saw you looking.'

'I *glanced* in your direction. A glance is not the same as a look. And *you* were looking at *me*.'

'Why are you standing here all by yourself? Can't you get anyone to ask you to dance?'

That annoyed her.

'I could dance if I wanted to. I'm choosing not to.'

'The war's over, you know. There's no need to look so *vexed*.'

Up close, she noticed that his suit was cut from a cheap cloth and had gone shiny at the elbows. But he stood in front of her as though he were wearing the finest Harris Tweed all the way from Scotland.

'Can I buy you a drink?'

She took a deliberate sip from her half-full glass. 'Not too perceptive, are you?'

'That's a big-city word. You a Kingston girl?'

'Close enough. Portmore.'

Winston Brown whistled in mock admiration, and she rolled her eyes.

'Where are *you* from?'

'Malvern,' he said casually, though she detected the slightest hesitation. 'I moved for work.'

'Kingston's full of boys that move for work. No need to be ashamed.'

'Who said I'm ashamed?' He smiled his beautiful smile and Precious noticed the way his eyes crinkled into half-moons. She felt punch-drunk, though she was still on her first drink, and put her hand to her temple.

'You alright?'

'I should find my friend. It was nice to meet you, Winston Brown.'

'Don't go. You never told me your name—' he placed

a bold, calloused hand on her shoulder, then yelped and snatched it away.

'Cho!' he exclaimed, examining the pinprick of blood that had bubbled up on his palm with surprise. 'You line *all* your dresses with pins?'

Precious was mortified. 'I'm *so* sorry—'

'It's okay.' He wiped his hand on his trousers. 'I'll forgive you. But only if you dance with me.'

She opened her mouth to protest but he held up a finger.

'One dance. Just one.'

The music changed. The band eased into a slow ballad and the frenetic atmosphere of the dance floor melted away. He held her close, his hips rocking against hers, his hand pressed tightly against her lower back. She felt the warmth from his palm through the thin material of her dress and breathed in his woodsy scent.

'Will you tell me your name now, or do I need to guess?'

'Precious,' she murmured. 'Precious Gladstone.'

Her real name was Amaretta, but the minute her poor mother had laid eyes on her she'd declared that her baby was the most precious thing to ever exist on God's green earth. No one had called her anything else since.

Winston winked at her appreciatively.

'Precious. It suits you. Pretty girls are as rare as diamonds in Kingston.'

She laughed. It was the type of compliment she had heard many times before, but from him it sounded like a sonnet.

'Are the girls prettier in Malvern?'

'Oh, sure. You haven't heard? Malvern has the prettiest girls on the whole island.' He spun her beneath his arm then pulled her back into his chest. 'It was a hard job tearing myself away from them.'

'Then why did you?'

'A man can't live on pretty girls alone. I needed work. I needed money. I've got big plans, Precious Gladstone.'

Errol had had big plans, too.

She came to her senses and loosened herself from his grip.

'One dance, like you said. Now, I really must find my friend.'

'That was only half a dance—'

But Precious was already gone, pushing her way across the crowded dance floor and grabbing Janice by her wrist and pulling her outside into the balmy night air. She filled her lungs and exhaled, clearing her head of the smoke and the slick talk.

'Jan, I'm going home.'

'But why? We're having a *good* time.' Janice's lipstick was smeared across her chin.

'You stay here if you want. But I need to go.'

The lane was silent and still when she arrived home, save for the tree frogs singing their own victory symphony in the bromeliads that surrounded the house. She let herself in and slipped into her aunt's bed, pressing herself against Luce's back and inhaling the familiar scent of rose water.

'What's this?' Luce muttered groggily, as Precious threw her slender arm across her aunt's heavy bosom. 'Wappn to you, chile?'

She wanted to tell her aunt about the boasy boy in the raggy suit, the one who had smiled at her from across the room and made her go weak at the knees.

Winston Brown. The boy with big plans.

'Never mind, Auntie. Go back to sleep.'

She woke up the next morning alone, the sound of dishes clattering in the kitchen below.

'Aww, shit.'

She had overslept.

'Mawnin,' Auntie Luce called out cheerfully as Precious entered the kitchen in her nightgown. 'I told your daddy you were sick.'

Precious worked in her father's grocery store, keeping a careful record of every pound of flour and every piece of fruit that was bought and sold at Gladstone & Son's. She had a head for numbers and it was easy work, but that morning she knew she would not have been able to concentrate on the tiny columns of numbers and dates. She sighed in relief and reached for a coffee cup.

'Thanks, Auntie.'

Luce turned from the sink, one eyebrow raised so high it practically kissed her hairline.

'Did you have fun last night?'

'Yes. No – I mean, it was fine.'

'Ahh. Who's the lucky fella?' Luce asked knowingly, and Precious knocked the milk jug over. The liquid seeped into the sleeve of her nightgown, and she set her empty cup back down.

'I think I'll go back to bed.'

Auntie Luce chuckled. 'Good idea. Get that boy out your head before you wreck my whole kitchen.'

'There's no *boy*, Auntie,' Precious insisted as she swept past. She meant it too. She had no intention of ever seeing Winston Brown again.

She hid in her room until her father and brother arrived home from the store. Janice appeared in the kitchen shortly afterwards; she graciously accepted Auntie Luce's invitation to stay for dinner and then pulled Precious into the pantry by the edge of her blouse.

'Who was that you were dancing with last night?' she hissed excitedly, clicking the door closed behind her.

'No one,' Precious replied, louder than was necessary (she'd bet her last doubloon that her aunt had her ear pressed against the pantry door). 'He was just some facety boy that wanted a dance, that's all.'

'He asked after you. Wanted to know where he could find you.'

'Janice Goodby, if you told him where I live, I swear—'

'Of course I didn't,' Janice replied hastily. 'He's *dappa* though, Presh.'

'How dappa are we talking?' Auntie Luce shouted, and Precious opened the door and shoved her friend out of the pantry, then slammed it closed again. Alone, she pressed her cool hands against her hot cheeks and stood silently in the dark as Janice and Auntie Luce whispered in the kitchen like a pair of pickneys.

He'd asked after her . . .

At dinner, her father wiped his mouth and gravely set down his knife and fork.

'A young man came by the store today, Precious. For you.'

Precious glowered at Janice, who pretended to choke on a chicken bone and excused herself from the table.

'Auntie Luce says you met him last night in Kingston—' Luce made a noise like a bullfrog and got up to 'check on Janice'.

'But I don't want strange men hanging around outside the store, it makes us look untidy.'

'It won't happen again, Daddy,' Precious said firmly. 'And if it does, I'll send him packing.'

* * *

'Nice to see you again.'

It was the very next day, and there was Winston grinning at her as she left work, looking for all the world like a starving man who'd just found a tree dripping with ripe fruit. It was too late to go back into the store, or pretend she hadn't seen him, so she nodded primly and stalked past him, willing her legs not to give out. Lord, his smile did *sumtin* to her . . .

'Where's the fire?'

Winston hurried to fall in step beside her. He had a broad nose and spirited brown eyes. She noticed a thin scar on his left temple, but rather than marring his face, he wore it dashingly. He was dressed in loose trousers held up by suspenders and a rough cotton shirt rolled up to his elbows. The shirt accentuated the muscles in his arms, and she remembered how it had felt to have those arms wrapped around her waist . . .

'Or are we running from your farda?'

Precious slowed down. 'I'm not running. I'm walking.'

'Oh, like you walked out on me at Sam's?'

He winked at her, and her heart began to beat as fast as a rhumba box. Don't let her daddy be watching from the office window, please God . . .

'Let me walk you home,' he said, taking her bag from her shoulder. 'It's the least you can do, after you stabbed me then left me on the dance floor like some kinda sap.'

'You stabbed yourself,' she said starchily. 'Putting your hands all over strange girls.'

'You're strange, alright.'

'And *you're* downright rude.'

'My apologies, miss,' he said, tipping an imaginary hat. 'Us country boys don't know how to talk to city girls. P'raps you could teach me some manners?'

Precious rolled her eyes in exasperation. 'You need more than manners.'

'Oh?' He shot her a sly, sideways glance. 'And what do I need?'

'A good hiding.'

He laughed and said she was probably right, and Precious began listing all the reasons why she did not like him in her head. He was vexatious, he was presumptuous, he was–

'Precious?'

'What?'

Winston turned his head towards her. 'What do *you* need?'

'I don't understand.'

He shook his head and smiled. 'What do you want from life?'

It took her a moment to realise she didn't know the answer. Before the war, her life had been neatly mapped out, as though drawn by a cartographer: she was going to marry Errol, his father was going to set him up in the export business and Auntie Luce would help look after the babies, regardless of whether they needed her help or not. But that map had been torn to pieces and she didn't know what to make from the scraps.

'Let me guess,' Winston sighed, noticing her hesitation. 'You'll marry a *nice* boy and live in a *big* house and have lots of babies and grow tired and homely, like all pretty girls do.'

'What's wrong with wanting lots of babies?' she asked, deflecting his accusation with a challenge of her own.

'Nuttin', I suppose. But I would have thought a girl like *you* would have wanted more.'

'A girl like me?'

He grinned. 'Pretty. Smart. Strange. You could have anything you wanted, Precious. You could have the whole world. I'm surprised you haven't realised that yet.'

'I . . .'

'Can I kiss you?' he asked, and her mouth fell open.

'Kiss me?' She crossed her arms and glared at him, a near-perfect imitation of Auntie Luce. 'Boy, you've got some *nerve*—'

'Whoa,' he said languidly, his hand brushing against hers. A jolt of electricity shot up her spine. 'It's just a kiss, that's all. A kiss from the prettiest girl this side of Malvern.'

He leant in. Precious couldn't help it. She tilted her head towards his.

'Your attitude stinks, of course,' he said, his mouth inches from hers. 'And I get the feeling you'll be a pain in the backside. But I'm willing to overlook it. 'Specially because I know you want to kiss me too.'

Precious stepped back. She'd had enough.

'*My* attitude? Look here, Winston Brown! You're not God's gift to women! And I think it's time that you walked on home and left me alone, you, you rude, ignorant—'

He smiled lazily. 'I like you, Precious Gladstone. You make a man work for it.'

He crossed the small distance between them and his mouth was suddenly on hers. Errol had *never* kissed her like this, hot, and hungry, scorching with passion. . .

The spell was broken by the Blackstock boy, who ran past and hollered 'Precious Gladstone's got a new sweetie puss!' at the top of his voice. She groaned and pressed her forehead against the rough cloth of his shirt.

'The whole lane will know by sundown,' she laughed breathlessly.

Winston raised an eyebrow but didn't release her from his embrace.

'You're not afraid to be seen with a boy like me?'

She turned her head towards him and kissed him again. 'I don't know, Winston. Should I be?'

* * *

The *Windrush* set sail right on time, easing out of the dock just as Bridget Lucille Brown slipped into the world, wet and wailing and unaware that across the harbour, a handful of men, women and children were sailing away from their homeland and into the history books.

Auntie Luce planted a fat kiss on the baby's forehead and left to spread the good news, though not before delivering a parting warning that she wouldn't be held responsible if they were all struck down with some calamitous disease and were carried home in coffins. She shook her head as she waddled through the corridors, rolling pin under her arm, and out the front door. As if Precious gave birth in a *hospital*.

As Precious slept, Winston gingerly scooped the child up and held her against his chest, rocking her back and forth in a gentle, if unexperienced, rhythm. She whimpered and stirred then settled down into his arms, staring up at him with bright eyes. He stood at the window and looked out into the distance, where the thin blue line of the sea glinted beneath a cloudless sky. In the distance the sound of cheers, as sweet and joyous as a summer calypso, took flight as the *Windrush* disappeared over the horizon.

# Three

## *2016*

The world outside the immigration reporting office was as Birdie had left it. The street had not disappeared into a sinkhole. The skies had not turned black. As she passed through the glass doors and out into the late summer sunshine, she half expected to find a world in chaos. Sirens blaring. But no: the sirens were all in her own head.

There was no mistake. That's what they'd told her. She had reached the counter and given her name and address and then said she had received a letter in error.

'It's not an error, Ms Brown.'

'It must be.' Birdie's legs wobbled beneath her. 'I'm not an illegal immigrant.'

'You are. You lack the documentation needed to remain permanently in the United Kingdom—'

'What documentation? I've never needed documentation—'

'All non-UK citizens need documentation. It is the law.'

'I'm *not* a non-UK citizen. I'm British. I've been here my whole life, practically—'

'So you say.' It sounded like an accusation. 'But we don't have a record of you in our system.'

'Can you check again?'

'I don't need to check again—'

'I arrived in the UK in July 1955,' she said in a rush. 'I travelled with my mother from Jamaica – it was allowed, we were British – we *are* British, I mean *I* am—'

The person behind the counter didn't even blink.

'Ms Brown. There is no record of you in our system. You do not have the correct documentation to remain indefinitely in the United Kingdom and as such, you are liable for removal back to Jamaica.'

*Back to Jamaica.* They might as well have said they were sending her to the moon.

'But . . . why?' Birdie whispered. The question was ignored.

'Your next appointment is in two weeks. Please ensure you are on time.'

She had to return to the Solihull office every two weeks to register until—

Until she was removed. Deported. Thrown out.

She had entered the building a British citizen and walked out an illegal immigrant.

* * *

Birdie drifted down the unfamiliar street, unsure of her surroundings. She had only visited Solihull once before, to visit the new John Lewis store with her daughter. They had marvelled over the homewares and cooed over Egyptian cotton linens and then baulked at the prices. *How* much for a stainless steel frying pan? Carmen, who'd been determined to buy *something*, purchased a bone china gravy boat from the cookware section on the ground floor. She was very proud of that gravy boat. Every Christmas it took pride of place in the centre of the table.

Birdie hadn't finished her Christmas list.

Would she get one last Christmas with her family?

She found her bus stop, eventually. The journey that morning had taken almost two hours in rush hour traffic, but the return felt like it was over in minutes. She hurried along the pavement towards her estate. If she was lucky, she could make it back to Clent House without having to say a word to anyone who knew her. Who might ask how she was, or where she'd been.

Out of the corner of her eye, she noticed a black van pull up alongside her, the engine humming idly as the driver checked something on his phone. He looked up as she walked past. His eye caught hers.

Birdie had a sudden vision of the doors of the van being thrown open and armed police snatching her from the street. She walked faster, her bunions aching, her eyes on her shoes, listening for heavy footsteps coming up behind her, waiting for a hand on her shoulder . . .

She darted into Purcell Close and risked a glance backwards. The van had made a U-turn and was already at the bottom of the street. She leaned against the alley wall and inhaled, the back of her neck coated in sweat. She reached beneath her good wig and wiped it away with her hand. *Just get home*, she thought. *Get home and then you can* . . . She didn't know how to finish that thought.

*Just get home.*

Clent House was a concrete block of post-war flats, seven storeys high, identical to the three other blocks that made up the estate, built in a utilitarian square with a scrub of fenced-in grass at the centre. There used to be a swing set, and a bench, but both had been set on fire so many times that the council had stopped replacing them. Not that Birdie had stopped complaining – her youngest grandson Jaxon, she would tell whichever receptionist she got through to, loved playing on that swing, and now she had to take him all the way to Victoria Park, crossing not one but *three* major roads. It wasn't on. The kiddies of the estate deserved somewhere to play. Her comments would be passed to 'higher-ups' at the council, the receptionist always said. 'You see that they are,' Birdie would say with a huff before hanging up the phone.

The estate had been a nice place to live, back in the old days, according to Mr Patel at number thirty-two. In those days people would grow flowers in pots outside their doors and you could leave your front door unlocked while you popped to Hardeep's corner shop for a pint of milk on credit. Now Hardeep's was a Spar and you locked your front door regardless of whether or not you had anything to steal. Every time Carmen came to visit she would complain that she felt unsafe in the car park, or moan about the broken lift. But Birdie would ignore her. What was that old saying? It's not much, but it's home.

'Yo, Mrs Brown!'

Birdie's hopes that she could get to her front door without being intercepted were sunk. Tyrone Middleton was limping towards her, in that strange, lopsided way that kids those days liked to walk, his tracksuit bottoms slung low around his waist. Tyrone lived on the first floor of Clent House with his mother and younger sister Scarlett. He was known around the estate as an up-and-coming hustler, though he looked, with his baby face beneath a shock of curly ginger hair, much younger than his sixteen years.

'Wagwan?'

'Hello, Tyrone,' she replied, trying to coax the muscles in her face into a smile.

'You don't look too good, Mrs B. D'you need help with the stairs or sumfin?'

Birdie waved his concern away. 'I'm just coming down with a cold,' she said, snatching an excuse out of thin air.

'Try Lemsip with a dash of Kahlúa. My mom swears by it.'

'Thanks Tyrone, I will.'

Tyrone looked around surreptitiously and dropped his voice. 'Do you want free Sky? A mate of mine can hook you up for a tenner. All he has to do is take a Stanley knife right, and strip the end of a HDMI cable—'

'That doesn't sound safe. Or legal.' Birdie shuddered to imagine the police at her door. An illegal immigrant who was *also* a thief? The papers would have a field day. 'Does your mom know about this mate of yours?'

He blushed the same colour as his hair.

'Don't tell her, will you? We're a bit short on rent this month. I'm just trying to help.'

Birdie promised not to tell, and he limped off with a cheery wave. She heaved a weary sigh. Please God, just let her get to her flat, uninterrupted—

'Birdie! Hey Birdie!'

God was not on her side. (*Course he's not*, she thought to herself. *Otherwise they wouldn't be trying to kick you out of the country.*) This was the problem (funny. When had she ever called it a problem before?) with living somewhere like the estate. Everyone knew you. Everyone always wanted to stop and shoot the breeze.

She squinted up into the sun. Delma Rees, who lived on the top floor of Kinver House, was hanging over the walkway, dressed in a sleeveless nightie, her hair ensconced in a silk bonnet the colour of grape soda.

'Was that Tyrone you was talking to just now?' Delma hollered, her voice echoing around the courtyard.

'It was,' Birdie shouted back. 'Did you need him to fix something?'

Tyrone often did odd jobs for people around the estate. It was cheaper than calling a plumber or an electrician and, with his GCSE in woodwork, he was qualified enough.

'I need him to fix my TV! Ever since his lickle friend fiddled with it, everything's blue! Phil Mitchell – blue! Eamonn Holmes – blue! That gyal with the fringe, whatshername, the one from *Strictly* – she's blue too! What's the point of free Sky if every raatid thing is blue?'

'I'll tell him next time I see him,' Birdie shouted quickly and waved goodbye, but Delma was even quicker.

'You're back late from bingo today. Did you win? D'you fancy coming up for a cuppa?'

'I can't chat right now, Delma. I need to call my daughter,' Birdie lied. A disappointed Delma disappeared back into her flat, and Birdie continued homewards. She felt bad. Normally she had a lot of time for Delma, who didn't like to leave her flat, but Delma was a blabbermouth. If she got wind of Birdie's troubles, the whole estate would know by teatime. Thankfully, she made it across the courtyard and up the stairwell that always smelled like weed, to her flat on the fourth floor without meeting anyone else.

Birdie lived alone, but she wasn't lonely. Her one-bedroom flat was full of odds and ends and uncoordinated furniture. The living room was dominated by a Welsh dresser of dark wood that had once been her mother's. It contained, among a collection of knick-knacks and mismatched wine glasses, four antique plates and photos of her children, and her grandchildren, arranged in order of age. Partially hidden behind a

Toby jug was a family photo from the late eighties: Birdie, flanked on either side by her daughter and her son, and then behind her, Jimmy. He was not the biological father of her two children, but he'd been their father in every way that mattered. Tall, and good-natured, they'd split up decades ago – an argument that couldn't be reconciled, a bitter heartache but a belief that she was doing the right thing – but his presence still remained: in songs Birdie heard on the radio, in photos. Luce would have recommended cutting him out of all the family photos, but Birdie didn't see the point in ruining a nice picture. Besides, tucked away as it was, she didn't have to look at it much.

Birdie put down her handbag and hung up her coat. The coffee table was littered with papers (the community centre where she volunteered twice a week was organising a bank holiday fête and she was in charge of the table plan) and her mother's urn was dusty. A bag of old clothes, donated by her best friend, Claudette, needed sorting for the jumble sale. Jaxon's toys were strewn across the floor – he'd left late the night before and she hadn't had a chance to put them away yet. She should tidy up before she worried about getting deported—

It was like a dam bursting. She sank into an armchair, buried her face in her age-spotted hands, and wept. Noisy sobs that felt like they would choke her. Hot, frightened tears, coming so fast she thought she might drown in them.

There was a sharp knock at the door and her head flew up. Was this it? Had they come to take her away?

'Birdie?'

She exhaled. It was only Rita, her next-door neighbour. She wiped her face on her sleeve and half rose out of the armchair, and then stopped. What if – oh Jesus, what if Rita was working for *them*? What if they'd asked her to knock, to create a diversion, to save them the bother of breaking down her front door?

'Birdie, open the door. I know you're in there – I can hear you crying.'

Rita had lived next door to Birdie for three years. Birdie occasionally watched her boys, Kian and Manny. They would share celebrity gossip and food, passing fragrant vegetable samosas and fried dumplings, fresh and warm out of the skillet, between their kitchens. Rita was her *friend*. And yet, Birdie remained cowering in the armchair.

'I have to pick up Manny from after-school club,' Rita shouted through the door. 'But we'll be back soon. I'll check in on you then, okay Birdie?'

Rita's shadow receded from the window and Birdie heaved a heavy sigh of relief. Then her mobile phone began to ring. She ignored it. It rang again. And again. Then the landline in the hallway blared. She ignored that, too. After seven rings, the answering machine beeped.

'Mom, answer the phone. I know you're there.'

Birdie stared at the phone as though Carmen might squeeze herself through the line and appear in her living room. She didn't want to speak to her daughter, not now.

'I'm not hanging up. Answer the phone. Mom? Mom? *Mom*—'

Maybe there was something wrong with one of the children. Birdie would never be able to forgive herself—

'Carmen, I'm here.'

'Why didn't you answer the phone? I've been calling and calling—'

'I don't know where my mobile is,' Birdie lied.

'Where did you last see it?'

'I don't remember—'

'That's not important,' Carmen interrupted. 'I got a text from Rita. Apparently you were crying so loudly she could hear you over *Escape to the Country*, but you won't let her in. What's going on?'

'Why does Rita have your number?'

'From when you took that tumble last year. I gave it to her for emergencies.'

Birdie clicked her tongue.

'I didn't "take a tumble". I fell off a stepladder.'

'You shouldn't have been painting the ceiling in the first place—'

'If Andy had come round when he said he would I wouldn't have had to paint the ceiling myself—'

'You're changing the subject. Why are you crying?'

'I'm not,' Birdie insisted, staring at her reflection in the hallway mirror. Her eyes were red raw. 'How are my grand-children?'

Birdie had always been able to tell when Carmen was lying to her. Unfortunately, it seemed to be an inherited skill.

'You're lying. Do I have to drive over there? It's not – you're not *ill* or anything, are you? Mom?'

'No, I'm not ill.'

Birdie felt her daughter's suspicion trickle down the phone line and nestle right into her ear.

'Then what is it? You weren't crying over nothing.'

Birdie swallowed.

'Mom?'

'I got a letter,' Birdie began quietly. 'From the Home Office.'

'What did it say?'

'It said . . . well. It said that according to them, I'm not a British citizen.'

'What?'

'More specifically . . .' she put one hand flat against the telephone table, as if to brace herself. 'They think . . . they said I'm here illegally.'

'*What*?'

Birdie flinched. How the roles had reversed – she remembered reacting exactly the same way when she'd discovered that Carmen had gotten a dolphin tattooed on her lower back at the age of seventeen. She half expected Carmen to tell her to get her batty ready for a beating.

'Mom? Are you still there? *Mom*?'

'I'm here,' Birdie said, tentatively bringing the phone back to her ear. 'No need to shout.'

'I think there's *every* need. You're telling me that you had a letter from the Home Office and this is the first I am hearing of it?'

'I'm telling you now.'

'Are you sure they got the right person? They could have mixed you up with another Bridget Brown, or—'

'I went to a meeting this morning. At the immigration centre, in Solihull. At least, I thought it was a meeting. It wasn't. But I spoke to someone.'

'And? What did they say?'

'They said that—'

*We have no record of you in our system.*

It had sounded so absolute. We don't have a record of you, so we're kicking you out of the country.

'What did they say?'

*You are liable for removal to Jamaica.*

'Mom?'

'I'm going to be deported,' she said. It sounded so strange, like the punchline to a joke she didn't get.

Carmen laughed incredulously. 'Come off it.'

'I'm being serious, Carmen.' Her voice began to tremble. 'The letter said—'

'Hold on. When did this letter arrive?'

'I can't remember.'

'Mom.'

Birdie recognised that tone. It was the same tone her mumma had used on *her* when she was a pickney and then she'd grown up and used it on her own daughter. And now her daughter was using it on her.

'Last week.'

'Last *week*? You've been sitting on this letter from the fucking Home Office for a *week*?'

'Language,' Birdie admonished, but she knew from experience that Carmen was like a tank. Once she got going, she would not stop until she ran out of ammunition or energy.

'My own mother is getting *deported* and she doesn't think to tell me—'

'Deported? Birdie's getting deported?'

Birdie had forgotten that Andy, Carmen's out-of-work husband, would be at home. Andy was not the sort of person she wanted on her side in a crisis. He lacked . . . well, Birdie could write a list as long as her arm detailing all the ways in which she found Andy Lloyd lacking, but she'd learned to keep them to herself. The only thing she could say about Andy was that he was consistent: he'd been *wutless* when Carmen married him and *wutless* he remained.

'If you don't mind,' Birdie interrupted. The stress of the day clung to her like a limpet, and she was utterly exhausted. 'I need to get my tea on.'

'Oh well, I'm *so* sorry, Mom.' The sarcasm slid down the line like treacle. 'You go get your tea on and we'll worry about you being deported tomorrow, hmm? I'm sorry for worrying about you, like I don't have enough on my bloody plate—'

Birdie remembered Carmen as a pickney, snub-nosed and loud-mouthed – cheeky yes, but with warm little hands she'd wrap around Birdie's waist, squeezing her tightly before dashing off into the school playground. Then came the rows, the rebellion. She had been such a surly teenager; nothing like Scott, who'd been sweetness and tropical syrup. Birdie had been warned that boys were more difficult than girls, but if you'd asked her back then, she would have said that Carmen would be the one to cause her headaches in her old age, not Scott. And yet . . . her son was halfway through a prison sentence. Eight years for burglary. It felt like a permanent migraine.

'I'm coming over,' Carmen huffed. 'I need to see this letter.'

She hung up without saying goodbye and turned to her husband.

'I need to go to Mom's. You'll have to sort the kids' tea. There's fish fingers in the freezer and some potatoes that are getting a bit wrinkly but they'll do for chips.'

Andy slipped a hand beneath his waistband and scratched himself. He was wearing an old pair of tracksuit bottoms and an Aston Villa shirt from four seasons ago that outlined the soft paunch of his stomach. His blonde hair was receding slightly around the temples.

'I'll send Saffie to the chippy.'

'I thought we said no more takeaways for the time being.'

'One bag of chips isn't going to break the bank, Carm.'

Her jaw set tight.

'Alright. Can you at least make sure the kids finish their homework?' Carmen and Andy had four children. Declan, the eldest, lived in London, but Saffie and the twins, Jade and

Lewis, were still in school. 'Jade needs her planner signing, she got detention again. And remind Lewis to put his P.E. kit in the wash, it stunk to high heaven this morning.'

'Sure thing love,' Andy said, one eye still on the television. 'Say hi to Birdie for me.'

'It's not a *social call*, Andy. I'm going over because they want to *kick her out of the country*.'

'Nanny's getting kicked out of the country?'

Saffie stuck her head over the balustrade, a pair of headphones looped around her neck, a mass of frizzy brown curls falling over her face. The cheap, tinny sound of drum and bass emanating from the headphones irritated Carmen. She exhaled, and tried to silently count to ten, like the stress expert had demonstrated on *Loose Women* the week before.

'Why is Nanny getting kicked out the country?'

She made it to four.

'What have I told you about eavesdropping?'

'I can't help it. You were rowing.'

'No one's rowing. You're in charge of dinner. There are potatoes that—'

'Dad said we could have fish and chips. Why's Nanny getting kicked out of the country?'

'That,' Carmen said, shrugging into her denim jacket, her lips set in a grim line, 'is what I am about to find out.'

* * *

Carmen blustered into the flat like an angry cat and held out her hand expectantly. Birdie passed her the letter and asked if she wanted a cup of tea. Carmen shot her a withering glance over the top of the rumpled piece of paper and made no response.

Birdie decided to make a pot anyway, the brown-and-red bead curtain clattering soothingly as she stepped through to the kitchen. She always thought it sounded like the sea. In that moment, she wished there was an ocean between her and her daughter. She poured a generous dash of rum into the teapot and carried it back through to the living room on her best lacquered tea tray, alongside a packet of custard creams. Carmen's favourite. A peace offering.

'I can't believe you didn't tell me.'

'I'm sorry.'

'Let me read it again.'

Birdie had read it so many times she had committed it to memory – whenever she closed her eyes, she could see it unfolding in front of her, the letters jumping off the page, rearranging themselves to scream a less restrained message in her face.

*You're not wanted here.*

'And this is the only letter you've received?'

Birdie took a sip of scalding hot tea to buy herself some time, but she felt Carmen's eyes boring into her. The teacup rattled in her hand.

'One arrived yesterday. About my pension.'

'They've stopped your pension?'

'They said it was under review. I meant to ask them about it today but I forgot.'

Carmen crossly ate a custard cream. 'Who else knows about this?'

'No one.'

'Not even Auntie Claud?'

'You're the only person that knows, Carm.'

Carmen made a noise. Birdie couldn't tell if it was a sound of approbation or disapproval.

'You should have told me as soon as the first letter arrived.'

'Sorry,' Birdie said again. She found one of Jaxon's action figures shoved down the side of the settee and began to fiddle with it, twisting the little plastic limbs around in her hands.

'What happened then? At this "meeting"?'

'Well. I told you. Not really much of a meeting.'

Carmen narrowed her eyes. 'How can a meeting not be a meeting?'

*When they've already made up their mind to kick you out.*

'It was more of a . . . formality.'

'But you spoke to someone, right? A member of staff?'

'Yes.'

'Who?'

'I don't know. I didn't get a name.'

Carmen pinched the bridge of her nose. 'Just walk me through it, okay? You got this letter and . . .'

And so Birdie recounted every minute of the experience in painful detail: the two buses, the surly security guard, the pink ticket and the waiting room, the conversation with the patient, desperate daughter and her sick father, the long march up to the counter, and then, 'And then they said – well, implied, really – that I couldn't prove I had moved here when I said I did. There's no record of me in the system.'

She still didn't know what that meant. What system? And why wasn't she in it? They had her address, after all. They knew she *existed*. So how could she exist outside the system? Suddenly, the arm snapped off the action figure, and she stared at the broken toy, trying to remember if it was one of Jaxon's favourites. Jaxon spent a lot of time at his nanny's. He was Scott's only child, and his mother wasn't . . . Tegan wasn't suited to life as a single parent. She needed a lot of support. Support that Birdie was happy to provide, even if it did wind Carmen up. Tegan, who was twenty-eight and stick thin, with frazzled, bleached hair, was a persistent source of tension in Birdie's relationship with her daughter. Carmen thought Tegan took advantage. Birdie was tired of explaining that everything she did for Tegan, she did voluntarily, just like she'd done for Carmen when *she'd* been an overwhelmed new mother. It took a village, after all. Just yesterday, Tegan had asked Birdie to watch Jaxon for a bit, two hours tops, and then didn't come back until well after his bedtime. Jaxon never seemed to mind being left with Nanny while his mommy got up to goodness knows what. Birdie supposed that at just four years old, he didn't really understand. Yesterday he'd been too engrossed in his new toy . . . the toy that now lay broken in Birdie's lap. Would he miss it if she threw it in the bin? And how much would he miss her, if—

'Are you listening?'

She looked up. Carmen's gaze was fearful, and Birdie saw her own distress mirrored in her daughter's expression. There was no denying that Carmen was her daughter. They were so alike: the same apple cheeks, the same brown eyes, the same wide nose, the same tight coils that were prone to breakage. Carmen wanted reassurance, Birdie knew, but the well was empty. How could she provide comfort to her daughter when she had nothing to offer but uncertainty and fear and that word, *removal*, going around and around in her head?

'Mom?'

'What?'

'I said, did you come here legally?'

'Of course I did!'

'Then why are they saying you didn't?'

'I . . .' The words caught in her throat. 'I don't know.'

'This isn't a joke, Mom—'

'I mean it.' Birdie's voice broke. 'I don't know why they're saying I didn't. I don't understand. I don't understand any of it.'

The tears came again.

'Oh, *Mom*. Don't cry. Do you have a number for the Home Office? I can call them tomorrow before my shift and get this all straightened out—'

Someone knocked on the front door.

'I'll get it,' Carmen said.

'Wait—' Birdie gasped, shrinking back into the settee, balling her best skirt up in her hands.

'Don't be silly, it's only Rita,' Carmen said exasperatedly, swinging the front door wide open and gesturing like a game show host. 'Come in, Rita, love. You've caught us at a bit of a bad time.'

'I don't mean to pry,' Rita said softly, 'I just wanted to make sure you were okay, Birdie. But if you're busy, I'll go—'

'Hang on, aren't you a lawyer?' Carmen looked over her shoulder at her mom. 'Maybe she can help us.'

Birdie didn't respond, and Carmen turned back to Rita.

'You *are* a lawyer, aren't you?'

'I'm a receptionist at a law firm—'

Carmen took Rita by the elbow and guided her towards the settee. 'Close enough. We're in trouble, Rita. Sit down, I'll pour you a cup of tea.'

'What kind of trouble?'

Carmen handed her the letter and Rita sat down, crossing her legs at the ankle. She read it quickly, uttering a little *oh*, then gingerly returned it to the envelope.

'Have they given you a timeframe?' she asked, placing her hand on top of Birdie's cold one.

'Timeframe?' Birdie asked dully.

'For your deportation, Mom,' Carmen said frustratedly. 'And no, they didn't Rita, love. They didn't give her *any* information whatsoever, according to her. Is that even legal?'

Carmen handed Rita a cup of tea and she balanced it on the knee of her navy trouser suit.

'I'll ask at work, but Alan doesn't deal with immigration law,' she said, tucking her long, shiny hair behind one ear. Carmen's hand went up to her own hair, subconsciously smoothing the frizzy flyaways. She'd been meaning to find the time to relax her hair for weeks.

'He's a family lawyer, so he won't be much help, I'm afraid.'

Carmen exhaled through her nose and ate another biscuit.

'He might be able to point us in the right direction though. I'm sure he has plenty of colleagues who work in immigration.' Rita took a sip of her tea and blanched, setting the cup back down on the coffee table. 'And you're going to need a lawyer.'

'I am?'

'Most definitely. A good lawyer will tell you what you need to do next. They didn't give you *any* instructions when you went in today?'

'No. Oh. They told me to go back in two weeks' time. To register again. They didn't say why.'

'To keep tabs on you, I suppose,' Rita said thoughtfully. 'In case you fled the country – although that doesn't make sense, does it? If you *did* leave, why would they care?'

'I'll go with you, next time,' Carmen said. 'And I'll call the Home Office first thing tomorrow. See if I can find out anything useful. You haven't exactly given us a lot to go on, Mom.'

'I've told you everything.'

'I know, I just want to make sure—'

'Make sure *what* exactly?'

They were interrupted by another knock on the door.

'That will be Kian,' Rita explained. 'I told him to come and get me once he'd dished up dinner. I'll only be a moment.'

She left them in the living room and an awkward hush settled like dust. Carmen looked around the room, her eyes landing on the family photos displayed in the dresser.

'I always hated that picture,' she said, in an attempt to fill the silence, gesturing towards an old school photo. 'You told me not to cut my own fringe and you were right. I wore a hat for weeks! Do you remember when Dean cut his fringe too so I wouldn't feel so bad? He looked ridiculous – hang on a minute! I bet *he* could help us.'

'Who could?' Birdie asked thickly.

'Dean. Dean Evans. Do you remember him?'

Birdie remembered him. Short, buck teeth and a face full of acne, he'd been besotted with Carmen all the way through secondary school, and then Andy had flicked his ridiculous hair in her direction and she'd dumped Dean three minutes later. Poor boy. In the weeks that followed the break-up he spent all of his pocket money on bunches of carnations from the petrol station, shoving them desperately into Birdie's arms and begging her to please ask Carmen to call him. One time he brought a mixtape.

'It's all the songs that make me think of her,' he said, his eyes thick with tears. 'It's mostly Duran Duran.'

Carmen had dropped the tape in the bin on her way to meet Andy at the youth centre.

'As in Dean Evans,' Carmen replied.

'Why, what can he do? Is he a lawyer?'

'He's a civil engineer, actually. I found him on Facebook a

year or two ago. He's doing really well for himself.' Carmen unconsciously smoothed down her hair again.

'How can a civil engineer help me?'

'He emigrated to Canada about a decade ago.'

'How can he help me from Canada?'

'He might have some advice,' Carmen replied hotly. 'About the system. He emigrated legally, of course, but—'

'So did I.'

'Sorry about that,' Rita apologised, returning to the living room. 'So, we have a plan of action, yes? Carmen is going to call up and get some more information, and I will speak to Alan and—'

'But *did* you enter the country legally, Mom? Because I don't want to call up and have them think I'm an idiot—'

'For the last time, *yes*.'

'Then why are they saying you didn't?'

'I told you I don't know! I'm not "in the system" – and I don't know what that means either, so don't ask!'

Rita placed a gentle hand on her arm. 'What I think Carmen means is that was all so long ago. No one could blame you if you didn't exactly follow the rules. And that would have been your parents' fault, not yours.'

'They *did* do it properly though,' Birdie insisted.

'How do you know that, Mom? You were six.'

'Seven,' she replied, but Carmen had a point. 'I think they did.'

Carmen rolled her eyes and took a gulp of lukewarm tea, then spat it back into the chipped Cadbury World mug.

'Jesus, Mom, what did you put in this?' Without waiting for an answer, she carried the teapot into the kitchen and dumped the remaining contents into the sink.

'Can I get you anything, Rita love? A cup of tea that's actually drinkable?'

'No thank you,' Rita said politely, then turned to Birdie. 'We're going to fix this, Birdie. But we need to know what happened. When you emigrated. Can you remember anything? Anything your parents might have said, or . . .'

*England's going to be good to us.*

Birdie hadn't thought about any of that in such a long time. An old sadness, one long buried, tugged at her heart. She didn't know if she wanted to open the door to the past. She didn't know if she'd be able to close it again if she did.

'Birdie?'

'You have to understand,' Birdie said shakily. 'My parents' generation didn't really talk about . . . they just got on with it. They took the bad times with the good. You emigrated, and you made the best of it, regardless of whether it . . . whether it worked out or not.'

'That sounds like it was tough.'

'It was . . . but it was also *exciting*. People all over were leaving the island for a better life. There wasn't much money in Jamaica in those days, you understand. But over in England . . . in England there was money flowing down the streets. That's what we *heard* . . . We were going to be rich. That's what my father said. He couldn't wait to go.'

Birdie's eyes glazed over. 'And neither could I.'

# Four

## *1954*

Auntie Luce was vexed.

The raatid butcher's boy hadn't come with the good cut of mutton she'd asked for, Miss Linda Next Door had promised some prime Portmore gossip and then failed to deliver (*everyone* knew that Alvita Whilby had been caught on her knees behind the general store inspecting a pecker that wasn't her husband's – Luce had put on a pot of coffee for *nuttin'*) and, if that wasn't bad enough, Winston Brown, that starry-eyed, empty-headed dreamer her niece had gone and married, had decided he was going to move his family – *her* family – to England, and nothing she did or said could make him see sense.

She'd *told* Precious not to marry him.

In part, Luce blamed herself, not that she'd ever admit that to a living soul, of course. She might have been able to prevent all of this, had she not made a rare error of judgement all those years ago. Precious had invited her new fella to dinner to meet the family, and immediately Winston Brown had made a poor impression. It might have been nerves. It might have been sheer bumptiousness. Whatever it was, Winston had sat at the table and listed all the ways in which Jamaica was falling to the dogs, and how he had the ambition and the brains to make it in this world, but no one on the island would give him a chance. He was going to make his fortune one day, though. You could count on it.

Aubrey looked at him over his glasses, his face unreadable. 'Tell me, son. Do you have a trade?'

'No sir.'

'A college education?'

'No sir.'

'I see.'

Aubrey said nothing more, apart from *pass the water pitcher please*, and Luce had turned her ample bosom towards Precious, raising one eyebrow as if to say *where'd you find this idiot?* But, to her consternation, Precious only looked mildly embarrassed.

'Winston moved to Kingston to make his fortune,' she said vaguely. 'Does anyone want more rice?'

She'd give her niece more rice. What was she thinking, bringing a boy like this to a respectable home like hers? His suit had gone shiny at the elbows. He held his knife and fork like he'd been raised in a tin shack.

He *was* a looker, though.

Aubrey asked where Winston came from. A country boy! Well, that made sense. Luce rolled her eyes and turned her attention to her bulla cake. Boys like Winston Brown flocked to the city like rats escaping a sinking ship. It wasn't that she couldn't see the attraction (Lord, if she'd been twenty years younger) but Precious was too special to give her heart away to a ragamuffin.

Luce scraped up the crumbs of her cake with the edge of her fork. Winston hadn't yet complimented her cooking, a dangerous oversight if you asked her. The boys Precious *usually* courted had college degrees and neat shirts and exquisite manners. They *always* remembered to compliment her cooking. But maybe, Luce thought, after losing her last sweetheart, maybe *this* was the kind of boy Precious needed to take her mind off her heartbreak. A handsome fella with a misplaced sense of confidence just might put a stop to her moping and her sighing and help her get her spark back. And then, she thought, warming considerably to the idea, Precious would have her head turned by the *right* sort of boy and Winston Brown would never again be mentioned around the Gladstone table.

She made up her mind. What harm could this fella do, with his head full of ambition and his pockets full of nothing? Precious was young. She deserved to have a little fun.

But then they'd had a little too much fun and here they were. A hastily arranged wedding and baby on the way to seal the deal.

She had to give Winston Brown *some* credit, though. She'd half expected him to run right back to Malvern, but he'd shown up to the church on time in the same suit with the shiny elbows he'd worn to dinner, and when he'd smiled at his bride Luce had surprised herself by going weak at the knees. What she wouldn't give for a man to look that way at her again . . .

For close to a decade, things worked out the way she wanted them to, with Precious situated in a single-storey house close by and Winston staying in line and keeping his handsome nose out of trouble.

Or so she thought. The problem was, Luce hadn't banked on that misplaced confidence of his finding a direction.

* * *

Winston Brown, born in a corrugated tin house on the outskirts of Malvern, a tiny village in the Santa Cruz mountains, had come into the world with a quizzical look on his face, as though he'd been expecting a whole lot more than the little he'd got. The youngest son of Ennis and Iciline Brown, he'd spent his childhood working in the family's field, tilling hard, stubborn soil and planting potatoes and carrots and yams and hauling them to the market, watching as his father's back stooped lower and lower, buckling under the burden of his meagre crops and his responsibilities. Ennis was a brittle man, quick to anger and incapable of warmth. When Winston was nine, his father had clipped him around the face without first loosening his grip on the awl in his hand and had been inches away from blinding his son. That was the Ennis they knew at home: a man who communicated through slaps and harsh words. In the market though, Winston had watched him bow and scrape to the wealthy white homeowners who had large houses in the hills, his hands hanging limply at his sides, as subservient as a house dog.

For a young boy unable to shake the feeling that he was destined for something more, the apathy of his father disgusted him. But it was a family affliction, and one by one, his older brothers left the farm to seek their fortunes. His oldest brother Ozzie went first, to Mandeville. Then Ika, to the bauxite mines in the north. Ral did one better and managed to get halfway to Cuba before anyone noticed him missing. Three days after Ral left, Winston's feet began to itch. At first just a tickle, nothing worse than a tick bite, easily ignored as he stuffed his feet into his boots and stomped about the yard, but day by day the itch grew until it felt like his soles were on fire. At sundown, he would plunge his dry, dusty feet into a bucket of cool water and sigh in relief. The itch would subside, for a moment or two, then his father would come round the side of the house and berate him for standing around in a bucket of filthy water like a yam head.

What kind of life could he achieve on the farm? Prosperity couldn't be cultivated like a banana tree. He made up his mind that he too would leave, like his oldest brothers had done. And then Ennis dropped dead in the field, his hands balled into fists and his mouth frozen open in one final complaint. There was no point sending for the doctor – flies had settled on his face by the time they found him. Fifty-seven and barely literate, the man had worked every day of his life and had never stepped beyond the mountain where he'd been born and raised.

Iciline sold the farmland to a neighbour and then turned to her two sons she had left at home, the two who had not made their escape in time. Lanzo was the man of the house now, she said. It was up to him and his baby brother to provide for their mother and sister. Lanzo, with a wisp of hair on his chin, had no intention of becoming the man of the house. He ran off in the middle of the night and sent a telegram from South America a month later.

'My family's disappearing before my eyes,' Iciline wailed, wringing her ashen hands and turning her face so that Winston might see the tears drying on her cheeks. 'Oh Lord, don't let me lose another one of my babies.'

He cursed the misfortune of being the youngest son; the others had left knowing they had a younger replacement at home to take care of the women. But the itch in his feet began to burn like hot tar and he knew that to stay would be to lower himself into an early grave, like his father. So he too left in darkness, the snores of his sleeping mother at his back like a breeze, propelling him down the side of the mountain and towards the sea.

He arrived in Kingston in early 1944. The first thing he did was walk right into the ocean, fully dressed, ignoring the snickers from passers-by. The warm water lapped around his ankles and the itch in his feet melted completely away.

He fast-talked his way into a job at the docks; hot, grimy work loading crates and barrels onto ships so big he had to crane his neck backwards to see where they ended and where the sky began, ships destined for far-flung locations he might have learned about in school, if he'd stayed in the classroom beyond sixth class. The job did not pay much, but he was tall and strong, and a hard worker. He had common sense coming out of his ears and he could take orders with an easy smile and a *right away, sir*. For the first time in his life, he was responsible only for his own needs. That felt good, to have money in his pocket felt good, but after a year he began to resent the men giving him orders. He was just as smart, just as capable, so why should they lord it over him? He was tired of feeling lesser. His whole life, he'd felt lesser.

And then he'd met Precious. A beautiful girl with a dress full of pins. She was clever, and beautiful, with manners like a fine lady. She listened when he shared his blurry yet bombastic dreams for the future with her, as delicate as silk and as fantastical as snow falling on Kingston. She didn't scoff, the way his father would have done. With her on his arm, he felt like a king.

And then she told him about the baby.

'Shit.' He swallowed and rubbed the back of his neck. 'Are you sure?'

'Course I'm sure. Auntie Luce reckons I'm about three months gone.'

He sat down next to her, not giving his legs the chance to run all the way back to Malvern. Then again, he wouldn't put it past Lucille to chase him all the way there and drag him back by his heels. The woman terrified him.

Precious was afraid, too.

'Winston. What are we going to do?'

He forced himself to look at her. Christ, she was beautiful. There wasn't another one like her on the whole island, he was sure. Which meant there was no one else who could make him feel the way she made him feel. Like he mattered. Like he was a man of consequence. He didn't want to lose that.

'Precious Gladstone,' he said, taking her slender hand in his calloused one. 'Will you marry me?'

* * *

Precious lost the baby three weeks after the wedding. She was told not to worry, that the good Lord would surely provide, but two years later, a second pregnancy was celebrated and then too mourned. Only then did Precious tell Winston that her own mother had had difficulties carrying a child to term. Amaretta had had a string of miscarriages, too. Precious's voice dripped with guilt. She knew the only reason they were tethered together was because he'd put a baby in her belly, but the crib was still empty and now there was no reason for him to stay.

'Maybe . . . maybe I can't . . .' she began. They stood at opposite ends of the kitchen, but they might as well have been standing at opposite ends of the island. He would not meet her gaze, so she closed her eyes so she wouldn't have to watch him walk out the front door.

But instead of leaving, he had crossed the short distance between them and wrapped his arms around her.

'Oh Presh,' he said softly, one hand on the back of her head. He tilted her face up to his. 'Look at me. Don't cry.'

'I'm sorry,' she sobbed.

'What for? I knew you would be a pain in the backside when I married you, didn't I?'

She laughed through her tears and wiped her nose on the back of her hand. 'I love you, Winston,' she said fiercely. 'I want us to be happy.'

'We *are* happy. Aren't we?'

She lowered her tear-stained eyelashes, but he tapped her gently on the cheek and she lifted her eyes back to his.

'*We're happy*. We're young, and healthy, and handsome.' He grinned roguishly at her. 'The world's ours for the taking, and one day I'll be so rich you'll bathe in diamonds as pretty as you.'

'But what about—?'

'No buts. We don't need anything else. You can be enough for me, and I can be enough for you. We're happy, Presh.'

She kissed him then, with fierce desperation. His lips tasted like salt and she breathed in his woodsmoke scent, gasping for air like a deep-sea diver breaching the surface of the water. *Winston*, she cried.

A month later, Precious told him she was expecting again.

* * *

The years fell away and baby Bridget grew up. Too fast, for some. She said her first word (*Puppa*) at eight months old and then did not shut up again.

'That girl,' Auntie Luce bellyached, 'is as chirpy as a bird. Give her a lickle sugar cane or something to stop her mouth.'

No one could deny she was her puppa's pickney; not only did she look just like him, right down to the butter-wouldn't-melt grin, but she'd inherited his curiosity – Precious had to keep a sharp eye on her at all times, lest she follow a stray dog out of the market or pull a pot of boiling beans down on top of her head. Winston heard these stories and laughed, much to Precious's vexation.

'She'll be the death of me.'

'Ahh, she's just bentasome,' Winston said, ruffling Birdie's hair affectionately. 'She wants to explore the world, that's all.'

And Winston wanted to give her the whole world, though money was tight and getting tighter. And then he lost his job at the dock, and no amount of smiling or *right away sir*-ing could sweet talk the foreman into changing his mind. It's just a temporary setback, he said. He would find another job before the month was up, and then spent seven weeks tramping the streets, like a mongrel after a bone held just out of reach.

'Can't compete with them city boys,' Winston grumbled over dinner. 'They take one look at you and turn you away before you get the chance to prove you're just as smart as them.'

One evening, he limped up the veranda steps, complaining about a pebble in his shoe that had plagued him all the way home. He sat down on the top step and Birdie pulled his heavy boots off his feet, tipping the right one upside down. Nothing. She slipped her hand inside and then held it up to her eye.

'There's no pebble, Puppa.'

He took the boot from her small hands and felt around inside. Then he inspected the sole of his foot. There was nothing there, no mark, no blemish, and yet the prickling sensation remained.

'Maybe I'm imagining things,' he said slowly, running his palm over his heel in contemplation. 'Nuttin' to worry about, Birdie.'

Birdie believed him. She had few worries in life. She was

small for her age, and skinny, with brown eyes that looked out at the world in wonder. She liked to play beneath the veranda, where there was just enough space for her to squeeze in with Abigay, her rag doll. She'd make neat little piles of red earth and panama berries and wait for the crunch of her father's boots above her head. Then she would wiggle out and chase him up the steps and into the kitchen, diving around the table to take a running leap and land in his lap. He was the person she loved most in the world. She loved her mumma too, of course, but Puppa was more fun. Not only would he play with her whenever she wanted, but he would let her ask as many questions as she liked – and would answer them all too.

After supper she would trot up the lane to Grandpa's, which was as much her home as her own house, or call on her little playmate next door; two years older and completely smitten with her, Anslow allowed himself to be bossed around, and primped, and prodded, smiling a shiny white smile and declaring to his mudda that him a gwine marry Birdie Brown someday.

Five days a week she went to Portmore Junior School in a navy-blue pinny. Every morning before school, she would join her father on the veranda, her bare feet tucked beneath her nightgown, and nestle into his side. He'd let her take sips of strong, bitter coffee from his mug and they'd listen to the chorus as the birds roused themselves in the trees.

On Saturdays she would accompany Mumma to the market, where food sizzled on top of oil drums and the air was heavy with the smell of jerk chicken and exhaust fumes. Auntie Luce was teaching her how to cook: how to tell a ripe ackee from a poisonous one; how to squeeze the liquid from grated cassava using the square of muslin that hung in the pantry; how to eyeball seasoning so she didn't waste time measuring with a spoon. Luce had taught Precious too, her great-aunt said, and one day it would be Birdie's job to teach her own daughters.

On Sundays they would go to church, and then to Grandpa's for lunch. There would be Guinness punch (of which Birdie was allowed a small glass, with a dollop of ice cream floating on the top) and fried snapper. Luce would slit open their bellies one by one and fling the guts into the bowl for the stray cat that hung around the kitchen door. The worst part of Sundays was having her hair washed but afterwards, to serve as a balm to ease her sore scalp, Puppa would tuck her into bed and tell her a story invented right out of his head, of mermaids and pirates and mariners who lived a life on the ocean waves, of pioneers who forged bold new paths in uncharted territory, and she'd fall asleep with sea shanties ringing in her ears.

She was the happiest child on the island.

How different her life might have been, how happy she might have continued to be, if it hadn't been for Niecy Campbell and her big, fat mouth.

* * *

A crowd of schoolgirls were gathered in a circle beneath the shade of a coolie plum tree, just out of sight of Miss Smith's prying eye. Niecy Campbell, a girl in Birdie's class, preened in the centre.

'My daddy's sailing to England,' she said with a pompous sneer, tossing her royal blue hair ribbons over one shoulder. They made a soft sound, like the wing of a bird taking flight, as they flew through the air.

'What for?' a fat little girl asked.

'To live, chupid. He's *emigrating*.' Niecy rolled the word

around her mouth, relishing it, as though it were a sweetie. '*And* when he gets there, he'll get a job that pays so much money we'll have new dresses and shoes and ice cream every day and we'll be rich and *then* he'll send for me and Junior and we'll live in a house bigger than Buckingham Palace.'

The girls gasped in admiration and Niecy grinned, a reptilian smile that stretched across her big ugly face, and batted her eyelashes. The school bell rang. Jealousy simmered right to the tips of Birdie's toes.

She knew where England was of course. She could identify it on a map, the tiny isle that had conquered so much of the world, the Mother Country, where their schoolbooks and their national anthem and their pretty young Queen came from. Birdie and her classmates were Children of the Empire, Miss Smith had read aloud from her Teacher's Edition, and had been since the day the explorers of old had sailed along the Middle Passage. Everyone knew that everything good about Jamaica had been imported from England.

And now Niecy was moving there.

'*My* daddy said they're *begging* for us to move to England, but not every man is smart enough to seize the opportunity,' Niecy said airily as they filed into the classroom. 'Some men just have more *gumption* than others.'

Birdie didn't know what gumption meant (neither, it had to be said, did Niecy). But if England wanted Niecy's puppa then surely they'd want Birdie's, too. He was better than Niecy's father in every way. She stared at the map of the world that Miss Smith had tacked beside the blackboard, her eyes greedily scooping up the small splodge of England, painted the same delicious colour as strawberry ice cream.

That evening, she swung from the veranda railing as she waited for her father to come home from another fruitless day looking for work, pouncing on him before he'd had the chance to knock the dust from his boots.

'Why won't you go to England?'

'What's this?'

She put her hands on her hips. 'Niecy Campbell's puppa's going to England and she's going to get new dresses and ice cream and—'

'Get back in here and set the table like I told you to,' her mother scolded from the kitchen, and Birdie reluctantly complied. She got another chance at bedtime. When Winston went to kiss his daughter goodnight, he found her sat up in bed, anxiously waiting for him.

'Why can't you go to England?'

'Are you trying to get rid of me, baby?'

'No,' Birdie fidgeted impatiently. 'But Niecy said her puppa said there isn't enough money on this raatid island and over in England they're *begging* for us to go and work there and that some men have more gumption than others and—'

'Is that so?'

'Uh-huh, and her puppa said they will have so much money they won't know what to do with it. They'll have ice cream *every* day—'

'Not *every* day, surely?'

'Every day, Puppa!' she insisted, and he whistled with appreciation.

'That sounds mighty nice.'

'So will you? Will you go to England?'

Winston looked at her out of the corner of his eye.

'I don't know . . .' Her bottom lip fell. 'England's pretty far away. How would I get there? I don't think I could swim that far—'

'You wouldn't *swim*, Puppa. You'd take a boat,' Birdie said frustratedly. Niecy hadn't shut up about her father's second-class passage aboard a ship called the *Riviera*. Her mother had ordered him a new suit especially for the journey because the captain was sure to want to dine with him—

'And then there's you and your mumma to think about. *She* can't swim, for one—'

'Puppa,' she whined, giving an exasperated wiggle in his arms.

'And what if England doesn't want me, hmm? You thought about that? Niecy's farda might give us all a bad name.'

'Oh, but Puppa.' She scrambled to her knees, her breath hot and sweet against his cheek. 'You have just as much gumption as Niecy's puppa does. *More*. I know it.'

He stroked his chin in casual contemplation. 'You know Birdie, people say that the streets of England are paved with gold.' His voice swelled with possibility. 'What do you think of that?'

'*Real* gold?'

'That's just what I heard, of course. But wouldn't it be something if we could see for ourselves?'

She clasped her hands around his. 'I want to see it! Please, let's go!'

His smile faded. 'But Birdie, what about your mumma? I don't think she would be that keen to move to England. Do you think I could convince her?'

'I *know* you can, Puppa,' Birdie said confidently.

'Leave it with me,' he said with a wink, and Birdie kissed his cheek. He chucked her beneath the chin and left the room, and Birdie drifted off into a satisfied sleep – no sea shanties in her head tonight, but her father's words echoing faintly, as through borne about her room on the night breeze.

*Wouldn't it be something if we could see for ourselves?*

* * *

'England? What you gwine do in England?'

'Work, Auntie.'

They were seated around the Gladstone dining table: Winston and Precious, Auntie Luce and Aubrey, and Peter, who had stopped by unannounced and had no idea he was walking into a powda house. Birdie was upstairs playing in Luce's wardrobe, draping herself in yards of black material and tottering about in her aunt's slippers with an ugly hat perched on top of her head. She'd been told to run along and play while the grown-ups talk.

'You only have to look in the papers to see there's jobs aplenty,' Winston reasoned. He had been out of work for six long months and both his savings and his pride had taken a battering. 'I need to earn a living. I have a family. I have to provide.'

'But *England* . . .'

Lucille was at her wits' end. She felt like she'd been ambushed – Winston Brown had sat at *her* table and had eaten *her* food and then said he wanted to take *her* family away. Well. Not if she had anything to do with it. At first, she tried belittling (*what would England want with you?*) and then she tried prognosticating (*Sonellie Martin's husband's brudda went to England and now he's dead*) but Winston refused to see sense. She had one tool left up her sleeve. Guilt.

'You'll be so far away. I'll never see you again!'

She let out a noisy wail and fished up her *other* sleeve for a handkerchief.

'It's just an idea,' Precious said hastily. 'Nuttin's been decided yet.'

'I think it's a good idea,' Peter said, and Luce glared at him from behind her man-sized hankie.

Aubrey rubbed his eyes wearily. 'I understand the appeal,

son. But it's a big decision, and one you can't easily walk back from. I've asked around for a job for you—'

'Couldn't *you* give him a job, Daddy?' Precious asked, but Aubrey shook his head.

'I've had to let two of my own boys go. Times are tight, Presh. The economy's not what it was. I'm sorry.'

Auntie Luce threw her hands into the air.

'So you're just going to let them go? You're going to let your only daughter follow *him* halfway across the world?'

Precious tried to take Luce's hand in her own. 'Auntie. Nuttin's been decided yet.' Luce shook her off, more out of disbelief than genuine anger. She'd never lost an argument before.

'And what about Birdie, hmm?' It was her last shot. 'What about your daughter? Have you thought about what this will mean for *her*? She's so lickle; she'll get pneumonia and die, I'm sure of it—'

Lucille did not know that for weeks, Birdie had been asking her father when they were going to England. They couldn't leave soon enough, if you asked her. Three days after the family dinner, she returned home from a visit up the lane to find her parents locked in a fierce argument, their voices floating through the screen door.

'It's done,' she heard her father say. 'I've got my ticket.'

'You march right down to that shipping office and get your money back right now—'

'And throw away the opportunity of a lifetime?'

'You'll find another job here, Winston. Just be patient—'

'And what will we live on in the meantime? I've been out of work for *six months* – if we wait even a few more *weeks* we won't be able to afford this house. It's a hunting ground for ready labour over there, and I'm *ready*. This makes sense, why can't you see that?'

'I could go back to work, I told you—'

Winston glowered. 'And I told *you.* What kind of man lets his *wife* provide for his family?'

'What about school?' Precious asked desperately. 'We can't just pull her out of school—'

'Schools are better over there. Everyone knows that. She might actually learn something—'

'But to buy a ticket *without discussing it*—'

Winston looked away.

'We did discuss it. You didn't like the discussion, but we discussed it.'

'Auntie Luce will have something to say about this—'

'Let her. She's not the boss of me—'

The screen door squeaked, and Birdie jumped back. It was too late to flee back down the lane. In three paces her father crossed the kitchen and opened the door.

'Come in, baby. We need to talk.'

'Don't go dragging Birdie into this,' her mother remonstrated as Winston guided her to her chair at the kitchen table. She wasn't tall enough to touch the floor and her feet swung freely in scuffed leather sandals. Her father sat next to her, his foot drumming against the wooden floor.

'She needs to know sooner or later. And besides, you want to go, don't you baby? You said so yourself.'

'Birdie said she wanted to go to England?' Her mother's voice was dangerously low. 'What ideas have you been putting in her head?'

'She's a free spirit, like her farda.'

Precious shook her head in disbelief.

'And she came up with it all by herself, did she?' She swivelled her eyes towards her daughter. 'So. You want to go to England, eh?'

Birdie opened her mouth, then closed it again. She didn't know what to say. A jumble of thoughts ran through her head: the sound of Niecy's laughter, the taste of strawberry ice cream, the wonder in her father's voice and the promise of having more money than they'd know what to do with . . .

'I . . .' Birdie began.

She looked at her mother. Precious's face was creased into a frown, her lips pursed together, tension pulsating in her temple. Then Birdie looked at her father. He smiled his sunshiny smile, the one that made her feel warm all over.

'I . . . I do,' she whispered, and Winston hollered and scooped her up in his arms.

'Whoooee! That settles it!'

Birdie giggled dizzily as he spun her round the kitchen. He planted a noisy kiss on her forehead as they came to a stop, and as the room came back into focus, her eyes found Mumma, sat with her back straight, her eyes expressionless.

'Oh *Presh*,' her father said softly, and pulled her into their embrace. At first, Precious stood there, stiff and unmoveable, but Winston snaked his arm around her waist and Birdie threw her arms around her neck, and she melted into them.

'Have faith,' Winston whispered into his wife's ear as she cried silent tears into the front of his shirt.

'England's going to be good to us. I promise you that.'

# Five

## *2016*

'This is ridiculous,' Carmen hissed out of the corner of her mouth. 'What's taking them so long?'

As promised, Carmen accompanied her mother on her next visit to the immigration centre. Birdie had spent the last two weeks in a strange kind of fog. She didn't know what she was supposed to *do*. How was a person supposed to get on with their life with the threat of deportation hanging over their heads, like an axe? The Home Office had not provided instructions.

She had tried to go about her life as usual – bingo on Wednesday, the community centre on Tuesdays and Thursdays – but it was hard. The Bingo Babs kept asking her if she was alright; she'd missed three numbers – no, *four* – and Birdie never missed a number. Something had to be up. The lie came to her quickly – *I'm due a hearing test* – because she'd rather they think she was going deaf than know the truth. Shame was eating away at her. Funny how two little words – illegal immigrant – could alter a person's identity. Or rob them of it entirely. Would people look at her differently, if they knew? She didn't want to risk it. She hadn't even told her best friend yet. She and Claudette had met as young black women, but their bond went far deeper than the colour of their skin: they had helped each other through bereavements, motherhood, mammograms and health issues. Claudette was recovering from a stroke and Birdie visited as often as she could, to sit with her and hold her hand and talk of better, happier days. How could she talk about this? She didn't have the words.

It was easier at the creche. A small place filled with small problems – *he took my toy, I hurted my knee* – where she could forget, for a few hours, the world beyond the baby-proofed doors. She took Jaxon to Victoria Park, watched him wave at her from the top of the metal slide that had been tagged by four rival graffiti artists, calling out to him to be careful as he dove down it headfirst. Jaxon had a mop of toffee-coloured curls, a tiny gap in his front teeth and struggled to say his Rs. He was just a baby. Who would look out for him, if they sent her away? Who would keep him safe? She was just as much a mother to that boy as Tegan was, really – and she was not the sort of parent who left. She'd made that vow long ago and she wasn't going to break it now. They *couldn't* deport her, she decided, her confidence galvanising. She was needed here.

That confidence came and went in waves. She would wake up in the middle of the night in a cold sweat – the government could do with her what it liked, they would chew her up and spit her out – and the sound of a car door slamming would leave her twitching like a shell-shocked soldier.

She was not the sort of parent who left – but what if the decision was taken out of her hands?

* * *

On the morning of her second appointment, Carmen texted Birdie to say she was waiting downstairs in the car. Birdie picked up her purse. Slotted neatly inside was a cardboard

ID card that had arrived by post, along with the command that she carry it on her person, always. If she were stopped by a law enforcement officer, she was to present it immediately, the letter said, which left Birdie wondering how likely it would be that she'd have police stopping her in the middle of her weekly shop.

Birdie had not put much thought into her outfit that morning. She was wearing a pair of maroon leggings with stirrups under her heels, a baggy T-shirt and a pair of slip-on shoes, the sort of clothes she would wear to pop to the shop or clean the bathroom. She'd not bothered with her wig, either. She wore her natural, greying hair short, as it was easier to manage. Carmen, in contrast, was wearing an electric blue blazer and lipstick the colour of burnt caramel.

'What are you wearing that get up for?' Birdie asked as she dropped heavily into the passenger seat.

'I borrowed this from Tina. It's her work jacket. It looks smart, doesn't it?'

'I suppose so. But why do *you* need to look smart?'

'Because these people need to know who they're dealing with. And besides, a good first impression is everything.'

'They're not deporting *you*,' Birdie muttered.

'They're not going to deport you, either,' she replied sternly. 'Right, let's get going. Do you have the address for the satnav?'

Despite their best intentions, they hit heavy traffic on the ring road and arrived in Solihull with only minutes to spare. Upon joining the queue to go through the security checks, Carmen complained when the guard asked for her phone, and then moaned that there was a line for the bathroom, so by the time Birdie took a ticket – sunshine-yellow, this time – from the dispenser, she half wished that her daughter had stayed at home.

Carmen checked her watch. 'Has it only been half an hour? God. Feels like it's been longer. Does it feel longer to you? It feels like it's been forever already. Why is it taking so long? I told Craig I'd be in by twelve. He'll go nuts if I'm late.'

'Who's Craig?'

'I *told* you. My manager.'

'I thought *you* were the manager?'

'I'm a department shift leader. It means nothing, really. I *could* be manager, one day. I could run that store with one hand tied behind my back. But not if I keep having to take time off . . .'

Birdie got the hint. 'Thank you again, Carmen. You didn't have to come with me.'

'Of course I did,' she said, and Birdie squeezed her arm gratefully. Carmen was temporarily mollified, until a man slid into the space beside her, pressing his thigh against hers. She tried to lean away from him, but he merely spread his legs wider. She tutted pointedly, then reached into the pocket of the borrowed blazer for her phone, before remembering she had surrendered it. Because clearly they wanted everyone in the room to die of boredom.

A short man with a thick neck lumbered past them, and Carmen nudged her mother in the shoulder.

'He looks just like Scott,' she said surreptitiously, but Birdie disagreed.

'Not as handsome.'

'Does he know yet, or . . .?'

Birdie sighed. 'How would he know?'

'I don't know, you might have—'

'Can we not talk about him please?'

'Fine.'

Carmen was silent for a few seconds, but she couldn't help herself. She nudged her mother again.

'Mom?'

'What?'

'Will you tell Jimmy?'

'*What*?'

'Don't look at me like that. I was only asking.'

'Don't ask me such stupid questions then.'

'Just trying to make conversation,' Carmen muttered under her breath. She fidgeted on the bench, the hard metal indenting grooves into her backside, and checked her watch again. 'Whoever's running this place needs to get their act together.'

'I told you, it takes a long time,' Birdie replied wearily. She understood Carmen's frustration – the last time she had been here, she too had been ready to complain about the lack of comfort. But that had been when she still believed she had the right to complain. Now she was terrified of saying or doing anything that would get her into more trouble.

'This is like an act of torture, forcing us all to wait like this. And look!' Carmen pointed towards the door. 'They keep letting more and more people in. Why? There's no room for them here.'

'How's Andy?' Birdie asked quickly.

'Oh. Well.' Carmen brushed a stray hair off her face. 'His back's still not right. He's thinking about calling one of those compensation lawyers – you know, the "no win, no fee" ones. But in the meantime he's found some work – or at least, his friend Jake knows a guy who knows a guy who's looking for some labourers. Just cash-in-hand stuff, but it's better than nothing. Jake said Andy needs to call the first guy who'll vouch for him.'

'Call who, Andy?'

'No, Andy needs to – never mind.'

'Oh. How are the kids?' Birdie asked, intuitively feeling that they were a much safer topic of conversation. 'Any chance of a visit from Declan soon?'

Declan, Birdie's oldest grandchild, was twenty-five and worked in something he called software sales. Birdie didn't understand it, but she was proud of him, nonetheless.

'Oh, you know Dec, too busy living the high life to remember his family. But apparently he and Angharad are posting the save the dates this week, so keep an eye out.'

'How lovely. Listen Carm, you haven't told the kids, have you?'

'No-o,' Carmen said, and it sounded like a lie. Birdie frowned.

'I hope you haven't told them. I don't want them worrying over this, it wouldn't be fair. They're too young.'

Saffie was seventeen and the twins were three years younger. They were all still babies in Birdie's eyes.

'I'm going to go say something,' Carmen interrupted. 'They shouldn't keep us waiting so long – some of us have jobs to get to.'

Her eyes scanned the room. The only people she could see who looked as though they might have any kind of authority were stationed behind the plexiglass.

'Carmen, don't—' Birdie pleaded, as Carmen rose to her feet.

'*Ticket number three hundred and one, to window five, please. Ticket number—*'

*Thank the Lord*, Birdie thought.

'That's us,' Carmen said needlessly. 'Have you got your evidence?'

Of course Birdie had her evidence. Bundled in her handbag

was a slim stack of bills and bank statements, one dating back ten years. She'd even managed to find some old payslips gathering dust in a Clarks shoebox at the back of the wardrobe – just two, but she hoped it was enough to prove she had, at one time, been in legal employment.

She had found other things in that shoebox. A letter from her father, dated October 1954, written from England. Another, which had reached her almost thirty years later, this time sent from Jamaica. She hadn't re-read them. Seeing his handwriting on the envelopes was enough to hurt, but she'd had an easier time looking through old photo albums. She had added a handful of photographs to her small pile of 'evidence': Birdie standing to one side of a department store Father Christmas while a two-year-old Carmen screamed in the old man's lap; Birdie squinting on Blackpool beach, Scott proudly holding up his new bucket and spade for the camera; Jimmy's fortieth; *her* fortieth; a barbeque in Carmen's back garden in 2009, Precious seated primly on a picnic blanket, surrounded by her great-grandchildren, not long before she entered the hospice . . .

There was a black and white picture of her father and mother too, taken on their wedding day, back when Winston's smile stretched from ear to ear and Precious could still remember her own name. She stared at her parents. She wished she could talk to them. Precious would know what to do in a situation like this; she had always been so cool, so unflappable. Not like Winston, whose emotions changed direction as quickly as the wind blowing over the Caribbean Sea. What would they say to her, if they could be there with her now? Would they have been able to explain? Would they have known why they were calling their daughter an illegal immigrant?

She set the photo down and continued on her trip down memory lane. It had to be endured if she was to convince the government of her right to remain. Proving she had been here since childhood was the only option she had, now that she knew legal aid would be denied to her.

Rita had done as she had promised and asked her employer for his advice. It was not good news.

'Alan had to google this, because, like I said, he's not an immigration lawyer,' she'd said, flipping open an A5 notebook. 'But he said that the cause of Birdie's specific issue is the amendments made to the Immigration Act in 1971, which is why the Home Office have legal recourse to remove her from the country.'

'Rita, love.'

Even over speakerphone, Birdie could tell her daughter was frowning.

'Can we please have that in terms we can understand.'

'It's like this. When Birdie arrived, in—'

'1955,' Birdie prompted.

'Right, in 1955, she and her parents had the right to remain indefinitely. You and all the other citizens of the Commonwealth, my own grandparents included. But since the 1950s, they've been trying to . . .' Rita gestured for the right words. 'To slow immigration down, I guess. The government didn't want an open-door policy anymore, so they changed the rules – more than once, according to Alan – so that after 1973, Commonwealth citizens no longer had the automatic right to remain, no matter *when* they'd arrived.'

'Meaning?'

Rita paused. 'Meaning that Birdie has technically been an illegal immigrant since the 1970s.'

Birdie's mouth fell open. 'But no one told me they'd changed the rules!'

'None of this makes sense,' Carmen said. 'If the rules changed in the seventies, why are they coming after her *now*?'

'I don't know. Alan had no idea, either. I told you, this isn't his area of expertise. You'll need to find an immigration lawyer to answer those kinds of questions.'

'Did he recommend anyone?'

Rita closed her notebook. 'Ahh. He *did* . . . but . . .'

Birdie had the prickly feeling she wasn't going to like what Rita was about to say.

'He said that because you're now officially classed as an illegal immigrant, you don't qualify for legal aid.'

'What does that mean?'

'You'll have to pay a lawyer's full fee, and he said it's not going to be cheap. You could try to find one to work pro bono – that means for free – but he said most immigration lawyers are probably inundated with such requests and time isn't on your side right now.'

'How much . . .?'

What was the point in finishing the question? Birdie could never afford to hire a lawyer. She had a few thousand pounds in a savings account and £250 stashed in a drawer, in case of emergencies or unexpected bills. But her pension only went so far.

There was an awkward silence.

'Mom,' Carmen paused, and cleared her throat. The sound reverberated down the phone. 'You know I'd help out if I could, but the twins needed new blazers for school this year and Andy's not working right now and—'

'It's fine, Carmen.'

'Maybe we could do a whip around the community? I could certainly stretch my budget a little—' Rita began, but Birdie quashed that suggestion immediately. She hadn't been raised to accept handouts.

'People around here have their own problems. And their own bills to pay. I don't want to burden anybody.'

'Alan is happy to put you in touch with someone, but he was very clear that the law prevents him from giving you any proper counsel, *even* if he did know anything about immigration law.'

'Thanks, Rita,' Birdie said, her shoulders slumping. She had been British all her life and now she was only British if she could afford to hire a lawyer who could plead her case.

'But,' Rita said, brightening. 'I asked him about the evidence. You know, what you said about that old man and his daughter, and he said it makes sense. They're claiming they don't know if you entered the country before or after 1973, right? But you can prove you *did*. You can prove that you have a life here. They can't argue with that.'

And so Birdie had spent the past two weeks combing her flat for every scrap of paper she could find that confirmed her name, her address, even her blood type – anything she thought might help. In an attempt to track down her school records she'd called up her old primary school and spent a very confusing twenty minutes on the line with the secretary.

'I don't know if we have records that go back that far. I've only just started working here.'

'Could you check anyway, please?' Birdie asked. 'And if you find anything, anything at all, I'd be grateful if you could post it to me. I'll even pay for the stamp.'

'I'll email you a screenshot, that'll be quicker than posting it,' the secretary said cheerily.

Birdie thanked her for her enthusiasm and then explained that digital records hadn't existed in the 1950s.

While she hadn't been able to confirm she had attended a British school (*how* had that young woman managed it? She wished she could find her and ask), she did have a letter from her GP practice, plus the birth certificates of both of her children, a clever idea of Rita's.

'Think about it,' Rita had said excitedly. 'Carmen and Scott were born right here in Birmingham. And you *had* to have been in the country to give birth here.'

Yesterday she had spread all of her evidence over the kitchen table and felt a bloom of hope. Here was irrefutable proof that she had been living in the country since . . . well, since 1966, the year Carmen was born. They *couldn't* argue with it.

She went to bed thinking that in twenty-four hours it would all be over. Then she had woken in the night, plagued by sudden doubt. The timeline she had piecemealed together was spotty, at best. There was nothing but the letter from her father to prove that he had emigrated to England a year before she did, and nothing to prove that she had actually followed him. But what could she do about that now? She couldn't go back in time and write herself a note . . .

She rolled over and closed her eyes, then opened them again. She padded into the living room. In the dresser was a stern snapshot of Auntie Luce wearing a *hideous* hat (she looked, Birdie often thought, like a pig in a wig) that had been bestowed upon a seven-year-old Birdie as a farewell gift. She turned it over. Written on the back of the frame, in a thin, spidery hand, was a parting message.

*Goodbye to my treasured Birdie. Safe travels to England.*
*Until we meet again, in this life or the next.*
*July 1955.*

Luce had always been so dramatic, she thought gratefully. Birdie dropped the photo into her handbag and went back to bed.

* * *

Carmen stared down the woman behind the glass.

'I'm here with my mother.' She was doing her posh voice, the one she used on bank managers and Angharad's parents. 'You have incorrectly labelled her an illegal immigrant, and I'd like to speak to your manager.'

The woman smiled nervously. She was wearing a cream pussybow shirt with a coffee stain down the front. The stain was still damp, and Birdie noticed a wad of mocha-coloured tissues on the woman's desk.

'Oh. I'm sorry, I'm afraid that's not possible. For you to speak to a manager, I mean. But I would be more than happy to help you today—'

Carmen laughed dryly. 'Help us? Help us? That's rich. None of you lot want to help us. I have been calling the Home Office *every day* and every single time I am put on hold for hours and then when someone *actually* answers they tell me that they're busy or they're closed and that I should speak to someone here instead. So – what's your name?'

'Maisie.'

'So, Maisie, I am here, and I want to speak to someone in charge.'

Maisie glanced over her shoulder, and then looked back at Carmen. 'I – I can answer any queries you may have—'

'You don't seem so sure about that. Is there someone else we can talk to?'

Maisie smiled harder, her eyes wide. Birdie realised that she wasn't a woman at all, not really. She didn't look much older than Saffie.

'No – no, I can—'

Carmen didn't wait for her to finish. 'My mother moved here in the 1950s when she was *seven*,' she said, jabbing her finger into Birdie's arm. 'She's no more an illegal immigrant than – than the prime minster. I don't understand why you're coming after her. No one will tell us anything. What we want is answers.'

*I want to not get deported*, Birdie thought. Maisie, whose smile was getting more and more strained by the second, asked for her name and address.

'I'll need to look you up in the system—' Maisie explained, and Carmen tutted angrily.

'The *system* you all care about so much is clearly broken and what you're doing here is barbaric. My mother hasn't done anything wrong.'

Maisie's hands flew over the keys. She hit the enter key four times in rapid succession.

'I'm sorry, my computer is running slow—'

'Is *his* running?' Carmen pointed to the man at the next window. 'Can *he* help me?'

Maisie turned in her chair – were those tears in her eyes, Birdie wondered in horror, or just a reflection from the harsh strip lighting overhead? – and called for someone called Geoff. Geoff had three fat strands of mousy hair combed over his shiny scalp, and the tip of his nose was red and chapped. He wiped it on a handkerchief and frowned at them through the glass.

'What seems to be the problem?' he said, his eyes fixed on Carmen.

'Are *you* in charge?' Carmen asked, unable to mask her surprise. Geoff straightened his spine – even in her trainers, Carmen was at least two inches taller than him – and adjusted his mustard-yellow tie.

'We have a strict no hostility policy here and if you do not contain yourself, I will call security and have you both escorted out of the building.'

'We're not being hostile!' Carmen spluttered. 'I'm just trying to get answers.'

Before Geoff had a chance to argue, Birdie began shoving her sheaf of papers and photographs beneath the gap in the plexiglass.

'I'm sorry. I'm so sorry. I just want to show somebody this,' she said quickly. 'It's my evidence. Proof that I've been here since the fifties. I have payslips – I worked in care homes for the elderly – and here, here's a council tax bill and, and my daughter's birth certificate – she was born in Dudley Road Hospital and I *had* to have been in the country to give birth here, right? And this note from my great-aunt, which proves—'

'I'm sorry,' Geoff held up one hand, his handkerchief balled into his fist. 'But none of that is sufficient.'

Birdie didn't understand.

'Not . . . sufficient?'

Geoff pushed his gold-framed glasses up his nose. 'The only evidence the Home Office can and will accept of your right to remain is proof of entry into the United Kingdom before 1973. That is when the law changed and—'

'Yes, we know all about the law changing. But what do you mean by "proof of entry"?' Carmen asked.

'Your mother's passport. Her travel documents,' he said slowly, as though speaking to a child. 'Bearing an official stamp from border control to show the date of entry. Without that we cannot substantiate her claim that she entered the country legally before 1973. It's the only form of evidence we will accept.'

'But I—' Birdie looked down at the mess of papers. 'I don't *have* any travel documents. I came to England on my mother's passport, and I haven't seen it in – in *years*. I don't know where it is.'

'Then there's nothing more we can do for you today,' Geoff

said dismissively. 'If you find it, please present it at your next appointment, the details of which will be posted to you in due course. Thank you.'

'Hang on,' Carmen objected. 'How come this is the first we're hearing of needing proof of entry? Not one of you have said *any*thing about it before now.'

'If you have any questions you can call the Home Office immigration support team—'

'I've been *trying* to call the Home Office immigration support team but there's never anyone there—'

'They'll be able to help with your queries. Good morning.'

Carmen muttered something under her breath as she grabbed fistfuls of papers, stuffing them back into Birdie's handbag.

'Thank you, Maisie,' Birdie said quietly, stepping away from the counter and making room for the next person, and then the next person, and then the next.

* * *

'I've got half a mind to go back in there,' Carmen said as they exited the building. 'It's a bloody outrage—'

Birdie wasn't paying attention. She was watching the young woman with purple braids lead her father slowly up the concrete steps. So, their evidence hadn't been enough, either. She tried to catch the woman's eye, but she was entirely focused on her father and if she recognised Birdie, she did not acknowledge it.

'Mom? Are you listening?'

'Don't go back in, for God's sake. Don't start a row. They could use that against me.'

'They can't do that,' Carmen said, but she had the decency

to sound chastened. She was silent all the way back to the estate, but when she pulled up outside Clent House, she turned to her mother and spoke with unabashed emotion.

'I'll find a way to fix it, Mom,' she said, leaning over to wrap her arms around Birdie. 'I'll fix it. I promise.'

* * *

Carmen ducked into the toilets and shrugged out of Tina's blazer. She felt a quick twinge of resentment as she changed into her blue polyester T-shirt, then slipped into the staff room as discreetly as she could. She'd told Craig she'd *definitely* be in by twelve but—

'What time do you call this?'

It had only *just* gone quarter past. She turned to face Craig, an artificially contrite smile plastered across her face.

'I'm sorry. My mother's emergency took longer than expected.'

Craig's facial expression remained stony. He was in his early thirties but looked fifteen, with a weak chin and dyed black hair gelled into spikes. She could smell his cheap deodorant from the other side of the staff room. Lynx Africa. She bet he bought enough boxsets with his staff discount every December to last him the whole year.

'I need you on the floor. And Carmen. This is the second time you've been late this month. I expect better from a shift team leader.'

'Prick,' she muttered once he was out of earshot. He hadn't even asked how the morning had gone.

'It went utterly shit, Craig, if you were wondering. My mom might get deported—'

Shit, shit, shit. What if it actually happened? She'd said

that she'd fix it, but what the fuck did she know? They could come for her tomorrow and she'd have no way of stopping it. She felt an overwhelming sense of guilt that clung to her as uncomfortably as her unflattering uniform. The worst part was how lost her mom had looked, how diminished, bleating out an apology when she had every right to tear that tosser with the terrible combover a new one for what they were doing to her. Her mom *never* took any shit from anyone. Carmen remembered when Mr Woodruff had singled her out for detention even though *three* other girls had been caught cheating too. The look on his face when her mom told him off at the school gates had been *epic*. Where had that version of her mom gone? Carmen hated seeing her look so . . . so *small*. She threw her handbag into her locker with vitriol, then heard the *ping!* of a new notification and retrieved it again. If it was the school saying Jade had gotten detention again then so help her—

It was Dean! Her first boyfriend. Her first love. She'd sent him a Facebook message a week ago, after scrolling through his photos for half an hour (he was so handsome. When had he gotten so handsome? And so *tall*) and drinking half a bottle of discounted red wine she'd hidden in the cupboard under the sink, where Andy wouldn't find it.

Hey Carm,

He still called her Carm! Her heart fluttered beneath her polyester T-shirt.

It's great to hear from you. Sorry to hear about your mom but I'm not sure how I can help, this is definitely a case for a lawyer. Do you remember Anna Derwent, from school?

Carmen *did* remember Anna – a prudish teacher's pet who'd grassed on her for smoking behind the science shed. As payback Carmen had written on the wall in the girls' loos that Anna had had three abortions already because she was such a slag. Of course, no one really believed that shy, speccy Anna, who spent every dinner hour reading in the library, had *actually* lost her cherry, but by the end of the day a group of year eleven boys were calling her Annabortion all the same.

She's a barrister now, and I'm sure she'd be happy to speak with you. I can give you her details if you'd like?

Carmen typed out an eager response.

Hi Dean its so great to hear from you! Id love it if you could put me in touch with Anna, that would be a big help, thank you! Are you planning on coming back to the UK anytime soon? Id love to see you! Let me know! Love Carmen xxx

She debated signing off *Love Carm* instead, but decided that that would be overkill. She sent the message and then, almost compulsively, went back to his most recent photos. Oh, Dean. She hadn't appreciated it at the time, but he'd been a lifeline during those troublesome teen years, when she'd had to contend not only with her body stretching and swelling in the most awkward of places but with her mom too, who would never let her do anything fun, who wanted to raise her like Nanny P had been raised and embarrassed her by being loud and *nothing* like her friends' moms. Dean had lived in a quiet house with his dad who worked in finance and his mom who made roast beef every Sunday. Carmen had always marvelled at how *calm* his upbringing had been. It was a soothing antithesis to her own childhood. If Andy hadn't asked her for a light that night at the youth club . . . well. There was no way of knowing what could have been.

She liked his last three photos, then heard a dry cough behind her.

'If you're not too busy, I need you in dairy produce,' Craig said scathingly. 'Someone's dropped a whole bottle of Cravendale.'

* * *

Birdie saw Carmen's face fall as she looked in the rear-view mirror. Carmen had promised to fix it, but what could she do, really? The situation seemed hopeless without – what had that man called them? – without travel documents. She didn't *have* travel documents. Who knew what her mother had done with the passport. She'd probably thrown it away, thinking it would never be needed again . . .

She made a small choking sound and hurried across the courtyard. Delma waved at her from the top floor and Birdie nodded in acknowledgement but didn't stop until she'd reached her flat.

A tiny mountain of post was piled up on the mat behind her front door and she stooped, with creaking knees, to scoop it up. She used to love to receive letters, when she was a little girl. Back then, letters were a luxury; someone had to deem you were worthy of not just the time it would take to sit down and write to you, but also the cost of the postage. Letters from across the sea were the most expensive of all, and the most exciting. She remembered waiting all morning on the veranda for the first glimpse of the postboy to come riding up the lane on his bicycle, the thrill of anticipation as he pedalled closer, holding her breath as she tried to determine if he was slowing down, or if he'd ride right on by to the next house –

She flicked through the pile distractedly. Takeaway menus, junk mail, *congratulations, you're a winner* – useless bits of paper, about as useless as the stack of so-called evidence that she had amassed for nothing. How could her proof not be sufficient proof? She'd been pre-approved for a credit card. Funny, she didn't suppose an illegal immigrant could apply for a credit card. And Carmen hadn't helped matters, carrying on the way she had – the save the date! It was about time. Declan had proposed to Angharad, his university girlfriend (a lovely girl, a bit horsey in the tooth but absolutely besotted with her grandson) two years ago, but every time Birdie had asked *when's the wedding?* he had shrugged sheepishly. Pickney these days. Thinking they had all the time in the world. Perhaps her nagging had finally paid off, but it might not matter anymore. She might not be around to see him wed.

She dabbed her eyes. She was going to buy them the best set of wedding china she could afford. Something they could keep for generations, a lasting reminder of their nanny—

There was one more envelope in the pile. She slit it open and pulled out the single piece of paper, embossed in the top corner with an official logo. The Department for Work and Pensions.

They'd stopped her pension.

Her heart stopped, too.

# Six

## *1954*

The ticket was purchased, the suitcase was packed, and word was spread, from veranda to veranda. Winston Brown was going to England.

He would be travelling to London alone. His wife and child would follow in six months, maybe twelve. Birdie's bottom lip had trembled when she'd heard the news. At no point had a separation been mentioned. Why couldn't she go too?

'I'll need to make enough money to send for you, first. Don't worry, baby. I'll find a job the minute I get off the boat. I bet you'll be with me in England before I've had a chance to unlace my boots!'

'Don't tell her that. It's going to take months,' her mother scolded.

'Months?' Birdie wailed.

'It'll fly by,' Winston promised.

As his departure date grew closer, his smile grew bigger. Not even Auntie Luce, and her constant remonstrations and prophesies of doom (*he'll fall overboard. Can he swim?*) could quell his excitement. She wasn't the only one who had their doubts, though. Neighbours and friends would stop him in the street and ask when he was planning on coming back. Three years? Five?

He baulked.

'*Back*? Why would I come back?'

Since the sailing of the *Windrush*, it was custom for those who had made the decision to emigrate to plan ahead for their eventual return, their pockets laden with enough money to prop up their families. Not Winston.

'I'm getting out of this country for a reason, boy,' he bragged, stuffing his hands in his pockets self-importantly. 'I'll have no need to come back.'

*But surely one day*, came the incredulous response.

'Maybe when I retire,' Winston said airily, his wallet already overflowing with imagined earnings. 'Buy a big white house in the mountains . . .'

'Who does he think he is, Dick Wittington?' Lucille grumbled, plucking a chicken with such ferocity it was lucky the unfortunate bird was already dead. 'Mister high and mighty thinking he's too good for this world . . .'

On the day of his departure, the Browns travelled to Kingston by bus, a new felt hat on top of Winston's head at a jaunty angle, tap-tapping his feet like a dancer warming up in the wings. Alighting the bus, they followed the busy road that sloped gently down towards the sea, Precious unconsciously catching onto the edge of Winston's sleeve, Birdie following behind, a half skip in her step as she struggled to keep up with her father's long legs. She wanted to see the ship that would carry him across the waves. Her father had told her the story of the day she'd been born, and she knew what to expect – the crowd, the atmosphere, the thrum of anticipation – but when they arrived at the docks, she was greeted by nothing but her own disappointment. There wasn't a crowd come to see Puppa off, just a small collection of folks saying goodbye to their own. Hers was the only hankie fluttering in the air (she'd started waving it the moment they had disembarked the bus). There was only one ship in the harbour, and it was not the sleek ocean liner she had been expecting.

'Is *that* the ship?'

'Sure is, baby.'

'Nuh-uh.'

Puppa's ship was small and shabby, with burnt orange rust leaking from its rivets.

'What's wrong with it? Don't you think it'll get me to England? Do you think it'll sink and I'll have to swim the rest of the way?'

'Hush, you'll give her nightmares.'

'It's fine, Birdie. The captain told me himself that she's seaworthy.'

Birdie wasn't convinced. All of a sudden, it became too much – the thought of her father climbing the rusty gangplank, the thought of their separation—

'Don't go.'

She dropped her hankie and buried her face into the front of his shirt. He smelled like stale tobacco smoke and carbolic soap and home. *Their* home. He should stay at home.

'Don't go, Puppa.'

He kissed her on her forehead. 'Be a good girl, and look after Mumma,' he said, then straightened up and kissed his wife.

'I'll write as soon as I make land. Money will follow.'

'*Please* Puppa,' Birdie begged, but he chucked her beneath the chin and picked up his suitcase.

'I'll send for you soon.'

*How soon?*

'You best go,' Precious advised. 'No point in dragging it out any longer.'

Winston nodded once and walked away. Precious took Birdie's hand in her own as they watched him climb the gangplank. He reached the top and presented his ticket, then disappeared into the belly of the ship.

'Puppa!'

He'd promised to wave to her from the deck of the ship, surely he hadn't forgotten – no, there he was, smiling and waving, one hand clasped tight to the railing. She snatched up her hankie from the ground – a little grubby, now, but Puppa wouldn't mind – and waved it with all her might. She wanted to stay and watch as the ship sailed away, but Precious tugged on her hand.

'Come.'

'Not yet—'

'Birdie, come. Now,' Mumma said in a voice that meant danger was still avoidable, but only just, and she had no choice but to let Mumma lead her away.

At least she had a hankie, grimy as it was, to mop up her tears.

The little wooden house felt incomplete without him, as though someone had taken away the kitchen, or part of the roof. Birdie would wake up each morning, expecting to hear him on the veranda, drinking his coffee, and then she would remember that he wasn't there and she'd begin the day with a fresh volley of tears. Every day she waited in desperate anticipation for the postman.

'He's only been gone a week, Birdie,' Precious said wearily. 'He's still on the ship. He can't post a letter until he arrives in London.'

Six slow weeks later, Birdie came home from school to find

an envelope propped up against a tin pitcher on the kitchen table and she tore into it so fast she almost ripped its contents in two.

> I've been told I'm lucky it's summer. I was expecting rain but not damp. The fog is so cold it cuts through you . . . I've found lodging in a place they call Shoreditch, and ditch is right. If I want water I have to carry it up three flights of stairs in a bucket . . . I've found work, too. Every day you go to the labour exchange and they tell you who's hiring and you go and ask for the foreman and if he likes the look of you, you've got the job. It took me three attempts – the first two times they told me the job had already been taken. I guess there's a lot of fellas looking for work and you need to be quick . . .

Winston wrote often. He told them about the strange things he encountered in London: the buses, the pubs, the beer (the quality varied from pub to pub. Last night he'd had a pint that tasted like water) and the English obsession with cricket, though everyone knew the West Indian team was superior.

He told them that there was plenty of work, but for some reason all the West Indian fellas ended up on the night shift (one foreman tried to tell him it was something to do with the time difference, so they'd feel more at home).

He told them he was going to try his luck further north, in a city called Birmingham, where there weren't as many immigrants competing for the same jobs. London was not for him, he'd decided. He did not say why.

More exciting than the letters was the sporadic arrival of the barrels. A barrel day was always momentous for a family with a parent or loved one overseas. Neighbours would gather to see what foreign treasures had been packed up and shipped across the ocean, veritable proof of the sender's good fortune. Puppa would send food, clothes, and the occasional toy – a teddy bear in a red waistcoat, and a skipping rope, with bright blue handles, that made Birdie the envy of every little girl in her class until it snapped in two during a vigorous playground game of tug o' war.

In December, he sent a Christmas cake that all but Auntie Luce complimented, a box of expensive chocolates and a Christmas card. Birdie pinned it to the wall beside her bed. There was smoke curling from the chimney of a whitewashed cottage, and a hedgerow dusted with snow, a tiny robin peering through the branches.

**It's snowing and I wish Birdie were here to see it,** Puppa wrote inside.

**This is my new address, and soon it will be yours, too.**

Next to the Christmas card Birdie pinned a picture of Buckingham Palace, carefully torn from the *Daily Gleaner*, and every night she leant out of her window and looked towards England (or so she thought – her bedroom was south facing) to say goodnight to Puppa and bid God to help him make enough money to send for her soon.

The letters and the barrels, as nice as they were, did not soothe the absence of her father. Precious was stricter than Winston, and games did not come as easily to her. Birdie's only comfort was the knowledge that it wouldn't be long, no time at all really, before she and Mumma left for England too, and they'd be with Puppa, and they'd all be so happy, and England would be so good to them, just like he'd promised.

The separation hurt Precious too, but buried deep beneath her grief was a tiny, niggling seed of doubt that threatened to sprout into something untameable. It was easy to ignore during the day, while she was cooking and cleaning, or chasing after Birdie, but in the still of the night, lying in her bed without her husband, her misgivings loomed as large as the shadows on the wall.

How *could* Winston be so sure of England? His letters may be full of bombast and excitement, but there was something hidden between the lines written in his rounded hand. The move 'further north' troubled her. He had done it without asking his wife's opinion. But Winston was well-rehearsed in ignoring his wife's concerns. What choice did she have but to trust him?

*Whatever your husband do, you do.* Most women (apart from Luce) were brought up to believe a woman's happiness was not important to a successful marriage. Pleasing the husband, that was the secret. They would stop her in the lane, women she had known all of her life, and say *I bet you miss him something terrible?* And she'd answer yes, which was the truth, and then they'd say *and I bet you can't wait to join him?* And she'd answer yes, and that was a lie.

On Sunday mornings she tried to pray her doubts away in church, muttering in rhythm with her own heartbeat. But if she were really being honest, Lord, what bothered her most was the change in Birdie. She'd been so morose since Winston left, spending all of her time moping beneath the veranda with the stuffed bear and the broken skipping rope. She knew it was an emotional upheaval, a child losing a parent that young, God knows she knew what that felt like. But she was jealous. Jealous that her daughter loved her father more than her . . . Sweet Jesus. She prayed harder.

But he'd asked for Birdie's opinion. As if hers did not matter. And then he'd left.

As if she did not matter.

Pastor Johnson asked everyone to stand and the choir, resplendent in their white robes, pitched their voices to the rooftop.

Birdie sang and clapped. Precious stayed on her knees.

* * *

## *1955*

It took a whole year, but the news they had been waiting for finally arrived.

On the last day of term, Birdie skipped home from school to find Mumma and Auntie Luce in the kitchen, their arms wrapped around each other so tightly that Birdie couldn't tell where her aunt ended and her mother began.

'What's wrong?'

'It's your farda,' Luce said. 'He's sent for you.'

'He – he *has*?' Birdie dropped her schoolbooks in excitement, feeling as fizzy as a carnival firework. She squealed and rushed off to start packing. She didn't notice that her mother was crying.

In a matter of weeks, the little wooden house was emptied of its contents. Barefooted boys had carried out the table, and the chairs, and the beds, in exchange for a penny each from Auntie Luce, who had appointed herself as the deputy of the move. If she couldn't keep her Precious then she'd make sure that she left the island in as organised a fashion as possible. After that – well, she'd be in the Lord's hands then. Space was a commodity in the heavy trunk, and choices had to be made. Precious's wedding china was packed, six beautiful plates spotted with tiny posies, but the sewing machine was given to a neighbour.

Birdie watched as the house was stripped bare. They were starting a new life and taking so little of the old one. All that was left behind were two tiny pinholes in Birdie's bedroom wall, and it felt as though the first seven years of her life had been wiped clean, like a blackboard at the end of the school day. For the first time, she realised the enormity of their situation. Someone else would live in this house now. Perhaps another little girl would call it home. Birdie wouldn't. Never again.

'Birdie? Hurry up, taxi come!'

She left the house for the last time. Grandpa had closed the store for the morning to see them off and Auntie Luce, who'd sworn the night before that she wouldn't be there because it would be too painful, was panting up the lane, her backside jiggling with every step. She swooped Birdie into a hug, squeezing the child to her bosom so tightly she left an imprint of buttons down one side of her face.

'Write the minute you get there, do you hear me?' Luce sniffed, doing a poor imitation of one whose heart was not breaking. 'The very minute. Do you have your passport, Precious? Did you pack those stockings I knitted? Remember to hold your breath as you take off so as your ears don't explode. I heard that happened to Abraham Somerville and now he's as deaf as a doornail and no one wants to hire a deaf West Indian—'

'Alright, Auntie. We need to go. We'll be late.'

Birdie felt like royalty, dressed to pussfoot and stepping into the taxicab. They were both wearing their Sunday best: Precious in a dress and jacket of cheerful fuchsia, and Birdie in a pink and white gingham dress with a matching bow at the waist. Birdie also carried a black patent leather handbag, a barrel gift that she hadn't let go of since it had arrived, though it was only large enough to carry a clean hankie and the Christmas card she had removed from her bedroom wall. From the back seat she blew kisses to her great-aunt and grandfather.

It had come as a great shock when Puppa suggested they make the journey to England by aeroplane, but it did not cost that much more to travel by air than by sea, and he'd had a feeling that Birdie would come to some sort of mishap on a ship. No one prepared her for the noise of the plane – even Mumma looked alarmed and gripped the armrests, muttering an *oh, Lord* and a hasty prayer – but the smiling stewardess in a red uniform had given Birdie a cherry-flavoured sweetie and encouraged her to suck it to stop her 'ears from popping'. It was delicious, and she asked her mumma if she was allowed a second one. Precious didn't know.

'Mumma!' Birdie squealed, pointing out the window, the second sweetie already forgotten. 'Look at that!'

'Hush,' Mumma said, her eyes screwed tightly closed. 'Don't bother me just now.'

Jamaica's green and rugged outline, ringed by an expanse of blue, was spread out beneath them, like a painting. It was pretty enough to hurt, but Birdie didn't feel sad. Soon she would be with her father, and that was all that mattered.

*We're coming, Puppa . . .*

The flight seemed to take forever. Birdie fidgeted, and napped, and asked her mother endless questions (*how do we stay up in the air? Can I talk to the pilot? What happens if he needs to use the pot?*) but eventually, they landed in England with an unceremonious bump. Birdie wiggled impatiently as Precious filled in a landing card and the stewardesses helped passengers with their luggage. When it was their turn to disembark, she bounded down the aisle, urging Mumma to hurry up, then stopped dead at the door.

'Whooeee! It's *cold*!'

The stewardess chuckled. *Welcome to England.*

Birdie clutched Precious's hand as they were swept across the tarmac and into the terminal. The queue at border control snaked up and down and back on itself and Birdie hopped impatiently on one foot, and then on the other, as they inched forward. When it was finally their turn, Precious smiled at the serious man in a neat uniform, but he didn't smile back, merely holding out his hand for her passport. He glanced up at Precious and then down at her photograph. His eyes slid over the desk to Birdie, and then he raised a stamp and brought it down on the page with a small thud.

'Can I see it, Mumma?' Birdie whispered.

From the moment it had arrived, the passport had been a source of reverent entertainment. An official declaration in a flourishing script stated that Amaretta Brown, by order of Her Majesty the Queen, was a citizen of the Commonwealth, and beneath that someone had written her mother's height (five feet and seven inches), eye colour (dark brown) and hair colour (black). Someone had also printed *BRIDGET LUCILLE BROWN, Female, DOB 24/5/1948* beneath her mother's name. Birdie had been disappointed to learn she wouldn't be getting her own passport, but Mumma had explained that she didn't need one, and thank goodness, because it was one less thing to pay for.

Precious handed the passport to her daughter and Birdie flipped it open. It was an official looking stamp, a big purple triangle, with the date embossed in tiny letters.

*23rd July 1955*. She gently touched it with her finger.

They had left the aeroplane in kind of a pack, a scrum of passengers all walking in the same direction, but once they reached the arrivals hall they melted away, one by one, carried off by family and friends.

'Noreen! Over here!'

'Larry Carpenter! Boy, did you get fat—'

'Sherlock! Yoohoo, Sherlock!'

Some of them, like themselves, had no one there to meet them. They had stood looking lost and unsure for a moment before squaring their shoulders and striding out of the airport to face their futures head on.

Mumma said that they needed to take a train to Birmingham, where Puppa should be waiting for them. Winston had wanted to meet them at the airport, but they'd decided against it. He'd be tired after the night shift, and Precious had said if they could manage the journey from Jamaica to England then surely they could catch a train by themselves. The only problem was, she didn't know where they needed to go.

'There must be a policeman or someone around here.' Her eyes scanned the concourse. A woman draped in a pale-yellow fur coat approached them, and Precious smiled gratefully.

'Missus, could you please tell me where the—'

The woman reached out and touched Birdie's hair. It happened so quickly – the woman made a small *hmm* sound, then turned and walked away.

'Who was that, Mumma?' Birdie asked, more curious than frightened. 'Why'd she touch my hair?'

'Just some crazy woman,' Mumma said, her eyes focused on the departing figure. 'You pay her no mind.'

Eventually, a guard pointed them in the direction of the train station. Aboard the train, they found empty seats in the third-class carriage. Precious dropped wearily into the seat and removed her hat, but Birdie stood at the window, eager to see everything the square view would afford. She fiddled with the latch and the window fell down and she jumped back, thinking she'd broken it. Precious sighed and closed it again, telling her not to meddle. The whistle blasted and the train began to move.

Birdie gasped and pointed to the biggest building she'd ever seen.

'Mumma! Is that Buckingham Palace?'

'No.'

'Are you sure?'

'That dirty old factory?' a strange voice said, and Birdie turned around. 'That's not Buckingham Palace.'

A poised West Indian woman stood before them, dressed in an expensive travelling suit of worsted red wool, a leather suitcase clasped in her gloved hand. She asked if she could take the empty seat opposite.

'Of course. Birdie, help the lady with her bag.'

'No need,' the woman said. She expertly swung it up onto the rack in one smooth motion, before sitting down and holding out her hand.

'I'm Eula-May Gray.'

Birdie let out an errant giggle then clapped her hand over her mouth. Precious shot her a warning look, but Eula-May laughed good-naturedly. She had angled eyebrows with a high arch accentuated by a kohl pencil and plump lips; a perfect cupid's bow painted a deep red to match her travelling suit.

'My parents like a joke,' she said, her eyes twinkling. 'My brother's name is Ray.'

Precious coughed. 'How . . . nice . . .'

'I'm come to live with him. He's been in England six months and he can't take care of himself, so he asked me to join him.' Eula-May rolled her eyes. 'I'm surprised he's lasted this long. Ray's never been what you might call resourceful.'

'Where are you from?' Precious asked politely.

'Little London. But having seen *proper* London now I can tell you which one I'd rather call home.' She shook her head. 'Spent my whole life thinking Little London was grand because all the shops in the town square had Delco generators. Have you seen London, Missus . . .?'

'My name's Precious Brown. And only what we saw from the train.'

'That's a pity.' Eula-May looked from Precious to Birdie with interest. 'Is it just the two of you?'

'My husband's in Birmingham. We're going to meet him.'

Eula-May clapped her hands together. 'Well you're in luck, because I'm heading to Wolverhampton. That's not too far from Birmingham, *if* Ray is to be believed. Here—'

She took a notebook and a stub of an eyeliner out of her handbag.

'Excuse the kohl. This is my address. Come and call on me some time.'

They began to discuss the people they knew back home, the differences between life on the east and west sides of the island (not many, it transpired) and the reasons for their departures. In Eula-May's case, those reasons were numerous.

'I was bored, sister. Tired of my job – I worked domestic at the sugar cane estate – tired of the people. Ray leaving was the excuse I needed to get up and *go*. I'm going to train as a nurse. England is crying out for nurses, or so the papers say.'

'Was there no young man that caught your eye?'

Eula-May tossed back her head.

'There was, which was the problem. Island men are all the same. Idle. Sitting on their backsides and refusing to let the world change. They're comfortable sinking into a rut and expect you to move in beside them.' She paused. 'No offence to your husband.'

'Winston's not like that. The world couldn't change fast enough for him.' Precious sounded wistful. 'He was convinced things would be better over here. But he didn't like London.'

'Your husband was smart – everyone gets off the boat train in London and says *well, I made it to England*, and they won't go a step further. The capital's overrun with immigrants. Not a spare pot to piss in for the likes of us.'

'Why do we need a spare pot to piss in, Mumma?' Birdie asked, and Precious told her to hush. She obediently turned back to the window. She hadn't seen a gold road yet, but she was determined not to miss them when they began to flash by.

'Now Ray,' Eula-May continued wryly, 'had no idea that Wolverhampton *wasn't* near London. Didn't think to look at a map before he applied for a job. How they trust him to drive a bus all day I don't know.'

'He *can* drive though, can't he?'

'Oh, sure – though his passengers don't believe he can. All these old white ladies would rather wait in the rain than be driven about by a West Indian. Don't they know we've been driving whites around for centuries?'

'Mumma, why have West Indians been—'

'Birdie please. It's been a long day. Can you hold your tongue for *five* minutes? I'm sorry. She's a chatterbox. You were saying—'

Precious and Eula-May's voices rose together, their tongues clack-clacking like the wheels of the train. Birdie sat down and rested her chin in her hands. She was getting tired, lulled by the gentle rocking motion beneath her, but she didn't want to sleep. She didn't want to miss a single thing—

'Next stop, Birmingham New Street! Birmingham New Street, next stop!'

Birdie sat up suddenly and rubbed her eyes as Eula-May sprung to her feet.

'That's us! Need help with your bags, sister?'

It was nearing the end of the working day and the train station was busy. Birdie clung to Precious's hand as they moved through a sea of weary commuters all dressed in drab, identical suits, and set their bags down beneath a giant clock. Almost immediately, a voice across the concourse shouted *Eula! Hey Eula!*

A young man, with the same thin nose and lively eyes as Eula-May, rushed over. He swept his sister into a hug, swinging her off her feet.

'Put me down, you idiot!' She cackled. A few commuters turned their heads in their direction as they trudged past. 'Anybody would think you hadn't seen me for a year. Raymond, this is Missus Brown and her daughter, Birdie. They're from the island.'

'Pleased to meet you,' Raymond said. 'Missus, huh? You waiting on your husband?'

'He's meeting us here. He'll be along any minute, I'm sure.'

Raymond shot a glance at his sister. 'We can wait with you, can't we, Eu?'

'Sure we can. Maybe we can all go get a bite to eat?'

Birdie tugged on her mother's sleeve – she was starving – but Precious shook her head.

'I don't want to keep you.'

'Well alright then. But hold onto my address, do you hear? I have a feeling we're going to be good friends.'

They left with a final backwards wave. Birdie yawned and perched on the edge of the trunk.

'I liked them. Where's Puppa?'

Precious didn't know. Her head turned from left to right as she scanned the station for her husband. Every so often, she'd glance up at the clock. Birdie slumped to the floor, the concrete chilling her legs through the thin material of her dress, and Precious didn't have the energy to tell her to stand up.

It was not the welcome either of them had been expecting.

'Maybe he's been held up,' Precious began for the third time, but then Birdie jumped to her feet and squealed, her voice echoing through the vast space.

'There he is! There he is!'

She ran at him, weaving in and out of commuters, and leapt into Winston's open arms. She buried her nose in the front of his shirt and inhaled deeply.

*Tobacco. Soap. Home.*

'So, you made it in one piece, eh?'

'We've been waiting almost an hour,' Precious complained as she caught up to them, dragging the heavy trunk behind her. Her legs were throbbing from standing for so long.

'It's these night shifts. I'm sorry.'

He reached in for a kiss and she presented her cheek.

'Well, you're here now. Let's get going, shall we?'

'Sure. But first, presents! I thought you might be cold—'

To his daughter he presented a navy anorak with shiny red buttons. She put it on and spun on the toe of one shoe, and Winston whistled and clapped. Then he reached into the bag and shook out a coat of unassuming beige felt.

'All the white sistren wearing them,' he said, draping it around Precious's shoulders. 'What do you think Birdie? Doesn't your mumma look grand?'

But she wasn't looking at her mother. She was looking at

her father. He seemed thinner. Shorter, somehow . . . and then she was crying, but she didn't know why. Her father wiped the tears away with his rough thumb.

'Tears for your old man, eh? What, you're not happy to see me?'

'She's tired. It's been a long day.'

'Then let's go home,' Puppa said.

*Home.*

It was a special day, Puppa said, so there was money for a taxi. Birdie spent the first half of the taxi ride wedged into Puppa's armpit, but even the overwhelming happiness at being reunited with a long-lost parent could not rival a small child's curiosity.

'Puppa. Why is everything so *black*?'

'That's the coal. This is coal country.'

'Oh. Puppa? Why are there so many factories?'

'She's been like this the whole way,' Precious complained, and Winston's smile stretched from ear to ear.

'I've missed her chatter. And they aren't factories, baby. They're houses.'

'*Houses*? But they all have chimneys! And where are the verandas?'

'Houses in England don't have verandas. None that I've seen, anyway.'

'Oh. Puppa, where are the gold roads?'

'Birdie,' Precious warned, and Birdie settled silently back in her father's embrace.

The taxi turned down Maltby Street and stopped outside a thin, Victorian brick house. It looked the same as all the other houses, like a row of glum children lining up to see the headmaster. There weren't any trees, or children playing in front yards. Two doors down, a net curtain twitched.

'Birdie?'

She turned her head from the twitching curtain. Puppa was stood before a black front door, his hands on his hips and a warm grin on his face.

'Are you going to stand on the pavement all night long or are you going to come inside and see your new home?'

# Seven

## *2016*

Streetlamps were flickering to life along the main road, and Birdie's flat felt warm, and safe. The trouble was, without her pension, for how much longer would she be able to call her flat her home? Without her pension, how would she be able to pay her rent? How would she look after herself?

And how would she pay for a lawyer?

She was seated at the dining table, half a bowl of oxtail soup at her elbow. She hadn't managed to finish it. She didn't have much of an appetite lately. In front of her was a to-do list. A few things – pay the electricity bill, make doctor's appointment for Jaxon, buy Rita a bunch of flowers – had already been ticked off. Those had been easy. But the rest of the list was proving much more difficult.

Find a lawyer (CHEAP)
Sort out finances – budget
Tell Scott

She tapped her pen lightly against the paper. Finding a cheap lawyer. Well. She might as well be trying to find the fountain of youth. She had already visited the library to use one of the computers, typing *immigration lawyers in Birmingham* into the search bar, then glancing over her shoulder, paranoid that someone might see. No one was paying her any attention – the man on the computer next to her was laboriously typing an email to someone named Bianca. She turned back to the screen and frowned.

Cheap immigration lawyers in Birmingham
Pro-bono lawyers in Birmingham
What is a retainer?

Carmen had sent Birdie a list of all the lawyers she'd found that *wouldn't* be able to help. 'So we don't waste time calling the same firms,' she'd said. It had been a depressingly long list.

Birdie's pen moved down the page. Sort out finances. She could live on a budget. She'd done it before. Money had been tight while she was growing up. Money had been tight while her kids were growing up, too. But she'd managed, hadn't she? She could manage now. She had her savings. But that money wouldn't last forever. Then what? Her chest tightened, a sensation that was becoming painfully familiar. She moved on.

Tell Scott. That would be hard, given that her son wouldn't let her visit him in prison, for reasons he'd never tried to explain. It stung, but she'd gotten the message and kept her distance, relying instead on Tegan for updates. Perhaps he wouldn't even want to know. Perhaps he wouldn't care. He'd already pushed her away . . .

Birdie would never, not in a million years, admit to having a favourite. Her relationship with Scott wasn't *better*, she used to say. Just different. Unlike Carmen, who had fought tooth and nail for any scrap of freedom that could be wrestled from her mother, often resulting in flared tempers and screaming matches, Scott was easy-going and easy to get on with. When he'd been very young, he'd always wanted to be near her: in her lap, or holding her hand, burrowing his way into her bed each morning and pushing Jimmy aside so he could have all of her warmth to himself. Jimmy wanted him to toughen up a bit, teach him to stand on his own two feet. He'd called Birdie soft. He'd said she would ruin him if she wasn't careful.

She set down her pen. The nights were drawing in now, slowly, the way they always did before clocks went back, so slowly that you might not notice it from one day to the next. Then suddenly it would be dark at four in the afternoon and all anyone would be able to talk about till March was *these bloody dark nights*. Did Jamaica have daylight savings time, Birdie suddenly wondered? She didn't know. She couldn't even remember the time difference. She should find out. It was useful information to have. She added it to her to-do list. It was probably the easiest task on there, much easier than finding a lawyer she could afford or convincing her son to let her visit him in prison. Then, abruptly, Birdie decided she didn't want to know if Jamaica had daylight savings time. She scribbled it out, her pencil making deep grooves in the thin piece of paper.

The doorbell rang.

She glanced at her gold wristwatch. She wasn't expecting visitors. It might be Tegan dropping Jaxon off again so she could go and do God knows what God knows where. Or it might be—

'Who is it?' she said tentatively as she approached the door. It was futile, really. As if immigration officers would politely announce themselves and wait for her to let them in.

'Nanny, it's me!'

'Saffie!' Birdie opened the front door. 'What are you doing here? *How* did you get here?'

'Bus,' Saffie said, bounding into the living room.

'Does your mom know you're here?'

'Course, I texted her on the way. And she said that you're not answering the phone again and wants to know why you're avoiding her.'

'I'm not avoiding her,' Birdie lied. Carmen wanted to know if she'd had her pension review yet. Birdie was keeping the news to herself a little bit longer. She didn't think she could deal with another Carmen meltdown.

Saffie grinned. 'It's okay, Nanny. She gets on my tits too. Got any biscuits?'

'What are you doing here, Saff?' Birdie asked as her granddaughter rooted around the kitchen cupboards, looking for biscuits that were not there. Her unfinished budget had identified essentials and luxuries; things she could afford to spend money on and things she could go without. Milk, bread and bingo were essentials. Biscuits were not.

'Can I have this?' Saffie held up a broken Penguin bar. It must have been one of Jaxon's. Judging by the state of the wrapper, it had been in the cupboard a long time.

'Help yourself.'

Saffie flicked on the kettle and noisily unwrapped the chocolate bar. 'Cup of tea, Nanny?'

'Thank you, Saff. Now will you tell me why you're here?'

Saffie returned to the living room, a steaming mug of tea in each hand and the last remaining bite of the chocolate bar wedged between her teeth. She placed the mugs down and then reached into her school bag, pulling out a dog-eared exercise book covered in doodles.

'Ignore that,' she said witheringly, indicating a giant love heart scored into the cover, embossed with the words SAFFIE LOVES BEN W in apple-green gel pen. 'Shabz wrote that, not me. She's projecting, she fancies the pants off him. Anyway, Mom told me what's happened. *Finally.* I mean, I already knew, sort of – that night she came over? When she got home she said it was all just a misunderstanding, you weren't getting deported blah blah blah, but she's been acting really sketchy ever since. I finally confronted her last night and at first she denied anything was wrong, but then I pointed out that she and Dad haven't exactly been rowing quietly—'

'They've been rowing?'

Saffie took a noisy slurp of her tea.

'Mmm. Mom said they should pay for your lawyer, but Dad said they can't afford it. And then Mom said maybe they *would* be able to afford it if he got off his arse and went back to work. She's been sleeping on the settee for the past couple of nights.'

'*She's* been—'

'I know, right? Not very chivalrous of Dad, even if he *does* have a bad back. *Anyway*. She told me everything. About that guy and what he said about you needing your travel documents.'

'She wasn't supposed to tell you!'

'Don't be cross with Mom, I kind of forced it out of her. And anyway, I'm glad she did. I've been doing some research for you, look—'

Saffie spread a stack of papers between them. Huge portions of the printed text had been highlighted in lurid pink, with frantic scribbles in the margin written in leaky biro. Saffie had always been a whirlwind of boundless energy, jumping from one idea to the next like a bullfrog. It was hard to keep up with her bright ideas, or her career aspirations, or—

'You've changed your hair,' Birdie said, noticing for the first time that Saffie's curls had been ironed straight. Saffie tucked a strand behind her ear.

'Oh. Yeah. We had mock job interviews today. This looks more professional.'

'I *like* your curls,' Birdie said reassuringly. 'I like all of you.'

Saffie had long, coltish limbs, a pert nose she'd inherited from her *other* grandmother and a smattering of freckles dotted across her fair cheeks. She had lighter skin than her siblings, which Birdie knew made her self-conscious. *You're just as pretty as Jade*, Birdie would tell her. *You're* all *gorgeous, and I'm not just saying that because I'm your grandmother.* Birdie could begrudgingly accept that Andy Lloyd made good looking children.

Saffie ignored her.

'There was some stuff that I couldn't print because I ran out of credits. And I would have brought my laptop, but Lewis downloaded dodgy porn again and now it's got a virus.'

'Saffie,' Birdie began slowly. 'It's not that I don't appreciate a visit. But I don't have a clue what you're talking about. And why is Lewis looking at *porn*? He's just a pickney!'

Saffie grimaced. 'He's fourteen. He's old enough to know how to delete a search history. Anyway—'

She flicked chocolate crumbs off the pile of papers. 'Okay, so Mom said that the Home Office said that they don't have a record of when you entered the country, right?'

'Right.'

'They've said it's *your* job to prove you're who you say you are, and that you arrived when you say you did, which isn't fair. It's like Mom said, who would hold onto someone else's passport? But that doesn't matter anymore, because . . .' Saffie took a pause for dramatic effect. 'You can write to the Home

Office and ask for a copy of your travel records. This is the address—'

'*What*?'

Birdie's mouth fell open, revealing two silver fillings.

Saffie read aloud from a highlighted paragraph. 'You can request personal information about you that is held in the Home Office's immigration records. This includes an electronic summary of your immigration history, a summary of your travel history, and *copies of your landing cards*.'

Her eyes gleamed.

'Nanny P would have filled in a landing card, right? On the day you arrived in England?'

'I think she did.'

Birdie closed her eyes and pictured a small yellow card being presented by the stewardess. Precious didn't have a pen, so the lady in the seat in front of them had lent her one, twisting round and keeping a beady eye on them until Precious handed it back. She had forgotten all about that. She opened her eyes.

'She definitely did,' Birdie said with confidence.

'Then that's your proof! Because the Home Office kept them, Nanny. There are probably thousands upon thousands of landing cards in some secret bunker hidden beneath London or something. And all we have to do is write and get a copy.'

Birdie couldn't believe it. There had to be a catch. It couldn't be *that* easy.

'And it only costs a tenner.'

Ten pounds? Was that it?

'Oh, Saff! How did you get so clever?'

Saffie shrugged bashfully and uncapped a chewed-up biro.

'Tell me what to write and I'll type it up for you tomorrow. I've got independent study first period, but I've already finished annotating all the chapters I need for English, so it's no problem.'

'Do you still want to be a teacher?' Birdie asked, her heart feeling lighter than it had in weeks.

'Maybe,' Saffie replied without commitment.

'I wanted to be a secretary when I was your age,' Birdie said offhandedly, and Saffie looked up with interest. 'But there's still plenty of time for you to decide what you want to do. You're young, you've got your whole life ahead of you. You can do anything you want to, my girl.'

'There's more,' Saffie said hurriedly, eager to get off the subject before university inevitably came up. 'Before I started looking into the Home Office stuff I was looking for a lawyer. One you could actually afford—'

'I'm not sure one exists—'

'I know. But *then* I found this charity that offers legal assistance and support services for illegal immigrants, completely free of charge but donations welcomed.' She waved a piece of paper at Birdie. 'This is the number to call for an appointment. They're open six days a week.'

Birdie barely glanced at the paper. She wouldn't need it, not now Saffie had presented her with a golden ticket – or rather, a little yellow landing card, worth more to her than the whole chocolate factory and a lifetime supply of Bournville.

'They're really easy to get to, too – their office is near the Custard Factory. I went to a great gig there last summer, this incredible grime artist—'

'You're not old enough to be going to gigs.'

'We went with Grace's older brother and it was perfectly safe. Not a single person offered me drugs.'

'It's not right for young girls to be gallivanting all over

town. Anything could have happened to you. And who is this older brother? Has your mom even met him?'

Saffie resisted the urge to roll her eyes. 'This isn't the Middle Ages, Nanny. Young girls are allowed their freedom nowadays.'

Birdie snorted. 'In my day,' she began, and Saffie pounced on it.

'Yeah?' she said eagerly. 'What *was* it like when you were my age?'

'What do you mean?'

'I mean, what was it like being a teenager in the sixties? I bet it was really cool. The music scene, and that.'

Birdie thought about it. She wouldn't exactly have described the decade as *cool*. There had been so much turmoil. So much loss . . .

'Well . . . I didn't have much time for the "music scene",' she admitted. 'I'd been to a few nightclubs and that. But . . . Saff, you know I was young when I had your mother.'

'Oh, so you had *your* freedom,' Saffie teased, and Birdie aimed a half-hearted swipe at her granddaughter, who dodged it easily. Saffie sat back and fixed her with a solemn stare. 'I can't imagine being a mom at my age. Was it scary?'

Birdie considered the question. 'No one's ever asked me that before.'

'Really? Not even Mom?'

'She was too busy arguing with me when *she* was that age,' Birdie said ruefully. 'But I was just glad she didn't make the same mistake I did – and don't you go telling her I called her a "mistake", either, because I'll never hear the end of it.'

Saffie laughed. 'I know what you mean. You just wanted better for her, that's all.'

'And *she* wants better for *you*. What's this I hear about you not wanting to go to university?'

Saffie really did roll her eyes that time. 'Not you too. Please. I beg you.'

'Saffie—'

Saffie groaned into a pillow embellished with the words *World's Best Nan*, a Mother's Day present from the twins, stained purple with blackcurrant squash.

'I'm just saying you should consider it, that's all. Your mom wants you to go.'

'Dad says it's a waste of time and money,' Saffie said as she came up for air.

Birdie stopped herself from saying something unkind. Instead, she said, 'You should decide for yourself. After all, someone told me that young girls today are allowed their freedom.'

In spite of herself, Saffie giggled. 'Okay. I promise I'll think about it.'

'Thank you. And thank you for all of this,' Birdie gestured at the papers. 'You're a good girl.'

Saffie grinned confidently. 'I'm not going to let them deport my nanny, am I?'

'Are you hungry? I've not done a big shop this week, but I'm sure I can rustle you up something.'

'I'll just have some toast, if that's okay. Unless you've got anything good in the freezer?'

'Dig around, see what you can find,' Birdie invited. She followed Saffie into the kitchen and washed up her soup bowl as Saffie foraged through the freezer drawers, yelling in delight like a triumphant prospector when she found a Wall's ice cream tub full of what Birdie identified as curry goat. Saffie defrosted it in the microwave and the smell made Birdie's mouth water. She was suddenly ravenous. They ended up sharing the leftovers together, eating the reheated curry off a single dinner plate, side by side on the settee, Saffie's legs curled up beneath the blanket she'd thrown over their laps, her pointed elbow digging into Birdie's soft stomach as they clashed their forks territorially over the largest hunks of meat. They watched *The Chase* together and Saffie sighed contentedly and declared it a delicious dinner, even though Birdie thought that the curry goat was not her best (she'd run out of Mr Brown's and had had to use generic curry powder), and then she rested her head on her grandmother's shoulder and Birdie didn't think she could love the girl more.

'Thank you, Nanny.'

'Thank *you*, Saff,' she said quietly, and kissed her granddaughter right above the ear.

* * *

Saffie wrote a short but polite request for any information pertaining to the arrival of Amaretta and Bridget Brown at Gatwick Airport in July 1955 (Birdie couldn't remember the exact date, but Saffie doubted it would matter) and dropped it in the postbox at the end of her road on the way to school. Then there was nothing to do but wait for the response. Birdie began stalking the postman, haunting the walkway, waiting for the red van to pull up into the courtyard below. It had been twenty days. It couldn't be much longer. She wondered how long it would take them to reinstate her pension. The first thing she'd do was buy something for Saffie. A new laptop perhaps?

'Morning,' she said eagerly to the postman, who wore shorts and a scowl all year round. He thrust a single letter towards her. She recognised the logo on the envelope immediately and tore it open.

Dear Ms Brown,

We have searched our records and we can find no trace of you in our files.

'How?'

Birdie had called the number at the bottom of the letter. 'How could there not be a trace of me in your files? My mother filled out a landing card. You should have it.'

The sound of typing filled her ear. The landing card was supposed to be her way out. It was supposed to make the nightmare go away—

'Ms Brown? I'm sorry, but there's nothing here—'

'Why isn't it there? Did you get rid of it?'

There was a long pause.

'Well?' Birdie's voice shook.

'All I can tell you is that there's no sign of you in our files.'

Birdie hung up. Perhaps it had been naïve to think that the Home Office would present her with the solution to the problem they had created. They wanted her gone, didn't they? But she couldn't sit around all day, staring at the thickly striped wallpaper, an idiosyncratic residue of the 1990s, hung by the previous tenant. She needed to make a call. Saffie had left the number around somewhere . . .

* * *

Birdie watched from the bus window as the Birmingham suburbs gave way to utilitarian apartment buildings, clustered together along the main road, all built from the same sandy-coloured brick. They reminded her of Jaxon's Lego blocks. He liked to build towers and then knock them down, over and over again, squealing with joy every time they collapsed at his feet.

'Thanks for coming with me.'

'Of course,' Carmen replied. 'Though I wish one of you had told me about this charity sooner. Are we sure they're genuine? You hear about all sorts of fake charities trying to scam old people.'

Saffie, on the seat behind them, leaned forward. 'They're genuine! I showed you the website—'

'Anyone can make a website these days,' Carmen rebutted.

It was Carmen's idea that they get the bus. It cost too much to park in the city centre, she said, and they could treat it like a girly day out – *we can have a mooch around the shops afterwards, Mom, won't that be nice? I want to start looking for a Mother of the Bride outfit* – as though they weren't on their way to plead a charity to take on Birdie's case. Saffie, who had arranged to meet her friends in the Bullring Shopping Centre afterwards, had assumed she was required to lead the way. She'd gelled her hair back into a bun this time, scraping it back so tightly that just looking at it gave Birdie a headache.

'You should wear your hair natural. It's so pretty.'

'I want to get it relaxed.'

'You'll ruin your gorgeous curls,' Carmen said with a tut. 'I'd give anything for my hair to grow as long as yours. What time are you meeting your friends?'

'Not till two. Shabz has to babysit and Grace is at the stables until twelve.'

Carmen and Birdie shared a glance, a moment of understanding between two mothers who couldn't afford riding lessons for their children.

The bus stopped at the edge of the city centre. Saffie directed them through a graffitied maze of former factories, bars and vintage clothing stores, bemoaning the demise of a cool shop that had sold jumpers made out of recycled carrier bags. Carmen gingerly stepped around a puddle of vomit and muttered under her breath that it was exactly the sort of location a fake charity *would* operate.

'There it is,' Saffie said, pointing to a dingy building at the end of a row of warehouses. The sign above the roll shutter door read 'Centre for Migrant and Refugee Wellbeing'.

Carmen opened the door and a bell tinkled pleasantly. A young woman with a crimson-coloured bob beamed at them from the front desk.

'Can I help you?'

'Good morning,' Carmen said authoritatively. 'My mother has an appointment. She's getting deported.'

Birdie cringed. 'No need to say it so loud!'

The receptionist smiled kindly. 'There's no judgement here – the centre was set up to help people exactly in your position. And we'll certainly do our best to help. Please take a seat, Marley will be right with you.'

Despite the early hour, the room was busy. They sat down in three worn but comfortable chairs placed in front of the window. It was a small, but cosy space. A stack of magazines had been fanned out on an Ikea coffee table, with a box of children's toys tucked beneath it. A tiny cactus sat on the receptionist's desk. It felt a world away from the immigration centre. There you couldn't even get a drink of water.

'Tea? Coffee?' the receptionist asked. Birdie shook her head.

'While you're waiting, I'll need you to fill this out,' she added, handing Birdie a clipboard and a pen. 'And if you change your mind about the drink—'

Carmen flicked through a copy of *Hello* as Birdie

methodically made her way through the intake form. It was fairly straightforward: name, date of birth, address – she hesitated. The form asked her to tick her nationality. For as long as she could remember she had ticked British. Her pen hovered above the box.

'Ms Brown?'

A young, black man with shoulder-length locs tied back in a loose ponytail stood in front of them. He was wearing modish glasses and a fitted T-shirt, and he had a smile that Birdie thought she recognised. Saffie looked up from her phone and blushed crimson.

'Do you want to follow me? You can finish filling that out later. I'm Marley,' he added, as he led them to a quiet corner.

'This is my daughter and granddaughter,' Birdie said.

Carmen extended her hand. 'Carmen. You know Marley, you look awfully young . . .'

Marley smiled bashfully. 'I graduated from university last year. I'm working here part-time while I do my LPC.'

Birdie didn't know what an LPC was, but it sounded important.

'Which university did you go to?' Carmen continued. 'My daughter is doing her A levels right now and we've been told the deadline for university applications is January, but she hasn't so much as opened a single prospectus—'

'Mo-om,' Saffie muttered, her neck reddening. 'We're not here for me, we're here for Nanny.'

'It doesn't hurt to ask, Saff!' Carmen looked knowingly at Marley. 'I'm sure you weren't as indecisive as this one. She says she doesn't even know if she *wants* to go to university—'

'Mom!'

'Alright! So, Marley. Can you help us? Please tell me you can help us, because I am at my wits' end.'

'Sure, sure. I don't know how acquainted you are with our services, Ms Brown—'

'Call me Birdie.'

'Okay, Birdie. I'll take some details from you and then we'll discuss ways in which we can help. How does that sound?'

It sounded fine. Better than, actually. Marley was confident, yet sincere. Birdie had only known him a few minutes, but she already felt like she was in safe hands, a rare sensation since this whole ordeal had begun.

Marley took a yellow legal pad out of his desk drawer and opened it to a fresh page. 'Whenever you're ready, Birdie.'

Birdie nodded tentatively and then began. She started with the letter, and then sidestepped to her arrival in England. She told him about her parents, and the story of the day she was born, and the immigration centre, and the missing landing card. Marley's pen flew down the page. By the time she had finished, he had ink smeared down the side of his left hand. Birdie was crying, and Marley looked grim.

'I'm not going to sugar-coat things,' he began slowly. 'We've had a few other cases like this in recent months that are identical to your situation – Commonwealth-born British citizens being told they're not citizens at all and threatened with deportation.'

'But *why*?'

'Because of the government's "Hostile Environment" policy. They've been trying – and, it has to be said, succeeding – to make life in the UK so unliveable for undocumented immigrants that they'll leave. They're stripped of any and all safety nets, such as access to legal aid, and employers are expected to turn in anyone they suspect of being undocumented or they'll face massive fines. And without a job, or a home, or any means of supporting themselves, they'll *have* to go back to their country of birth, won't they? Or better yet, they won't attempt to enter the UK in the first place. But people of Birdie's generation, those who *did* come here legally but never naturalised, are being caught in the crosshairs of this policy. They are unintended victims.'

Birdie wiped her eyes on a hankie. She'd dealt with plenty of hostility in her time, but nothing as cruel as this.

Marley scanned his notes. 'You said the passport you travelled on is missing?'

Missing, disposed of, rotting away in a landfill somewhere – who could say?

'I couldn't tell you the last time I saw it. My mumma – mother – only used it once, when we came to England. I have no idea if she even kept it after she got a British passport. I don't remember seeing it when we cleared out her house after she died.'

'When did she get a British passport?'

'Ehh . . . sometime in the early sixties, when my great-aunt died. My mother's Jamaican passport had expired, and she needed a new one to go back for the funeral. I didn't go with her. It was too expensive.'

Marley made a note on his pad. 'And your father? Did he have a British passport?'

'I don't know,' Birdie said.

'Is he still living?'

Another funeral she had missed.

'No.'

'Okay.' He crossed something out with a scratch of his pen.

'I never had a passport of my own,' Birdie said. 'I never needed one. We could never – I could never afford holidays abroad and things like that. When my kids were little we mostly went to Blackpool.'

'I *love* Blackpool,' Carmen said, the lie so obvious that all Marley could do was cough politely. 'So don't go beating yourself up, Mom.'

'Yours is an extraordinary situation, Birdie,' Marley said. 'It's impractical that the Home Office expects you to still have your mother's passport, but—'

'Why is it the only proof they'll accept, anyway?' Carmen interrupted. 'Why wouldn't they accept her tax records and her payslips and stuff? They wouldn't even look at them.'

'I'm not sure. And believe me, we've asked. But we had one unfortunate case where the Home Office took the individual's collection of payslips as proof that he'd been working illegally for forty-eight years—'

'Oh, come off it!'

'It's true. So you might be glad that they didn't look too closely at them, as frustrating as that is. Now Birdie, you said you had requested a copy of your landing card, but the Home Office said it was *missing*?'

'They said it didn't exist,' Birdie corrected.

'Ahh. That makes more sense. In all likelihood they've probably been destroyed, though why they weren't digitised first is anyone's guess.'

'So now what? Is there *anything* you can do for us?' Carmen asked.

'Well, the good news is that Birdie's chances don't rest solely on the landing card or the passport. Yes, she was supposed to naturalise in 1973. But there's nothing stopping her from naturalising *now*.'

'What do you mean?'

'She applies for British citizenship.'

Birdie let out a squeak. 'I can do that? How? What do I do?'

'First, we'll need to apply for Indefinite Leave to Remain,

which will grant you the right to live in the UK. Once you have ILR you can then apply for naturalisation and then you'll be a bona fide British citizen. I know, it sounds complicated. And it's not an overnight fix, either. These things can take months. But I can print out the necessary paperwork for you immediately and get the ball rolling. There *is* the matter of the cost though—'

Of *course* there was a cost.

'How much is it?'

'Two thousand pounds. For the ILR application. When the time comes for you to naturalise there will be an additional fee.'

Carmen drew in a breath. 'That is *extortionate*. Is that another deterrent, or is it just a blatant cash grab? As if we don't pay enough tax as it is!'

'I know it's a lot of money—'

'What if she can't afford it? Wait. Mom, *can* you afford it?'

'I—'

'Is your pension still under review?'

'What's that?' Marley asked.

'Oh. It's – yes, it is. I haven't heard back from them,' Birdie lied.

Marley frowned slightly, but he didn't press her for further details. Instead, he said, 'Remember, you only need to pay for the ILR application now. You can worry about naturalisation later.'

There were so many bridges to cross, so many hoops to jump through. Such a price to pay to reclaim what she thought had always been hers.

'Will submitting the application stop them from deporting me?'

Marley looked Birdie straight in the eye. 'No. But without the passport, it's the only chance you have.'

* * *

Birdie blinked as they stepped back outside into the autumn sunshine. The shops were busier now; teenagers milled around on skateboards and happy couples sat outside a colourful vegan café, taking advantage of the unseasonably warm weather.

'Well,' Carmen said brightly. 'I think that went well, don't you? We have a clear plan of action now.'

Marley promised to get started on the paperwork right away, and Birdie was to return on Monday with her cheque book. It was going to cost almost half of her savings. Her budget would need to be reviewed again. She might have to live without bingo after all.

'It's not much of a plan,' Saffie said doubtfully. 'Hope that Nanny's application gets accepted *before* she gets deported? What we need is a backup plan, just in case.'

'I think Marley is more than capable of handling it, don't you Mom? Besides, you need to focus on school, Saff. And maybe start booking some open days too?'

Saffie didn't reply but stared off into the distance, her eyes narrowed in thought.

'Anyway, shall we go have a cup of tea and then a mooch around Selfridges?'

So Birdie let her daughter steer her into the city centre, where they would spend the rest of the afternoon traipsing around the Bullring and looking at designer dresses and handbags and other things that neither of them could afford.

# Eight

## *1955*

'Are you going to stand on the pavement all night long or are you going to come inside and see your new home?'

Birdie stared up at the brick house. The house stared balefully back. '*This* is our house?'

'What's wrong with it?' Puppa asked, fishing in his pocket for a set of keys.

'It looks nothing like the card!'

Winston paused, his hand around the key in the lock. 'Card? What card?'

Birdie opened her patent handbag.

'The Christmas card,' she said expectantly, holding it out for him. Winston looked at it and then tipped his head back and laughed, the sound reverberating down the silent street. The net curtain two doors down twitched again.

'Birdie, that was just a painting! You can buy whole boxes of Christmas cards with that picture on it. Did you think that's where we *lived*?'

'But you said "this is my new address". You *said*.'

'I'm sorry. But this house is nice too, I promise.'

She cocked her head and looked at the house again. It might not be a quaint cottage with a sorrel-red door, but, she conceded, it *was* huge. Two whole storeys – taller than Grandpa's house! And the glossy black door had a smart brass knocker hung proudly at its centre. She'd bet her left foot that Niecy didn't live in a house as big as theirs.

Winston jiggled the key up and down in the lock (*it sticks sometimes*, he said) and then the front door swung open. Light flooded into the dim hallway.

'Go on,' Winston stood back and beckoned his daughter forwards. 'Straight up the stairs and to the left.'

Birdie stepped gingerly over the threshold. The floor was patterned with terracotta and blue tiles and the hallway was flocked in wallpaper with a delicately faded floral motif. To her right, a narrow staircase stretched upwards. Birdie climbed the stairs, her hand gripping the wooden banister. It felt rough beneath her palm. She paused at the top.

'Puppa?'

'Through there,' he said, nudging her gently in her back. One door sat ajar, a chink of light carving through the dark of the landing. She went towards it, full of anticipation to see what was on the other side—

'It's a kitchen!' she exclaimed.

'What did you expect? A swimming hole?'

The kitchen was big enough to fit a circular Formica table and four chairs in its centre, with a square window directly above an enormous enamel sink. In the Portmore house the window had been by the stove – and that was on the wrong side too, Birdie thought. *And* it was the wrong colour, a sort of muted cream, with rusted legs and blackened hob grates. Precious, who'd brought up the rear of their procession up the stairs, bent down to inspect it. She opened and closed the stove door, then ran her forefinger over one of the grates and rubbed it against her thumb. She wrinkled her nose as she looked in each of the cupboards in turn, then peered into the larder, which was, she noted, too small and narrow to stand up in.

The kitchen didn't interest Birdie in the same way.

'What's behind the other doors?'

'Go and see,' Puppa said.

At the other end of the hallway, she found a bedroom – her parents', clearly, judging by the double bed that had been pushed up against the chimney breast (the fireplace had been boarded up and painted over. The room still smelled like paint). A chest of drawers stood in one corner, and in the other, a sagging chintz armchair. Against the window Winston had set up a dressing table, another present for his wife. A cheap yet pretty set of combs sat waiting for their new owner to claim them. This room didn't interest Birdie much either. It felt cool, almost damp, compared to the kitchen. The smell of paint tickled her nose. She closed the door carefully behind her and then ran back down the hallway, past a wardrobe that protruded out into the hall like a barnacle clamped to a briny rock. She was certain that her bedroom lay behind the last door. She gently pushed it open.

The room was tiny. The door scraped against the edge of the single bed frame, and she had to force it to open all the way. A small chest of drawers had been wedged beneath the window; on top Winston had placed a comb set for her, too, a miniature version of her mother's. The handles were made of a shiny, pearlescent material, decorated with tiny rosebuds, each no bigger than her little fingernail. She stroked them reverently. Two presents in one day – and it wasn't even her birthday. Her father had been right about England all along. The money flowed like honey, just like he said it would.

She ran giddily back into the kitchen, and straight into her father's waiting arms.

'It's lovely,' she said, and Winston grinned. He didn't realise she was talking about the set of combs, and not the flat. 'I'm going to explore downstairs.'

She took a step towards the kitchen door, but Winston caught hold of the hood of her new coat and pulled her back.

'You can't go bursting into Pat's place unannounced,' he said.

'Who's Pat?'

'Patricia. She lives on the bottom floor.'

Birdie's hands flew to her hips. 'Why have you let someone live in our house?'

'It's not our house, baby. We rent the top floor. Pat has the bottom.'

'But . . .' Something was wrong. She'd seen every room on 'their' floor and there was a glaring omission. 'There's no pot.'

'Aha,' Winston said, and led her to the kitchen window. He pointed down to the yard. 'The privy is outside. We share it with Pat.'

'Do we share toilet paper with her, too?' Precious asked. Her voice was oddly tight. 'Come on. We best get the trunk upstairs.'

Birdie took off her new coat and draped it carefully over a wooden chair. She sniffed the air. The kitchen smelled funny, like the time she'd forgotten to mind the stove and burned a hole in the bottom of one of Mumma's pots. The back of her legs tingled as she replayed the memory. She absent-mindedly scratched at a bloom of mildew in one corner of the sill and looked out the window. The sun was setting, casting long shadows across the roofs of the houses opposite. It didn't seem possible to Birdie that it was the same sun they'd left behind in Jamaica – this one didn't seem to give out as much heat. From the window, she could see the roof of the privy – a squat, brick appendage, with a green wooden door – and beyond that, a high wall embedded with shards of brown glass that separated their yard from the neighbour's. A woman was in the neighbouring yard, her hair done up in rollers and a cigarette hanging limply from her mouth, unpegging grey shirts from the line. Their yard – or did it belong to the woman called Pat? – was tiny, empty save for a ratty piece of string that had been strung up for washing. Birdie doubted there was room to swing a skipping rope, let alone a cat. She was about to ask Puppa if she could go outside and play when she heard a soft, feminine voice on the stairs.

'You sure you don't need help with that?'

'We can manage. But go on through to the kitchen and meet Birdie.'

Birdie was struck by sudden shyness. In a panic, she darted into the pantry and pulled the door closed behind her. Mumma was right. It *was* small. Standing with her eye pressed against the crack, she saw a young woman, with blonde hair curled bouncily around her forehead, step into view. She wore tan slacks and a tight jumper that accentuated her plump frame, and she carried a brown casserole dish wrapped in a chequered tea towel. She was pretty, Birdie decided. Not beautiful like Mumma, but she had nice clothes. She especially liked Pat's pink satin slippers with a soft, fluffy trim.

'She's not here, Winston.' Pat's accent sounded strange to Birdie's ears.

'That's funny. She was here a second ago. Birdie?'

'This place is too small for her to have gone far,' Precious said. She carried in her arms the small jars of spices that had been wrapped in newspaper and nestled inside her second-best pair of shoes – Auntie Luce had insisted they make room for 'a lickle taste of home' in the trunk. She opened the pantry door and nearly dropped her bounty in surprise.

'Birdie! What are you hiding for? Come on out this minute.'

'You must be Birdie,' Pat said in her peculiar, rounded accent. 'I've heard a lot about you.'

Birdie whispered a hello.

'I brought you something.' Pat proffered the casserole dish towards Precious. 'Thought you might be hungry.'

'Oh. That's kind of you—'

'It's a shepherd's pie. I know Winston isn't the best at cooking—'

'How do you know that?'

Pat laughed. 'He'd been living here a fortnight before he asked me how to light the oven. He'd been surviving on bread and butter and cold tins of soup. I wasn't surprised when he caught that terrible cold, the way he was carrying on.'

'You didn't tell me you were sick,' Precious said reprovingly.

'Didn't want to worry you.'

Precious took the dish from Pat's hands. 'This is very generous of you, Pat. I'll bring the dish back as soon as I've washed it.'

'There's no rush. I'll leave you to get settled, but if you need anything, just knock.'

Pat fluttered her fingers and bounced out of the kitchen. Winston turned to his family with a grin spreading from ear to ear.

'Let's eat while it's still warm, eh?'

* * *

'And we flew up and up and up and through the clouds!'

'Weren't you scared? Not even a little bit?'

'Nuh-uh,' Birdie replied smugly. 'Mumma was though.'

'Is that so?' Winston turned to his wife with a smile.

'Are you finished?' Precious asked, pushing her chair away from the table and gathering the plates. The linoleum beneath the legs of her chair puckered slightly.

'You've barely touched your dinner,' Winston remarked as Precious covered her plate with a tea towel and put it in the fridge.

'It was kind of her,' she said diplomatically. 'But I'll be happy when I've stocked my *own* cupboard. You said there was a West Indian store around here?'

'It's expensive. It wouldn't hurt you to cook the sort of food Pat cooks.'

Precious snorted but said nothing more, and Winston turned his attention back to his daughter.

'No work tomorrow, so we can all spend the whole day together. What would you like to do? We could go into town, or visit the picture house, p'raps?'

'Can we go and see Eula-May? And ride on Ray's bus?'

'Who?'

'We met Eula-May on the train. She's nice and she's going to be a nurse. Ray is her brother. He drives a bus though white folk don't believe he can. He's nice too.'

'You have a friend already?' Winston said to his wife's back. Precious, who was scrubbing the casserole dish with force, didn't turn around.

'So do you.'

'So that's what this is about, eh?' he asked, standing up and snaking his arms around her waist. The silk of her dress slid against his palms and he could feel the warmth of her stomach and the gentle expanse of her ribcage beneath the thin material.

'You're worried that I spent the last month in Pat's embrace and not lying in my lonesome bed and thinking about you every waking second?' He dropped his voice to whisper. 'Missing you. *Wanting* you.'

'Winston,' she scolded, fighting to hide her smile.

'I've *longed* for you, Presh. Promise we won't ever be apart again?' He brushed the baby hairs that curled at the nape of her neck with his thumb and she shivered, then pushed him off.

'Winston Brown, you must be the chupidest man in the country—'

'And you followed me all the way here, so what does that say about you?' he replied, and in spite of herself Precious laughed. 'Well? Now you *are* here, what do you think?'

'We hardly saw anything from the train—' she began, but he shook his head in earnest.

'No,' he said, spreading his hands like a pastor offering up thanks to God. 'I mean *this* place.'

Precious floundered. 'It's – well – smaller than I was expecting.'

'Small? You should have seen what I was living in in London—'

'I know, you told us all about it—'

'West Indians are stacked on of top of each other down there, packed into boarding houses like sardines. I knew of a whole family living in a *corridor*.'

'I don't doubt it.'

'*And* I knew two fellas taking turns in the one bed – one on the day shift, the other on the night. One slept while the other was at work. *And* I bet the landlord charged them both full rent.' He looked at his wife. 'Are you disappointed?'

Precious shook her head. 'It just needs sprucing up a bit. To make it feel more like home. Some new linens on the beds. And maybe some new furniture? And a good scrubbing. And shelves for my plates, too—'

'Don't get carried away spending my money,' Winston said, but he looked pleased. 'This place, it's just temporary. We can save up and buy a place of our own. Think of that.'

'Oh, Winston. Do you really think we'll be able to buy?'

'I know it. Now you're here I can start saving again. We won't be renting forever. Not many landlords willing to rent to—'

He coughed and looked over his shoulder at his daughter.

Birdie was asleep at the table, her head propped up in her hands.

* * *

Winston woke them up early the next morning. They would go into town, he said, so he could show them everything – and show *them* to everyone. His beautiful wife and his lovely daughter. He'd be the envy of every man, black or white, he said. They caught a bus (*not* driven by Raymond, to Birdie's disappointment) into the city centre. Winston, as jolly as a sailor, pointed out the landmarks – Centenary Square and the town hall and the pub where that fella wanted to fight him for saying that England didn't deserve to win that last test – and Birdie walked beneath her parents, feeling small and overwhelmed by the noise, the buildings, the people. It didn't smell the way she thought a city smelled – not hot and acrid and spicy, but damp and sooty and smoky. None of the roads were gold, not one. And everyone, she whispered to her father, was staring at them.

'They've just never seen such a happy, handsome family before,' he replied breezily. 'They wish they could be as happy as us.'

Birdie believed him. She was so happy, despite the tarmac roads – happier still when Winston steered them into a restaurant for ice cream and Coca-Colas. It was cool and quiet. A lone man sat at one table, delicately deboning a fish with the precision of a surgeon, and three women, all with stiffly lacquered hair, sat drinking tea at another. The Browns sat at a table covered with a crisp, white tablecloth that had been pressed smooth by a harried waiter and shared a bowl of strawberry ice cream. Birdie shovelled a spoon of the creamy confection into her mouth and made a long sound of satisfaction, and Winston laughed loudly. Several heads turned in their direction.

'Winston,' Precious murmured beneath her breath, but he would not be cowed.

'We have just as much right as anyone else to be here. My money is as good as theirs.'

Precious frowned, but the comment sailed right over Birdie's head – her greedy eyes had spied the waiter approaching their table with a second bottle of Coca-Cola, just for her. She slurped it up and then leaned back in her chair, her hands resting on her stomach.

'How d'you like England so far?' Winston asked indulgently.

'Lots and lots,' she said contentedly. It was time to leave then (*if sir isn't going to order anything else*, the waiter said in a reedy voice) and they walked back to the bus stop, hand in hand. Although the ice cream had been deliciously cold, a warm feeling had spread from the top of Birdie's head right down to her toes. If every day in England was like this, if every day was as beautiful . . .

* * *

On Monday, Winston stayed in bed. Their jaunt to town the day before had disrupted his sleep schedule, he said, and while he was on the night shift he would need to get his rest during the day. That meant Birdie would have to be quiet, he added, something she couldn't ever remember him saying before. She and Precious hovered in the kitchen, unsure of what to do once the breakfast things had been cleared away. Their silence made the small flat seem smaller.

'Can we play a game, Mumma?'

'A game?'

'Blind Man's Buff. Or Follow the Leader—'

'You'll make a racket and wake your farda. Let's go to the market.'

'Without Puppa?' Birdie asked, but Precious was already changing into her outdoor shoes.

'We can manage without him,' she said, slipping into her new, shapeless coat. 'And it won't do us any good to stay cooped up in here all day. We can make a nice supper for when he wakes up. How about oxtail stew?'

Oxtail was a favourite of Winston's. Birdie's too. She ran to fetch her coat out of the big wardrobe in the hallway and together they tiptoed down the stairs and out the front door. Precious thought it would be easy enough to retrace their steps into the city centre – it was, after all, just a short bus ride – but after twenty minutes she realised they were going in the wrong direction. Flustered, she rang the bell and they got off the bus, wholly unsure of their surroundings. The street, with its small, grey houses, looked both familiar and unrecognisable all at once. In a nearby garden, a woman in a striped housedress was pruning a rose bush. Precious approached her with a tidy smile.

'Excuse me. Could you help me, please? We're lost – I'm trying to get back to Maltby Street.'

The woman almost dropped her pruning shears in

surprise. 'You speak English?' she asked, her eyebrows leaping off her face in shock.

'We're from Jamaica,' Precious said, her smile faltering.

'You've done well to learn the language so quickly,' the woman replied, before retreating quickly back into her house, her basket of roses only half full. Precious grunted with mild annoyance and bade Birdie to come.

They trudged along the street for another forty minutes, Precious half believing she recognised every street corner, every lamp post, until she spied, with relief, the striped awning of a greengrocers. At last, here was familiar ground. The bell tinkled softly as she pushed open the door; like her father's store, the shelves were stacked high with tins and jars and boxes, arranged in regimented rows by precise hands. The dark mahogany counter had been polished so brilliantly she could see her reflection in it. She breathed in the dry, earthy scent and thought of her father. She must remember to buy some stamps, so she could write home.

'I suppose you'll be wanting some bananas?'

Precious looked up from a crate of potatoes, all small and green and unappetising. The greengrocer was eyeing her, his arms folded across his girth. Behind him stood a shop girl with her hand clapped to her mouth. Her shoulders were shaking.

'Excuse me?'

'Nothing, missus. Find everything you're looking for?'

Precious straightened up and reached into her handbag for a shopping list. 'I'd like a pound of flour, please, and a pound of butter, and—'

The shop girl spluttered through her fingers and rushed through a darkened recess into the back room.

'Can't understand a word you're saying, missus. You'll have to slow down—'

'A-pound-of-flour,' Precious repeated slowly. 'A-pound-of-butter. Bread. Eggs.'

'Right away, missus.'

While the greengrocer busied himself at the weighing scales, Birdie eyed the jars of sweets behind the counter: inky-black liquorice wheels and jagged pieces of pink and yellow rock and crystallised pear drops, all displayed in glass jars too high up for grubby little hands to reach. There was money for sweets as well as ice cream now they were in England, wasn't there? Her mouth watered.

'Mumma. Can I have some sweeties please?' she whispered.

'I suppose so. Just a few, mind. Which ones?'

Birdie shyly pointed to a jar of red and yellow and green boiled sweets, as pretty as a necklace of jewels. The shopkeeper weighed out a small handful on a brass scale and deposited them into a brown paper bag.

'Anything else, missus?'

Precious asked for carrots, onions and, after a small hesitation, potatoes.

'Is there a butcher, around here? I'd like to get some meat—'

'I don't sell meat,' the greengrocer said. 'You'll need to go to a butcher, for that.'

Precious held out her hand for her groceries.

'Thank you very much,' she said as they exited the shop. As the door swung shut behind them, a peal of laughter exploded at their backs.

Precious didn't say very much on the walk home, other than to decline an offer of one of Birdie's sweets. Birdie was struck, once again, by how quiet the streets were. She was used to neighbours calling out from their verandas – casual greetings and messages for her mother and *you tell*

*Auntie Luce to stop telling everyone I don't make my own bun* – but on these English streets, front doors remained resolutely shut. The houses silently stared down at her on either side. She had the prickly sensation that she was being watched.

The jute shopping bags cut grooves into Precious's palms. She couldn't believe how expensive a few basic ingredients had been. Work might be more plentiful in England, but she didn't see how a man could look after a family *and* save for a house at the same time, as Winston seemed to think he could. Especially after all the presents he'd insisted on buying them, coats and combs and Coca-Colas. She'd rather go without trinkets if it meant getting out of that flat sooner rather than later. She didn't doubt that her husband had done his best to provide them with a roof over their heads, but she'd be mortified to welcome guests – Jesus, she thought, could you imagine what Luce would say if she saw the place? *I told you not to marry him. I told you not to go.*

She banished her aunt's voice from her thoughts. It was temporary, Winston said. They'd move somewhere better before long – he was confident the foreman would promote him to the day shift any day now. Her eyes shifted sideways to her daughter. Birdie was skipping alongside her, a boiled sweet bulging in her cheek. Had Winston disappointed her, too? Probably not. The man could do no wrong in her eyes.

She wished she'd been able to find a butchers, but there was a tray of chops in the fridge that Winston had bought a few days ago, and there was only one missing, so they would do for dinner. Besides, even if she'd found one, perhaps the butcher would have laughed at her too. Winston hadn't said anything about being laughed at. Had Birdie heard the laughter? And if she had, would she ask her what it had meant? They wouldn't be going back to *that* greengrocer at any case. Nasty man.

They turned a corner and Precious noticed that they had reached the top of their road. She exhaled with relief. It was then she realised she'd forgotten the stamps.

* * *

It had felt like a holiday, at first. Like the time they'd piled into Grandpa's car – Birdie in the back seat, squashed between her mother's bony frame and her great-aunt's ample one – and spent a week in the countryside. At the end of the week, though, they'd gone back home, back to her familiar bed and familiar friends. Birdie hadn't grasped that moving to another country would be more permanent than a holiday.

'Can we go out for ice cream today?' Birdie asked, hopping from foot to foot. They'd been in England exactly one week, and, after the excitement of the first two days, they'd settled into a routine as dull as the weather. Puppa slept all day and Mumma cleaned.

'No,' was Precious's echoey response. She was on her hands and knees, her hair wrapped in an old shirt of Winston's, her head in the stove. Her arms ached as she scrubbed at the build-up of blackened grease. After the oven, she'd scrub the floor again. She was determined to rid the kitchen of its peculiar scent, even if that meant cleaning it from top to bottom every single day.

'Tomorrow then?' Birdie asked hopefully.

'We're going to church tomorrow.'

'After church?'

'I said we'd go see Eula-May.'

'Eula-May can come for ice cream,' she replied generously, and Precious sat back on her heels.

'We can't be going for ice cream every single— Birdie, do you need the toilet?'

Birdie shook her head unconvincingly. It wasn't that she was *afraid* of using the privy, exactly. It was just that two days ago she'd opened the door and caught Pat with her knickers around her ankles – white, voluminous things – and she didn't want to repeat the incident.

'Then stop jigging about.'

'I'm bored,' Birdie whined. Until she started school, she had little opportunity to meet children her own age. Pat lived alone (there *was* a husband, she'd heard her father tell her mother, but he had a problem with drink and had not been seen in years. Not even Pat knew where he was, the poor woman) and had no children of her own. Birdie had seen a group of boys kicking a battered leather football down Maltby Street, but Precious wouldn't let her out to join them. *This isn't the lane, Birdie. You can't go running around the streets. It might not be safe.* It was a new and strange feeling, to be tethered to the home, but she knew well enough than to argue. Instead, she played alone in her room, quiet games, like Cat's Cradle, with only Abigay and the barrel teddy bear for company. She wished she had someone to talk to. Even Niecy Campbell would do.

'Why don't you write back to Auntie Luce? There's paper and stamps in my dressing table. But don't wake Puppa.'

Birdie tiptoed into the darkened bedroom. Her father was an unmoving form beneath the blankets. He was snoring lightly, his mouth open, the corners of his eyes crusted with sleep. The day before, Precious had caught Birdie sitting in the armchair, her arms wrapped around her knees, staring at him as he slept. She asked her what she was doing. Birdie whispered back that she just wanted to sit with him for a while. Precious hadn't known what to make of it.

This time though, Birdie didn't linger to listen to his snores but collected up the writing supplies and hurried back into the kitchen. Luce had posted a letter to them before they'd even left the island – she had wanted it to be waiting for them when they arrived in their new home, the kind of housewarming gift that only a person like Lucille Barry could think up. But she'd overestimated the speed of the mail steamer and it had only arrived the day before. Precious said she was surprised Luce hadn't sent a second letter to ask why the first one had gone ignored. But then again, it was probably already on its way.

Birdie spread fresh sheets of paper out on the table and began to write, her tongue poking out between her teeth as she concentrated on her letters. There was so much to tell. A description of the flat had been requested, along with information pertaining to their neighbours (a desire to gossip about the neighbours transcended distance) and, Luce had added in a begrudging hand, Winston's health. Was it cold? Were they remembering to eat well? Did they think they would be happy? Birdie dutifully answered each question: she described the flat and her mother's efforts to clean it; it was cold but not that cold, at least according to Puppa; they were eating recipes from a book called *Mrs Lowes' Hearty Family Recipes and Other Household Tips* that Pat had lent to her mother (the worst 'hearty family recipe' so far had been faggots and peas, which even her father had turned his nose up at); and yes, she was sure that they would be very, very happy, only—

Homesickness hit like a freight train.

'I want to go home,' she wailed. 'I want to see Auntie Luce and Grandpa.'

'Hush, chile,' her mother said gently, setting her scrubbing brush on the floor. 'Puppa's sleeping.'

But she couldn't stop the tears, not even when she heard the sound of Winston's weary footsteps in the hallway.

'Wappn?' he said blearily, his long johns crumpled from sleep. 'Is the house on fire?'

Birdie hiccupped guiltily. 'I'm sorry, Puppa. It's just that I . . . I . . .'

'She's feeling homesick is all,' Precious said.

'Homesick?' he repeated, as though his wife had spoken in a foreign tongue. It wasn't something he'd ever experienced – not when he'd left the farm, and not when he'd left for England. Of course, he'd missed his wife and his child something terrible, but he'd never once sickened for the *island*.

'It'll pass, Birdie. Give it time.'

'I want to go *home*,' she repeated.

'*This* is your home now.'

'But I miss Grandpa and Auntie Luce and Anslow and Miss Smith,' she took a noisy gulp of air. 'And Uncle Peter and Miss Linda Next Door and the cat that lived under her porch and—'

'Anyone else?' Winston asked.

'And *you-uu*.'

He raised his eyebrows.

'I'm right here.'

'But you sleep all the time.'

Winston and Precious shared a glance above Birdie's head. She shrugged, and he sat down and pulled Birdie onto his lap, wiping her wet cheeks with the heels of his hands.

'Oof. You're getting too big for this. Now look here, baby. Jamaica isn't our home anymore. We live in England now.'

Her bottom lip began to wobble again.

'But let me tell you a secret. Home is wherever your family is – your *real* family,' he added quickly. 'Me and Mumma. *That's* your real family. And that means you're already home.'

She let out one last squeak of a sob and nodded.

'And as for me sleeping all the time – I told you. It's just temporary, till I find a better job.'

'Promise . . .' she began. She put her mouth next to his ear, so close that her breath tickled his neck. 'Promise that you won't go away again.'

He chucked her gently beneath the chin.

'I promise. Although I heard Timbuktu is pretty nice this time of year—'

Birdie giggled and Winston grinned delightedly.

'Listen, baby. I know it might be hard, being in a new place. But it won't be hard forever, you'll see. As long as we stick together – all we need to be happy is us three.'

Birdie nodded and threw her arms about his neck. She kissed him on his cheek and then jumped off his lap – she *really* had to go to the bathroom, or else she'd have an accident right on Mumma's clean floor – and ran down the stairs two at a time, bursting through the door of the privy and not stopping to check if it was occupied first. She had to get back upstairs and finish writing her letter home – no, finish writing her letter to her relatives that lived overseas.

She was already home.

# Nine

## *2016*

The cheque cleared, the forms were signed and dated, and the request that Bridget Brown be granted Indefinite Leave to Remain in the United Kingdom was sent off to be reviewed by the Home Office. Birdie imagined a faceless official plucking her application off a conveyor belt and reaching for a stamp (in her nightmares, the stamp was brought down on her forehead and she was branded with the word ILLEGAL in bright red ink), but Marley said it didn't really work like that. Birdie didn't care how the process worked, just as long as it *worked*.

A week passed, and then a month. She made a Halloween costume for Jaxon – sewing the sleeves of a blue T-shirt to a red one and drawing a spiderweb on the front – and took him trick-or-treating up and down the walkways of Clent House. She watched the leaves change. She watched the news. Donald Trump speaking at a rally. A double stabbing in Birmingham city centre, two black teenagers, two lives cut short on the same day, and the world kept turning like it was no big deal. She waited, and kept waiting, for her application to be approved, a lump of anxiety, growing like a tumour, in her stomach. Marley said it could take a long time for a decision to come back. She was to sit tight, continue going to her fortnightly 'meetings', and keep her head down. Birdie wanted nothing more than to keep her head down. She had no intention of shouting her worries from the roof of Clent House. The fewer people that knew the better.

Carmen couldn't understand it.

'You need to tell someone. Talking about it will make you feel better. And it's too big a burden for just me to carry.' Carmen's eyes widened as she realised what she'd said. 'I didn't mean it like that! I just mean that there are other people who'd be willing to help too. You know Auntie Claud loves you like a sister.'

Birdie didn't tell Carmen this, but she'd almost told Claudette. She'd gone round to visit her friend with the intention of getting everything off her chest, at last. Carmen was right – the burden was *too* heavy for one person to bear. But in the end, she couldn't do it.

Claudette lived in the end terrace house on a street near Guru Nanak Gurdwara Smethwick. Her daughter Michelle opened the front door and pecked Birdie on the cheek.

'How are you, sweetheart?'

'I got sixty-eight per cent on my last essay,' Michelle said proudly. 'But then today Alfie Jenkins tipped a plate of beans over Skylar Hadley's head. They congealed in her hair and I was the one who had to clean her up. Children are disgusting.'

Michelle worked as a dinner lady and was halfway through a part-time Open University degree in Social Work. She'd moved in with her mother after her stroke, because Claudette couldn't afford a paid carer.

'Well done on the essay, I'm proud of you. How's your mom?'

'The muscle weakness isn't any better, and on top of

everything else she's developed a chest infection—' there was the sound of wet, hacking cough from the living room. Michelle dropped her voice to a whisper.

'She'll be furious if she knows I told you, but the doctor isn't happy. He said if it gets any worse he'll have to admit her, but you know how much she hates hospitals.' She chewed on the end of her Westlife hoodie drawstring. 'I'm really worried.'

'I know you're talking about me out there,' Claudette wheezed. 'Come talk about me in here where I can hear you.'

Birdie rolled her eyes and went through to the living room. A single bed was tidily made up in one corner, because Claudette still couldn't manage the stairs. She was sat in an armchair before the electric fire, wearing her favourite jumper, a bright yellow one with white knitted daisies, and her hair was neatly brushed into two short, grey plaits. The left side of her face drooped slightly, making her look out of focus. Birdie reached down to kiss her.

'You're looking a little better.'

'Bullshit,' Claudette slurred. 'I look terrible and I know it.'

She looked Birdie up and down.

'So do you. What's wrong?'

'Nothing's wrong,' Birdie said, accepting a cup of tea from Michelle and sitting in the other armchair.

'Is it Tegan?'

'Tegan's fine, Claud.'

'Then it's Carmen.'

'She's fine too. Actually, Michelle, that reminds me,' Birdie twisted around in her chair. 'She said to tell you that Yorkshire Tea and Heinz Beans are on offer this week.'

Michelle shuddered. 'I don't think we'll be eating beans for a while, but thanks.'

Claudette wasn't so easily distracted.

'We've been friends for forty-four years, Birdie. I know when there's something wrong. Come on sis. Spill the beans.'

'Enough with the beans!' Michelle groaned. 'Just tell her, Auntie Birdie, whatever it is.'

Birdie turned her mug of tea in her hands, feeling Claudette's eyes on her. She opened her mouth.

'The thing is . . .' she began, but then Claudette began to cough and splutter. She dropped her mug of tea and it splashed in her lap, soaking through her pyjama bottoms. Michelle and Birdie both jumped to their feet. It took ten minutes to strip Claudette of her wet pyjamas, check her for scalds, dress her again and get her comfortably settled. By the time they were finished Birdie was sweating, and she thought of the time she could lift and manoeuvre the elderly care home patients she and Claudette had once looked after with ease.

'How many times have I told you to use the non-spill cup?' Birdie reprimanded Michelle.

'She refuses to drink out of it!'

'We always served cold tea to the rude ones,' Claudette said weakly. 'Do you remember? Now I'm starting to think we were doing them a favour.'

Birdie tucked a crocheted blanket around Claudette's legs. They were as thin as toothpicks.

'Are you doing your physio every day?'

'Course I am. I don't want to be stuck in this chair forever. I've got a mountain to climb.'

'You and that bloody mountain.'

It had all started after the death of Claudette's husband in 2008. She'd watched some film or another about a bucket list and had been inspired to compile her own. Some items had already been crossed off: go on a *Sound of Music* tour in Salzburg; see a West End musical (they saw *Les Misérables* and Birdie, Claudette, Carmen and Michelle had all been in floods of tears at the end); meet a celebrity (Gino D'Acampo at a book signing). Some of them – like climb to the top of Snowdon – were proving harder to accomplish.

'It's important to have a goal, it aids recovery,' Michelle said. Birdie looked down at the frail figure of her friend and wondered if she'd ever recover.

Claudette winced slightly.

'Will you rub my back?'

Birdie began to rub slow, rhythmic circles beneath Claudette's cheerful jumper. She could feel each vertebra beneath her fingers, could count every rib. *Thank God for that* Sound of Music *tour and Claudette's British passport*, she thought. Had Claudette been in her position, Birdie knew that she would not survive the ordeal.

'What were you saying before?' Claudette asked, as though reading her mind.

Birdie hesitated, and then said it was nothing. Claudette was too tired to press any further, and Birdie had left the house determined not to say a word of the truth to her friend, not while she was in such a bad way. She said as much to Carmen.

'She'll want to help, and then she'll find out she can't, that *no one* can, and then she'll be devastated. She's already so poorly – I'm not going to do that to her. I'll tell her when it's all over – when my application has been approved.'

'Okay, not Auntie Claud. What about Nancy? I don't think she'll judge you for what's happening to you.'

Birdie didn't think she would either, but then, Nancy's husband had voted for Brexit.

'Bingo is one of the few joys I have left,' she said doggedly. 'It's an escape. And it won't be if the girls are looking at me with pity every week.'

Or worse, if they looked at her with condemnation.

Carmen sighed. 'Fine. But we need to make a decision about the kids. Saffie knows, obviously, but I think Declan should too.'

'I don't want to worry him. He's got a wedding to plan.'

'He'd want to know, Mom. The twins too. They're old enough to handle it. And you should *definitely* tell Tegan. You have no excuse for not telling *her*.'

Birdie gave in and let Carmen break the news to Declan and the twins. She told Tegan herself, who immediately offered to tell Scott. Birdie thought of her to-do list and almost said yes, but then stopped herself and said she wanted to wait a bit longer. *It might still come to nothing*, she said. In a perfect world, her application would be approved and he would get out of prison and everything between them would be as it used to be, and then it would be something she could casually drop into the conversation one day. *Did I ever tell you about the time I almost got deported?*

While she waited for approval, she took solace in her grandchildren. Every Monday and Friday, Birdie picked Jaxon up from school and took him back to hers for tea, an arrangement she had made with Tegan to allow her, in her own words, some 'me time'. They'd walk home together, Jaxon's hand clasped in hers, Birdie listening indulgently as he chattered away about twucks and Mr Tumble, and she'd feel a brief wave of calm wash over her. They played together, sprawled out on the carpet, the way she used to do with Scott when he was that age. Sometimes, and without helping it, she saw Jaxon as something as a do-over. She could keep her grandson out of trouble, she could do better—

She had long chats on the phone with Declan, who apologised profusely for not visiting since Easter. Jade made her a card, writing inside that she hoped Birdie didn't get deported, and she and Lewis both signed it, filling every inch of available space with kisses. And Birdie spent more time with Saffie, too. Her granddaughter began dropping by two or three evenings a week to 'revise', because, she said, Birdie's flat was much quieter than the Lloyd household and it was easier for her to concentrate. The subterfuge didn't last long, however. After a few visits she stopped bringing her schoolbooks and instead brought a stack of DVDs from the library, all the films they'd watched together when Saffie was a pickney – *National Velvet*, *Mary Poppins*, *The Wizard of Oz* – and Birdie cried when Dorothy clicked her ruby heels together and declared that there was no place like home. Saffie poked her in the stomach and said *aww, you big softie*, and then Birdie tickled her granddaughter beneath the ribs until they were both breathless with laughter and her tears were forgotten.

One time Saffie asked if they could look through her photo albums together and requested a backstory for every single picture – the wheres and whos and whens of Birdie's life.

'When was this taken?' Saffie asked. In the photograph, Birdie was stood next to a Ford Anglia, holding a child-size handbag with two hands and smiling broadly. The photo was in black and white, but Birdie could remember that the car was green with a white hood.

'Puppa bought that car about a year after we moved to England. He'd wash it every Sunday morning, his sleeves rolled up to his elbows, whistling as loudly as he could. He wanted everyone on Maltby Street to know that he had a car.'

'Maltby Street,' Saffie repeated slowly. 'Your first home. We should go and visit sometime.'

'What for?'

'I want to see where you grew up. Where your dad washed his car. Did you live there long?'

'Until I was about seventeen.' Birdie turned the page.

'Did you always want to live in Birmingham? I mean, did you ever think about moving anywhere else?'

'What's with all the questions, Saff?'

'Just interested. I got a book out of the library about immigration. Did landlords really have signs saying "no dogs, no Irish—"'

'"*No blacks*",' Birdie finished for her. 'Yes, it was common.'

'So, why did you stay in Birmingham? You should have gone somewhere better.'

Birdie turned another page. 'Back then, lots of people had an issue with immigrants. They didn't want us living in their neighbourhoods and they weren't quiet about it, either. A boy I went to school with had dog mess shoved through the letter box. His family ended up moving.' She paused. 'I can't imagine it was any better anywhere else.'

'But that's so unfair.' Saffie looked at her grandmother with such horror in her eyes that Birdie regretted speaking so candidly.

'Here,' she said, pointing to another photo. 'Have you ever seen this one before?'

In the photo, Carmen, Birdie and Precious sat shoulder to shoulder. Carmen had the hint of a baby bump beneath her sparkly top, and the three of them were laughing, their heads tipped back, unaware of the cameraman. The photo was damaged though. A long crease ran down the centre and a half-moon coffee stain marred their faces.

'It's lovely,' Saffie said. 'Can I have it? Please.'

'If you want. It's so tatty though.'

'You all look so happy. It's nice.' Saffie traced the stain with her finger. 'There's so much I don't know about your life.'

'My life hasn't been that interesting.'

'I don't believe that. You have *great* stories – like your dad and his car. I want to know more about your parents and your friends at school. And what it was like moving to England. I bet it was a massive culture shock. In fact . . .' her eyes flashed. 'Oh Nanny, I've just had the most *incredible* idea. I want to interview you.'

'Interview *me*? What for?'

'As a kind of . . . a living record. An archive of your life!'

'Something to remember me by?' Birdie said, a little ruefully, but Saffie vehemently shook her head.

'Nooo. I didn't mean it like that. I just think it would be nice, that's all. Oh please, Nanny. Say yes!'

Luckily for Birdie, Andy arrived at that moment to pick Saffie up. Neither Birdie nor Carmen wanted her catching the bus at night, and Birdie had never learned to drive.

'Evening, Birdie,' he said jovially as Saffie let him in, and then he sniffed the air. 'Have you had your tea already?'

'Nanny made bangers and mash,' Saffie said, nodding towards two gravy-smeared plates on the coffee table as she carefully placed the photograph between the pages of her homework diary.

'Smells good. I love sausages,' he said hopefully, licking his lips. Birdie half expected him to lift off the ground and float towards the kitchen, like a cartoon character lured by a cooling pie on a windowsill.

'Carmen's got us on another one of her stupid diets. She wants to lose a stone by Christmas. I don't suppose there's a sausage going spare?'

'Brother, can you spare a sausage?' Saffie quipped, and

Andy looked put out, but it gave Birdie an idea. On the spot, she told him she wanted them round for dinner that Sunday.

'Are you sure? I know Carmen wouldn't want to inconvenience you—'

'Nonsense,' she said firmly. It had been ages since they'd done a family dinner together. Sunday lunch at Nanny's had been a regular occurrence until last Easter, when a petty argument between Carmen and Tegan had blown to such ridiculous proportions that Birdie had told them they could roast their own bloody Sunday dinners from then on if they didn't apologise to one another. Carmen had called her bluff and Birdie, who could be just as stubborn as her daughter, had stuck to her word. But it would be better to capitulate now and get some quality time with her family, she reasoned. She could stretch her budget to one family dinner. It wouldn't cost much – Precious had taught her how to dress up a scrawny cut of mutton and turn something as simple as rice and beans into something spectacular. Good food didn't have to be fancy, it just had to be *filling*.

'I won't take no for an answer. And tell Carmen none of this talk about diets. Be here at two.'

* * *

Early on Saturday morning, Birdie went to the indoor market to buy vegetables and a cheap beef joint, to marinate with thyme and a can of Guinness (*they're not for drinking*, she'd said haughtily to Saffie, when her granddaughter found the six pack at the back of the kitchen cupboard. *I've never touched the stuff. They're for cooking, girl*). The vegetables would be steamed in a saucepan that was probably older than Declan, and the potatoes would be deep fried, a Precious speciality, because her mumma couldn't bear a bland, boiled potato.

On her way out of the market, she stopped to buy a spiced bun from the nice fella with greying dreads who ran a small but well stocked Caribbean food stall, because the kids loved the stuff. Sunrise Bakery had been established in Birmingham in the sixties and the Browns hadn't made their own buns since.

As she made her way back to her bus stop, she heard her mobile phone ringing in the bottom of her handbag.

'Hello?'

'Hi, Birdie.' It was Marley. 'I'm sorry but your application has been rejected. I just got the email.'

'Oh.' She leaned against the handle of her tartan trolley bag, her breath coming in short, painful bursts. 'I see.'

'Birdie? I'm really, *really* sorry about this.'

She believed him. She'd never heard a person sound more devastated.

'I know this is a blow, but I promise you, it's not over—'

'It isn't?'

'We have avenues open to fight this,' Marley continued earnestly. Birdie could hear loud music in the background, and a voice saying 'We're approaching a hill, now climb! Climb!'

'Birdie, can you hear me? I said we have avenues open to fight this, and I'm going to do everything that I can to—'

'Can I appeal?'

'No. But we *can* reapply for ILR – I'm going to get another caseworker to join us on this to make sure your application is watertight. The grounds of rejection are ludicrous; they said that because you were born in Jamaica you shouldn't have any difficulty in returning there—'

She cut him off.

'If I reapply, will I have to pay another fee?'

He paused.

'Yes. I'm afraid you'll have to pay the fee again.'

The pain in her chest, squeezing, choking—

'I'm sorry,' he said again.

'It's not your fault. Thank you for letting me know. You take care now.'

She hung up and tried to get her breathing under control. Marley had said they had avenues to fight the decision, but she felt like she'd already gone a few rounds with a heavyweight champion and the crowd still wasn't satisfied. She was being asked to drag herself off the ropes and step back into the centre of the ring. She didn't know if she had the strength. How was she going to afford a second application? How could she cope with more, endless uncertainty? And what would she do if they failed a second time?

She was stood stock still in the middle of the pavement, she realised. Other shoppers were giving her a wide berth, steering around her without making eye contact. They must think she was a crazy old lady. Her phone buzzed in her hand and she jumped, like she'd been electrocuted. Perhaps it was Marley – perhaps he'd been wrong, perhaps her application had been accepted after all—

> Guess what mom? Declan is going to drive up from London and join us for lunch tomoz 😍😍😍

Oh yes. Sunday lunch with her family. She'd almost forgotten. Well. It would be easier to tell them all at once, wouldn't it?

* * *

They gathered at two o'clock as instructed. Carmen brought a bottle of wine. So did Declan. Tegan showed up empty-handed, but on her way to the bathroom she pulled Birdie to one side and surreptitiously handed her a ten-pound note.

'What I owe you for Jaxon's new trainers,' she said proudly. She rarely had the funds to pay Birdie back. Birdie pushed the note back into her hands and silently wondered who would lend Tegan the money the next time Jaxon needed new shoes.

Carmen, noticing the expression on her face, asked her what was wrong.

'Nothing,' Birdie lied. She'd planned to tell her family the news before dinner was served and then changed her mind the minute they were all gathered in the living room. Better to do it after dinner, she surmised. Bad news was always easier to digest on a full stomach.

*At least we're all together*, she told herself, and then immediately corrected that thought. Scott wasn't there. She remembered something her father had once said about home being where your family is. She wasn't sure she agreed. Distance didn't trump family ties, did it? How wonderful it would be to see Scott on the sofa with his son, bouncing him on his knee the way Jimmy used to bounce him when he was small. Jimmy had been great with the kids. Birdie instinctively felt that Scott would be a good dad too. It was what Jaxon deserved. It was what any child deserved. She allowed herself to indulge in the fantasy for a moment – her family all under one roof, laughing together, loving one another, and perhaps . . . perhaps Jimmy calling from the kitchen that the potatoes were done . . .

And then Jaxon dived headlong off the sofa and screamed until he was placated with cartoons and a second glass of orange squash.

* * *

'So what happened then, Declan?'

'Why do you think something happened?' Declan asked around a mouthful of sweet apple crumble (his favourite, which Birdie had made especially). His father gave him a knowing look.

'Oh I don't know, you visit out of the blue, you've left Angie in London—'

'She doesn't like being called Angie, Dad.'

'Is she here to hear me?'

'That's not the point. And anyway I told you, she's on a hen do this weekend.'

Andy winked. 'If you ask me, I'd say there was trouble in paradise. What's the matter Dec, lovers' tiff?'

'I told you, no. Can you drop it?'

'Then is it money you're after?'

'Course not,' Declan said, reddening. Andy banged his spoon on the table in triumph.

'Aha! It *is* money. Is Angie demanding a big wedding?'

'I came to see Nanny,' Declan insisted. 'Mom said you were coming for lunch and I wanted to join you, that's all.'

'A likely story. I don't know why *her* parents aren't paying for the wedding. They're rich enough.'

'They're not rich, Dad.'

'They bloody acted rich when we had that lunch together last year. I saw the way Angie's mom was putting on airs and graces. She called the lav the *powder room*. Didn't she, Carm?'

'She was wearing such a lovely coat,' Carmen said wistfully. 'That's all I noticed.'

'And her dad pretended he knew where Smethwick was. Ha! As if he'd ever been to Smethwick before. He wouldn't last a second around here. I'd show him stuff that'd have him running all the way back to Conwy.'

Carmen tutted. 'You've gotten him all worked up now, Declan.'

'Me?' Declan spluttered. 'He's the one that started it. And for your information Dad, Glynn *does* know where Smethwick is. He got lost once on the way to Birmingham Airport—'

Andy shook his head. 'God knows what Angie sees in you, Dec. Unless she's the type that likes to slum it?' He sniggered. 'I know what your first dance should be. "Common People" by . . . was that Pulp or Blur?'

'Leave the boy alone,' Birdie chided, stirring her apple crumble round and round in the bowl until it turned to a viscous mush. She'd barely eaten anything. 'Angharad is a sweet girl. And they make a lovely pair.'

Declan smiled at her gratefully. He looked exactly like Andy had looked at twenty-five, only with darker hair and a warmer complexion. It still shocked Birdie to see how big her little Dec had gotten – when he walked through her front door she'd declared that he must have grown another foot since she'd last seen him.

'Still only have two feet, Nan,' he'd said with a grin, presenting his stubbly cheek to be kissed. That had been their joke ever since he was nine years old. Birdie had tried to laugh, but her stomach had churned unpleasantly, as if she'd eaten too many mangoes.

'She's got him wrapped around her little finger. He should rein her in a bit. *If* he has the balls to do it.'

Andy loved to needle his eldest son – whether it was about his football team not doing as well as his dad's, or the fact that he'd dropped out of Cardiff University in his second year, or his decision to follow Angharad to London (*it's full of posh wankers mate, you won't fit in. You're* just *a wanker*) – but if Birdie was in earshot she'd jump to his defence, like a mother hen defending her chicks from a fox in the hen house. She couldn't help it. She loved all of her grandchildren equally, but there was something extra special about the first one. Every milestone had been a major event – first steps, first words, first day of school – and now here he was, planning his wedding. Where had the years gone? Oh, she'd always known her grandchildren would grow up eventually, that they'd no longer need her to fight their battles or soothe their tears. But there had always been great-grandchildren to look forward to, to be petted and spoiled and showered with love. There would be fresh milestones to relish in. But now, unless Marley could work a miracle, she'd miss out on the rest of their lives. Her great-grandchildren might not know her. Might not even meet her.

'The Bank of Mom and Dad won't be able to fund a fancy wedding,' Andy continued. 'Don't know why you don't just do what we did – go down the registry office and then to the pub afterwards. That was good enough for your mom and me and – Birdie? Everything alright?'

Seven pairs of eyes swivelled towards her. Birdie swallowed and dabbed her eyes with the piece of kitchen roll beside her bowl. Might as well get it over with.

'I have something to tell you all. It's about my application . . .'

It was funny, how she'd been dreading this moment all day, so sure that she wouldn't be able to get the words out. But when it came down to it, she found that they flowed quite easily. When she finished speaking, there was a long pause, no sound apart from the roar of a deafening exhaust. Someone was driving a quad bike around the courtyard again. A squeal of tyres. An angry shout. Carmen was the one to break the silence. She swore and asked why they'd put their trust in Marley instead of a real lawyer.

'Because I couldn't afford a real lawyer,' Birdie reminded her, feeling as protective of Marley as any one of her grandchildren. 'And it's not his fault. He did everything he could.'

'But you can apply again, right?' Declan asked, his brow furrowed. 'You said that he said you can apply again.'

'I can,' she said, hoping they could not hear the tremor in her voice. 'So there's no need to worry.'

'Can you afford it?' Saffie asked, and the tension in the room became heavier.

'Yes,' Birdie said, as convincingly as she could. It was technically the truth – she had enough left in her savings account to cover a second application. The problem was that there would be hardly anything left after that. Certainly not enough for her to survive on indefinitely. No one spoke, and the tension became too much. She stood up and began to noisily gather the empty bowls.

'You're all looking at me like I'm dying. Everything's going to be alright. I just wanted you all to know, that's all. I'm going to put the kettle on. Anyone want a cuppa?'

She stacked the bowls on top of each other and escaped into the kitchen, the bead curtain rattling like rain in a violent storm. She dumped the bowls in the sink and gripped the edge of the kitchen counter. Because it might not all be alright. And they didn't all know, did they?

* * *

Birdie couldn't work out where it had all gone wrong with him. Her sweet boy. After the first time Scott had been caught stealing, he'd promised her he would never do it again.

Looked her in the eyes and sworn it. She hadn't realised she'd raised a liar.

After Scott's arrest and sentencing in 2012, she vowed that she would visit him regularly. She and Carmen argued about it, of course – he'd made his own bed, Carmen said, and he could rot in it. Birdie didn't agree. It was the worst row she'd ever had with her daughter, even worse than the time Andy referred to his wife as "the old ball and chain" in earshot of his mother-in-law. But no matter what Carmen said, it couldn't change the fact that Scott was still her son, and she was still his mother. Scott had an opportunity for rehabilitation, and she was determined to help him. Her sweet boy was still in there somewhere. He just needed to come back to her.

Her very first visit had taken place during a heatwave, the heat radiating off the tarmac. *Imagine being locked up in this*, she thought, as she gazed up at the wall that surrounded the prison, too high to see what lay beyond it. Imagine being kept away from the sun. She couldn't think of anything worse.

She'd entered the visitors' hall and spotted him straight away, sitting listlessly at a table close to the door. It was funny. Whenever she thought of Scott she thought of her little man. But on that first visit, she'd been shocked at the change in him, and in such a short space of time, too. He'd filled out (what were they feeding him?), the muscles in his arm bulging beneath his plain, grey T-shirt. She'd held out her arms to him – she knew she was allowed to hug him at the start and end of the visit – and he'd stood up reluctantly and embraced her, but pulled away before she'd had a chance to get her arms all the way around him. She told herself it was just because of the heat. The visitors' hall was stifling.

'Have you been working out?' she'd asked as she took the chair opposite him.

Scott shrugged.

'Not much else to do in here,' he'd said, his gaze fixed over her head. His face had changed, too. His eyes had lost all of their boyish softness.

'A lot of time for thinking, I suppose.' Birdie had meant it innocently, but Scott's face had immediately clouded.

'What's that supposed to mean?' Sweat beaded on his upper lip.

'Nothing,' Birdie said, nonplussed. 'Nothing at all.'

'No, come out and say it. You think I've had long enough to think about the error of my ways, don't you, while I've been banged up in here? That it's high time I got down on bended knee and apologised?'

'I never said that—'

'Well, it's only been a month. Seven years and eleven months to go. Then you can ask me if I've had enough time to *think*.'

'I just wanted to come and see you,' she insisted.

'I can see it in your eyes. Your *disappointment*. You look just like *him*.'

'Scott, please!' Birdie chided. 'This isn't like you.'

'You don't know me at all,' he'd said. And Birdie, looking long and hard at her boy over the table that separated them, realised that he was right. She visited him a few more times after that, and the conversation was always strained and awkward, no matter how cheerful or positive she tried to be. And then, five months into his sentence, Tegan said that he didn't want Birdie to visit again. What was a mother to do but comply with his wishes? Never mind that it broke her heart a little bit more.

* * *

Birdie asked Tegan to pass on a message to Scott that she wanted to see him. Could she please tell him it was important? To her surprise, Scott said yes. She worried that Tegan had said something – she swore she wouldn't, but Tegan wasn't always the best at keeping secrets (like the time Birdie had paid Tegan's rent for six months. Tegan had accidentally mentioned it in front of Carmen. Carmen had been furious). But even if she had, Scott still had to hear it from her.

The prison, a long, red brick building, was located behind the hospital where Scott had been born. Birdie stepped off the bus and shivered. She couldn't tell if it was because of the wind or her nerves. She joined the back of the queue as it moved forwards. She felt like she was on a conveyor belt, taking slow, mechanical steps forward. Then Birdie was inside. She followed a prison guard down a long corridor that smelled like Domestos to the visitors' hall where her son was waiting. He sat at a table in the centre of the cavernous room.

'Hi Mom. Long time no see.'

Birdie looked at him. Was he being facety? *He* was the one who hadn't let her visit all these years. There was a long pause. The couple at the next table – a woman with thick, blue eyeliner and an older man with sallow skin – were blowing wet and noisy kisses to each other. He growled like a tiger and she meowed back. Was anything private in here, Birdie wondered? She asked how Scott was. He was fine, he said. How was she? Fine. Small talk felt like the safest ground, even though the clock was ticking and Birdie, who still had not gotten used to living on borrowed time, was avoiding doing what she had gone there to do.

'And Carmen, how's she?'

'She's fine. She sends her love.'

'Doubtful,' Scott said, but Birdie refused to admit the lie. Instead, she said, 'Jaxon's getting more and more like you every day, you know.'

He rubbed the back of his closely cropped head. He'd asked for all of his curls to be shorn off at the age of eleven and he'd never grown them out again. Birdie had mourned them for an embarrassingly long time.

'Tegan says the same. I hope not, for his sake.'

'Don't say that.'

He stared at her. He had a tattoo peeking above the collar of his beige sweatshirt that she was sure hadn't been there the last time she'd seen him. That sort of thing went on in prisons, didn't it? Tattooing, coded ink to be flaunted as badges of honour. At least that's what happened in the dramas she used to watch on ITV, the ones she'd enjoyed before her own son got banged up. Before she could stop herself, she told him not to tattoo his face. He was still a handsome man, she said. It would ruin his looks. Scott chuckled.

'Alright Mom, I won't.'

'You've got your grandmother's cheekbones. Did I ever tell you that?'

'Yeah, loads of times.'

'Oh.'

He cleared his throat. They both started speaking at the same time.

'Go on.'

'No, you—'

'Something's the matter, isn't it? You . . . something's happened. Something bad. What is it? Are you sick?'

Birdie blinked. 'Oh, Scott. I have something to tell you.'

When she finished, he was silent for a few seconds. Then he

said, 'Shit, Mom. I mean . . . fuck.' He looked devastated. 'Can you afford another application?'

This time she didn't see the point in lying.

'Not really,' she said.

'Can't Carmen help?'

'No, Scott.'

Carmen had offered, of course, chewing on the inside of her cheek, silently totting up earnings and outgoings in her head. Declan offered too, and so did Saffie, who had, according to her, one hundred and twenty eight pounds and seventy-four pence in her bank account saved up from babysitting jobs. Tegan said something about getting another payday loan, but Birdie wouldn't hear of it. Not with Carmen struggling to make ends meet, and Tegan with a child to take care of. And as for taking money off her grandkids! Absolutely not. *I didn't invite you round here to beg for money*, she had said. *I can manage.*

'But I have options . . .'

Scott shook his head darkly. 'Don't fuck with money lenders or anything. Trust me. It won't matter that you're an old woman. They'll hurt you if you can't pay.'

He shook out his wrist absent-mindedly, as though shaking out an old injury, and the gesture made Birdie's stomach turn. She had, in fact, thought about going to a money lender – desperate times called for desperate measures, and she didn't want *much* money, just enough to tide her over – but the sharpness of his tone made her immediately reconsider that option. Had someone hurt her son over an unpaid debt? When had he gotten mixed up with money lenders, anyway? And what else had he kept from her, over the years?

'I might know someone who can help,' he said, not giving her the chance to ask a question that, on reflection, she might not like the answer to. 'On the outside, I mean. It wouldn't be strictly legal, and I'd have to make sure it didn't get back to me, but—'

'Then no thank you,' she said firmly. 'We're both in enough trouble as it is, don't you think?'

'Thanks for the reminder,' he said wryly, and she winced.

'Oh Scott, I didn't mean—'

'Nah Mom, it's cool.' His fingers twitched on top of the table, as though he were about to reach out and take her hand, then thought better of it. 'I appreciate you coming to tell me, though. You didn't have to.'

'Yes, I did. I wanted you to hear it from me.' She tried to make her voice sound lighter. 'But that's not to say I'm going to be deported anyway . . .'

The woman at the next table burst into theatrical sobs, and several heads turned in her direction. Blue rivers were running down her cheeks. She looked like she was enjoying herself.

'Mom . . .' Scott swallowed. 'I should . . . that is, I want to . . .'

He looked at her and suddenly she saw her little man again, peering from behind the lines in his face, afraid that he was going to get into trouble.

'What is it?'

He took a deep breath, his shoulders shuddering. 'I want to apologise. For everything. And for . . . not letting you visit.'

'Oh.' Birdie had not been expecting that.

'It's just . . .' he tucked his chin to his chest and mumbled something into his collar.

'What?' Birdie leaned in closer across the table. 'I can't hear you.'

He fidgeted in his chair, looking as though he regretted starting the conversation.

'Please, Scott. Whatever it is, you can tell me—'

'I was ashamed,' he said and Birdie sat back in surprise. 'Ashamed that you had to see me in here. Ashamed of what I'd done. To you. And Jimmy.'

'I see.'

'You'd always stuck up for me. Even when everyone was telling you I was a waste of space—'

'You're not a waste of space—'

'You were always there for me. And then I fucked things up and you were still there for me.' He blinked, hard and fast, as though he were trying to stem the flow of tears. 'And I hated it. You made me feel guilty—'

'That wasn't my intention.'

'I know that. But that's how I felt. Every time you looked at me, all I could see was you counting all the ways I'd fucked up—'

'Scott, I *never*—'

'Let me finish.' She fell silent. 'I felt so fucking guilty, all the time. And I hated it. So I figured if I didn't see you, I wouldn't feel that way . . . shit. I've wasted so much time, haven't I?'

Birdie instinctively wanted to tell him no, but she couldn't. Visiting hours were almost over. They were running out of time.

*She* might be running out of time.

Birdie reached out and took her son's hands in her own. They were so much bigger than hers, the fingertips rough, the nails ragged and chewed. A childhood habit he'd never grown out of. She didn't want to worry about past regrets. If she did that, there wouldn't be time left in the day to do anything else.

She gently squeezed his hands. 'Let me tell you a funny thing Jaxon said the other day . . .'

# Ten

## *1956*

The Browns had been in England for a year. They celebrated with a trip to Weston-super-Mare, leaving early in the morning and arriving at the seaside in time for lunch. They ate fish and chips on the seafront, seagulls squawking overhead, and then strolled along the water's edge, shoes in hand. With her blue smocked dress tucked into her knickers, Birdie splashed about in the seaweed-coloured waves, shrieking with delight as sea spray burst over her bare legs. Winston rolled up his trousers and joined her.

'How about a donkey ride? Shall we get your mumma up on a donkey?'

Birdie laughed so hard she lost her balance and disappeared beneath the waves. Winston fished her out, dripping wet, a huge grin plastered across her face. Precious rolled her eyes. *Both as bad as each other*.

On the drive home, Birdie slept across the back seat of the car, the taste of sea salt on her lips, a blanket tucked around her bare shoulders. Winston, one lazy hand on the steering wheel, smiled at his wife.

'It's been a good day,' he said.

'It has.'

That was how they measured the first year. Good days and bad days. To Winston, a bad day was a blip, nothing more. A good day was proof that the decision to emigrate had been the right one. Precious didn't see it the same way, but she reminded herself that with any kind of upheaval, bad days were to be expected. It was only natural that it would take time for them to settle. The question remained though. Were they settling?

No one could blame them if they weren't. Up and down the Mother Country, West Indian families were discovering that the Promised Land wasn't so adept at keeping her promises. Sure, there was plentiful work, but they were tough, thankless jobs. A man with a degree in engineering might be employed to sweep the streets. And then there was the inhospitality of their so-called English bredrin to deal with, too. If they were lucky, it might amount to nothing more than a few long stares or uncomfortable, if well-meaning, questions. (Take Mrs Richards, who lived on Maltby Street, for example. She viewed the Browns as a source of entertainment. Her sister might have a television set, but *she* had exotic neighbours that she could watch from her windows. And get this – coloureds drank milk, just the same as them. Who would have thought it.) But some West Indians reported hostility. Cruel words and crueller actions. Some deemed the experience a failure and returned to the warm embrace of the island. Not Winston. He wouldn't dream of giving up so soon.

'There's nuttin' for us, back there,' he'd say to his wife. 'Here, we're contributing to the economy. Here, there's money. We'll get the country back on her feet, and we'll be rewarded. It'll get easier. Have faith, Presh.'

It was easy for Winston to say. He meant it when he said there was nothing left for him back in Jamaica (and he profited from those who couldn't hack it – the car, Winston's pride and joy, had been purchased cheaply from someone returning to the island). But the same couldn't be said for Precious. She missed the sound of bird song and the breeze in the palm trees. She missed the ease in which she could find the foods she liked to cook. She missed singing in her church, and she missed her people. Luce wanted to visit, but the flat, with its persistent acrid odour, was too small for guests. Letters from home made her heart ache. Yes, there were good days, but every bad day – every slur, every snigger – made her wonder if it was all worth it. She was trying though. Winston asked her to have faith and she loved him enough to try.

For Birdie, there were good days and bad days too. On a good day, there would be ice cream, or a trip to the picture house. She liked *The Gamma People* best, a film about a mad scientist who turned people into subhuman creatures (*What's subhuman mean?* she'd asked on the drive home, and Puppa explained it meant a lower class of people. *But it's just a film*, he'd reminded her. *It's all just make-believe*). On a bad day, Precious would make faggots and peas. She still experienced homesickness sometimes (especially during their first winter. The novelty of snow had not lasted long) but her puppa was always ready with a comforting word that soon made her forget her sorrow. He talked endlessly of the house he would buy for them, describing the luxuries they would have, the space they would command. What reason did she have to doubt him? He would buy them a house just as soon as he got a better job. It was taking longer than expected, that's all. Another period of waiting. Birdie didn't mind. At least, this time, they were all together.

And so, the first year passed quickly. Birdie was now eight years old – *she's growing up and I'm not there to see it*,

Luce bemoaned in a letter – though she was still small for her age, one of the shortest in her class. She liked to read *The Famous Five* books while sat in the privy, waiting for her father to wake up and pound against the wooden door. Every evening, she would join him at the kitchen table, her feet in thick woollen stockings, and he would let her take sips of his coffee from his mug before he left for the night shift and she was sent to bed. She had decorated the walls of her tiny bedroom with drawings she'd done at school and illustrations she'd cut from Pat's fashion magazines, willowy white women with serious faces and golden hair arranged in fantastical styles, dressed in beautiful ball gowns and bathing suits. Auntie Luce watched over her from the photograph on the dresser, and she slept with letters from her family beneath her pillow.

On Saturdays she would accompany Mumma to the market, where vendors shouted over one another in the accent her ears had finally gotten used to. On Sundays, they would go to church, a black-bricked building with chilly pews and an organ that sounded like a wounded animal. And, for a whole year, she had attended an English school, wearing a white shirt, green and blue striped tie and black shoes that her father polished for her every morning when he returned from work. There, Birdie got the education Winston had been so keen for her to get.

* * *

Greenfields was bigger, noisier, and more chaotic than the two-roomed schoolhouse she had left behind. Her teacher, Miss Butler, was a pretty woman, with rosy cheeks and chestnut brown hair. On Birdie's first day she had frowned and said that she already managed a class of thirty – another coloured was a distraction she could frankly do without.

'Well,' Miss Butler had said with a sigh. 'They've put you with me. What's your name?'

'Bridget, miss.'

'At least I can pronounce that,' Miss Butler said, handing Birdie a blank exercise book and a pencil and indicating an empty seat at the back of the class. Birdie sat down next to a West Indian child with big ears that stuck out from his face. Birdie smiled at him.

'I'm Birdie. What's your name?'

'Who is talking back there?' Miss Butler called from the front of the class. 'Was that you, Bridget? I don't know what it's like where you come from, but in *my* classroom, you do not speak unless spoken to.'

'Yes miss,' Birdie said obediently. Miss Butler narrowed her eyes, then turned back to writing sums on the blackboard. The class fell silent; the only sound that could be heard was the squeaking of pencils against paper. Birdie copied out the sums as neatly as she could, absent-mindedly chewing on the end of her pencil as she added and subtracted and divided in her head. She noticed that the boy beside her was still stuck on the first problem, so she nudged her exercise book over to him so he could look at her answer. Miss Butler called for pencils down and then read the answers aloud.

'Stand up if you got ten out of ten correct,' she called. No one left their seat.

'Nine? Very good, Kenneth. Eight?' Birdie stood up. Miss Butler made a small noise of surprise, then continued to call out the scores, admonishing those, including the boy sitting next to her, who scored less than five out of ten. After arithmetic Miss Butler said, in a gloomy manner, that they were to practise diction. She thumbed through a book of poems and handed it to a bespectacled girl in the front row.

'Everyone is to stand and recite a line. Starting with you, Lorraine,' she said. Lorraine began in a slow, halting manner, and Birdie felt the thrill of recognition. She knew the poem, had learned it off by heart in her old school, and when Miss Butler called on her to take her turn, she stood up so quickly that the desk rattled.

> *Cannon to the right of them, cannon to the left of them, cannon in front of them—*

Miss Butler cut her off. 'I can't understand you. Say it slowly.'

Birdie nodded and took a deep breath. 'Cannon to the right—'

'Sit down Bridget,' Miss Butler said, her hand to her forehead, as though she had a headache. 'Ada, please continue.'

Birdie passed on the book and sat down in confusion. She'd read better than half of the class. So why couldn't she understand her? Perhaps, Birdie thought, Miss Butler just didn't like poetry that much. She hadn't seemed that enthused to listen to the whole class read aloud – no, not the whole class. She'd forgotten to call on the boy with big ears.

The bell rang, and the children fled the classroom. Like animals released from captivity they took off, running and shouting and jumping over one another. Birdie followed the horde outside and spotted the boy with big ears standing by himself, his back against the brick wall of the school, staring at his scuffed shoes. He looked lonely, his too-large school jumper hanging down almost to his knees. Birdie approached him.

'I'm Birdie,' she said. 'What's your name?'

'Arnold.' His voice was low and he refused to meet her gaze.

'When did you get here?'

'Last year.'

'Do you like it?'

Arnold didn't reply, his eyes on his shoes.

'Do you want to play?'

Birdie was itching to join the other children, longing to jump and run and spin as they did.

'Come on,' she implored. A handful of children were playing hopscotch in one corner of the playground. Birdie loved hopscotch. At her old school she was the best hopper in her class: once Niecy had dared her to hop on one leg all around the schoolhouse and Birdie had done it *twice*.

'Let's go play with them.'

Arnold stuck his bottom lip out. 'No.'

Birdie put her hands on her hips. 'Why not?'

'Because they'll run away.'

'What do you mean?'

Arnold looked up at her from beneath his eyelashes. 'If you try to play with them, they'll run away.'

'Don't be silly.'

Birdie's eyes swivelled over to the children playing hopscotch. She took a step forward, then hesitated. They wouldn't *really* run away from her, would they? Perhaps . . . perhaps it would be better to just watch, for now.

'Why is it called Greenfields?' she asked, turning away from the game and taking in the rest of the playground. It was nothing more than a concrete square, unforgiving against school shoes and knees, boxed in by a tall fence. There wasn't a green field in sight. Arnold shrugged. He placed a finger up his nose, then put it in his mouth.

'That's disgusting,' Birdie said reproachfully. She wasn't sure she wanted to be friends with Arnold after all.

'Do they put doodoo through your letter box too?' he said, his finger finding his nose again.

'What do you mean?' Birdie demanded, but Arnold's finger had returned to his mouth. He didn't say another word to her for the rest of the day.

The bell rang at three o'clock and Birdie retrieved her anorak from her peg and skipped into the playground. Precious was easy to spot – she stood a little away from the other parents, holding herself stiffly upright, as though she were worried the children streaming past her might knock her to the ground. Birdie ran to her and threw her arms around her middle.

'Did you have a good first day?' Precious asked, taken aback by the embrace.

' . . . Yes,' Birdie replied, after the briefest of hesitations.

'Did you make any friends?'

Birdie spotted Arnold waiting by the school gates, and she nodded uncertainly.

'What's your teacher like?'

'Umm . . . she's pretty.'

Precious tutted. 'Let's hope she can teach you something.'

As it happened, Birdie learned a lot in Miss Butler's class. She learned that if she put her hand up to answer a question, Miss Butler would never call on her. She learned that she would never again be asked to read aloud from *The Standard Book of Poetry*, and her best artwork would never go up on the classroom walls. She could never quite pinpoint the root of Miss Butler's coldness. It wasn't as if the teacher was *nasty*. She didn't shout, or point the finger, or accuse Birdie of being a troublemaker, like she accused Gregory Smith on a daily basis. In fact, she barely acknowledged Birdie's presence in her classroom at all, preferring to act as though the desk at the back of the room was empty. Birdie was too young then to understand a word like prejudice, but she would, in time. It was a lesson that began in Miss Butler's classroom.

Miss Butler didn't like Arnold, either. Every playtime, they stood next to one another in the playground, their backs against the wall. He transferred his mistrust of the other children to Birdie, and she kept her distance from them, afraid that they'd reject her for reasons she couldn't quite understand. She'd never been afraid of anything, or anyone, until her first year in an English school.

* * *

The day after the trip to Weston-super-Mare was a bad one. Precious received a concerning letter from Peter: Luce had fallen – or fainted, depending on who you asked – in the market. She wasn't too badly hurt, just a black eye the colour of a ripe plum, and she'd refused to see a doctor, instead slapping on a comfrey poultice and going about her day as usual, still as sharp as ever even with only one good eye in her head. But she'd gone to bed early that night, complaining of a pain in her chest, and Aubrey had told his son that these pains were getting more frequent. Could Precious write to her, Peter asked, and tell her she must see a doctor? *Everyone knows you're her favourite*, Peter wrote. *If anyone can convince her, it's you.*

Precious showed the letter to her husband the moment he woke up and, to Winston's credit, he tried to appear interested.

'You should write to her,' he said from beneath the blankets. 'Get the doctor to extend her life another seventy-five years. What a gift that would be to the world.'

Precious frowned. Winston should know better than to joke about something as serious as this.

'Writing won't do much good. You know how stubborn she can be.'

Winston muttered something to the effect of he knew *exactly* how stubborn Lucille Barry could be, the pomptious old—

'If only I was there *with* her. I'd be able to convince her in person,' Precious said, and something in the manner of her voice made Winston feel uneasy.

'We can't afford for you to go back, Presh. Not right now.'

'You could afford the car,' she said accusingly. Winston threw the blankets aside in irritation and swung his legs out of bed. The argument had become repetitive and he was tired of explaining himself.

'You know full well that Lester was *giving* that car away. It cost a whole lot less than a ticket back to Jamaica—'

Precious began to cry, and Winston's anger vanished. He pulled her into his arms and she clung to the back of his string vest, her shoulders shaking.

'Don't cry, Presh,' he said soothingly, stroking her hair.

'I'm just so worried. We're so far away. And for what?'

'You know why.'

Precious didn't say anything, but cried into the crook of his neck. After a few minutes, her sobs quietened and she pulled away.

'We can't stand here all evening. You need to get to work.'

'You alright Presh?'

'I'm fine. I'll write to Auntie tonight. And I won't tell Birdie, it will only worry her.'

'Alright.'

'She'll want to go see her aunt . . .' Precious said, but Winston didn't reply.

'I don't think she's happy,' Precious continued. 'She doesn't want to go back to school in September.'

Winston sat on the end of the bed, the mattress groaning beneath him, and put on a pair of socks. One had a hole in the toe and he pulled it back off in annoyance.

'Cho. No child wants to go back after the holidays. You're worrying for nuttin'.'

'This time last year she couldn't wait to buy her new uniform, but I had to *drag* her to the shop last week. I tell you, she doesn't want to go back.'

'And I tell you, she's fine.'

'Is she?'

'*Isn't* she?'

Precious crossed her arms.

Winston sighed. 'Hand me my trousers, will you?'

'Talk to her.'

'What, and ask her if she hates school and wants to go back to Jamaica?'

'Ask her if she's happy. And I don't mean manipulate her into saying what you want to hear—'

Winston was rummaging through the chest of drawers, looking for another pair of socks. He slammed the drawer shut and turned to face his wife.

'That's a rotten thing to say, Presh.'

'Talk to her,' Precious implored. 'She tells you things she doesn't tell me.'

'Fine,' he sniffed. 'I'll talk to her. And you'll see that she's perfectly fine.'

'I hope so,' Precious said. 'I really hope so.'

* * *

On Sunday, Birdie woke up to a silent flat, sunlight streaming through the curtains Precious had sewn by hand. Even after a full year, Birdie was still struck by how quiet Maltby Street was.

She padded into the kitchen in her nightgown to find her father drinking coffee at the table.

'Mawnin, baby.'

She rubbed the sleep from her eyes. 'Where's Mumma?'

'Church. Want some porridge?'

'She's gone without us?' Birdie asked in surprise, and her father smiled at her.

'I thought we could have some time to ourselves this morning. Unless you *really* want to go—'

Birdie emphatically shook her head and Winston laughed and ladled porridge into two bowls. He sprinkled a generous spoonful of sugar on top of each bowl and winked at her. She grinned back.

'Porridge tastes nicer in England, doesn't it?' He shovelled a large spoonful into his mouth and made an exaggerated noise of appreciation.

'Yes,' Birdie agreed, even though she thought it tasted exactly the same.

'In fact, lots of things are better in England. You still like it here, don't you?'

'Uh-huh.'

'And you're looking forward to going back to school?'

'Uh-huh.' She swallowed. 'Only . . .'

'Only what?'

'I'd like a *real* friend. Someone to play with.'

'I thought you had a lickle friend. What's his name?'

Birdie wrinkled her nose. 'Arnold. He's not really my friend.'

'What's stopping you from making another one?'

She shifted in her chair, her bare toes skimming the linoleum.

'I don't think they like me,' she said, and Winston frowned.

'Why? What have they said? Are the other pickney – do they say mean things to you? Call you names?'

'No,' she said, and she saw her father visibly relax.

'Then I'm sure they *do* like you,' he encouraged. 'You just need to give them a chance. Like your mumma did with Pat. They're thick as thieves now, aren't they?'

'You sure, Puppa?'

Winston smiled softly and chucked her beneath the chin. 'I'm sure. Who wouldn't like you?'

Birdie did her best to believe him. On the first day of the new school year, she looked for Arnold in their usual spot, but he wasn't there. He wasn't anywhere to be found in the playground, nor in the cloakroom. His family had left Birmingham – though where they went, she would never find out.

There were other changes, too. She was now in fourth class, and her new teacher arranged her pupils in alphabetical order, regardless of the colour of their skin. Birdie sat next to a girl named Nancy Bower. Nancy had a thick, brown fringe that brushed the top of her glasses, and pudgy cheeks, like a hamster. When the lead in Birdie's pencil snapped, Nancy shyly pushed her sharpener across the desk, but she didn't say anything, not even when Birdie whispered thank you, and when the bell rang, she ran off with a girl with yellow hair named Bette Hicks. Birdie stood against the wall and pressed her back against the bricks. She felt bereft, standing there without Arnold. It hadn't been much, their friendship, but it had been better than nothing. Her puppa seemed to think that making friends would be easy, but Birdie felt as though there was an invisible barrier in between her and the other children, a divide wider than a playground that seemed impassable—

'Do you want to play?'

It was Nancy, arm in arm with Bette. Both little girls looked at her expectantly.

'Yes,' Birdie replied breathlessly, hardly daring to believe her luck.

'Come with us,' Bette demanded. As though in a trance, Birdie peeled herself off the wall and followed the girls into the cloakroom. There, they sheltered themselves behind the coats and drew their legs up to shield themselves from view. Birdie did the same, a glow spreading from the top of her head to her toes.

'Do you want to be our friend, Bridget?' Bette asked.

'Yes, please. And . . . I'm Birdie.'

'You sound so lovely. Say it again.'

'Birdie.'

Bette giggled with delight.

'And your skin is pretty too,' Nancy said in a half whisper. She reached out and stroked Birdie lightly on the arm. 'Arnold *never* let us touch him. He was *so* odd. I'm glad he's gone.'

Birdie nodded in agreement, feeling only slightly guilty, and held both of her arms out, inviting them to press their fingers to her skin. Their caresses felt like sunshine, and the invisible divide melted away.

* * *

Winston made a new friend, too.

'Fella at the pub told me about a job going at his factory. It's the day shift and better pay than I'm on now. What do you think of that, eh Presh?'

Winston had bonded with Keith over a pint of Guinness, Keith being of the opinion that any man who preferred the black stuff to a pint of bitter was alright in his book, no matter the colour of his skin. There were plenty of pubs in Birmingham, but many had adopted a colour bar and segregated its customers. The Red Lion though, had an indifferent landlord, and as long as Winston and his kind behaved themselves, they were welcome to drink in the main bar with the white patrons.

Keith looked much older than his forty years, with thinning hair and a smoking habit so deeply ingrained he'd been known, he'd tell anyone who'd listen, to light up in his sleep. Set fire to the bedspread he did, once. His missus would never let him hear the end of it. Keith took a liking to Winston, with his easy smile and good nature. Keith told Winston that if he bought him a drink, he'd tell him about a job that was going at his workplace. Buy him two and he'd recommend him to the foreman.

'I like you, Winston,' Keith wheezed. 'I'm glad I could do you a favour.'

They were in the pub, celebrating Winston's first week on the day shift, their pockets flush with their earnings.

'I like you too, Keith,' Winston replied easily, licking the thick, cream foam from his upper lip and accepting a cigarette.

'And now I'd like you to do a favour for me.'

The pub was noisy, packed to the rafters on a Friday night, and Keith motioned for Winston to put his head closer to his, exhaling a cloud of smoke through his red nose. The skin was a roadmap of broken capillaries.

'That fag you're enjoying . . . a carton of those fell off the back of a lorry, if you catch my drift.'

Winston didn't, and Keith tutted.

'I thought you were smart, Winston. Anyway, there's going to be another lorry tomorrow night. I could use your help liberating it of its contents.'

Winston caught on, and he was appalled. 'You want me to steal cigarettes?'

'Keep your voice down, you stupid – yes. Seeing as you need me to spell it out for you, that's exactly what I want you to do. You'll get a cut of the loot, don't worry about that. How about two cartons? I think that's fair.'

'No way.'

'Okay, okay . . . four cartons.'

'I don't want any cigarettes. I'm not interested.'

Keith narrowed his eyes. 'I did you a favour, don't forget. I didn't have to recommend you for that job.'

'And I appreciate it,' Winston said. 'But I'm not interested in helping you teef a lorry. I'm sorry.'

Keith drained his pint and stood up, wiping his lips on the back of his stained pullover sleeve. 'You will be.'

The following Monday, Winston left the house for work at six in the morning. He returned within the hour.

'Been laid off,' he said thickly, sinking into a kitchen chair and unwrapping his scarf from the lower half of his face. The weather was bitter for September, and he hated the way the English cold bit at a man's extremities like an angry dog.

'What?' Precious froze in shock, one arm suspended in mid-air. A thick dollop of porridge dripped from the spoon and landed on the tablecloth. 'Why?'

'Because of Keith.'

'Keith? I thought he was your friend.'

'I thought so too.' Winston rubbed his eyes, trying to erase the image of Keith sneering at him. 'I don't know what that bastard told the foreman, but it was his word against mine.'

'Oh, Winston. I'm sorry. Can you go and ask for your old job back?'

'I'll try.'

Perhaps it was because of the cold, but Precious heard something in Winston's voice that hadn't been there before. It sounded like defeat. Things had been tense since their last argument, but she pushed that aside in the face of his desolation.

'You're a good man, Winston Brown,' she said, standing behind his chair and bending at the waist to wrap her arms around him. 'Good and loyal and a hard worker. You'll sort it out. Have faith.'

He patted her on the arm and she kissed him on the top of the head.

'You might as well go see your old foreman now while you've still got your boots on,' she said pragmatically. 'Birdie, finish your breakfast before it gets cold.'

'Can I have a spoon of sugar on top?'

Precious clicked her tongue in response, so Birdie obediently shovelled porridge into her mouth and swallowed.

'I'm sorry you lost your job, Puppa. Why would Keith do something like that?'

'I don't know,' he said.

'But he was your friend. Wasn't he? I thought that he was your—'

'Well, he's not,' he barked. 'I was a fool to trust him.'

Birdie flinched. He father had never once raised his voice to her before.

'Listen to me, Birdie. Don't be too trusting with folk. You don't know what they might do—'

'Winston,' Precious said warningly. Immediately his face changed.

'Ahh, ignore me, Birdie. That's just the cold talking. Whooee, it's cold out there today!' He stood up, his joints cracking, and reached over the table to place an icy finger on the tip of her nose. She squealed and batted his hand away and he smiled at her.

'See, I told you. Presh? Give me a kiss for luck?'

And with a cheery backwards wave, he left the kitchen to go and beg for the job he'd hated.

# Eleven

## *2016*

'I don't know what to tell you. It's not making much sense to us either.'

The office was busy. A small child cried and the phone rang, and kept ringing, but Birdie did her best to drown out the noise and concentrate on Marley.

'It says that because you spent your formative years outside the UK, it is considered that you are "familiar with the cultural, social and economic aspects of life in Jamaica",' he continued, his tone reminiscent of a doctor delivering bad news.

'I was *seven*,' Birdie said weakly. 'How much does a seven-year-old know about the economy?'

'It's nonsense, I know. But in your new application, we've really driven home the fact that you remember so little about your childhood, that you've considered yourself British since infancy, that you have very little to do with Jamaican culture—'

Birdie shifted uncomfortably. It felt like she was being asked to pick a side, to renounce her own heritage. Before she had been both Jamaican *and* British, a blending of both identities that went together as easily as curry goat and Yorkshire pudding (a surprising combination, but it worked). Now it felt like her two halves no longer fit together.

'And you've mentioned Jaxon? That I need to look after him?'

'I've mentioned that you have a number of familial responsibilities, yes. But I have to warn you, as you're not his primary carer . . .'

Birdie's face fell.

'But I've had Ruth look over the paperwork and it's iron clad, there's absolutely no reason for them to reject it again. All we need is the cheque.'

Her hand shook as she took it out of her handbag.

'Are you sure there's no other way? Because Marley, this is almost every penny I have . . .'

'I'm doing everything I can to help you, Birdie. You have to trust me.'

'I do,' she said, and handed it over.

It was the truth. She trusted Marley with her life. But a person couldn't survive on trust alone.

* * *

Birdie took a light blue envelope out of her dresser drawer and thumbed through the crumpled contents. She had £220 left of her emergency fund. There was just enough in her bank account to cover next month's rent, which was due in a week – but what about the month after that? And the one after that? And then there was Christmas to think of . . . If she could make a little bit of money, just to tide her over . . .

She caught the 54 to West Bromwich, feeling as furtive as a spy creeping into enemy territory. A lot of shiny new buildings had gone up since she'd last made the journey, and a giant

Tesco Extra too, but Sheltered Brook Assisted Living Facility looked exactly the same. Birdie pressed the intercom and waited for it to crackle to life.

'Yes?'

'I have an appointment with Julie McKay,' she said, and the door buzzed open. She was hit with the familiar scent of steamed vegetables and nonenal. Birdie gave her name and pinned a visitors' badge to her coat, then walked down the familiar corridors, past the canteen and the day room. She turned right at the staff station. A few looked up at her curiously as she continued down the corridor, but no one stopped her.

*They probably think I belong here.* If she'd been wearing a pair of slippers, they might have taken her by the elbows and deposited her in an empty bed. Come to think of it, she thought, knocking on a door marked 'Administrator', that wouldn't be such a bad thing. Three hot meals a day and peace and quiet—

'Birdie! It's *so* good to see you! How's your retirement going? Enjoying yourself, I hope?'

Julie, her old boss, swept Birdie into a hug, then pushed her down onto an imitation Chesterfield settee.

'How are you, Julie? How's the family?'

'All good, thank you. Harry's doing *marvellously* at Oxford and Charlotte's married to a London banker. You should see the size of their *house*!'

'That's nice,' Birdie smiled forcefully.

Julie fluffed out her yellow hair. She'd had work done since the last time Birdie had seen her. Her crow's feet had disappeared.

'She and Edward live next door to Marcus Parker – you know, the Olympic gold medallist who won *Strictly* last year. Apparently he's *very* nice – gives them extra veg from his garden from time to time. Last Christmas he gave them a hamper of homemade *chutney*. Have you seen his Instagram lately?'

'Er . . . no—'

'He's rescued a chihuahua called Finn and posts about him non-stop. Charlotte says he's the cutest little thing, though a bit *yappy*. The dog I mean, *not* Marcus Parker!' Julie tittered delightfully at her own joke. 'So, to what do I owe the pleasure, Birdie? You're not thinking of moving in *here*, are you? I wouldn't have thought you were old enough!'

Birdie took a deep breath. 'I'd like to come back to work.'

Julie looked askance for a second, then threw her head back and laughed.

'Oh Birdie, you *are* funny.'

'I'm not joking.'

Julie frowned – or at least, Birdie could see that she was trying to.

'But . . . you left. *Years* ago. To look after your mother.'

Birdie had forgotten that Julie spoke with that funny little affectation, overenunciating every other word to sound posher than she really was. Someone, it might have been Diane, said they'd overheard her on the phone to her husband once and in private she sounded as yam yam as they come.

'I know.'

'Then why on *earth* would you want to come back?'

Shame stabbed her in the belly. But, in the six years she had worked for Julie, she had never known her to be cruel, or judgemental. Despite her superficial silliness, she had been a good woman to work for, never treating the residents as though they were babies. Or worse, a burden.

'Because I need the money,' she said plainly. 'My pension has been stopped, and . . . well Julie, I'm desperate.'

'Why have they stopped your pension?'

'I've had some trouble. With the Home Office.'

The news was spreading beyond her immediate circle now, and that scared her. If she couldn't keep it contained then it might become a part of her, just as much as the fact that she had two children, or that she was afraid of spiders, or that she'd been born in a different part of the world.

'I can clean. Or cook.'

But Julie shook her head. 'I'm *sorry* Birdie, but I can't—'

'I'm a hard worker. You know that. And any time you need me, I'll be right here—'

Julie cut her off. 'I couldn't even if I *wanted* to. The government is cracking down on people who hire undocumented workers. Have you *seen* the papers? They're handing out huge fines and even *prison* sentences. If we got caught, I'd lose my *job*.'

'You could pay me cash in hand, no one needs to know—'

'Birdie.' Julie's tone was firmer. 'I'm sorry, I truly am. But I can't bend the rules for you. It's not worth the risk.'

Well. So much for her great idea. Perhaps she could find an employer who wasn't as scrupulous as Julie McKay. There must be someone . . .

On the bus home, she got a text from Nancy. Coming today, it said, followed by a string of question marks. Birdie hadn't been to bingo in weeks, making up an excuse each time to justify her absence.

I can't, she texted back. She had to contain it. She couldn't let it out. Jaxon still sick. Nancy replied with a little yellow face that looked like it was crying.

*Join the club*, Birdie thought.

* * *

December arrived, and three things happened. Firstly, Birdie paid her rent and then tried to buy a packet of spaghetti only for her debit card to decline. She muttered something under her breath – *there must be a mistake, I need to call my bank* – and then rushed out of the shop, dragging Jaxon behind her. For tea that night they had bolognese mopped up with bread, and she wondered how she was going to tell Tegan that she couldn't feed her grandson twice a week anymore. So much for familial responsibilities.

Secondly, she learned that there *weren't* any unscrupulous employers out there, at least none that she could find. Her age seemed to preclude her from most of the jobs she called up about, and even if she managed to sidestep any polite suspicion (*sorry if this is rude, but you sound, well, like you're getting on a bit . . .*) she couldn't circumnavigate the big question – did she have permission to work in the UK? What did it matter, she wanted to ask? All she wanted to do was push a mop around and get paid for it. But no. It was impossible.

The third thing was the worst of the lot. She learned that Carmen didn't have the same sort of qualms about containing the truth and was running her mouth to anyone who would listen.

Birdie hovered outside Holy Trinity Church, trying to muster up the courage to go inside. According to another one of her library computer searches, the church ran a community food bank once a month. She could get three days' worth of meals, if only she could swallow her pride and go inside—

'Mrs Brown?'

Birdie looked up from beneath the hood of her parka. A buxom woman in a Burberry coat stood on the pavement in front of her, arm in arm with a man with a thick brown beard.

'Mrs Brown! I thought that was you! It's Tracey!' Tracey smiled, showing off fleshy, pink gums and artificially whitened teeth. 'Remember me? I was in Carmen's form at school—'

'Oh, right!' Birdie nodded in comprehension and pushed her hood back further. 'How are you doing, Tracey?'

'Fine thank you. Me and Mark are back in Smethwick because of my mom. She's not doing so well, bless her, and we think it might be time for round the clock care. In fact, we've just toured a nursing home up the road. I wasn't impressed with it. Mark wasn't either. Were you, Mark?'

The man named Mark shook his head, and Birdie took a small step to the left, trying to angle her body to hide the 'foodbank today' sign that had been pinned to the church notice board.

'What a shame,' she said, inching over a tiny bit more. 'About your mom. I hope she'll be well looked after.'

'It's so funny, bumping into you like this!' Tracey reached out and patted Birdie's arm in what she obviously thought was a sympathetic manner. 'I ran into Carmen just last week in Tesco and she said you were going through some legal problems—'

Tracey's eyes slid to the notice board. Though the ink was running in the rain, the sign was still perfectly legible.

'And I'm really sorry. This government's lost the plot, hasn't it, Mark?'

Mark nodded sombrely, and Birdie made a noise like a strangled goat. 'Lovely to see you Tracey,' she bleated. 'But I must be off. Give my love to your mother.'

She rushed across the road without looking. She was going to *kill* Carmen. What was she thinking, blabbing about her private business to any Tom, Dick or Tracey? How many other people had she told?

'Are you *trying* to get me deported?'

Carmen denied it at first, but she'd always been a terrible liar, even with all the practice she'd had in her teen years.

'Tracey won't say anything,' Carmen insisted down the phone. 'And besides, I didn't tell her *that* much. It's just that – she was complaining how long it was taking for her passport renewal to come through. Mark's taking her to *Aruba*, apparently.'

'And what has that got to do with me?'

'Nothing. But then she mentioned her mom and how sick she was and how much she was sacrificing to support her and she was droning on and on and—'

'And you wanted to one up her? Her mom's sick but your mom's getting deported?'

'I am single-handedly taking care of you and this, *this* is the thanks I get? I bet Tracey's mom is going down on bended knee to thank her!'

Birdie felt the anger that had been festering in her body for the past few months begin to bubble over, like pressure building up behind a blocked storm drain.

'Do you want a medal, Carmen?'

'You have no idea how much stress you've caused me!' Carmen continued. 'You have no idea about the sacrifices I've had to make, or the sleepless nights, or the rows I've had with Andy about—'

'About what, money? What has Andy got to say on that subject? You're the one earning it, not him. He's the laziest man I've ever—'

'How dare you speak about my husband that way! How we choose to spend our money is none of your concern—'

'I know it's not, because you haven't given your own mother a single penny.'

'You're one to talk. Any time Tegan comes begging you bend over backwards to help her, no questions asked. You'd give her your last penny if you had the chance. *And* she'd let you, the selfish cow.'

'And I wouldn't do the same for you, if you asked?'

'I don't know. I'm not Tegan. I'm not so thick I can't take care of myself—'

'This isn't about Tegan, this is about you. You go on about sacrifices Carm, but you have no idea the sacrifices I've made. Year after year. For you *and* your brother—'

'What a great job you did there,' Carmen spat. 'Really, I bet Jimmy is *so* pleased that you kicked him out for nothing.'

Birdie exhaled. 'Shut your damn mouth, Carmen. You have no idea what you're talking about.'

But Carmen didn't stop. 'First you ran off our *actual* dad and then you did it to Jimmy. Maybe if you hadn't been such a fool, he wouldn't have left you.'

'I said shut *up*—'

'And maybe if you'd been a better mother, I'd want to help you.'

The storm drain burst, flooding her body with bile.

'Maybe if you were a better daughter, I'd like you more—'

'I hope they deport you!' Carmen screamed down the phone.

Birdie reeled as though she'd been slapped. The silence that followed was deafening. She waited a few moments for Carmen to say *I'm sorry* or *I didn't mean it*.

'Hello? Carmen?'

The line had gone dead.

* * *

Christmas had come to the estate. In frost-speckled windows, fairy lights flashed blue and green and red and Tyrone limped from door to door, selling frozen gammons and turkeys that were probably stolen, but no one was going to turn their nose up at a discounted Christmas dinner. Birdie didn't buy one. Even with Tyrone's 'super saver Christmas mates' rates discount', she couldn't afford it. And it wasn't like she had anyone to feed, anyway. Tegan and Jaxon would not be joining her on Christmas Day like they usually did. Tegan had broken the news that they'd be going to her parents' instead.

'But Jaxon hardly knows them. Is this a good idea?' Birdie had said, full of concern for her grandson. Tegan was not close to her parents. Having Scott's baby had only increased the distance.

'Mom said it's time to mend fences,' Tegan said, twisting the hem of her baggy jumper in her hands. 'Besides, you're struggling, Birdie. You said you can't help me as much anymore. I thought this would be easier for you—'

'Oh. Oh, yes. That makes sense. It's what's best for Jaxon.'

She knew that, in her own way, Tegan was trying to help. But still, it *hurt*.

'And you'll see Carmen on Christmas Day instead, right?'

'Right.'

Wrong. She and Carmen hadn't spoken since the row. She'd spoken to Saffie, who wanted to know what was going on, and Birdie had explained that she and her mom had had a disagreement, which was putting it lightly, but Saffie wasn't to worry about it.

'Can I come over tonight? She's doing my head in about UCAS deadlines.'

'I've got a rotten cold,' Birdie lied. She didn't want Saffie coming over and seeing her empty cupboards. 'So you best stay away for a bit. Don't want you getting poorly too.'

'I thought you sounded a bit bunged up. I hope you're better in time for Christmas! Are you coming to the "non-denominational, multi-faith winter pageant" this year? Lewis is doing a *rap*—'

'Ah. I'm not sure, my girl. If I'm better—'

'Well, we'll see you on Boxing Day at least, right?'

'If I'm better,' Birdie repeated, not knowing what else to say.

'I hope so, because I have had the *best* idea. Remember when I said I wanted to interview you? At first, I was thinking it would be nice to have a record of your life for the family to enjoy, but *then* I realised that if we take your story *public*, then I could—'

Birdie cut her off. 'I've got such a headache, Saffie. D'you mind if we talk later?'

'Of course not. Love you, Nanny.'

'Love you too.'

If only Carmen was as sweet as Saffie. She couldn't imagine her granddaughter saying such terrible things.

*Maybe if you hadn't been such a fool, Jimmy wouldn't have left you.*

She knew how much Carmen had loved Jimmy, so much so that Birdie didn't think she'd ever missed her real dad. But Carmen was a mother. Surely she understood the position he'd put her in – and surely she'd do exactly the same? She couldn't imagine her daughter ever putting Andy Lloyd, that great lummox, above her own flesh and blood. But perhaps not. Perhaps she and Carmen were alike in appearance only. Carmen had said such terrible things—

But she'd said terrible things too. She'd let her anger get the better of her and she'd said things she didn't mean to her only daughter. Of *course* she didn't mean them. Carmen knew that, right?

But what if she didn't?

And worse. What if Carmen meant the things *she'd* said?

Birdie shivered. She'd turned the heating off a week ago in an effort to save money, but she couldn't tell if she was shaking from the cold or from fear.

* * *

Another week passed without any word from Carmen. Birdie was almost too hungry to care. She lay in bed one morning and stared at the ceiling, unaware of how many hours had passed since she'd fallen asleep. Two, maybe three. She exhaled and watched the misty cloud of condensation disappear above her head, the noisy din of children on their way to school filtering up from the courtyard. They were singing something – an off-key but joyful rendition of "Step Into Christmas". It was Jimmy's favourite. She remembered him sweeping her into his arms, drunk on Snowballs, and spinning around the kitchen as he crooned into her ear about how nice it was to have her here. She remembered other Christmases too. A party in the flat on Maltby Street, the cramped space alive with laughter and the smell of spiced ham; Carmen waking her at the crack of dawn, desperate to see what Father Christmas had left her; presenting Jimmy with a shirt she'd made herself – it was a soft mauve colour, with wonky button holes and love stitched in every seam, and he'd smiled and said he'd save it for best . . .

She rolled onto one side and listened as the sing-song voices faded away. She was wearing long johns beneath two nighties, a woolly jumper and her dressing gown on top in an effort to keep out the cold. Her stomach growled like a savage dog. A few days ago, she'd taken some of her treasures to the pawn shop, handing over her mother's plates with trembling hands and asking what they were worth. Nothing, came the reply.

'Please. I'm desperate.'

'Can't help you love,' the man behind the counter said.

'What about this?' She unclasped her watch and handed it to him. He gave it a cursory glance.

'Thirty quid.'

'But it's real gold. And it's probably well over fifty years old.'

'Thirty quid.'

'Deal,' she said, and walked out of the pawn shop feeling like she'd lost far more than she'd gained.

She needed to make the money last as long as possible. Yesterday all she'd had to eat was two slices of bread, a hoary-looking carrot she'd found in the bottom of the fridge and a can of Guinness, for the iron in it. Today she'd have a tin of cold new potatoes and another can. She longed for something hot and soothing, like her mother's beef and dumpling stew, but she didn't have money for stewing beef and besides, having the hob on all day was out of the question. If she wanted something warm, she could make a cup of black tea with a teabag she would dry on a cracked saucer, so it could be used again. Still, her mouth watered at the memory of her mother's stew: the tender cuts of meat, the thick slices of green banana and the soft, starchy texture of the cornmeal dumplings, swimming in a thick broth. Precious would make a pot so big it would last for days. Birdie liked to crumble cream crackers into it, the way her father did.

If only she could feast on memories.

* * *

Here she was again.

The room was the same, the guard was the same, the hollow, miserable faces lined up in rows were the same. She wasn't the same though. That was the irony of it. The Home Office wanted to deport a person who didn't exist anymore. They'd taken so much from her, so much *of* her. She felt like a puzzle with half of its pieces missing.

Birdie recognised some of the faces in the waiting room, though she never spoke to them: the Slavic-looking man, the Chinese woman, the fella in the Adidas tracksuit. She hadn't seen the young woman and her father in weeks, though. Had he been deported? Granted a reprieve? She had no way of knowing.

Her ticket number was called and she shuffled to the counter.

'May I have your name please – oh, it's you!' The girl behind the counter smiled timidly. 'I – I saw you a few months ago. You were with your daughter. I'm Maisie. But you probably don't remember me—'

Birdie remembered. The man in charge had gotten shirty with Carmen. Had that only been a few months ago?

'I wanted to say . . .' Maisie paused, then appeared to think better of it. 'Never mind. I'm supposed to give you this.'

She pushed a glossy piece of paper beneath the partition. Birdie peered at it through glassy eyes. A border patrol officer, resplendent in his neat uniform, smiled up at her from the brochure. An aeroplane took off against a bright blue sky. The words 'dignified departure' leapt out at her.

**A guide to self-deportation.**

'What's this?'

'Self-deportation will be much easier for you in the long run.' Maisie began to half-heartedly tick off the reasons on her fingers. It sounded as though she were trying to convince herself of the benefits. 'There's less stigma involved if you self-deport. You won't be arrested, for one. Or put in an immigration removal centre. And you'll get a weight limit of twenty kilos, and accommodation for the first thirty days in Jamaica—'

Birdie didn't want to hear the rest. She whispered her thanks and tucked the brochure in her handbag. Before she turned away, she remembered to wish Maisie a Merry Christmas.

It was clear now, what she had to do. She got off the bus and crossed the courtyard, her footsteps ringing wetly against the ground, her vision swimming. She regretted spending her life savings on fruitless applications when she could have used that money to set up a new home in Jamaica. Maisie said self-deportation was the dignified option, but there was nothing dignified about begging on the streets of Kingston. A memory – Saturdays in the market, Mumma steering her well clear of the begging bowls proffered pitifully skyward—

She climbed the stairwell to Clent House, her back wet with sweat, and reached the fourth floor just in time to see Rita manoeuvring Manny and a load of shopping bags through her front door. Birdie had been avoiding her neighbour, even going as far as inventing a lengthy absence. She hadn't had to worry about Rita hearing her – she hadn't turned the television on in weeks. But it was too late to hide, to retreat.

'Birdie!' Rita waved, her keys in her hand. 'I haven't seen you in ages, I thought you were still at Tegan's . . . Birdie? Birdie, what's wrong?'

The walkway pitched sideways, like the deck of a ship in rough seas, and Birdie lurched too. Rita rushed forward to catch her.

'Where are your keys? Come on, let's get you inside.'

Rita gently guided Birdie into her flat and deposited her on the settee, then offered to make her a cup of tea. Birdie was too weak to protest and Rita cried out in alarm when she opened the empty fridge.

'I wish you'd told me!' Rita said, when Birdie had explained. 'I could have helped, I could have— it's okay Birdie. We'll figure something out.'

Birdie pulled the brochure out of her bag. 'They gave me this today. They told me it's for the best.'

Rita was aghast. 'You can't possibly think that.'

'It's better than getting dragged out in handcuffs. Besides, my rent is due and I don't have the money to pay it.'

Manny crawled across the carpet, pushing his toy police car in front of him and beeping at imaginary traffic violations.

'What about that nice young lawyer you were telling me about, Marlow? Can't he do something?'

'It's Marley. And there's nothing else he can do. If my second application is denied I can't afford to apply again. And I can't prove when I entered the country. This is the only option I have left.'

Birdie shivered. 'It's the "dignified option". And I'll get twenty kilos.'

Twenty kilos. Manny probably weighed twenty kilos. It didn't seem that much, now. How much did her mother's urn weigh? She wouldn't be able to leave her behind. And what would she do with the rest of her possessions? Perhaps she could sell them. That was one way she could keep herself off the Jamaican streets.

'What does Carmen think?'

'I don't know . . . we had a row. She's not speaking to me.'

'Oh *Birdie*.' Rita reached out and touched her on the arm. 'You're freezing! Have you eaten at all today?'

'No.'

'Wait here. Let me put my frozens away and I'll come back with lunch. Do you mind watching Manny for five minutes? I'll be as quick as I can.'

Birdie watched Manny crawl, army style, across the floor, his car snagging on the thick weave of the carpet. He made *pew pew* noises, aiming the truck at an army of invisible monsters, then looked up.

'Have you done a bad thing?'

'No.'

'Then why do they want to put you in handcuffs?'

'Because they said I did a bad thing. But I didn't mean to.'

Manny pushed his car up the leg of the coffee table. 'You shouldn't lie,' he said reproachfully.

'I'm not.'

'Can I have a drink please?'

'Of course,' Birdie said.

She stood up, and her world went black.

When Rita returned seven minutes later, she found Birdie lying on the floor and her son driving his car up the side of the armchair.

# Twelve

## *1962*

'Bloody hell, Nora. There's more of them.'

Mrs Nora Tebbit was stood in her open doorway, her mouth working hard, as though she was sucking on a bitter caramel. Precious said she felt sorry for Mrs Tebbit, who talked to herself and sometimes went out without shoes, even in winter, but Birdie thought she was a witch. Mrs Tebbit liked to stand sentry outside her house halfway up Maltby Street where she could watch the comings and goings of her neighbours and pass ferocious judgement.

She licked her dry lips with distaste. 'Another lot of darkies moving in. I won't stand for it.'

A young West Indian couple were struggling to carry an iron bedstead through the front door of their new abode. She set her end down, exhausted, and he attempted to rally her with a bleak warning about leaving her to sleep on the street if she didn't put her back into it. *It's not going to fit!* she railed, her voice echoing down the street.

The Browns had been the first West Indian family to move to Maltby Street, but now there were fourteen such families within spitting distance. The same thing was happening in neighbourhoods all over the country. The newspapers referred to it as an 'invasion'.

Her school bag bouncing against her hip, Birdie trudged past Mrs Tebbit and the couple arguing in their new doorway. *Her* old doorway.

They had moved the week before. Not, as Winston had promised, into a house of their very own, but to another rented flat that was, at least, more spacious than their last. They now had a living room *and* a kitchen, and Birdie had a bedroom that was big enough for both her *and* a bed. They'd not moved far, either. Their new home was right next door to their old one. It had been previously rented to an Albert Hutchins, a widower who'd moved to Maltby Street after a German bomb destroyed his house and killed his wife, and it had taken every ounce of Precious Brown's cunning to secure it.

When old Mr Hutchins was found dead in his bed by his landlady, it barely registered among his neighbours. In life he had kept to himself, preferring his own company, and that of the small white mice he kept in a cage, and when he died few could be called upon to grieve him. The only people to pay much attention to his passing were the morbid little boys who pressed their noses against the living room window – Mr Hutchins was, for most of them, their first real corpse (apart from Mick McDonald, who bragged that he'd lost *both* of his grandfathers) – and entertained each other with gruesome stories about how he'd been carried out of the house missing his nose and his fingers, on account of the mice breaking loose in search of sustenance.

The day after Mr Hutchins was laid to rest, Precious intercepted his former landlady, her hair tied up in a spotted handkerchief and carrying a mop and a pail, to pass on her condolences.

'Such a shame,' Precious said genteelly. 'Did he have any family?'

'How the bleedin' hell should I know?' She set the pail down. 'I suppose not. No one's come to claim any of his belongings.'

The landlady knew this because she'd already picked through them and taken anything of value. The mice had been let out of their cage and they'd scampered down the road and out of sight.

'Had he been *very* sick? I hate to think of that poor man, suffering alone . . .'

'He didn't die of nuffink catching, if that's what you're asking. He had weak lungs,' the landlady added gruffly. 'An old war wound, I suspect. He served in the first war.'

She'd already pawned his medals.

'Goodness. I'd never have imagined—'

'Did you want something? Only Mr Hutchins weren't too clean and I've got to scrub this whole bleedin' flat before I can even think about renting it out again—'

'How much is the rent?' Precious said quickly.

The landlady looked her up and down. 'I've got a lot of people interested,' she said, dragging out the words, no longer in a hurry now that money was involved.

'Oh, I'm sure. A nice place like this—'

The landlady snorted. 'Nice? It was nice before Mr Hutchins moved in. I kept this place spotless, when I lived here. But the floor is caked with dirt and he had stuff piled up in every corner. I don't know why I didn't toss him out years ago. It's going to take me *weeks* to clean it and in that time I'll be losing money—'

'I can clean it,' Precious said confidently. 'For a reduced rent, of course.'

Winston arrived home from work that evening and found his wife already packing.

'And how much is the rent, exactly?' he asked.

'Same as what we pay here – I worked it all out, don't worry. We'll still have enough to pay into the pardner—'

Each week, Winston paid a portion of his wages into a pardner scheme. A banker collected the money from the participating families and then they all took it in turns to claim the whole pot. It was a common way for West Indian families to save up enough to buy a house (or, on occasion, flights back home) and they worked, providing the banker wasn't a *teef*, like the man who'd scammed Winston out of two years' worth of money back in 1959. *That* particular banker was living the high life back on the island at Winston's expense.

Winston was wiser now. He was not the kind of man to be caught out twice. There were other changes in him, too: his body had grown leaner, and his face harder, though the rogue, easy-going twinkle in his eye could be coaxed out by his daughter or a bottle of rum. There were premature flecks of grey in his hair and his smile had lost some of its youthful swagger. Physically changed, he might have been, but his mind – that was still as sharp as ever. Nor had his ambition dulled. He was single minded in his desire to buy a house. He pictured himself in a two-storey property, with a three-piece suite, like the kind he'd seen in Rackhams. A house of his own would prove to everyone, including his wife, that he'd made the right decision. It was just taking longer than he'd planned, that's all.

'But we'll have more space,' Precious continued eagerly. 'There might even be enough room for a sewing machine. I've already told the landlord we'll be moving out at the end of the month, and—'

Winston held up his hands to stop her giddy stream.

'Whoa, Presh. You told the landlord already? Without talking to me first?'

'I had to move quickly. She said she had a lot of people interested.'

'But without discussing it, Presh—'

He paused. They both remembered a similar conversation they'd once had, in a different kitchen. Precious shifted her gaze and began to wrap her plates in newspaper.

'This place is not fit to raise our child in, Winston. Birdie's bedroom is full of damp.'

'But the house—'

'We can still save for a house. But it's taking a lot longer than you said—'

His face fell.

'And I know that's not your fault. You weren't to know that Chilton was a crook. But we have a chance to better our situation. Wasn't that the whole point of emigrating? To better our situation?'

Though it bruised her husband's ego, Precious got her way and they moved into the flat next door. She worked non-stop for two weeks, a rag tied over her nose and mouth, to clean any trace of Mr Hutchins from their new home, and they moved just in time for Birdie's fourteenth birthday. Winston told his wife not to get too comfortable.

'We'll get the house soon, Presh. There probably isn't any point in unpacking—'

'It's nice to have more room though, isn't it?' Precious said, her fingers tracing the buttons on his shirt.

'I suppose so,' he admitted with a grin. 'But that's the last time you decide anything without me, you hear?'

He kissed her, and her hands groped wildly for the light switch.

* * *

'No. *No*. Absolutely not.'

'But Winston—'

'A man is entitled to a bit of peace and quiet in his own home, Precious. But how can he find peace and quiet with Lucille Barry breathing down his neck?'

Winston was striding from room to room, his hands in the air. Precious followed behind him, hiding her smile with the telegram that had arrived that afternoon.

'I'm sorry. I wrote to her about our new place and she went and invited herself. She says she's booked her ticket. There's nuttin' I can do.'

'Yes, there is. Tell her to un-book it,' Winston said petulantly. 'Is she bringing your farda? Or any of the neighbours? I bet they all want to come and gawk—'

'Daddy doesn't want to get on a plane, so it's just Luce.'

He groaned.

'It'll be fine. It's only for two weeks,' she said soothingly, standing on tiptoe to kiss him.

'I'm warning you, Precious. If she gives me *any* grief she'll be sleeping outside—'

Lucille arrived with all the bluster of a summer squall. She brought with her two bulging suitcases, one full of food ('You told me the West Indian store round here was too expensive') and the other full of her warmest clothes ('Holifay Mundle said that Delyse Bailey said that English summers are as warm as a well digger's backside.') They spotted her immediately in the arrivals hall, marching across the terminal as though she owned the place, but it took her a minute to believe that the awkward fourteen-year-old stood in front of her was her little Birdie.

'You're all grown up, chile!' she exclaimed, her eyes filling with dismayed, dramatic tears. Then she pointed out that Winston had more grey hair than the last time she'd seen him.

'So do you,' he muttered under his breath, forgetting that Luce had the ears of a bat.

'I'm old, boy. What's *your* excuse?'

Luce had grown older, but her manner hadn't softened with age. She could not be convinced that England was impressive enough to warrant a holiday, let alone worth staying for seven years like the Browns had done, and she passed judgement on everything – the weather, the fashions, the *food* – like the dinner lady at Birdie's school, spooning out lumpy mashed potato. It didn't matter if you wanted it or not. It was going on your plate all the same.

It felt strange to have someone who had known them before show up in their lives again. Luce settled herself into the flat like a piece of antique furniture – but the problem, Birdie thought, was that she didn't match their other furniture. She'd forgotten how *loud* Lucille was. Her aunt was full of stories of people that they'd once known – so-and-so had gotten married, someone else had moved to Spanish Town, and cranky Cedella Dale – 'You know, the one with the wart smack between her eyes' – had visited the Obeah for a spell to make her beautiful and now her hair was falling out – but Luce didn't know any of the people from their stories, and kept losing track of the names of Birdie's friends. Birdie talked more than ever, getting louder and more animated, worried that she was losing her aunt's focus. Lucille said, with a hint of disappointment, that she sounded like a proper little English pickney, so Birdie did her best to reclaim the accent she hadn't even realised she'd lost. No one had told her she sounded English before. She felt oddly suspended between the past and the present, especially because Luce was still treating her like a seven-year-old, cutting herself off in the middle of a particularly juicy story because 'lickle ears were listening'.

'I'm grown-up enough,' Birdie grumbled, and Luce laughed, her whole body jiggling.

'Hark at her. What do you know of the world, chile? You don't have titties yet.'

Birdie clamped her arms over her chest, her face burning, then left her mother and aunt to gossip.

Her father was lying on his bed, his hands folded beneath his head, listening to the record player he'd won in a dominoes game. He was listening to The Drifters, his and Birdie's favourite band, and she crawled onto the bed next to him and lifted his arm so she could nestle beneath it, her desire to be treated as a proper grown-up temporarily suspended in favour of comfort.

'You enjoying having your aunt here?' Winston asked.

'Ye-es,' she said slowly, wanting to explain how peculiar she felt, but not able to find the right words. 'Are you?'

He gave her such a look that she couldn't help but laugh so loudly her aunt yelled and demanded to be included in the joke. That just made them laugh harder.

That summer belonged to Lucille. She extended her visit from two weeks to six and took over the kitchen with her suitcase full of canned goods, rearranging all of Precious's cupboards without asking. She argued with Mr Rattray, the proprietor of the sole West Indian food store in their neighbourhood, and threatened to open up an establishment right next door and undercut him unless he charged what she considered a fair price. She disappeared entirely one day and Precious was sick with worry, thinking her aunt was lost in a strange city, or kidnapped ('No man would kidnap Lucille Barry,' Winston said. 'And if he did, he'd bring her back within the hour') or bleeding to death in a hospital somewhere. But Luce was fine – she was at their old flat next door, where she'd turned up unannounced and uninvited, because she'd wanted to see if it really was as small as Precious had described.

There was a real emergency too though, when Luce had a dizzy spell and fell to the ground like a sack of potatoes, skimming the skin clean off both knees. Precious wanted to call an ambulance, but Luce poured derision over that idea and said all she needed was a little drop of Tia Maria to set her to rights. Birdie was sent to Mr Rattray's to procure it and when he discovered that 'that aggravating woman' was sick, he insisted Birdie take the Tia Maria for free.

Another incident occurred when Luce met Birdie's school friends. Bette and Nancy called for her one afternoon to go to the park, but her aunt would not hear of them going off alone, despite Birdie's assertion that she was too old for a chaperone.

'Mumma lets me go out by myself all the time, Auntie,' Birdie whinged, but Luce was already lacing up her shoes.

'Who will keep you pickney safe? Could be any kind of white man lurking about the streets!'

'Don't you mean "mad man", Mrs Barry?' Bette asked innocently.

'What did I say? You know, where I'm from we don't let young gyals roam about. I should talk to your parents – don't they care about white pickney in this country?'

Birdie saw Bette and Nancy exchange glances, and she burned with embarrassment. Luce was a loud and unremitting reminder of the differences between Birdie and her peers and, for the first time in her life, she was ashamed of her aunt. Luckily, Precious intervened and Birdie was allowed out, though Luce warned her that if she were carried off by a lunatic she would not be to blame.

Birdie kept her friends away for the rest of her aunt's visit. Luce couldn't stay forever, to Winston's relief and Precious's resignation. They drove her to the airport and waved goodbye as she dragged her two suitcases (one full of clothes, the other full of souvenirs) behind her.

'I told her she has to go and see Doctor Elliot the minute she gets back,' Precious said, standing on tiptoe to wave at Lucille's departing figure. 'I don't like it, Winston. It was a shock to see her looking so thin.'

Winston snorted. 'Thin? There's enough meat on her backside to feed the five thousand. If the plane goes down, they'll be able to use her as a life raft.'

Birdie choked back a giggle.

'It was nice having her here,' Precious said softly, as though she didn't hear. Her eyes were straining to find her aunt's vanishing figure among the horde of strangers. 'And she'll be back again, God willing.'

* * *

## *1964*

God didn't will it. Luce died eighteen months later, despite her protestations that she still had three scores to settle and a baby on the lane to name. But there were some things that were out of even Lucille Barry's control.

The news arrived by telegram one cold, Saturday morning, three little words that made Precious faint dead away in the kitchen.

LUCILLE'S GONE STOP

Birdie ran next door for Pat, and together they carried Precious to the settee, a shiny lump protruding from her temple.

'Is she dead?' Birdie whimpered.

'Course not. She'll have a sore head tomorrow though. Where's your father?'

Birdie didn't know. He'd likely been in the pub the night before, or else in somebody's crowded kitchen – he and his friends would share a bottle of rum around a Calor gas heater and discuss the pertinent topics of the day: who was too soft for English weather; who knew of a better job going elsewhere; the trouble they were having with wives and sweethearts. It wasn't unusual for him to stay out all night. When he *did* arrive home, with a hangover so vicious he thought he might never see straight again, Birdie had to explain three times what had happened.

'Where's your mumma?' he asked blearily.

'I *told* you. She's in bed. She fainted. Auntie Luce is dead.'

'Oh, that's a shame. A real shame. What's for dinner?'

'Didn't you hear me, Puppa? Auntie Luce is *dead*.'

'Shh! No need to shout, baby. My head is killing me. Make me a cup of tea, will you?'

He passed out next to his wife before the kettle had finished boiling. Birdie tiptoed into the bedroom with the cup of tea and stared down at her parents. At nearly sixteen years old, she was old enough to recognise the changes in her father, but not old enough to understand them. It had all started after Luce's visit. Winston had lost another job and, though he'd soon found work elsewhere, his gloom had failed to lift. *Different factory, same shit*, he'd said and Birdie had laughed, thinking it was a joke, but then she'd caught sight of the expression on his face and her laughter had petered out. Since then, he'd been drinking more, saying that rum was the only thing that eased the ache in his joints. That, and soaking his feet in the tin bath, his nightly ritual, sighing in relief as he topped up the hot water. Mumma must have noticed the change in him too – why else would her face be folded in a permanent frown? Mumma even frowned in her sleep, Birdie noticed, a deep crease running vertically between her eyebrows. She set the cup of tea down on the nightstand and silently retreated.

The next morning, Precious leapt out of bed, despite the throbbing in her head. There was no time to lose. She used Pat's telephone and spoke briefly with her father, who said that Luce had passed quickly, if not peacefully, and made plans to return for the funeral.

'I'll need a new passport,' she said to her bleary-eyed husband. The one she had travelled to England on had expired four years earlier.

'How much is that going to cost?'

'It will cost what it costs.'

First thing on Monday morning, Precious donned her coat and caught the bus into town. The travel agent advised she get a British passport as it would last longer than a Jamaican one. She could pay a rush fee and be back in Jamaica by the end of the week. Was that amenable, the travel agent asked?

'It's not.' Winston folded his arms and planted his feet firmly on the kitchen floor. 'You know we don't have that kind of money lying around, Presh.'

'There's the—'

'Don't even think about it. You're not using the pardner.'

Precious flared her nostrils, but Winston was unmoved.

'It's not like Luce was your mudda.'

'She *raised* me. And if you think I'm going to let my farda bury her alone you have another thing coming, Winston Brown.'

Precious threw herself at the mercy of her church. Some years earlier, Eula-May had introduced her to a congregation of West Indians who made her feel much more at home than the dour-faced English pastor who'd offered half-hearted prayers up to God. The parishioners scraped together to cover the cost of a new passport and a return ticket, though there was not, to Birdie's disappointment, enough money to send her too.

Precious was apologetic. 'I can't ask for more, Birdie. Not when they've already been so generous.'

Birdie was helping her mother pack her suitcase, and she longed to cram herself inside it, to fold herself as thin as a black crêpe dress and unfurl herself in Jamaica.

'Luce loved a funeral,' Precious sighed wistfully. 'Said they were better than listening to the wireless. Especially the older she got. She was determined to outlive all of Portmore.'

'How old was she?'

Precious handed her a nightgown and shrugged. 'She always said it was impolite to ask a woman her age. "Old enough to know better than you" is what she'd say.'

Birdie laughed, and then she was crying in her mother's arms.

'Don't cry now. Luce wouldn't want tears,' Precious soothed, as hot tears of shame spilled down Birdie's cheeks. How could she have ever been embarrassed by her aunt? Luce had done nothing but love her, and now she wouldn't get one last chance to beg forgiveness.

'I wish I could go.'

'I know, but you're too old to travel on my passport now

and we can't afford to buy you one of your own. She'd understand.'

Precious left early the next morning. Her journey back to Jamaica was the same one she'd taken in 1955, but in reverse: the train to London, the airport, the aeroplane. Only this time she was dressed in black, and she didn't have Birdie chatting nineteen to the dozen in her ear. And this time, she was certain what lay at the end of the journey. There were no nerves to quell, no qualms to ignore. She was going home, to be with her aunt one last time.

She was going home.

Birdie was inconsolable. Pat did her best to comfort her, bringing round records, iced buns from the bakery where she worked, and magazines, gently encouraging Birdie to put aside her grief, if only for a little while. The night before Precious returned, Winston took them all to the picture house to see *The Pink Panther*, and Birdie laughed for the first time in weeks. On the drive home they all hummed the theme song, and as they pulled up outside the house, Pat leaned over and kissed Winston on the cheek.

'Thank you for a wonderful night.'

'Thank *you*. You've been a big help this past fortnight.'

'Would you care to come in for a nightcap?'

'That's mighty kind of you. Birdie, put yourself to bed.'

Birdie yawned and bid Pat a goodnight. She knelt to say another prayer for her aunt's soul and was asleep long before her father made his way to his own bed.

* * *

A change had come over Precious. Upon her return to England, she began scouring the *help wanted* sections in the papers, eventually taking up a job in a factory making flimsy nightgowns and chemises. It was time she had money of her own, she said to her husband. She wanted to be able to fly home whenever she needed to.

'*This* is our home, Presh.'

'I'm worried about Daddy,' she continued over him. 'Some hussy was sniffing after him the whole time I was there . . . remember Miss Vea? Delroy Glenmore's widow? She's got her piggy lickle eyes on him.'

'He's a grown man, he's single, and he's just lost his housekeeper. I say good on him.'

'Luce was more than just his housekeeper!' Precious replied indignantly, and Winston sighed. *You're right*, he wanted to say, *she was also a meddling heifer*, but he was worried if he gave his wife the chance she might up and run all the way back to Jamaica. He took her by the hand – the flesh around her wedding band looked swollen, like rising dough – and brushed a finger along her cheekbone.

'Your farda doesn't need you to take care of him. But *I* need you.' He dipped his nose towards hers, his lips puckered—

'He told me himself how nice it was to have me home,' she said, and he pulled back.

'Precious.' His tone was entreating. 'This is our home.'

'It might be where we live, but it's not where we *belong*.' She looked into his tired, worn face. When had he gotten so old? And when, for that matter, had she? She'd been so thin, so beautiful on her wedding day, but now . . . It was all she had heard while she'd been back on the island. *Goodness, Precious. I would never have recognised you.*

'We're not happy Winston. Not truly.'

He let go of her hand.

'Says who? *I'm* happy.'

'You should try telling your face some time. When was the last time you smiled, eh?'

'When was the last time you gave me a reason to smile? All I hear is *I want to go back to Jamaica, Winston. Nuttin' you do is good enough, Winston.* Tell me why I put up with it?'

'Winston—'

He pounded his fist in his palm.

'There are men like Griffiths trying to run us out of the country. Saying we've outstayed our welcome. He'll win the election and take his seat in parliament – and then what happens to the likes of us? You've seen his campaign slogan, Presh. *If you want a nig—*'

'Don't,' Precious winced. 'Don't say it.'

'All I want is that house, Precious. Then I'll know it's been worth it.'

'And then what, Winston? Once we have the house, then what?'

He did not know what to say. He realised that the big plans of his youth had somehow contracted over the years, shrinking like a favourite pullover washed in hot water. His focus was on the house. It had to be the house. After that, everything would fall into place.

She reached out to him and he flinched, but she refused to let him pull away from her. She ran her fingers across his temple and down the sides of his face, tracing lightly over his scar.

'We've wasted so much time being unhappy, Winston. Time we can't get back—'

'I can't give up now. I won't.'

'You're acting like it's you against the world.'

She looked into his eyes and sought a trace of the man she

had married. She stared at her reflection and looked for the young girl she once was.

'It feels like that,' he said eventually. 'And the world seems to be winning.'

Precious dropped her hands from his face and turned on her heel. Winston let her go.

* * *

## *1965*

Though the summer that year was cool, with dismally low temperatures, there were two hot topics of conversation. The first was the Race Relations Act, Howard Wilson's pioneering idea to ensure that Commonwealth immigrants received equal treatment in shops and pubs. The second was the Beatles' world tour. Depending on who you asked, one was far more important than the other.

Birdie was seventeen, and no longer a scrawny child with ashy knees. She had left school with three O Levels, despite teachers like Miss Butler assuming that she was stupid, not worth teaching, or intellectually obtuse. She wore short skirts her mother didn't approve of, plastered posters of Paul Newman over her bedroom walls, donated her ribbons to the church rag bag and teased her hair back into a bouffant, the way The Ronettes wore their hair. She felt *grown*. She was old enough to work; she'd gotten a job at the factory where her mumma worked, sweeping the floor with a long broom that made her arms ache (but the job was only temporary. She was saving her money for something better – secretarial college, or maybe a hairdressing apprenticeship. Something that would offer a steady income). And she was old enough to go to nightclubs with her friends, though sometimes she was turned away at the doors. The Race Relations Act might be being discussed and debated in parliament, but there was very little room to discuss and debate discrimination in real life. It was just something else they had to get on with.

The Browns had been in England for ten years, but there would be no celebratory trip to the seaside to mark the occasion. In fact, Winston didn't see the point in celebrating at all, but Precious said they should at least have a family dinner.

'With any luck, this will be our last year in the flat. We should celebrate that,' she said, and Winston shrugged and said fine. Birdie helped her mother cook. Precious was making oxtail stew, an apron protecting her new dress. She was making an effort to mend the cracks in the marriage. She'd even left a pin in the sleeve for Winston to find later, a present she hoped would make him laugh – only it was half past six, and her husband wasn't home yet.

'He's late this evening,' she said distractedly, then exclaimed in frustration. 'Cho, we're out of salt. Run next door and borrow a spoon from Pat.'

Birdie ran round to their neighbour's and knocked on the door, but there was no answer. She pressed her ear against the door and heard the record player, so she knocked again.

'Pat? Pat, it's me. Mumma needs—'

The door opened and Birdie found herself face to face with her father.

'Puppa!' she exclaimed in surprise. 'What are you doing here?'

Winston sighed heavily.

'I had a feeling you knew.'

'Knew what?'

'Fetch your mumma, will you?'

'Knew what, Puppa?'

'Birdie. Fetch your mumma.'

Birdie backed away from Pat's door, a terrible feeling in the pit of her stomach, and went home to fetch her mother. Precious didn't understand. What did she mean, Puppa was next door?

'He said he wants you. That's all he said. He wants to talk to you,' Birdie said stupidly, the implication taking hold, like a bad cold. She shivered. Precious took off her apron and silently left the kitchen, but Birdie didn't follow her. She turned down the flame beneath the Dutch pot of oxtail stew and dampened the intoxicating smell with the lid. She waited, though she hardly wanted to admit to herself what she was waiting for. Then she heard her mother scream and ran next door.

Winston was sat stiffly on Pat's velveteen settee, his faded brown cap on his lap, his arm around Pat's shoulders. Pat's eyes were on her avocado shag pile rug.

*Get up, Puppa*, Birdie wanted to say. *Get away from her*. But she didn't. She hovered in the doorway, feeling like a little girl again, eavesdropping on an argument that would once again change their lives.

Precious was stood before Winston, an accusatory finger pointing in his face. He pushed her hand away.

'Don't act surprised, Presh. You've been saying it for ages – we're not happy. I wasn't happy.'

'And Pat makes you happy?'

He didn't respond.

'How long?'

She turned to Pat, her eyes angry and hard.

'How long?'

'I'm sorry, Precious. It just sort of – happened—'

Precious slapped Pat cleanly across the face. Birdie flinched, as though she'd been slapped too. Her mother raised her arm again, but Winston stood and grabbed her by the wrist.

'Don't act like this is Pat's fault, Precious. If you hadn't been so miserable all the time, if you hadn't—'

Precious did not want to hear the rest. She shook herself free from his grip and marched out of the flat, her head held high, her cheeks speckled with tears. Birdie turned to her father in desperation.

'Puppa?'

'Ahh, shit, Birdie.' He rubbed the back of his neck, but he didn't move.

'You're not staying here, are you?'

'Go with your mumma,' he said slowly. 'Make sure she's alright.'

Birdie stared at him for a few seconds, then retreated through the open doorway and out into the street.

He didn't follow her.

He didn't even try.

# Thirteen

## *2016*

Inches away from Birdie's nose, a posse of young women gyrated on exercise bikes, their sleek ponytails swinging from side to side as they stared seductively into the camera. She scoffed.

'*This* is what you call music?'

Saffie was stretched out like a cat alongside her grandmother, her long legs thrown over Birdie's, the single bed barely big enough for the two of them.

'I thought you'd *like* this one.'

'Hmm. Can you get Janet Kay on that phone?'

'Of course I can. But it wouldn't kill you to get with the times.'

'Humph.'

Birdie lay back and looked at the ceiling. Posters of moody looking girls stared poutily back.

'Who are they, the Spice Girls?'

Saffie laughed so hard she almost fell off the bed. 'Oh *Nanny*. They're Little Mix. They're *amazing*. They've got this song that's like, all about taking the power back from the men that have hurt you. Listen—'

Birdie stared at Saffie's soft, innocent features, lit up in the glow of her mobile. What did she know about men and the hurt they could inflict?

Saffie wiggled her behind in time with the beat and sang along in a sweet, girlish voice.

'They're not exactly The Supremes, are they?'

'Who?'

Birdie was dismayed. 'Surely you've heard of Diana Ross?'

'Oh, right. She did that James Bond song, yeah?'

'That was Shirley Bassey.'

'Oh.'

Birdie waggled her finger. 'You want empowerment, you listen to Diana Ross, Tina Turner, Lulu. Then you'll understand.'

A memory came to her – sitting in front of the television for Eurovision, waving the little flag they'd given away free in the paper, Lulu smiling out of the screen in a pink mini dress and Carmen on her lap, her feet kicking.

'Where can I watch Lulu's Eurovision performance?'

'YouTube.'

'You'll be able to find it?'

'You can find anything you want on – oh!' Saffie sat up. 'That reminds me. Remember a few weeks ago, when I said I wanted to take your story public?'

'No,' Birdie said, and Saffie rolled her eyes.

'I knew you weren't listening.'

'I'm listening now.'

'Great, because,' Saffie pushed herself into an upright position, a crease from her pyjama top running down one side of her face. 'Because I'm going to interview you about your life. *Properly* interview you, like Louis Theroux. I'm going to ask you questions about your childhood, and what it was like moving to England—'

'No one's going to care about my childhood, Saff.'

'They *will*. I'm going to highlight your plight and—'

Downstairs, Carmen bellowed that breakfast was ready. Saffie wiggled off the end of the bed and paused in the open doorway.

'We'll talk about this later,' she said, in a vaguely threatening way, before thundering down the stairs. Birdie gingerly followed.

She had moved into Carmen's house four days before Christmas. There had been no discussion and no arguments – she hadn't been in any kind of state to protest. Rita had called Carmen shortly after discovering her on the floor, and once she'd regained consciousness, she'd been forced to confess everything.

She'd never seen Carmen so angry.

'You should have called me!'

Carmen was pacing back and forth in front of the glow of the electric fire. The room reeked of burning dust.

'How could you have done something so bloody stupid? What would have happened if Rita hadn't found you? You could be dead, Mom! Dead!'

She was used to Carmen's hyperbole, had been dealing with it since her daughter had learned how to talk, practically, but there was an edge to her voice that felt entirely alien.

'And look at you – you've lost so much weight!'

'Who needs Jenny Craig?' Birdie quipped shakily, but Carmen slammed her hand down on the mantlepiece so hard the photographs rattled in their frames.

'This isn't funny, Mom. You could have . . .'

*She's scared*, Birdie realised, and she felt a sharp pain in her chest. *I've scared her.*

'I . . . I didn't think you wanted to talk to me.'

'Just because we're not speaking doesn't mean you can't call me – I mean – oh for fuck's sake, you know what I mean. You didn't need to shut me out like this—'

'You said you hoped I'd get deported.'

Carmen winced, her face contracting into a concertina. 'It doesn't matter what I said. I didn't mean it.'

That was her way of apologising, Birdie knew.

'What matters is what we're going to do next. You're not self-deporting, for one. I'll call Marley and figure out our options. There has to be *something* we haven't tried—'

'Carmen, it's no use—'

'And you're coming home with me, obviously. Andy can come round later with the van for your things, and I'll get on the phone to your landlord—'

'I want to stay here,' Birdie said.

'It's not up for debate. You can't stay here, can you?' Carmen softened. 'At least until after Christmas. We can work out your next steps in the new year. It's not like they'll deport you over the holidays.'

So, Birdie had moved in with her daughter and now they were walking around each other on eggshells, Carmen full of artificial enthusiasm about how nice it was to have Birdie stay for Christmas, as though she were on holiday, and not homeless. She had been established in Saffie and Jade's room, with Saffie relegated to a blow-up mattress on the floor. Jade believed the lie about Nanny coming for Christmas, but Saffie had weaselled the truth out of her mother in the time it took her to carry Birdie's suitcase up the stairs.

Birdie shuffled into the kitchen. There she found a cacophony of ordered chaos, her family weaving around one another with the familiar movements of an established morning routine.

'I've sent another email to the Home Office,' Saffie was saying to Carmen. 'That's twenty-three so far. I've not had a single response.'

'Lewis finished the Cheerios!'

'Then have Bran Flakes.'

'I don't want Bran Flakes—'

'Are you listening, Mom? I said I've sent another email but—'

'Where are my keys, love?'

'Jade licked my spoon!'

'You're so autistic!'

'Jade, your brother isn't autistic. Andy, your keys are on the coffee table. Mom! There you are.' Carmen guided Birdie to the breakfast bar as though she were a waiter in a fine restaurant. 'What can I get you? We have cereal, toast, fruit—'

'I'm not hungry.'

'You need to eat. I can't have you taking a funny turn again, not when you're refusing to see a doctor.'

Birdie had allowed Carmen to install her in her house, but she drew the line at seeking medical attention. Marley had told her once that hospitals were supposed to report illegal immigrants to the government. It seemed safer not to risk it.

'Toast,' Birdie conceded, and Carmen busied herself with the toaster. Andy drained his mug of tea and wiped his lips.

'Right, I'm off. Where'd you say my—'

'Coffee table.' Carmen proffered her cheek for a kiss. 'Andy's got some work today. Just a bit of labouring, but every little helps.'

Birdie thought she heard a hint of frustration in Carmen's voice. She offered to do the washing up, but Carmen wouldn't hear of it.

'Of course not! You're our *guest*. I can manage.'

'Then I'll do the dusting. There's an inch of dust on the TV. Or I can do the laundry.'

'I said I can manage,' Carmen replied, sliding a plate of hot buttered toast in front of her mother. 'Now, eat up before it gets cold.'

* * *

Only Carmen wasn't really managing. The mental load was a heavy one: Andy hadn't had a proper job in months and Jobseeker's Allowance was not the saving grace that those who used terms like 'benefits scrounger' made it out to be. For the past fortnight, she'd been working double shifts whenever she could. Luckily, in the run-up to Christmas, there were hours to spare: everyone knew the temporary staff they drafted for the holiday season were next to useless. Craig was worse than ever, barking orders and rushing them all off their feet, acting as though he were preparing not for Christmas, but an apocalypse.

He cornered her in the staff room the minute she arrived for her shift.

'I'm going to need you on veg restock today, it's flying off the shelves – but I also need you to give the girls in homeware a hand, it's an absolute catastrophe. Half the Yankee Candles are already missing their lids.'

'Okay,' Carmen replied.

'You look tired,' he said.

She waited for him to ask why. But all he said was *chop, chop*, then flounced out of the room. Carmen stuck her fingers up at his departing figure, fished her phone out of her pocket and checked her Facebook messages. He'd caught her on her phone three times in the past week. Once on the shop floor, too. But she didn't care.

> You're right, it's been too long since I came home. Maybe next year, all being well.

For the past month she had been messaging Dean every single day. Not about her mom's situation – Anna Derwent wasn't able to help, apparently, and besides, Carmen didn't want to have to think about *that* every minute of the day. She wanted to know about Dean's life instead. *The life I could have lived lol*, she'd typed out once, before deleting it. He didn't always reply right away – he was busy with work; he was taking a weekend trip to Algonquin National Park; his phone had died and he'd left his charger in the office – but Carmen had fallen into the habit of messaging him good morning and goodnight every day, despite the time difference. He posted pictures of ice hockey games and poutine and gym selfies – nothing that implied he had a wife, or a girlfriend. Carmen liked every single new post. At night, as her husband snored beside her, she stared at the cracked screen of her phone, the tension in her neck easing as she watched the ticks turn blue.

> I hope you have a great Christmas and New Year Carm.

She hugged the phone to her chest and smiled, before rolling back her shoulders and turning her attention to the veg restock.

* * *

'About my idea, Nanny . . .'

Birdie set the knife down on the kitchen counter and swept a handful of carrot peelings into her hand. The children survived on junk food, as far as she could tell. Well, tonight they were getting shepherd's pie – she'd found a packet of mince in the back of the freezer (according to the expiry date, it had been there for a year, but it smelled okay once she'd thawed it out).

'If this is about interviewing me again, Saff—'

'Just listen. We need to tell your story. You heard what Marley said, about innocent people being caught in the crosshairs. But people don't know that this is happening. And change can't happen if people don't know that change is needed.'

'Who said that, Mandela?'

Saffie blushed. 'I made that up.'

'You're so clever. But the answer is no.'

'I've got it all planned out. A whole series of videos covering each chapter of your life, with a timed release on YouTube—'

Birdie opened her mouth to protest but Saffie clasped her hands together like a damsel in distress.

'Please?' she begged, and Birdie could hear the excitement underpinning her desperation. *She really thinks she can change the world*, Birdie thought. And then, *why shouldn't she think that?*

'Alright,' she said slowly, and Saffie squealed. 'But I don't know what you think it's going to achieve. And I'm going to carry on with my peeling if that's alright with you.'

'It's not very professional . . . but I suppose it adds an element of "real life" to it. Okay, fine.'

Saffie propped her phone up on the kitchen table and cleared her throat.

'Can you give me your full name please?' she said, slowly and clearly, as though she were a television presenter.

'You know my name.'

'It's for the video.'

Birdie stabbed a potato. 'Bridget Lucille Brown.'

'And how old are you, Bridget?'

'How old are you, *Nanny*. Sixty-nine next May.'

'Where were you born?'

'*Saffie*—'

Saffie stopped the recording.

'Nanny. We have to do this properly. Pretend you don't know me.'

'Alright,' Birdie replied grumpily. 'We don't have to start again, do we?'

'Nah, I can edit it later.'

'Really?' Kids today and their fancy technology. 'How?'

'On my laptop. Stop interrupting.'

Birdie exhaled and Saffie resumed the recording.

'Where were you born?'

'Portmore, Jamaica. Well, technically I was born in Kingston, on account of that's where the hospital was, but we lived in Portmore.'

'What was it like in Jamaica?'

'Like?' Birdie looked up from the small hill of half-peeled potatoes.

'Your childhood,' Saffie prompted. 'Tell me about your childhood.'

'Eh . . . it was . . . fine.'

'Can you tell us anything specific? About where you grew up – or your school—'

'I don't really remember . . . My school was small. It had a yard outside, with trees . . . the teacher was real strict about uniform, I remember that. My father shined my school shoes for me every morning before he went to work.'

For a second she thought she could smell the leather polish.

'What was your neighbourhood like?' Saffie continued, and Birdie squinted as she tried to peer into the past.

'Nice, I think. We had a small house. Grandpa Aubrey lived nearby . . .' She floundered and waved the knife in the air. 'I'm sorry. I don't know what you want to know. I don't remember too much.'

Saffie leaned forward. 'Can't you remember anything specific about the country where you were born?'

'Not really. I'm sorry—'

'Don't be sorry. The fact you can't remember your life before you moved here is all the more reason why they shouldn't send you back. You left when you were seven, right? Because your parents wanted economic stability.'

'That's right.'

'And you haven't been back to Jamaica since?'

Birdie shook her head.

Saffie touched her phone screen and zoomed in on Birdie's face.

'And you don't have *any* family left in Jamaica, do you? Or any friends? No one who'd be able to help you find somewhere to live, for example? All of your family are here in England. Your life is in England, right?'

Birdie gazed at the wall but didn't respond.

'Nanny? Nanny, are you alright?'

* * *

'Merry Christmas Eve, Scott.'

'Merry Christmas Eve, Mom. How's Carmen's?'

'I'm enjoying spending time with the kids,' she said diplomatically. She heard Scott chuckle, a low, rumbling laugh that betrayed his smoking habit.

'I think I'd rather be in here than spend Christmas with Carmen.'

'Scott!'

'I'm just kidding. I'm glad she's taking care of you. I wish . . .' He tailed off.

'What is it, Scott?'

'It's nothing. I just wish I was the one taking care of you. I wish a lot of things, actually.'

* * *

'Tell me about my grandfather,' Saffie said. Birdie looked up from the stack of presents she was wrapping at Carmen's frazzled request ('It's Christmas Eve and *nothing's* been wrapped!') to find Saffie's phone pointed at her. She'd been following Birdie around the house, firing off questions about Birdie's journey to England, her first impressions of the country, the flat she'd been brought up in, her first experience of an English school – Birdie couldn't get a moment's peace. That very morning, Saffie had asked her, in her newsreader voice, what 'home' meant to her. Birdie still didn't know what the answer was.

'My puppa? What do you want to know?'

'No. Not him. Mom's biological dad.'

Birdie hesitated, a pair of *Iron Man* boxer shorts in her lap. 'Why?'

'Just trying to build a full history of your life . . .'

Birdie raised an eyebrow and Saffie smiled sheepishly.

'And . . . I'm curious. Mom never talks about him.'

Birdie kissed her teeth. There were plenty of good reasons not to talk about him.

'How did you meet?' Saffie persisted.

'Saffie,' Birdie said warningly.

'What was he *like*?'

Birdie bopped her on the head with a flimsy roll of wrapping paper.

'You're not too old for a smacked bum, you know.'

Saffie held up her hands in defeat. 'Okay, okay, we don't have to talk about him specifically. Can I ask though . . . what was it like being in a relationship with a white man? I imagine there were people that didn't like it.'

'Plenty.'

'Did you experience a lot of racism?'

'I reckon no more than the average person – can you hand me the tape? Thanks.' Birdie tore off a strip with her teeth. 'You had to learn to let it roll off your back, but it was harder once I had children. I wanted to protect them from that. I remember once, I was out walking with Carmen and Tony and—'

She stopped short.

'What's your next question?'

Saffie stopped the recording.

'We don't have to talk about him on camera. But I'd really like to know more about him, if you felt comfortable . . .'

There were few people on earth Birdie felt more comfortable with than Saffie, but she also wanted to protect her granddaughter from the ugliness of life – the ugliness of *her* life. But Saffie was a brave girl. There was something of Winston's spirit in her, Birdie could see. And Precious's strength. And perhaps . . . perhaps if she shared that part of her life with

Saffie, she could teach her granddaughter how to recognise her own worth.

'I was seventeen when I met him . . .' Birdie began. Saffie hung onto her every word. So did Carmen, who had just returned from work and was listening from the other side of the door.

* * *

On Christmas morning, Lewis woke up at six thirty and scampered down the stairs. Andy shouted for him to go back to bloody bed, but it was too late. Jade, her dressing gown inside out, dashed out of the bedroom in pursuit of her brother.

'Stick the kettle on!' Andy shouted.

'Merry Christmas Nanny,' Saffie said sleepily from the air mattress on the floor.

'Merry Christmas Saff.'

Jade re-appeared with three cups of tea balanced on a *Santa Stop Here* tray and Birdie accepted hers with relish. They were all going to have a lovely day, she decided. For one day, she would forget about the Home Office, and enjoy a nice, normal Christmas with her family. She wasn't even going to let Andy wind her up.

'Thank you, Jade sweetheart. Ask your mom and dad if they want bacon or sausage, will you? I'll go turn the grill on.'

Half an hour later, the Lloyd family were gathered in the living room, still in their pyjamas, the floor strewn with wrapping paper. Lewis gave a yell of delight – the new Xbox game he'd wanted! – and Saffie wriggled under the white artificial tree, the white and silver baubles trembling precariously, and emerged with two identical boxes topped with giant gold bows.

'Here, Nanny,' Saffie said shyly, handing the first box to her grandmother and the second to her mother. 'You open yours too, Mom. Merry Christmas.'

Birdie carefully lifted the lid off the box. Nestled on a bed of shredded gold tissue paper was a large photo in a shiny black frame. She recognised it instantly – Precious, Carmen and her, their heads tipped back, laughing at some joke she didn't remember. The coffee stain had disappeared, the crease smoothed out. She turned to Saffie in wonder.

'How did you . . .' She was so amazed she could barely speak. 'How did you fix it?'

'Grace's brother is really good at Photoshop. He got rid of the stain,' she explained, hardly able to contain her satisfaction. 'Then I had it blown up and framed. Do you like it?'

'Oh Saffie, I love it.' Birdie enveloped her granddaughter in her arms. It was one of the sweetest gifts she had ever received.

'Who were you pregnant with there?' Andy asked, peering over Carmen's shoulder.

'Saffie,' Carmen replied, placing a gentle finger against the glass. 'This was at Leslie's birthday party, remember? Down The Shakespeare. Christ, we look so young . . .'

'No way,' Saffie exclaimed, looking at the photo again with completely fresh eyes. 'I didn't realise I was in this too. That's really cool.'

'Can you remember what we were laughing at?'

'No, but I do remember thinking I might wet myself if I wasn't careful,' Carmen said. 'It's beautiful, Saff. Thank you. I'll have to find a place to hang it up.'

'Where will you put yours, Nanny?' Jade asked innocently, and Birdie said she didn't know yet. Saffie suddenly looked aghast.

'I'm sorry Nanny,' she whispered in Birdie's ear. 'I didn't think—'

'None of that, thank you,' Birdie said firmly. 'We'll have no mopey faces on Christmas Day. Go on, finish opening your presents.'

'Who wants another bacon sarnie?' Andy volunteered, and Carmen told him not to ruin his appetite. The turkey was already in the oven, filling the house with the warming scent of sage and onion.

'It's Christmas!' Andy rebutted joyfully. 'If we can't indulge today, when can we?'

For once Birdie agreed with him. After a second round of bacon sandwiches, Carmen was convinced to prise open a tub of Celebrations and they tucked in, Lewis and Jade arguing over the Galaxy Caramels, in front of a sweet children's film about a trio of plucky orphans and knee-high yellow monsters. Birdie was on her third cup of tea – this one with a dash of rum in it – when Declan video called. He was spending the holidays with Angharad's parents in Conwy but was due to visit on his little sister's birthday. Saffie would turn eighteen on New Year's Eve.

'Merry Christmas!' he bellowed joyfully, a champagne flute of Buck's Fizz in his hand. He and Angharad were wearing matching snowman jumpers. Carmen pulled her baby blue dressing gown tightly around her throat.

'You said you were calling *after* lunch, Dec,' she said self-consciously. 'I'm sure Sue and Glynn won't want to see us in our pyjamas. Quick, Andy, go and get dressed. I'm sorry, Angharad.'

'Don't worry!' Angharad said with a kind smile. 'Mum's on the phone to her sister and Dad's having a nap. He was up all night making sure the foxes didn't steal the turkey out of the brine bath. But they said to wish you Merry Christmas.'

'And Merry Christmas to them as well,' Carmen said regally, before Andy could make a remark about foxes and brine baths. 'And thank you both for the scarf, it's lovely.'

She held the silky purple material up to the camera to show it off. Birdie had an identical one in periwinkle blue.

'Angharad picked it out, not me, but I'm glad you like it. What else did you get, then? What did Dad get you?'

Carmen's smile faltered.

'Ah, well. We agreed not to buy each other presents this year, didn't we Andy? We'll go shopping in the sales and get something for each other then. Something we actually need, not tat—'

'Smart move,' Declan said. 'Right, got to go, we've got spuds to peel. We'll see you all in a couple of days, yeah?'

Carmen's mood dipped after the call. She left her family in front of the television and slipped into the kitchen, ostensibly to check the turkey. Her phone buzzed in her dressing gown pocket, a flurry of Christmas greetings and Facebook messages from people she didn't speak to for the rest of the year. She scrolled through a morning's worth of status updates. Jackie was making her traditional Christmas Day chilli. Dawn down the road had a new Pandora charm, a tiny heart inscribed with the word 'wife' in a flowery font. Terri had done one better and unwrapped a shocking pink alligator handbag by that designer all the footballers' wives favourited. *#luckiestgirlintheworld* Terri boasted. Good for Terri, Carmen thought enviously. Dean hadn't replied to her last message. She sent another one – All I want for Christmas is you lol – then stashed her phone back in her pocket. She needed to get the potatoes in the oven and make the cauliflower cheese. And the pigs in blankets and the sprouts and the gravy—

A loud crash brought Birdie hurrying into the kitchen. She found Carmen on her knees, holding the broken pieces of her beloved gravy boat. The handle had snapped clean off.

'It slipped out of my hands. What will I do now? Dinner is ruined!'

'There's no use crying over spilled gravy.'

'That's not funny and you know it,' Carmen snapped, then looked shamefaced.

'I'm sorry,' they both said at the same time. Birdie held out her hand and helped her daughter to her feet, and then gently patted her on the shoulder.

'Dinner isn't ruined, Carm. And you should ask Andy to buy you a new jug in the sales.'

'Good idea Mom. Thanks.'

Later, Andy asked why the gravy was being served in a giant Sports Direct mug. Birdie signalled to him from across the dining table to change the subject.

'This is all absolutely delicious, Carm,' he said, with an unusual amount of tact. 'You've outdone yourself.'

'The turkey's a little dry.' Carmen paused and waited for Andy to contradict her – *no it's perfect, babe* – before continuing. 'I'll be glad to have a day off tomorrow, though. Are you sure you're up for cooking, Mom?'

'Of course I am. It's tradition.'

The Lloyds usually spent Boxing Day at Birdie's, and she'd serve chicken, rice and peas, with carrot juice topped with frosty scoops of vanilla ice cream.

'Can I help, Nanny? I've always wanted to learn how to cook,' Saffie said.

'You've never asked *me* to teach you,' Carmen said, looking injured.

'You never cook Jamaican food. I want to learn Nanny's recipes.'

'I can teach you both,' Birdie said. 'Frankly it's about time you learned.'

After a tea of turkey sandwiches and trifle, and board games, which Carmen had unearthed from the loft especially, Birdie taught her daughter and oldest granddaughter how to make a marinade for the chicken. If it wasn't ultra-processed the twins weren't interested, so while they watched a Vin Diesel film with Andy, Birdie showed Carmen and Saffie how to clean the chicken pieces in lemon juice, the way Auntie Luce had taught her, then rubbed garlic powder, onion powder, cayenne and plenty of salt and black pepper into the meat.

'I can't give you exact quantities,' she said, adding a dash more thyme. 'It's just something you learn over time. Almost like instinct.'

The chicken was left to marinate in the fridge overnight and, one by one, the Lloyds went to bed, leaving Carmen alone in the living room with her mother. She topped up their glasses of sherry and stretched out on the sofa. It was peaceful, them sitting together, the lights on the tree twinkling on and off in a pretty pattern.

'Mom?'

'Mmm?'

'Why did you never teach me to cook before?'

'I tried to, but you were never interested. Too busy chasing boys, I think.'

'Oh.'

'But I can write down all the recipes you want. That way you won't need me to teach them to you—'

'Don't say it like that,' Carmen implored.

'You know what I mean.'

'Oh. Well. Thank you.'

They sat in silence for a few minutes longer. Birdie's eyes found the photograph that Saffie had temporarily propped up on the mantlepiece.

'Carmen.'

'What?'

'You're a good mother,' she said, and Carmen blinked in surprise. 'You did a good job raising your kids. You shouldn't worry what Angharad's parents or anyone else might think of you.'

Carmen thanked her, her voice quivering.

'And . . . and I'm sorry. You were right. I wasn't always the best mother to you.'

'Oh *Mom*. You have nothing to apologise for—'

'I do,' Birdie insisted, determined to properly clear the air between them. 'We haven't always gotten on, have we? I . . . I was so young when I had you. I don't regret it – I love you and your brother – but . . . it was tough. You were too young to remember—'

'I remember all the rows. You and my . . .' Carmen struggled to say the word 'dad'. She swallowed. 'I asked Nanny P about him once. I was probably about nine or ten. She told me he was a waste of space and I shouldn't worry about him. She said "you have a mother and a father who love you. Blood isn't always thicker than water".'

Birdie's eyes lingered on the photograph.

'She said that?'

'Yeah. Wise woman. I can see where you get it from.'

Carmen squeezed her mother's hand. She thought about telling her what she'd overheard the night before, but decided against it. All she said was, 'I don't blame you for leaving him. I'm glad you did.'

Birdie squeezed back.

'It's true that when I was a kid it bothered me that our family didn't look like everyone else's. I was embarrassed, I suppose. But now I wouldn't change it for the world.'

She followed Birdie's gaze and nodded her head towards the photograph. 'Jimmy took that, you know.'

'I know.'

Carmen fiddled with her wedding ring. 'Mom?'

'Mmm?'

'I'm in touch with him. Jimmy. On Facebook. Oh, we don't message a lot,' she added quickly, seeing the shock on her mother's face. 'But we check in from time to time. Birthdays . . . and Christmas. He's divorced.'

Birdie exhaled. 'I didn't know that.'

'He seems pretty lonely.'

'Carmen.'

'What? I'm just saying.'

'You're never *just saying*. When were you going to tell me that you'd kept in touch?'

Carmen shrugged. 'I don't know. When the time was right, perhaps?'

Birdie shook her head but managed a smile. 'The timing's never right.'

'Exactly.' Carmen stood up and stretched. 'I'm turning in. You coming?'

'In a bit. Night, Carm.'

'Night Mom. I love you.'

'Love you too.'

Alone, Birdie scrolled through the photos Tegan had sent her, Jaxon grinning up at the camera, dressed in a reindeer onesie and a paper crown falling over one ear, and she smiled. He looked just like Scott had done at that age. And just like Carmen, too. How like her daughter, to keep a secret like that from her. She wondered what Jimmy was doing for Christmas. She wondered if she should do as Carmen had hinted and reach out to him. She remembered what Scott had said about wasting time. Wasn't she guilty of the same? But what would she even say, after all these years? The words *I'm sorry* didn't seem big enough.

She zoomed in on Jaxon's face using her finger and thumb like Saffie had taught her to. He had her eyes. Winston's eyes. How strange it was, to see the past staring back up at her. At least she would be leaving a part of herself behind, if the worst happened. Oh, none of them had come out and said it, but she knew they'd all been thinking it. *Birdie's last Christmas.* It wasn't fair. She'd do anything to stay with them. It was true what Carmen had said, that their family didn't look like everyone else's. Birdie had learned that the day she arrived in England and she'd been navigating that difficulty ever since. But it had been worth it, hadn't it? Her family might be big, and messy, but it was worth it. She didn't want to lose them.

She was tired, and she ought to go to bed, but instead she began writing out recipes for Carmen. It would be a late Christmas present, she decided, writing *Brown Stew Chicken* at the top of a fresh page in her notebook. Maybe she could get that smart brother of Saffie's friend to turn them into a proper book, wouldn't that be nice? And then one day Carmen could pass it down to Saffie and then Saffie would give it to her own children—

There was a pounding at the front door and Birdie jerked awake. Her notebook was lying open in her lap, the biro was still in her hand. The clock on the wall said it was ten past five in the morning, and her muscles were stiff with cold. She sat there for a moment, disorientated, her mouth dry, convinced she was dreaming—

*Bang bang bang bang.*

She heard Andy's heavy footsteps as he heaved himself out of bed and down the stairs. She heard him open the front door and then she heard four, no five, no *six* strange voices, and then she heard Andy shout.

'Look here, what right do you have to barge in—'

'It's the middle of the night!' Carmen screamed from halfway up the stairs, her eyes crusty with sleep, her children cowering behind her. Lewis was crying.

'She's an old woman, have some fucking decency!'

'I just need five more minutes,' Birdie said, though no one could hear her over the noise. 'I haven't finished the first recipe yet.'

# Fourteen

## *1965*

Winston wasn't coming back. He imploded their lives like a ship's captain who had run aground, swimming away from the wreckage without checking for survivors.

Birdie was in shock. Her once steadfast conviction that her puppa was the best man in the whole world had been shattered, and from the broken pieces had emerged a new, sombre reality. It wasn't going to be like the time he had left her behind in Jamaica. There wasn't going to be a joyful reunion this time.

Birdie and Precious moved into a gloomy basement bedsit in north Birmingham, sleeping top-to-tail in a double bed that groaned every time they rolled over. The bedsit was too small to comfortably accommodate their devastation – the air was thick with it, like a bad odour that could not be expelled. One of Precious's plates broke in the move, but she'd just laughed, a rasping sound, and said it didn't matter. Wedding china was for brides, not for women who couldn't hold onto their husbands.

Winston had been wrong – Birdie had not known about the affair. She'd not had an ounce of suspicion. Would she have been able to persuade him to stay if she'd known? Would she have been able to keep them together? Winston moved to Coventry with Pat. He'd never felt further away.

A whole summer passed, though to Birdie it seemed like very little sunlight reached them in the basement. She worried endlessly about her mumma, who was not sleeping or eating. Birdie did her best to cheer her up, cooking her favourite meals and borrowing Eula-May's bonnet hair dryer and hot comb so she could do Mumma's hair. Trying to distract her mother from her grief provided a respite from her own.

Precious sat cross-legged between her daughter's legs. Birdie hummed a tuneless song as she carefully separated the sections of hair and glided the hot comb from roots to ends. A curl of blue smoke flickered upwards. The smell of singed hair and Vaseline tickled her nostrils.

'Birdie?'

'Mmm?'

'I've been thinking . . .'

'Don't wriggle. I almost burned your ear.'

'I want to go back to Jamaica.'

'Ouch!'

The hot comb made searing contact with Birdie's finger, and Precious jumped up and pulled her over to the sink.

'Is it bad? Here, run it under some cold water—'

Precious held Birdie's hand beneath the cold tap, but Birdie could hardly focus on the pain.

'Back to Jamaica? Mumma! You can't be serious.'

'I am.'

Of course she was being serious. Mumma was not one to crack jokes or poke fun. That was Puppa's style . . .

'But this is your *home*,' Birdie implored, her fingers growing numb from cold. 'You can't just *leave*—'

'Why not?' Precious's voice cracked. 'Why not, after everything he put us through?'

'What about your job?'

'The factory? I'm not staying in England to work in some raatid *factory*.'

Birdie felt like her world was turning upside down. Her mother *never* swore.

'Mumma. I understand how you feel, but . . . here. Why don't we go back for a holiday? We could stay as long as you liked—'

Precious kissed her teeth. 'I don't want a *holiday*. Don't you see, Birdie? We don't belong here, and we never have. It was all for *him*. But we can go home now. There's nothing stopping us.'

'We?'

'You'll come with me, of course,' she replied, as though it were the most obvious thing in the world. 'Is your hand better?'

She turned off the tap and dabbed Birdie's hand dry. Birdie let her. She was too stunned to say anything more.

* * *

Birdie was not a child any longer. Her parents could no longer make decisions for her – what to wear, what to eat, where to live. She was old enough to enrol in secretarial college, to marry, to stay in England, if that's what she wanted. What *did* she want? It was a question without an answer. There were aspects of life in England that she loathed – the cold winters, the grey skies, the casual way some people liked to wear their bigotry as though it were a badge of honour – but she wasn't sure she belonged back in Jamaica, either. Ten years was a long time. For better or worse, England felt more like home than the island.

On Saturday, she left her mother in bed and went to the market. In the early days, Precious had had to improvise dishes using readily available ingredients, because the West Indian store had been too expensive. But now the foods she liked to eat were more obtainable, so perhaps Birdie could cook something that would sate her mother's hunger to leave. Tinned ackee and saltfish, perhaps, with red and green peppers to add a burst of colour. Or stew peas, glossy and rich—

'Are you going to buy those onions, or just look at them?'

Birdie looked over her shoulder. A young man stood beside a blanket on top of which he had arranged various pairs of women's shoes, each pair held together with an elastic band. He cocked his head appreciatively.

'You look like a girl with good taste. Come and see what I've got for you. I'm here for today only, ladies.'

This last remark was directed to a pair of women in stiff, buttoned up coats, who walked past without stopping. One of them muttered 'Stolen, I bet,' to her companion, then looked disapprovingly at Birdie, as though *she* was the one who had broken the law. Birdie turned away, but the young man called after her.

'Hey, come back. I'm talking to you. Don't they teach your kind manners?'

'Excuse me?'

He winked, and she felt an unfamiliar heat creep up her neck. He wore stained jeans and a leather jacket that gleamed with newness. His black hair had been slicked back away from his face.

'Dancing shoes?' He picked up a pair of high heels and held them out towards her.

'No thanks. I don't need new shoes.'

'Then how come I saw you eyeing up my wares?'

'I wasn't—'

'So you were eyeing *me* up then?' He looked her up and down. 'D'you like what you see?'

'Oi, Tony.' A man in dirty overalls signalled to the end of the row of stalls. Birdie caught sight of a policeman's helmet bobbing among the crowd of shoppers.

'Cheers, Badger.' Tony bent down and grabbed the four corners of the blanket, bundling up his ill-gotten goods. He slung them into the boot of his car and then linked arms with Birdie, speedily leading her in the opposite direction before she had a chance to protest.

'What's your name?'

'Birdie.'

'Birdie, eh? Do you sing like a little bird too?' He grinned at her. 'There's a bostin' bakery round the corner,' he said. 'Come on, Cuckoo. Let me buy you a sausage roll.'

* * *

To hear Tony Gibson tell it, he'd had a life marred by misery and hardship, and he'd had to learn at an early age to rely on himself. His mother was dead and his father as good as, he said, over two cups of tea and a sausage roll cut in half.

'That's terrible,' Birdie said, and he brushed the back of her hand with his thumb.

'I can't remember the last time a pretty girl showed me kindness,' he said, and her heart fluttered. It was the first time a man, other than her father, had called her pretty.

The way Tony Gibson told it, she was bound to fall in love.

She followed him around like a puppy. If he had money,

he would pick her up in his Morris 1100 and take her to the pictures, where he would sling his arm around her neck and they'd take turns sipping from the bottle of dandelion and burdock he'd smuggled in in his jacket pocket. If he didn't have money, which was more likely, then he'd drive them to a secluded street somewhere and his hands would be all over her before he'd even turned the engine off. Had Winston still been around, and had she not felt so adrift, Birdie might not have given her heart to him, and so freely. But on the back seat of his car, as he trailed kisses and compliments from her sternum to her stomach, she decided that she wanted to stay in England. She wanted to stay with him. She hoped her mumma would understand . . .

* * *

Precious realised that Birdie was pregnant before she realised it herself. Her daughter began to complain of an ache in her breasts, a lingering nausea that would not be soothed by ginger tea, fatigue that could not be banished by sleep. A trip to the doctor's confirmed it.

'I'm sorry, Mumma,' Birdie said, as they walked back to the bedsit. Precious stared ahead, her shoes clacking so forcefully on the pavement that Birdie had to pant to keep up.

'I love him,' Birdie stressed. 'This is a *good* thing.'

Precious walked a little faster.

'Mumma, please. Say something.'

What could Precious say? Her first thought had been to cuss out her daughter for being so *chupid*. She thought she'd raised Birdie better than that, to not fall victim to a load of pretty, meaningless sweet talk. Winston came to mind then, holding out his hand to lead her onto the dance floor . . .

Her second thought had been to blame Birdie's father. If he hadn't been so duplicitous, selfish, *nigretful*, then none of this would have happened.

'Mumma?' They were almost home. Precious hadn't said a word since they'd left the doctor's office. 'Mumma, please don't be angry with me.'

'I'm not angry,' Precious said. Her third and final thought was one of resignation. It was too late for warnings. Even later for blame. Her Birdie was in love. She knew what that felt like. She knew, too, there was no point trying to convince her daughter to give the fella up. Could Luce have persuaded her to give up Winston? For better or worse, Birdie had made her decision. Precious made her mind up, too. She stopped and turned to her daughter. Birdie looked back at her with wide, worried eyes. She was the spitting image of her father and Precious wondered for a moment if that was the reason she'd struggled to bond with her only living child. Winston and Birdie had always been two peas in a pod. She'd always been on the periphery, feeling like a weed in the flower bed. She took a deep breath.

'I love you, Birdie. If this is what you've decided then . . . then I'll support you. You *and* the baby.'

Birdie didn't care that they were stood in the middle of the street. With a little choking sob of gratitude, she dived into her mother's arms.

* * *

Birdie's stomach swelled like a watermelon and she quit her job at the factory when she could no longer stand on her feet for a full shift. Tony, who had no fixed abode of his own, moved into the bedsit, but he quickly tired of the arrangement. He disliked having to sleep on the settee, for one, and he found Precious far too concerned with his affairs. She wanted to know where he was going and who he was meeting and when he was coming home – it was enough to drive a man crazy. Precious found him equally exasperating. He left his grubby underwear on the floor. He came home at all hours. And worst of all, he made no attempt to make an honest woman of her daughter.

'Don't tell me you can't afford it,' she snapped. She didn't trust Tony Gibson as far as she could throw him.

As a matter of fact, he couldn't afford it. Birdie had had to spend her own money on things for the baby. But that didn't mean that Precious had a right to nag him. She wasn't *his* mother. After yet another comment about his finances, or lack thereof, Tony stomped out of the bedsit and Birdie was beside herself, convinced that her mumma had driven him away forever. However, he came back all smiles and announced that he'd secured them new lodgings. They could move in immediately, he said.

'Where?' Birdie spluttered.

His reply was vague.

'It's far. Two buses and then a twenty-minute walk.'

'But you can't live together. You're unmarried,' Precious said, horrified, but Tony merely grinned.

'We're living in a modern age, Mrs Brown, and I'm a modern man. Hurry up and pack, Birdie. I want to get there before it gets dark.'

Birdie hesitated and looked between him and her mother. 'I don't know . . .' she began. 'It's not really respectable . . .'

Tony shrugged. 'Then I'll go without you.'

That was all Birdie needed to hear.

'It's important we're together, Mumma,' she said, all worries about respectability forgotten. 'But don't worry. I'll come and visit all the time. And you can come and visit us.'

'You don't have to rush out of here. Take all the time you need,' Precious said, but Tony was already tossing an armful of clothes into a suitcase.

'Best to get out from under your feet, Mrs Brown,' he said genially.

Two buses and a thirty-minute walk (Birdie couldn't walk very fast, in her state) later, they arrived at a shabby boarding house on the outskirts of the city. It had been painted white, but badly, and the paint was peeling, revealing the dirty red bricks beneath. As Tony hurried her up the steps, Birdie remembered the days when she thought every home in England would be as grand as Buckingham Palace.

Their new landlady, a fearsome woman from Belfast, addressed them as 'Mr and Mrs Gibson'. Tony had rented a flat on the third floor. Birdie was out of breath before they'd reached the first landing.

'Going to be hard to manage this with a baby,' she puffed, but Tony told her to stop complaining.

'You sound like your mother,' he criticised.

The room was sparsely furnished, though cleaner than Birdie had expected. Tony went back downstairs for the rest of their luggage and she eased herself onto the bed and exhaled with relief. The mattress was comfortable, there wasn't any mould growing up the walls and there was plenty of space for a crib. She could be happy here, she decided. They would be happy here.

'This is our *home*,' she said as he came through the door, suitcases in hand. The baby kicked. 'I love you so much, Tony.'

'That's sweet. Put the kettle on, will you?'

* * *

## *1969*

Motherhood was harder than Birdie expected. Life with Tony was harder than expected. She hadn't realised the experience would be so isolating, that the only person she could rely on for unconditional support was her mumma. Her friends had lives of their own: Bette was engaged to a young man called Norman Flowers and Nancy was training to be a teacher. In the early days, they would come to visit and coo over the baby, but she felt they didn't approve of Tony, or their situation, and as the months went by, Birdie felt herself slipping out of their orbit. Her days were filled with nappies, teethers, potty training and screaming matches at bedtime, and some days she missed the factory. She certainly missed having money of her own.

Tony wasn't very good with money. He had a devil-may-care attitude to everything in life and Birdie found that charming, at first. He would sing to her, rolling his hips from side to side like Elvis, kicking up imaginary blue suede shoes to make her laugh. Tony didn't take himself seriously. The problem was, he didn't take anything else seriously either. He didn't always feel the need to come home on time for dinner. He didn't always feel the need to pay the rent on time, and Birdie would have to dodge their landlady, Mrs Murray, in shame, tiptoeing up and down the stairs and praying that Carmen wouldn't cry or scream and give the game away. The money Birdie had been saving for secretarial college was long gone, but Tony didn't seem to care.

They were walking back from the shops. Carmen was three years old – much too big for the pushchair, but Birdie had not been able to face another tantrum that morning and had given into her daughter's demand.

'I don't see what the big deal is,' Tony said. 'Borrow it from your mother if you're so worried about the rent.'

Birdie glared. Sometimes, she thought, it was like she was dealing with two babies.

'I already have. We owe her three months already.'

Tony opened his mouth and then closed it again. Two skinhead teens were walking down the pavement towards them, their feet sheathed in heavy black boots laced up to the knee, their faces contorted into twin sneers.

'Should stick to your own kind, mate,' one of them said to Tony. His friend spat into the street, the foamy globule landing in the gutter, and looked Birdie straight in the eye.

'We don't want you or your golliwog baby here,' he jeered. 'Why don't you go back to your own country and take the half-breed with you?'

Birdie almost flew over the pram handlebar in a rage, but Tony put his hand on her arm.

'Leave it,' he said, but he was talking to her, not the skinheads, and the boys laughed and swaggered away.

'Why didn't you say something to them?' Birdie asked.

'Are you stupid? There were two of them and only one of me.' Tony shook his head. 'You know what we look like to people like that, Cuckoo. Sometimes you can be really naïve.'

Birdie was too stunned to say another word. She could not believe that he hadn't defended her, hadn't defended their *child*, and later that day, after he'd disappeared down the pub, she dragged her suitcase out from under the bed and began flinging clothes into it. But then she caught sight of Carmen, playing on the rug with the rag doll that had once been hers. She didn't want her child to grow up without a father. Winston had been her closest friend when she'd been Carmen's age. They'd been joined at the hip, practically. The wound still smarted. She didn't want that for Carmen.

Slowly, she hung the clothes back up in the wardrobe. She would stay, for the sake of their child.

She just wished she wasn't so lonely.

* * *

## *1971*

One bright February morning, Birdie heard a crash on the stairs, followed by a bang and a loud '*Arse!*' She surreptitiously poked her head out into the hallway. A sandy-haired man was halfway to the fourth floor, a suitcase under each arm. The source of the commotion was the third suitcase, the heaviest of the lot, which had evidentially proved too cumbersome to carry; it had burst open on the bottom step and its contents had spilled all over the landing. A black-bottomed saucepan clattered noisily all the way down to the ground floor, bouncing off each step with a metallic *ping*!

'Do you need help?' Birdie asked. A pair of his underwear had caught on the newel post, hanging sadly like a white flag of surrender.

'Shite,' the man muttered in a Scottish accent. 'I mean, no thank you. I can manage.'

He hastened back down the stairs and tripped on a pair of his trousers, ending up in a tangled heap at Birdie's feet.

'Are you sure?'

'Aye,' he said through gritted teeth, using the banister to pull himself upright. He was tall, with hair that stuck up in all directions, and his movements were awkward (*all limbs,*

Birdie thought to herself), as he stuffed shirts and shoes and books back into his broken suitcase.

'Don't forget your underwear,' Birdie said, and he snatched them off the newel post without saying another word. Then, with a suitcase clamped under each arm and the third one hugged tightly to his chest, he carefully made his way back up the stairs and disappeared around the corner.

When Tony came home that evening, he told Birdie to close her eyes for a surprise.

'Ta-da!' In his hands he held a dented saucepan. 'Found it downstairs, can you believe it? Give it a scrub and it'll be as good as new.'

* * *

'Hello,' said a broad voice. 'D'you need a hand?'

It was a week later, and Birdie was trying to transport a shrieking Carmen and a week's worth of groceries up the stairs. Carmen was having a tantrum; she clung to the banister, her loud wails echoing up and down the stairwell, and no amount of coaxing or scolding could induce her to walk under her own steam. Birdie looked up to see her new neighbour watching her from the first-floor landing.

'She wants me to carry her,' she explained irritably. 'Even though she's a big girl and she can walk by herself. Up the stairs *now* or you'll get a good hiding—'

'*Ca-aa-an't*,' Carmen wailed, crocodile tears pouring down her cheeks.

In a flash, he was at the bottom of the stairs. He picked Carmen up, threw her over his shoulder and then proceeded to take the stairs two at a time, not giving her time to protest. Birdie followed with the shopping bags.

'Thank you,' Birdie said gratefully, fishing in her pocket for the key. Carmen's mouth hung open in surprise as he set her down on her feet. 'Would you like to come in for a cup of tea?'

He smiled and said a cup of tea would be grand. Too late she remembered the ill-gotten saucepan; she steered him to the settee, out of view of the kitchenette, and told him to make himself comfortable. Carmen sidled up next to him.

'Pick me up again,' she commanded, and he obliged, flipping her upside down and shaking her like a rattle. Carmen squawked with delight, and Birdie used the distraction to toss the saucepan into the cupboard under the sink.

'Milk and sugar?' she called, sniffing the bottle. It was *just* passable—

'Aye, thanks. How old is this one?'

'She'll be five in April.'

He put Carmen down and she teetered dizzily on the spot, a huge smile stretching from ear to ear.

'Again,' she demanded, and he would have obeyed, but Birdie told her to hush. She handed him his cup, handle first, and their fingertips brushed together.

'The milk's fine, I promise,' she said, aware of a residual tingling in her fingers.

'Have you lived here long?' he asked.

'Since before Carmen was born.'

'Is it just you and the bairn?'

'No, I . . . her father.' Birdie cleared her throat. 'That is to say, my—'

'Right you are,' he said kindly. 'Well as you know, I've just moved in. I didn't intend on introducing myself by showing you my breeks, but I've always been terrible at first impressions. I suppose you're wondering how a clumsy Scottish oaf like me ended up in Birmingham?'

'I hadn't wondered at all,' she replied truthfully. She didn't like to nose into people's backgrounds the way people liked to nose into hers. She'd grown up with enough undisguised curiosity – she could hear it in their voices when people asked her where she was *really* from. *Jamaica*, she would say, and then add, unprompted, *but I've lived here most of my life*, as though she needed to offer some sort of explanation for why she looked like she did while sounding like someone else. She presumed he wouldn't want to offer explanations either, but to her surprise, he looked hurt.

'I don't mean that I hadn't thought about it,' Birdie said quickly.

'It's alright,' he said amiably. 'I wouldn't be interested in me either.'

'I am,' Birdie insisted, but he drained his tea and held out the mug.

'I best be off. I need to pop into town for a new saucepan. Mine disappeared.'

He stood up, and Carmen's bottom lip began to wobble, a sure sign that another tantrum was imminent.

'Don't cry, Carm, there's a good girl. Say goodbye to . . .' Birdie tailed off. She'd had the man in her home and she didn't even know his *name*. But he smiled and held out his hand.

'I'm Jimmy.'

'Birdie.'

'Like the custard?' He reddened. 'That was a bad joke, sorry. See you around, Birdie.'

He left with a cheery wave.

That afternoon, as Birdie scrubbed potatoes at the kitchen sink, she absent-mindedly thought about Jimmy. He'd known exactly how to handle Carmen. Perhaps he had children of his own, but then, he would have mentioned them, wouldn't he?

Perhaps he was just a friendly person. How nice it had been, to talk to someone her own age . . .

'Stay in tonight.' It was later that evening, and Tony was mopping up gravy from his plate with a piece of bread and butter. Birdie said it as nicely as she could, reaching for his free hand. 'Please. You've been out every night this week.'

He batted her hand away, as though it were a fly buzzing around his ear.

'Can't, Cuckoo. I'm expected down The Anchor.'

Birdie bristled. 'And I expect you to spend time with your family every once in a while. Aren't we more important?'

Tony didn't answer. Instead, he crossed over to the mirror that was hung on the wall and began to comb his hair.

'We'll do something on Saturday, alright?'

'It's not alright. You're never here. Your daughter misses you. *I* miss you—'

'I said we'll do something on Saturday. Don't start, Cuckoo.'

'I'm not starting.'

'Yes, you are. D'you know why I'd rather spend my evenings down the pub? It's because whenever I'm here all you do is nag. I won't put up with it much longer, Cuckoo. I mean it.'

'What's that supposed to mean?'

'Christ. Here come the waterworks. I suppose you'll run off and complain to your mother now. Or maybe your dad – oh wait, he couldn't wait to get away from you either, could he?'

If it hadn't been for the mirror, Tony would not have seen Birdie's plate come sailing towards his head, but he managed to duck just in time. It hit the mirror with a sharp crack, splintering it into pieces. Carmen began to scream. Mushy peas ran down the wall.

Tony roared and advanced on Birdie, his face purple, his fist cocked. She threw up her fists and swung wildly—

'Somebody being murdered?'

Jimmy stood in the doorway, dressed in a pair of crumpled pyjamas.

'It's nothing to do with you,' Tony said, but Jimmy ignored him and looked towards Birdie, who had picked Carmen up and held her tightly in her arms.

'You alright, hen?'

'I told you, this has got nothing to do with you—'

Jimmy stretched himself to his full height. He was much taller than Tony, who looked him up and down and then grabbed his jacket off the hook by the door.

'I've had enough of this,' he muttered. 'I'm leaving.'

'No one's stopping you,' Jimmy said, standing to one side to let him past. 'Good riddance,' he muttered, as Tony hurtled down the stairs. The landlady shouted something. Jimmy closed the door with a gentle click.

'Did he hurt you?'

Birdie shook her head. In her arms, Carmen quietened to a soft whimper.

'Does he get like that a lot?'

She shook her head. 'Not usually. We argue sometimes, but . . .'

Jimmy began to gather up the largest shards of broken glass.

'My mam's second husband was a bad 'un,' he said. 'Worst of the lot. Yelling. Cussing. Breaking things. He liked to use his fists. Used them on my mam more than once. It wasn't until she ended up in hospital that she realised she was better off without him.'

He sat back on his heels. 'I'd say *you* were better off without him.'

'He's never hurt me. Or Carmen.'

Jimmy rolled his eyes. 'Good for him.'

'That's not fair.' Birdie tried to swallow the lump in her throat. It felt as though a sliver of broken glass had gotten lodged in her windpipe. 'You don't know him. You don't know me, for that matter.'

'I know, but—'

Birdie couldn't take it anymore. His pity. It made her feel like a fool.

'Please go.'

'What?'

'Please. Just go.' She held Carmen a little tighter. 'I can clean up.'

'As long as you're alright.'

'I am,' she insisted. He nodded and left Birdie alone. As soon as the door had closed behind him, she let out a sob so loud that Carmen started crying again.

Tony didn't come home for two days, but on the third, he brought flowers. They fell into an exhaustive cycle: he would be sweet for weeks at a time, coming home at a reasonable hour, playing with Carmen, kissing Birdie the way he'd kissed her on the back seat of his car. She fell pregnant again and she hoped that things would be different. But the sweetness and kindness and kisses would never last long.

One afternoon, Mrs Murray came to the door. She was a thickset woman who wore men's shoes and a starched apron around her waist, in which she carried a hammer, her reading glasses and dog biscuits. As far as Birdie knew, she didn't have a dog.

'Hello, Mrs Murray. How are you today?'

'Rent.'

'Tony's already paid,' Birdie said, massaging her lower back. This baby sat lower than Carmen had, pressing against her spine. The ache radiated into her hips and thighs, and she was exhausted, though she still had four months to go.

'He hasn't.'

'He said he did.'

Mrs Murray crossed her arms. 'You have twenty-four hours. Otherwise, take your things and go.'

'Tony will pay you when he gets in from work, I promise.'

All afternoon she paced back and forth, like a tiger trapped in a cage. The minute Tony walked through the door, she pounced.

'You didn't pay the rent again.'

'Christ, Cuckoo, let me get my boots off—'

'You need to go and pay Mrs Murray. You need to go right now or else she'll put us out—'

'Then she'll have to put us out, because I don't have it.' Tony put his hands into his pockets and turned them inside out. 'Not a penny.'

'How can you not have any money?'

Tony shrugged. 'What's for dinner?'

'Tony.' Her blood boiled. 'I asked you a question.'

He pulled a bottle of beer out of the fridge, popping off the top with his key, and took a long swig.

'Nag, nag, nag. I don't know why I bother coming home.'

'Why do you? It's obvious you don't care about me.' She placed her palms on her stomach. 'About any of us.'

'Don't give me that. I've looked after the kid, haven't I? I'll look after this one too. I don't have to.'

'Of course you do. You're their father—'

'Am I?' His words were as sharp as a bee sting, and just as venomous. 'For all I know you've had it off with half of Birmingham.'

'You don't mean that. You *know* they're yours—'

Thank God, Birdie thought, that Carmen had gone to Precious's for the day. Imagine if she was around to hear him.

'Everyone knows coloured girls are loose.' Tony drained the bottle. 'They go after white men and get knocked up on purpose to trap them—'

'A minute ago, you were claiming this baby isn't yours and now you're saying I trapped you,' she said with disdain. 'You're the stupidest person I've ever met.'

Tony moved with the sudden grace of a dancer. The slap rang out, clear and sharp, and Birdie felt her teeth rattle. She lifted her hand to her cheek and probed about her mouth with her tongue to see if any of them had come loose. Tony just watched her, his arms hung limply at his sides.

'I was wrong,' she said finally. Her ears were still ringing. 'I guess I'm the stupid one.'

* * *

Birdie, weighed down by her suitcases and her sadness, made the long trek across Birmingham. No one had seen her leave the boarding house. She knocked on her mother's door and heard Carmen whoop and holler. Precious opened the door and caught sight of Birdie's swollen face.

'What happened, chile?'

'I left him. It's over.'

Precious guided her into the living room.

'There, there, don't cry now.'

'What am I going to do, Mumma?'

'It's going to be alright. Sit down, I'll make some tea—'

She sat down on the settee and Carmen began climbing all over her, her sticky fingers accidentally brushing against the bruise on her cheek. Birdie winced. Then she heard hushed whispers in the hallway and the front door open and close. Precious returned with two cups of tea and a glass of cordial for Carmen.

'Was someone here?' Birdie asked.

'Just a friend from church,' Precious said offhandedly. 'He was dropping off some coats for the clothes drive. He's from the island too. But never mind that. Tell me what happened.'

'Oh, Mumma. I feel so *foolish*.'

'No daughter of mine is a fool,' Precious replied sternly.

'But what am I going to do? I don't have any money, or anywhere to live—'

Precious grabbed hold of her hands. 'Birdie. We can do it. We can move back to Jamaica. There's nothing holding us back now.' Her mother's voice sounded so full of promise, so full of hope. 'We can save up and go.'

Somewhere in the back of Birdie's mind, a memory stirred. Her puppa at the kitchen table, the light shining in his eyes as he stared past her and towards an invisible horizon . . .

*England will be good to us.*

Birdie looked down at Carmen. Her daughter was too small for her legs to reach the floor and they dangled off the edge of the settee. She slurped happily on her cordial. The baby in her belly would be fine, Birdie thought. It wouldn't know any different. But what about Carmen? Could she take her from the only life she'd ever known? Looking back, she could see how Winston had influenced her. How he'd planted the idea of immigration in her head and watered it until it bloomed. But it had come with an enormous price, and his dream had withered and died while they still clung to the vines, scrambling for a foothold.

She took a deep breath.

'I can't do it, Mumma. I'm sorry. The upheaval – it's too much for a child. I'm sorry.'

Precious didn't say anything for a moment, and Birdie couldn't bring herself to look into her eyes. Would she see betrayal there again, like she'd seen all those years ago, when she'd sided with her father?

'Okay then,' Precious said matter-of-factly. 'We'll stay here.'

Birdie looked up. 'We?'

'Did that boy knock *all* the sense from your head?' Precious rolled her eyes, then put her arm around her daughter. Birdie sank into her, and Carmen wriggled in between them.

'I've stayed here all these years because you needed me. Do you think I'd leave you now?' Precious placed a gentle hand on Birdie's stomach. 'Jamaica will always be there. It will always be my home. But I'm right where I need to be.'

# Fifteen

*2017*

Birdie had rung in the new year in an immigration removal centre on the outskirts of London.

They had come for her at dawn on Boxing Day. If any of the neighbours had looked out of the window they would have been treated to a ridiculous show: Andy posturing menacingly in his boxers; Carmen, blubbering like a baby, unaware that her dressing gown had swung open and she was giving the street an eyeful; the children in the doorway, unwilling spectators, shaking and ashen faced. A Christmas pantomime gone terribly wrong. Birdie felt like she was a spectator herself, suspended above the scene, watching as the door of a black van swung open to swallow her up . . .

They treated her like she was an object, lifting her off her feet to place her in the back of the van. The handcuffs chafed her wrists. Would she be driven straight to the airport? The van was soundproof, and she could hear nothing but her own heart drumming in her ears. It sounded too loud. What if she had a heart attack and died on the way? Would they let Carmen bury her in England, or would they fly her body back to Jamaica? She pictured a coffin left on the runway at Kingston Airport with no one coming to claim it, the heat from the sun seeping through the wood, the coffin cracking and splitting open. She shuddered.

The journey was over quickly – was she being flown out of Birmingham Airport? No. The officers removed her, dizzy and disorientated, from the van, and marched her inside a police station. They deposited her in a waiting room with breeze block walls painted a dull shade of magnolia. Two officers sat behind the front desk, yawning and fiddling with their phones as they made their way through a pile of paperwork, not paying the slightest bit of attention to her. She didn't suppose she was, at her age, a flight risk. How far would she get in her dressing gown?

'How many this morning?' one of them asked.

'She was the seventh,' his colleague replied, jerking his head towards Birdie.

The first one sighed with exaggerated exhaustion.

'Merry flipping Christmas.'

* * *

A female officer had been assigned to search her. Her hands were cool as she ran them up and down Birdie's legs, across her back and under her armpits. She told Birdie she'd be there for a few hours.

'And then . . . I'll be deported?' Birdie asked.

The officer peeled off her gloves and tossed them in a bin, a well-practised move.

'This is a temporary holding location, for local detainees. You'll be transported shortly to one of the immigration removal centres. Probably Yarl's Wood.'

They put her in handcuffs again and checked her identity before taking her outside to the van. The sun had risen, though it was impossible to see through the thick, grey clouds. Birdie had always hated English winters. Dour days and dour, wind-chapped faces, the misery of knowing that the sun had migrated and wouldn't be back until spring. Muddy fields and naked trees – nothing like the Christmas card . . .

**It's snowing and I wish Birdie were here to see it.**

Birdie remembered the first time she'd seen snow. She had rushed out into the backyard, barefoot, and yelped so loudly that Pat had almost fallen off the toilet. The snow had burned her bare skin with breathtaking intensity, and she had hopped back up the stairs, outraged. Puppa had said the snow was *cold*, she whined. But it was hotter than Mumma's curry. Puppa had laughed until he cried.

The memory made her want to cry, too.

Birdie was not the only detainee in the van: three other women, their hands cuffed and their eyes glued to the floor, sat beside her, crammed shoulder to shoulder, like cattle on the way to slaughter. No one spoke; there was no solidarity to be found in degradation. The small space reeked of body odour and fear.

They rumbled along the motorway for hours. Birdie's bladder ached and her mouth was dry. Eventually, the van eased to a stop, and the doors were thrown open. Birdie heard a plane overhead, but she couldn't see it. She had not been on a plane since the day she'd arrived. She'd been given a sweetie, she suddenly remembered, the phantom flavour bursting across her tongue. The stewardess had given it to her to stop her ears popping.

She got her first glimpse, then, of the removal centre. It was a large, modern-looking building, with a sloping grey roof. It looked more like a school than a prison, she thought. How long was she to stay here? Did her family know where she was? When would they put her on a plane? Instead of answers, she was peppered with questions. Name? Date of birth? Place of birth? *Keep it moving*, someone said. Someone else handed her a small bundle.

'You're allowed your own clothes in here,' they said. Birdie wanted to ask where *here* was, but they'd already moved down the line.

Marley had said that immigration removal centres were not prisons, that the government was keen to differentiate between the two. If Scott were here, perhaps he'd look around and say *Sweet, Mom, you don't have it so bad*. She wished she could ask him.

She was given an ID number and shown to her cell. It was a small room, smaller than the kitchen in her old flat. It contained a set of bunkbeds, two plywood wardrobes and a metal toilet without a lid. The window, which did not open more than a centimetre, looked out onto a patchy scrub of grass. The walls were painted a sky blue. It may have been a cheery colour, for some, but it made Birdie feel cold.

She shook out the bundle of clothes and it unravelled into a plain, navy tracksuit of shiny polyester. The bottoms were too big – they flapped comically around her thighs, even with the drawstring tied as tightly as she could manage it – but the top would not zip past her bust. There was a T-shirt too, washed to an off-white colour, and a pair of rubbery flip-flops in a sealed polythene packet.

*One size fits all.*

Birdie had arrived too late for breakfast, they said. At lunchtime, she joined a queue in the windowless dining room, her stomach rumbling so loudly she would have eaten anything placed before her, even faggots and peas. The dining room smelled like overheated food and dirty dishwater, just like . . . her nostrils flared as she chased the memory. Just like the dinner hall at Greenfields.

'Meat or vegetarian?'

Birdie looked down at the food coagulating in two stainless steel food warmers. She couldn't tell which option was which.

'Meat, please.'

The meat option, square pieces of chicken served in sweet and sour sauce, came with a soggy serving of unseasoned rice and a portion of chips. The rice tasted like Styrofoam. The chips were cold. Birdie devoured it.

After lunch, she waited for someone to tell her where to go or what to do. Women – all of the other detainees were women (that made sense, Birdie supposed. They had men's prisons and women's prisons, so why should detention centres be any different?) – were leaving the room in lethargic groups of twos and threes and, after waiting for permission that was not forthcoming, she followed them.

There was a rec room, of sorts, with bookshelves and a few computers. A sign-up sheet stated that computer time was limited to twenty minutes per person. A sign wonkily fixed to the wall with Blu Tack reminded residents (residents! Birdie scoffed) that certain websites were blocked. Someone had helpfully scribbled beneath the note: *Can't access Facebook*.

*No porn either*, someone else had written.

* * *

'I sleep on the bottom.'

Birdie had survived her first day. How many more would she endure? If she had a pencil she could keep a tally on the walls, like they did in old prison movies, but she didn't have one. Her cellmate didn't look like the type who would lend her one, either. She was a tall, thin woman, with long nails sharpened into points. She had buzzcut hair, and her eyes flashed with irritation.

Birdie surveyed the top bunk with weary dismay.

'There's no way I can climb up there. I'd get stuck.'

The woman looked askance for a second. Then she shrugged.

'Fine,' she sniffed. 'But you owe me.'

Birdie did not like the sound of that. She'd seen enough episodes of *Bad Girls* to know that you didn't want to be in someone's debt in prison. You'd be forced to do all kinds of terrible things—

The woman pulled down her jeans and sat on the toilet. Birdie turned her head away, but the woman did not seem to mind the lack of privacy. She flushed the toilet then stripped off her clothes and stretched her arms above her head, showing off a taut stomach and toned limbs. Birdie wondered if such a nonchalant attitude was afforded with time. Maybe after a few weeks she wouldn't have such hesitations about a forced sense of intimacy with a complete stranger. The thought was not comforting.

The woman climbed into bed, the frame above Birdie's head shaking as she shifted about on the thin mattress. Within minutes she was asleep. Sleep was harder to come by for Birdie. The building echoed with intrusive sounds – footsteps receding, gentle snores from the bunk above and somewhere, a baby crying. Or was it just the wind? Even though she was surrounded by hundreds – maybe thousands – of sleeping bodies, Birdie had never felt more alone in her life.

*Please let Carmen know where I am*, she prayed silently as she rolled over onto her back, covering her face with her hands. Her fingers still smelled faintly like garlic and spices.

*Please get me out of here.*

* * *

Someone was calling her ID number.

'Brown? Bridget Brown? You've got a visitor.'

Birdie sat up so quickly she hit her head on the bed above. Four days had passed since her arrest, and she hadn't had any contact with what she was already calling *the outside world*. There were pay phones, but she didn't have any money. She practically ran to the visiting room, holding up her too-large tracksuit trousers with trembling hands.

'Mom!'

Carmen grabbed her, her grip as tight as a wrench.

'Christ. What have they put you in?'

'I didn't have any other clothes—'

'Don't worry about that. I've brought clothes for you. And pyjamas and toiletries, and your new slippers and those biscuits you like. I've left it all with the people in the reception bit. They said they need to check it before they can give it to you.'

'Thank you, Carm.'

'And I brought you *this*,' Carmen said, presenting her with a mobile phone the size of a small brick. 'I've loaded it with credit, so now you'll be able to talk to me whenever you'd like. I can't believe they still make these old phones. The twins were fascinated—'

'How are the kids?'

'They're holding up. Saffie won't come out of her room.

She said she's working on some sort of plan to get you out. I don't know what she thinks she can do, bless her. If *I* haven't managed to . . .'

'Have you spoken to Marley?'

'I *finally* got in touch with him yesterday.' Carmen's irritation was obvious. 'The whole office was closed and he wasn't answering his phone—'

'It's Christmas, Carm. He was probably with his family—'

'But when I *did* finally get through to him, he was quite helpful. He was the one that recommended the cheap phone. He said calls are expensive in here, but you're not allowed smartphones. And he told me to bring these—'

She took out a cardboard folder containing photocopies of all of the letters from the Home Office, plus the applications and all of the evidence Birdie had amassed. 'And he said that you should give my number to as many other detainees as possible. His too.'

'Why?'

'So someone can get in touch if they . . . if the worst happens. If we left it to the government, I'd probably be the last person to know if . . .' Carmen sniffed and looked around. 'It's not so bad, is it? I was expecting something much worse.'

The visiting room was bright, with individual tables set out in neat rows. One wall had been painted with a colourful mural, bold splashes of pink and blue and yellow paint that almost leapt off the wall. Visitors like Carmen might find it pleasant, but Birdie thought the mural sardonic.

'*Is* it bad, Mom?' Carmen asked, gnawing on her bottom lip.

'The food's not great,' was all she could say.

'But they *are* feeding you? And you have – you have a bed and stuff? And your own room?'

'I share a room with someone else. I've got the bottom bunk.'

'Is she nice?'

'She doesn't talk much.'

'You should try and make friends. Marley said so. He said it can really help you feel less isolated. I'm not going to be able to visit you every day, as much as I wish I could—'

'It's enough that you came today,' Birdie said, her voice catching. 'I was worried you'd forgotten about me.'

'Don't be bloody daft. I want you to call me every day. *Twice* a day. Marley said they could keep you here indefinitely, but—'

'Indefinitely? What does that mean? I could be locked in here *forever*?'

Carmen gave her hand a reassuring squeeze. 'I know it sounds scary, but he said we can use the time to our advantage. And until they actually put you on a plane there's still hope. Okay, Mom? There's still hope.'

* * *

A day slipped by, and then another. They were all the same. Birdie got up when she was told to and ate what she was given. She urinated two feet away from where she slept, and did slow, plodding laps in the 'garden', feeling like a rat in a cage. It was as if an invisible countdown was ticking above her head and there was no way of knowing when her time would run out. That was the worst bit. The not knowing.

*They could keep you here indefinitely.*

It made no sense. They wanted to get rid of her, so why would they hold her indefinitely?

'I have been here for six months and they will not tell me what will happen to me. Am I staying or am I going? Why won't they tell me?'

Birdie had joined a sort of unofficial support group that convened in the rec room every morning, a collection of women bonded by circumstance and misery. Marley had said that it was important she make friends and she understood why. Just a few days in that place was enough to make a person feel like they were going mad.

There were a few hundred women in the centre. But, for such a large cast of characters, their stories were frighteningly similar. Fatme had fled an escalating conflict. Maliha had travelled to Bradford to get married, but the government had declared it a scam. Urfi had overstayed her student visa. Hiza had the wrong visa altogether, relying on the advice and expertise of traffickers who had only cared about lining their pockets.

*That happened to me too.*

*And me.*

*And me.*

It had happened to Birdie's cellmate, too. She returned to their shared room one evening after dinner (chicken in mushroom sauce, rice and chips) to find the woman sat on Birdie's bed, rifling through the photocopied papers Carmen had brought.

'What do you think you're doing?' Birdie snatched the papers out of her hands. 'These are mine.'

'I was just looking.'

'Well, don't,' Birdie replied lamely. Had this woman gone through her other possessions? She did not have much to steal – some clothes and a few home comforts that had been handed over in a clear plastic bag having been cleared by security. But her own clothes provided a thin thread of normalcy; a metre of black polyester or a half a yard of viscose may not seem like precious items, but they made her feel more like herself.

She eyed the woman. 'What's your name?'

'Victorine. Those papers, they are from your lawyer, yes?'

'Not exactly. He's not fully qualified yet, but—'

'Can he get me papers?'

'Oh,' Birdie said, understanding. 'No, these are just a record, of sorts. Of my case. See?'

She showed her the photocopies of the letters from the Home Office. Victorine looked sullen in her disappointment.

'I do not have letters.'

'Where are you from?'

'Cameroon.'

'Does anyone know you're here?' Birdie asked, but Victorine did not wish to say anything further. She climbed, fully dressed, into her bunk and pulled the covers over her head. Birdie slowly put the papers back in the cardboard folder as the soft sound of weeping filled the small space. Victorine's tears sounded like summer rain, splashing against the roof of a little wooden house . . .

* * *

Carmen felt deflated. She had made the two-hour journey back to the detention centre to hand over more clothes and dispatch more flowery optimism, but the self-help audiobook she'd been listening to in the car didn't have a chapter on how to stay positive when your loved one gets detained. Saffie had insisted on joining her. Carmen had protested at first, but feebly – *it's no place for a child, you don't want to see your nanny like that* – and secretly she was glad of the company. She hated everything about it: the metal detectors, the guards, the sadness that draped the building, like a funeral shroud. The image of her mom in a cheap, ill-fitting tracksuit. The other images she couldn't erase from her mind: Birdie tickling her stomach on Nanny P's carpet as she shrieked with laughter; Birdie's hand in hers, soft and reassuring, on her first day of school; Birdie mopping her brow as contractions tore her in two. This couldn't be the end. She couldn't lose her mom.

'Did you bring my summer stuff?'

'Mom . . . it's January. Why would you need your summer clothes?'

'For when they send me back.'

Carmen looked like she was going to throw up. 'I don't want to hear that kind of talk! We need to think positive thoughts—'

'What we *need* is action.' Saffie's eyes were darting around the visiting room, trying to commit it to memory. Cameras and recording devices were strictly prohibited. Birdie saw her counting under her breath.

'There's a lot of people in here,' she muttered.

'There's a lot of people to deport,' Birdie replied, her voice flat. 'They'll get to me eventually. I hadn't realised it would take so long.'

'Mom!'

'They took the woman who shared my room. Her name was Victorine.'

Saffie, blinked, momentarily stunned, and then took out a notebook and pen.

'Any last name?'

'I don't . . . she didn't say.'

'Shit.'

'Language.'

Saffie ignored Carmen and flipped open her notebook. 'I'm sorry about your friend, Nanny—'

'She wasn't my friend. Not really—'

'But I have some questions. Have you noticed any issues of overcrowding? And how long are you left in your room each day? Different detention centres have their own guidelines for how much "free time" detainees are allowed to have. I read that this place was one of the better ones, but there have been budget cuts. And have you been offered work? You should have the opportunity to make some money while you're in here—'

Birdie kissed her teeth. 'You can clean. Pound an hour.'

*Now* she could work. It was fine as long as the government wanted something from you.

Saffie scribbled in her notebook, her tongue poking out between her lips, then flipped back through the pages, a slight crease appearing between her eyebrows.

'I think that's everything. You've answered all of my questions . . . oh. Apart from this one. *What does home mean to you?*' She looked up at her grandmother. 'You said you'd answer it later, but we never got around to it.'

'I don't know, Saff.'

'You can dictate the answer and I can add it to one of the videos as a voice over, or something,' Saffie said, her pen poised ready in her hand. 'Ready when you are.'

'I don't know.'

'But—'

'That's enough with the questions, Saff,' Carmen said wearily. 'Your nan doesn't need an interrogation right now. What she needs is *positivity*.'

She turned the corners of her mouth up in what she hoped was a convincing smile.

'Rita sends her love. She said to hang in there. And Declan said he'll visit on Thursday; he's booked the day off—'

Saffie turned to the last page in her notebook. 'I'm drawing up a rota so that you don't have to go more than two or three days without a visit. Look – us today, Dec and Angharad on Thursday, and Auntie Michelle on Saturday. I'm going to look after Auntie Claud. She's furious you didn't tell her, by the way. She said she's going to give you a good hiding the minute she sees you.'

'And I'm bringing Tegan next time,' Carmen added. 'And she said she's told Scott but to let her know in the meantime if there's anything else she can do.'

'A photo of Jax would be nice,' Birdie said. 'To take with me.'

'Mom, stop it—'

Birdie stared into her daughter's eyes. 'Bring my summer clothes next time, please.'

* * *

When they got back home, Saffie went straight to the garden shed. She scrambled over the exercise bike, Andy's tools, the lawnmower and a dismantled bed frame until she found the boxes filled with her grandmother's belongings. Birdie's flat had been emptied and the keys handed back to the landlord. Saffie positioned a pen light between her teeth and began ripping parcel tape from one box after another. Carmen curiously followed her down the garden path.

'What are you looking for?'

'Nanny's things,' Saffie mumbled around the pen.

'Not her summer clothes Saffie, I won't have you taking those to her—'

Saffie removed the pen from her mouth and rocked back on her heels on the dusty floor. 'Of course not. No, I'm looking for her *things*. Her photo albums, keepsakes, that sort of thing. To remind her of the life she has *here*. To remind her how loved she is.'

'Oh, sweetheart—'

'She sounded so defeated today,' Saffie said fiercely, screwing up her face in a futile attempt not to cry. 'She's ready to let them deport her, but we've got to get through to her somehow. And I've got a plan to help her, I just need a bit more time – urgh, the bottom of this one is all wet—'

Bending at the waist, she picked up a box and stretched over the lawnmower, motioning for Carmen to take it. But just as her mother's fingers grazed the edge of the box, the bottom, soggy from the shed floor, fell open. There was a smash of broken glass, a tinkling of broken porcelain—

'I always hated that photo,' Carmen said, nudging the wreckage with one fluffy slippered toe. 'Oh, but your nanny *loved* those plates—'

'I can glue it back together,' Saffie said frantically, gathering the pieces of the shattered plate in her hand. 'We have superglue, right?'

'I don't think that will work. But it's okay. It was an accident—'

'No, I can *fix* it,' Saffie insisted forcefully. 'You have to let me try. I can fix it.'

'Oh, love. Come here,' Carmen said, pulling her daughter into a tight embrace.

Saffie wept in her arms.

* * *

Birdie had lost count of the days.

She woke up and rolled over onto one side, her back stiff,

her hips aching. Her cell had felt eerily quiet since Victorine had been deported. She couldn't get used to being able to urinate in peace.

After breakfast, the only meal where chips weren't an option, she went along to the rec room to join her support group, dropping distractedly into a chair in the corner. She was vaguely aware of a whisper rustling about the room, hushed voices and sad shakes of the head, but her mind was far beyond the walls and metal fences of the detention centre, her thoughts a confusion of memories knotted together. She should have self-deported when she'd had the chance. She'd put her family through so much pain already. Her poor daughter. Her troubled son. Would Carmen pass on a message to Jimmy, if she asked? Would he care what was happening to her?

Someone nudged her shoulder, and Birdie looked up.

'Sorry, I was miles away. What's happened?'

'It's Maliha,' Fatme whispered. 'She was deported last night.'

Birdie closed her eyes. It was like they were being picked off, one by one . . .

'Has someone called her family?'

Each member of the group was responsible for passing on the message to someone else's family, if the worst should happen. Hiza nodded.

'I called this morning.'

'Poor Maliha,' someone else said, but all Birdie heard was *you could be next*.

# Sixteen

## *1972*

'Bridget Brown? You're next.'

Birdie stood up, smoothed out the non-existent wrinkles in her best trousers (the wide-legged plaid pair her mumma had made her) and plastered on her best smile. She entered Mr Newhall's office with as much confidence as she could muster, running through all the reasons why she'd make an excellent receptionist in her head. Twenty minutes later, with one final, firm handshake, she left the offices of Mr Newhall, a local businessman who ran a growing double-glazing empire. Her smile vanished the moment she reached the street. Not qualified, he'd told her. As if she needed qualifications to answer the phone and pour coffee!

She walked home dispiritedly. She was a young woman in her twenties, but to hear her slow, heavy footsteps along the pavement, a passerby would be forgiven in thinking she was much older. She *felt* old. Old and worn out, unable to get a job despite her best intentions.

She and her two children lived with Precious and Leslie in their house in Winson Green. Birdie liked to joke that her mother hadn't stayed in England for her but rather for Leslie, her 'friend from church', who was, by that time, Precious's second husband. It had been a small wedding – the bride beaming in an orange suit with gold buttons as large as the new ten pence pieces, the groom taking her arm with a giddy sense of pride – because Leslie didn't like fuss. Happiest in his garden among his roses, he was a shy, docile man, a fact which wouldn't be believed if you'd heard him on his market stall, yelling with a clear, strong voice that carried above the competition. They'd married on a Saturday and by the following Monday, Leslie was back at work at the market. Precious kept his books for him. It reminded her of the work she did for her father in her youth, though Aubrey's store was long gone and he spent his days in a rocking chair on the back veranda of his Portmore house, sipping dogwood tea to ease his arthritis, deaf and blind to everything but the feeling of the sun on his face.

Jamaica still came to Precious on hot nights and in wistful dreams. She and Leslie discussed retiring to the island, eventually, when Birdie was settled and their debts were paid off, and a large glass jar in the corner of the bedroom grew heavy with loose change, crumpled notes and heartfelt plans. Birdie never thought of the island. Her mother would frequently begin a sentence with 'remember when' – *remember when Auntie Luce threw her shoe at Mr Martin and hit him square on the backside? Remember when you got your head stuck in the veranda railings? Remember that time you were convinced a duppy was hiding under your bed and you went to sleep with a butter knife?* – but Birdie rarely remembered. Jamaica was as hazy to her as the mountains in springtime, hidden beneath a blanket of mist. Had she really found an injured tody hiding under the veranda, or did that happen to a little girl in her class? Could her puppa really throw her as high as the house? And what was the name of the boy who'd lived next door? Her childhood felt like it belonged in a book of fairy stories – whimsical, beautiful, but not *real*.

A real concern was her children, and their future. Tony had had no interest in seeing them, and he had no interest in providing for them either, so it was up to Birdie. She knew they couldn't stay with Precious and Leslie for ever, so every day she scoured the newspapers and circled help wanted ads. She was determined to pay her mother back all the rent money she'd borrowed over the years and make her children proud at the same time. It was just proving harder than she'd imagined.

Birdie arrived home and did her best to shake off her frustration at the front door. She rounded up the children, strapping Scott into his pram and wrestling Carmen into a woolly hat, and smiled down at them.

'Ready to see Grandad, kids?'

They occasionally met up with Winston. A tentative sort of peace had developed between father and daughter in the last year; he'd expressed a desire to get to know his grandchildren, and she couldn't deny her kids that, no matter what had passed between them. It was bad enough they were growing up without a father (although Leslie was a wonderful substitute. He spoiled them both rotten), and though Birdie wanted to ask Winston why he hadn't been there for her when she'd needed him, she bit her tongue for the sake of Carmen and Scott.

Scott dozed peacefully in his pram, his long, black eyelashes fluttering, like strands of silk. He could sleep through anything, which Birdie considered both a blessing and a miracle. Carmen was a handful, with boundless energy and a belting voice that belied her size. Her daughter was just like she had been at that age, apparently – rambunctious, inquisitive, too garrulous for her own good – how had her parents coped?

'Your mumma exaggerates. You weren't *that* bad.'

She met Winston at the park around the corner, and they sat on a bench and watched Carmen climb the slide. A little boy was sat at the top and refused to go down.

'It's my turn,' Carmen said assertively.

'No girls allowed,' the little boy countered.

'Play nice, Carmen,' Birdie called out. Her daughter ignored her and shoved the boy in the back. He slid down the slide headfirst and began to cry, more out of surprise than anything else. Winston chuckled, and Birdie clucked her tongue.

'Don't encourage her. Carmen, say sorry.'

'He deserved it. And now he knows not to mess with my granddaughter. She's got confidence in spades, hasn't she? Just like you.'

'I don't feel confident anymore,' Birdie sighed.

'You've had a few knocks. You'll get back up.'

They sat and watched Carmen defend her position as ruler of the playground.

'Your mumma always wanted a big family,' Winston said suddenly. This was unusual. They never talked about her mother. They never talked about the past at all, a tacit agreement they had both instinctively come to, and Birdie was torn between curiosity and the perverse sensation that she was talking about Precious behind her back.

'I know about the babies,' Birdie said slowly. 'There were two before me, weren't there?'

'I'm sure there might have been more, if we'd stayed,' Winston said, and Birdie didn't need him to explain further. *If we'd stayed in Jamaica*. Had they stayed, her mother might have had the big family she'd apparently always wanted.

Birdie might have had brothers and sisters. How different things might have been.

'Found a job yet?'

Birdie sighed. 'It's impossible. The minute I mention needing flexible hours because of the children they show me the door.' She scowled and looked, unintentionally, like her six-year-old. 'It's not fair.'

'They will always have plenty of reasons not to hire us,' Winston said casually. 'Reminds me of when I was looking for work. I was desperate. You were just a pickney, you wouldn't remember—'

'I remember. You lost your job once.'

'I lost it more than once. Do you remember, when you first came here? You were so disappointed that none of the roads were made of gold.' He laughed cynically. 'I think I was disappointed, too.'

* * *

'Birdie, there you are! Eu, tell Birdie what you were just telling me.'

They arrived home to find Precious and Eula-May sipping coffee in the kitchen. Eula-May's three-year-old twin daughters were playing at their feet with the frilly basket of tiny seashells that usually sat on the back of the downstairs toilet. Carmen immediately snatched up the basket and claimed it as her own.

'Your mudda said you're still looking for work.'

'Uh-huh,' Birdie nodded distractedly as she divided the shells into three equal piles for the girls.

'Raymond's wife just got a job in a nursing home. It's hard work, she says, but the pay is real good.'

'I don't have the right qualifications,' Birdie said, but Eula-May laughed.

'Bless you. They took Chandice on and she's as chupid as dey come. I said to her, "Chandice, do they know how badly you messed up the food at Richard's wake? You might poison one of those old folk". The chicken was raw!' Eula-May gave Precious a knowing look. 'She and Ray are perfect for each other. Neither of them has anything but cotton wool between their ears—'

Eula-May was right – not about Chandice poisoning the old folk, luckily – but about how easy it was to get paid to look after other people's parents. Birdie interviewed at a local nursing home and was offered the job on the spot. Adequate training and a uniform would be provided. She requested the night shift, so she could work while her children slept, and three evenings a week she would put her children to bed, don her light-blue tunic and slip out of the front door, returning home in time to see her daughter off to school. Then she would fall into bed and sleep as the sun moved across the sky while her mother watched Scott.

On her first night on the job she'd been paired with a woman called Claudette Thompson, who immediately took Birdie under her wing. *This is a tough job, but it's easier with friends*, she'd said, and Birdie soon came to appreciate the truth in those words. The work was gruelling. There were patients to wash, and lift, and feed. There were soiled sheets to strip, bed sores to treat and, hardest of all, grief to grapple with. But there was laughter, too. Claudette made sure of that. She was five years older than Birdie and married to her childhood sweetheart, a barber named Walford. They had a daughter around the same age as Carmen, and the girls played together on weekends. Birdie and Claudette would sometimes get a quick breakfast together in the greasy spoon around the corner after their shift, drinking enormous mugs of tea and eating bacon and eggs, the only women among the early morning crowd of builders and tradesmen. Birdie had not had a close friend in years. Her mother had tried to encourage her to forge a social life, but Birdie had said she preferred to be at home, with the children. That was not a lie. But it wasn't the whole truth, either. The truth was that she found it hard to trust people. *People aren't always who you think they are*, she said once to her mother. She didn't need to elaborate.

But Birdie could trust Claudette. She was tall, with curves that Birdie coveted, and wore her hair in a beautiful afro. It framed her face like a halo, but Birdie quickly learned that she was no Mother Teresa, not when it came to the patients that objected to the colour of her skin. There were some patients who were vocal in their distrust of yet another black member of staff, how their kind had ruined the country, how much better things had been before the government had opened the floodgates. It was exhausting, having to deal with that on top of everything else. But in Claudette, she'd found someone who understood. That alone made the friendship worth its weight in gold.

'They're old and sick,' Claudette said, when she found Birdie silently raging in the supply cupboard. 'They don't know what they're saying, or how ignorant they sound. And if you accidentally serve them cold tea – well, no one ever died from a cup of cold tea, did they?'

Birdie's laughter echoed down the corridor.

Not all of the patients were racist, but plenty of them were difficult. One evening, Shaz, the senior state nurse, approached Birdie as she was clocking in for her shift.

'Mrs Milne took a funny turn this afternoon.'

Shaz sounded completely worn out, and Birdie understood why. Mrs Milne was exhausting. Cantankerous, quarrelsome and always complaining of non-existent bedsores, she bossed the staff around as though they were her personal servants. Nevertheless, she'd taken a shine to Birdie, who apparently reminded her of 'an ebony queen' she'd once met on her travels. Birdie was the only one who could convince her to take her pills and settle each night.

'She'll pull through,' Shaz continued, 'but her son's still with her. She won't let him leave until she's fallen asleep and—'

'She won't fall asleep until I've brushed her hair. I'll go right to her now.'

'Thank God she doesn't like me,' Claudette muttered. 'I'd much rather deal with Mr Cartwright's roaming hands than *that* woman.'

Mrs Milne's unmistakable voice rang out as Birdie approached her room.

'I've already told you James, *no*,' she was saying in her clipped, English accent. 'You brush it too hard; I won't have you yanking on my hair. Bridget knows how to do it the way I like, she's gentle – Bridget! There you are. You're late.'

'I'm sorry, Mrs Milne,' Birdie said agreeably. 'I didn't mean to keep you waiting, I— it's you!'

Birdie couldn't believe her eyes. Sitting in the easy chair beside Mrs Milne's bed was Jimmy. He looked just as astonished to see her as she was to see him, unfolding his long legs and sitting up straight in surprise.

'You're acquainted with my son?' Mrs Milne asked grandly. The resemblance was so uncanny – they had the same long nose, the same broad jaw – that Birdie was surprised she hadn't seen it before.

'We used to be neighbours. How are you? And Carmen, how is she?'

Birdie was about to answer when Mrs Milne let out a comically spurious groan. She bit back a smile and adopted a suitably grave manner.

'Now then, Mrs Milne. What's this I heard about you taking a turn?'

Mrs Milne sighed dramatically. 'I thought it was the end, Bridget. I closed my eyes and didn't think I'd ever open them again.'

'You're fine now though, aren't you Mam? The doctor said you're going to be okay—'

'This time, perhaps. But what about next time?'

'Enough of that, Mrs Milne,' Birdie said with authority. 'It won't do you any good to worry. Let's get you nice and comfortable.'

Mrs Milne obediently settled back onto the pillows and closed her eyes, folding her hands across her heart. Birdie began to brush her hair and within minutes she was snoring lightly, a small, fluttering sound escaping from between her lips.

'Birdie . . .' Jimmy said in a hushed whisper, his eyes as wide as a child's.

'It's alright, she's asleep. How've you been, Jimmy?'

'Never mind me, how are *you*? You just disappeared. I thought—' he leaned forward and ran his hands through his sandy coloured hair. It still stuck out in every direction. 'I can't believe it. Here's me spending all this time wondering where you'd gone and you were *here* all along.'

'Your mother talks about her son James all the time. I never imagined—'

'And she talks about *you* all the time. Every time I visit it's

Bridget this and Bridget that. Had I known it was *you* I would have—'

He tailed off and rubbed his bloodshot eyes.

'She won't wake up now. You can go, if you want. You look exhausted.'

He shook his head and hunched his broad shoulders, as though he were turning his back against the wind.

'I'll stay a bit longer, if that's alright. You might think she's being a bit silly. But she really was frightened today, I could tell.'

'Alright.'

'I know she's difficult,' he continued. 'And she probably makes *your* life difficult. But I'm all she has . . .'

Birdie set down the hairbrush. Mrs Milne didn't even stir. Neither did Jimmy. He was fast asleep, his mouth slightly parted, the same soft, fluttering sound issuing from between his lips. *Like newly hatched chicks in a coop*, she thought with a smile. She decided to leave him be, gently draping a blanket across his knees before tiptoeing out of the room.

'Who's that?' Claudette asked, coming up behind her, her arms full of clean sheets.

'Mrs Milne's son.' Birdie felt her cheeks warm. 'We used to know each other a little.'

Claudette opened the door to Mrs Milne's room and poked her head through to get a good look.

'Quiet, you'll wake them.'

'Hmm. It's hard to tell what he really looks like with his eyes closed.'

'They're blue.'

'You sure I can't wake him up?'

Birdie pulled her back by her tunic. 'If you wake her up *you* can deal with her.'

Claudette immediately closed the door. 'I hope he's nothing like his mother, for your sake.'

'What's that supposed to mean?' Birdie asked, but Claudette just winked at her and went on her way.

That night was a busy one, and Birdie didn't have time to think about Jimmy Milne again. She left the nursing home as dawn broke, yawning and putting her coat on over her tunic, thinking longingly of her bed. A voice called out to her.

'You know, that's the second time you've disappeared on me. I'm starting to think you're doing it on purpose.'

She squinted in the early morning sunlight. Jimmy, his clothes crinkled with sleep, was leaning against his car and smiling at her.

'Sorry. I thought it best to let you rest. You seemed so tired—'

'And I'm grateful for it. I probably would have fallen asleep behind the wheel and crashed into a tree if I'd tried to drive home. Can I give you a lift? To say thank you?'

'It's really not that far—' Birdie began, but he was already holding the passenger door open for her.

'Are you hungry? Only I've just realised that a lift isn't really fair recompense for preventing a road accident, is it? Breakfast should be included too. If you want to do these things properly, I mean.'

'I could eat. It'll have to be quick though. I need to take Carmen to school.'

'I can be quick!' he exclaimed. Birdie raised her eyebrow, and he laughed ruefully. 'Aye, I know just what to say to impress the ladies. It's one of my finer skills, if you can believe it.'

In the front seat of Jimmy's car, over cheese and onion cobs, purchased in haste from the greasy spoon, he requested the truncated version of events that had led to Birdie's disappearance from the boarding house.

'You make it sound mysterious. *Disappearance*.'

'One day you were there, the next, there's a Greek family moving in. What's that if not mysterious?'

'Things ended badly with Tony—'

'Never liked the wee fella—'

'And now we live with my mother and Leslie—'

'Her cat?'

'Her *husband*.'

'So, you live with your mother and Leslie.' He gave her a sideways look. 'Is there another fella in your life, or . . .?'

'Yes. My son. Are you almost finished? Only it's nearly half past—'

'Right you are. I'll drop you off. Tomorrow, you can ask me all the questions.'

'Tomorrow?'

'Sure. I'll pick you up from work again. If that's alright? We can get to know one another. Properly, this time.'

She thought about it for a second. 'Alright.'

The next morning, over bacon sandwiches that Jimmy had made especially, he told Birdie all about himself. An only child, his father had died when he was five years old. They'd moved around a lot, he said, to escape his mother's creditors – or else her second, third, or fourth husband. He had been born in a small mining town in Scotland, and Mrs Milne had moved them to Birmingham some time around his fifteenth birthday. Her English accent appeared overnight.

'When did she travel the world? Before you were born?' Birdie asked. Jimmy looked at her in puzzlement.

'She's never been on a plane in her life. I don't know why

she feels the need to lie all the time. Her own life was a melodrama.'

Jimmy worked as a mechanic at Derek's Garage and Car Repair. He'd developed a love of cars from his third father and had ambitions to open his own garage one day. As an adult, he hankered for stability – all he had wanted as a child was a home rooted in permanence and the reassurance he could sleep through the night without being shaken awake and forced to do another moonlight flit.

'I can understand that,' Birdie said with a small sigh. 'Kids shouldn't have to deal with that kind of upheaval. Sometimes I worry about mine. That I haven't done right by them . . .'

'Don't say that. And leaving Tony was the right thing to do. I *really* didn't like him.'

Birdie smiled softly. 'Thank you. And thanks for the sandwich.'

'Perhaps on Saturday I could take you to the pictures?' The tips of his ears turned pink. 'There's a new *Carry On* film that I'd like to see.'

'I can't, sorry. I've got the kids.'

'How about we do something with them then? Take them to the park or something?'

Birdie wanted to say yes. She had no doubt that Carmen would enjoy herself, and she would enjoy spending an afternoon in Jimmy's company, too. But still, she was cautious. Tony had broken her heart. Tony had also had an issue with the colour of her skin. She didn't think that Jimmy was like that. But people weren't always who you thought they were . . .

He sensed her hesitation. 'We don't have to if you don't want to.'

'It's not that I don't want to . . .' she took a deep breath, unsure of how to put her reservations into words. 'Would your mother be okay with you going out with me?'

'Of course,' he said with a little laugh. 'She loves you.'

'She loves me as her *nurse*,' Birdie stressed. 'I'm asking you if she'd be okay with you going out with *me*.'

He understood then, and his eyes went wide. 'Would that really matter?'

'It matters to a lot of people.'

'Does it matter to you?'

'Yes, Jimmy. It matters to me when people are giving me abuse in the street in front of my kids.'

He squirmed uncomfortably. 'Right you are then. I understand.'

'I'm sorry. It's just . . . complicated.'

'Right you are,' he said again, and started the engine.

It was for the best, she told Claudette. It was okay for her; she and Walford had had the same kind of upbringing. She and Jimmy were too different. She said the same thing to her mumma. Besides, she had her children to think about. She had to put them first.

On Saturday night, she sat at home, alone. Precious and Leslie had gone dancing, and the children were asleep. The house was quiet and calm, but Birdie felt restless. She wondered if Jimmy had gone to the pictures without her, then chided herself for thinking about Jimmy at all. *You made your decision*, she thought. A little voice at the back of her head asked her if it was the wrong one, and she closed her eyes. *Do not think about Jimmy Milne.*

There was a knock at the front door. Birdie slowly stood up and stretched, wondering if Leslie had forgotten his keys again.

'You should sew them into your jacket,' she said as she opened the front door.

It was Jimmy. His hair stood up in all directions and his eyes were rimmed with red.

'You shouldn't be here,' she began, and he started to cry.

'Mam's dead. She died this evening.'

'Oh, Jimmy.' Without thinking, she threw her arms around his broad back.

'I got there just in time to say goodbye. I'm sorry. I didn't know where else to go—'

She ushered him off the doorstep and into the front room. It was the room that was kept for best – only the pastor, or the doctor, or other such guests of great importance were allowed to cross its threshold. Birdie thought that Jimmy counted. The back and arms of the settee had been draped with pristine white doilies that Precious had crocheted herself. The wallpaper was mustard yellow and flecked with gold, though little of it was on show – the walls had been covered with family photographs, decorative plates, embroidered bible verses and a velour map of Jamaica. In one corner sat a drinks trolley made of highly polished wood – Precious and Carmen dusted the room every Saturday morning – and in the other, the Blue Spot radiogram. In the centre of the coffee table sat a bunch of plastic flowers of vibrant colours rarely seen in nature.

She sat Jimmy down on the settee, encased in clear plastic, and left him to make him a cup of tea. When she came back he said, 'Mam has a clock just like that one. Had. She had one . . . D'you know the last thing she said to me?' He turned his watery eyes to hers. 'She told me she wanted me to be happy.'

'Jimmy,' she began, but he held up a finger to silence her.

'I love you, Birdie. I know I don't know what you've been through and I know you think it's too complicated, but that's the truth of it. I love you. And I'm not saying it's going to be easy, but I do think it's worth it because you . . . well, you make me happy. And I think I could make you happy, too.' He tentatively reached out and placed his hand on top of hers. 'I'm sorry. I've never really been all that eloquent.'

'I think what you're saying makes perfect sense,' Birdie said, and then she kissed him.

* * *

Six months after Mrs Milne's funeral, Birdie, Jimmy and the children moved into a house of their own. On the day they moved in, Jimmy didn't carry Birdie across the threshold – instead he carried both of the children, one under each arm, through the door. He also gave Birdie his mother's gold watch as a present. Rather shamefacedly, Birdie reunited Jimmy with his saucepan, and he laughed so hard he thought his sides might split.

With Jimmy, Birdie found constancy, a gentle love that was nurtured as carefully as one of Leslie's roses. He'd trace his finger down her nose, or run his hands tenderly over her stretch marks, shushing her whenever she said that her hips were too wide, or that her bottom was too big, whispering that he loved every inch of her and there was nothing she could say that would change his mind. They talked about having children of their own but, for whatever reason, it didn't happen for them. It was okay, Jimmy said, after months of disappointment. Scott and Carmen were enough for him. And he was a *wonderful* dad. He didn't get grumpy, like she did. He never shouted, like she did – when Jimmy was upset, he'd explain it in frank terms, but he never once raised his voice. It was as if his placidity complemented her spirit, like a dollop of cream on top of a slice of tart apple pie. With Jimmy by her side, she regained the confidence she'd had in her youth.

He demonstrated, with words and with actions, that she could trust him. He didn't overstep with the children. Precious and Leslie adored him.

'And he's *nothing* like his mother,' she laughingly told Claudette. 'Can you believe I almost made the wrong decision?'

* * *

## *1982*

Aubrey died in his rocking chair, and Precious and Leslie flew back to Jamaica for the funeral. Birdie didn't join them. Jimmy had just taken ownership of Derek's Garage (a new sign had been ordered), and money was tight. It couldn't be helped, and Birdie mourned her grandfather from a distance like she had done for Luce nearly two decades before.

Precious had only been gone a few days, but Scott missed her terribly. He was a loving child but felt his emotions quietly, as though he didn't want to cause alarm or make a fuss. At bedtime, he asked when his nanny was coming back. Birdie brushed his curls back from his forehead.

'I told you. First there's nine night, and then they'll have the funeral. Then Nanny and Uncle Les will come home.'

'Do you remember your grandad?' Scott asked sleepily.

'Of course I remember him.' Birdie could picture Aubrey's glasses and his moustache, and the shirt and tie he wore every day. She could remember how pleased he'd sound to see her whenever she ran up the lane and burst through his front door. In her memory of him though, his voice sounded echoey and far away, the way it had sounded on a long-distance phone call to Jamaica.

'But Carmen said you were very little the last time you saw him.'

'That's true.'

'Does that make you sad?'

'Very.'

Scott and Carmen were lucky, she thought as she climbed into her own bed that night. They were growing up surrounded by adults who loved them, whereas she'd been cut off from the majority of her family at the age of seven. She rolled over and nestled her head onto Jimmy's shoulder, lulled by the steady rhythm of his breath. How difficult had it been for her parents to make the decision to emigrate? To make that leap without a safety net? She should ask her father the next time she saw him.

The opportunity came sooner than she expected. The next morning, Winston called and asked if they could meet. He was going into Birmingham city centre on business that Saturday, he said. Would she be free?

'What business?' she asked curiously. He declined to answer and suggested they meet in a café near the bus station. When she arrived, a shy Scott and a grumpy Carmen in tow, the only other customer was an old man sat at the table by the window, a steaming cup of strong black coffee in front of him. He had a stooped back, greying hair and a thin scar at his temple.

'Hey, Puppa.'

Winston smiled at his daughter and for one, brief moment, he looked like a young man again. Birdie sat down opposite him and ordered a cup of tea and two orange juices.

'No hello for your grandad?'

Carmen muttered a sullen hello (Andy Lloyd and his mates were, at that very minute, skating at Silver Blades and if she didn't hurry up Tracey Carmichael and her big tits would get there first) and Scott leaned bashfully into Birdie's side and whispered a greeting to the plastic tablecloth.

'Nuttin' like each other, are they?' Winston said observingly. 'Strange, how two pickney can be so different. She looks just like you,' – Carmen's face was an expression of horror – 'whereas *he* must take after his farda.'

'How's Pat?' Birdie asked, changing the subject.

'She's fine. How's Jimmy?'

'He's fine.'

Winston cleared his throat of phlegm. 'I was sorry to hear about Aubrey. He was a good man, and he raised your mumma to be a fine, upstanding woman.'

Birdie raised her eyebrows. There was something peculiar about his manner: the way his hands fidgeted with the sugar packet, the unexpected compliment of her mother. He seemed nervous, brimming with energy, and once again she was reminded of the father of her youth, a man overwhelmed with big ideas and unresolved ambitions.

'Puppa—' she began, but he nodded his head towards Scott. 'How old is this one now?'

'Almost eleven.' Birdie would have to remind him of Scott's birthday a few days before, like she did every year.

'Boys are harder than girls.'

'I don't know about that,' Birdie said, tousling her son's hair. 'Scott's a good boy. Aren't you, little man?'

Carmen glowered beneath her fringe. 'What about that football he stole?'

Birdie fixed her with a hard glare. 'It's not nice of you to bring that up. It was a misunderstanding, he said sorry and he won't do it again.'

'Yeah, but Dad said you let him off too easy and that you coddle him—'

'That's enough, young lady. Do you want to be grounded again?'

Carmen pulled a face, but said nothing more.

'Kids!' Winston said. 'More trouble than they're worth. Not that *you* were ever any trouble. A chatterbox, sure, but you never caused a moment's grief.'

'Did you want to talk about something in particular, Puppa? Only on the phone it sounded urgent—'

'Nuttin' in particular, baby. I just wanted to see you.'

So they chatted about nothing in particular for an hour, and then, when the dregs of his coffee had gone cold, he announced that he'd best be on his way.

'Not without getting something to eat, surely?' Birdie said. She sensed there was something he was not saying, some underlining tension that was gagging him. The problem was she didn't know how to draw him out. Long gone were the days when he would trust her to be the keeper of his secrets.

'I need to get going. It's a long bus ride home—'

'What happened to your car?'

'I sold it.'

Winston's left leg was bouncing up and down beneath the table. The empty cups rattled in the saucers.

'You alright, Puppa?'

'My foot's gone to sleep. Shoe must be too tight.'

He was reaching for his coat when she remembered what she'd wanted to ask him.

'Before you go, Puppa. I wanted to know—'

'Yes?'

'How hard was it? Leaving the island, I mean. Did you know at the time that you'd never go back, or—'

'Not that hard.'

That surprised her. The speed at which he'd responded surprised her. He hadn't even needed to think about it.

'Really? Leaving everyone behind? It seems so . . . it seems crazy now, to think about it.'

'That's just how it was done,' he said nonchalantly, buttoning up his coat. 'We weren't the only family to do it.'

'I know that. But how did you know it was the right thing to do? Especially with everything that – that happened afterwards. *Was* it the right thing to do?'

He looked at her for a few seconds and then spread his hands in capitulation.

'You can't ever really know, baby. You just have to hope for the best.'

She had more to say, but he pulled her into a long hug. He smelled like stale tobacco smoke and carbolic soap, and something, buried beneath all of that, from her childhood, that she couldn't quite place.

'Let's do this again,' she said, and he chucked her beneath the chin and said he'd call her soon.

But a week passed, and then another, and she did not hear from him. She called his house, and then again, and again. Finally, on the fifth try, Pat answered.

'Winston's gone.'

Birdie's heart stopped.

'*Gone*? You mean he's—'

Pat began to cry, a soft, ugly sound.

'He's gone back to Jamaica. He went into Birmingham a fortnight ago to buy a ticket and he's gone. Just upped and left. How could he *do* this to me? How could he do this to *me*?'

*Oh, Pat*, Birdie thought, as she hung up the phone. A sharp, familiar ache began to spread through her body. *It's what he does.*

'Winston's going to be running for the rest of his life,' was Precious's epitaph. 'He won't have any rest until he's dead and buried. And even then, he'll still probably still keep twitching. God help whoever he's buried next to. They'll never get a moment's peace.'

A letter arrived, eventually, with Winston's new address and an entreaty for her continuing good health, but no explanation, no apology. He'd purchased a plot of land in the hills and was building a house, high above the treeline and far, far away from the sea. If Birdie ever wanted to visit she'd be welcome, he'd written, but he wouldn't be coming back.

*How many times*, Birdie wondered, folding the letter up and sealing it back in the envelope, *can one girl lose her father?*

# Seventeen

## *2017*

Saffie was eleven and dancing to her favourite Beyoncé song at the Christmas disco with uninhibited confidence. Boosted by a candy necklace sugar rush, purchased at the tuck table in the school foyer, Saffie swung her hips and flipped her hair in time with the music, a Ribena-stained smile on her lips. But then the song ended, and Saffie noticed Tanika Jenkins, a year ten girl with a fearsome reputation, eyeing her up and down, and her euphoria fizzled out like a damp firework. Tanika waved her over.

'Oi. Titch. Come here.'

Saffie timidly complied.

'What's your name?' Tanika demanded.

'Saffie.'

'You can dance, Saffie!' Tanika said, with a level of congeniality not usually ascribed to her character.

'Yeah, you can really dance,' Imani Sullivan parroted, her stick-on eyelashes hanging on for dear life.

'Oh. Thanks.' Saffie blushed right up to the roots of her curls.

'Can I give you some advice though?'

Tanika leant down so that her glossy lips were inches away from Saffie's face. She smelled like bubblegum and cheap body spray.

'Stop trying to dance like a black girl.'

'Oh. Umm. Okay.'

Saffie turned and scuttled away. For the rest of the night, she was too self-conscious to do more than sway on the spot, and she texted her dad to ask him to pick her up early.

Saffie was fourteen and it was the first day of a new school year. Lewis and Jade, nervous in their oversized blazers, followed their older sister across the playground like anxious ducklings waddling after their mother. At breaktime, Oliver Chapman, the most popular boy in Saffie's year (a rumour was circulating that over the summer holidays he'd dumped Kylie Mitchell for Michaela Porter, a girl in sixth form who had her provisional) approached her in the playground.

'Hey,' he said, and tossed his hair. It was a move he practised in the mirror each morning. 'You're Saffie, right? I want to ask you something.'

Saffie hoped she didn't have food stuck in her teeth. He'd never spoken to her before.

'Sure.'

'Are you adopted?'

'What?'

'Your mom dropped you off this morning, right? She's black. And your brother and sister are black. Must be weird for you, being adopted by black people. Is that even allowed?'

A year and a half later Oliver Chapman spoke to her again. He asked if he could copy her Business Studies homework. She said no. He got an F.

Saffie was eighteen, finally, and staring at herself in the foggy bathroom mirror. She had her dad's eyes, and his ears, and her mouth turned down in the corners just like his did. She turned her face from side to side, trying to find a trace of her mom's genes in her reflection. She smiled. She frowned – *then* she could see something of Carmen, they had the same crease that appeared between their eyebrows – but there was hardly anything, a distinct lack of physical evidence, that linked her to Birdie Brown. But her nanny's family had to be in there *some*where, right? They had provided half of her make-up, they took up half of her family tree. They had to share *some* of the responsibility for the person staring back at her.

She pulled her hair back into a messy bun, then changed her mind and left the curls her nanny loved so much loose. She dressed, then poked her head around her parents' bedroom door.

'I'm going into town,' she said to the two lumpy, sleeping forms beneath the duvet.

'What time is it?' Carmen groaned.

'Nearly eight. See you later,' she replied, and left before Carmen had the chance to call her back.

Her nanny had been in the detention centre for three weeks.

Saffie had a plan to get her out.

She caught the bus to Digbeth, her headphones nestled over her ears, her head bobbing absent-mindedly in time with the music. She watched houses and factories flash by, imagining she was her nanny seeing Birmingham for the first time. She had been amazed, Birdie had said in one of their interviews. She couldn't believe the size of the place compared to where she'd grown up. Saffie had looked Portmore up on a map, but Birdie couldn't remember what street she had lived on. *It's not fair*, Saffie thought as she stared out of the grimy window. She might question her own identity sometimes – or have people question it for her, which was way worse – but no one could ever *take* it from her. Her nanny didn't have that security.

The last time Saffie had been to the Centre for Migrant and Refugee Wellbeing, it had been early September. Now it was

January and the sky was sleet-grey, and she shivered in her old coat. Grace had received a downy white skiing jacket for Christmas and had worn it to school on the first day of term. She'd been so hot that she'd sweated off her foundation and now the collar was stained tawny-orange.

The red-headed receptionist asked if she had an appointment.

'No, but it's an emergency.'

'I'm sorry, his diary is fully booked today—'

'It's okay, Becca.' Marley was striding towards the front desk, a steaming cup of coffee in his hands. 'My first appointment isn't for another ten minutes.'

He offered Saffie a drink. She shook her head.

'I know you're busy, so I'll be quick. I want to tell you about an idea I have. To help Nanny.'

'I've already started the paperwork to appeal her arrest—'

'And that's great. But that could fail, right?'

'Right,' he conceded.

'Which is why I want to launch a campaign. A public one.'

Marley raised one eyebrow. 'What kind of a campaign?'

Saffie could hardly contain her excitement. 'We take Nanny's story public. You said she's not the only one of her generation in this situation, right? But it's being swept under the rug. So, we need to bring it out into the open. Let the whole world know what's happening. But I'll need your help. You have media contacts and stuff, right?'

A large part of her plan depended on the expertise she had presumed Marley could offer, but to her dismay, he shook his head.

'Media contacts? This is a small charity, Saffie, and a woefully underfunded one at that. I doubt anyone in the media knows we exist.'

'But you must know other lawyers who have contacts—' she began desperately. She'd put in so much work and now Marley was going to tell her it had all been for nothing.

'I can ask around, but . . .'

'But it's over before I've even begun?' She blinked rapidly, trying her best not to cry. He'd think she was a total baby. 'That's it?'

He steepled his fingers in thought and brought them up to his chin.

'No,' he said, after a moment, and Saffie's heart soared. 'It's not over. Tell me about this plan of yours. I'll do whatever I can to help.'

* * *

'*Where've* you been, Saff?'

Saffie sailed through the front door, her cheeks flushed and her curls fighting to escape from beneath her bobble hat. She left a trail of coat and scarf and gloves behind her as she flew into the kitchen and made a beeline for the breadbin.

'I went to see Marley,' she replied, her mouth full of bread and peanut butter.

'Don't speak with your mouth full. Why did you go and see Marley?'

Saffie chewed and swallowed. 'Because I told him about my plan to save Nanny.'

'What plan?'

Saffie took a deep breath. It had taken her weeks, but she finally had it all worked out.

'Step one. I am going to make Nanny go viral.'

She had amassed tons of footage from the interviews she had conducted with Birdie over the Christmas holidays, and she'd spent the last week editing it into short videos that she planned to release across social media. Each video covered a different period of her nanny's life, from the story of her birth and her arrival in England to the footage she'd filmed on her phone of the Boxing Day dawn arrest. She had listened, transfixed, as Birdie recalled memories of people and places long gone, her story captured through a camera lens. Her grandmother thought that she'd lived an unremarkable life. Saffie couldn't believe she'd lived through so much.

She pulled up the same video on her phone that she'd shown Marley and pressed play. A black and white photo of Winston, beaming at the camera, one arm raised to shield his eyes from the sun, faded in as Birdie's voice rang out, clear and full of emotion.

*We were separated for a year. My puppa sent letters and presents but I missed him so much. Every day I waited for the letter to say that he was sending for us, and when it finally came I nearly died with happiness.*

'Wow. That looks really professional,' Carmen exclaimed. 'Isn't Angharad's brother doing Film Studies at Bristol? You should get his number from Dec, find out what it's like there—'

Saffie glowered. 'Not the time, Mom.'

'I'm just saying, you clearly have a knack for this sort of thing—'

'I'm going to share one video a day on Facebook and Twitter,' Saffie continued, ignoring her mom. 'And I've come up with a hashtag. #FreeBirdie. It's short and snappy, don't you think?'

'What's a hashtag?' Andy asked, and Carmen shushed him.

'Step two,' Saffie continued, starting on another sandwich, 'I'm going to start a petition to have Nanny released. We need ten thousand signatures just to get a response from the government—'

'Ten *thousand*?'

'The *real* goal is one hundred thousand signatures, which is what we need to get a parliamentary debate—'

'Don't you think that's a bit ambitious?'

Saffie's bottom lip stuck out. 'You're the one who is always telling me to be ambitious.'

'About your future,' Carmen stressed. 'And your education – which is what you should be focused on. Leave all of this to the grown-ups.'

'I'm eighteen,' Saffie responded hotly. 'I'm an adult. And Nanny's in jail, and nothing anyone has done so far has helped.'

Carmen nodded slowly. 'Alright. What's step three?'

Saffie's eyes shone and Carmen realised that the rosy redness in her cheeks was not because of the cold.

'Step three,' Saffie said boldly. 'We stage a protest.'

'A *protest*? How? And where?'

'At Nanny's old flat – in the courtyard bit in the middle. We can get all of her old friends and neighbours involved, and we can make signs—'

'That's not a good idea, love. You can't go starting a riot—'

'It will be a *peaceful* protest Dad, not a riot. I'm thinking it will have more of a carnival vibe, with music, and food.' She turned to her mom with pleading eyes. 'Marley thinks it's a *great* idea. He said his priority is getting Nanny out of the detention centre, but *our* focus should be making sure she's not put back in there again, because the only thing that's going to ensure she can stay in this country is getting her Indefinite Leave to Remain.'

'Alright,' Carmen said, so matter-of-factly that Saffie nearly fell off her stool. 'How do we organise a protest?'

'Carm, we shouldn't be encouraging this—'

'Yes, we should,' Carmen snapped. 'But if you don't want to help, fine. You know where the front door is.'

There was a tense silence, Andy's face frozen in an expression of surprise.

'I'm only saying, Carmen love,' he began cautiously, 'that Saffie has her future to think of. She can't go getting mixed up in political protests—'

'A *peaceful* protest. But you can row with Mom later, okay? We don't have time to waste right now.'

Andy looked from his wife to his daughter. Carmen's expression was stony, Saffie's determined.

'*Please*, Dad.'

Andy tried to catch his wife's eye, but she refused to meet his gaze.

'Fine,' he said eventually, and Saffie squealed a triumphant *yes!* And thundered up the stairs to fetch her laptop.

'But don't expect me to bail you out if you get arrested!' he shouted after her, and forced out a chuckle. Carmen refused to crack even a smile.

* * *

*We couldn't go to salons to get our hair done, so we'd do it ourselves in the home. Our friend Eula-May had her own bonnet hair dryer and we'd sit and gossip as we waited for our turn. We built our own communities that way.*

'She's so cute!' Shabz exclaimed. 'She looks *just* like your mom.'

Saffie and her friends were sat at the back of English. Miss Simmons had stepped out to 'have a talk' with Sam Robinson (he claimed that while his dog hadn't eaten his essay, Buster had done something far more unmentionable *on* the essay and that's why he needed an extension) and Saffie was using the disruption to check the stats of her latest YouTube video.

'How many views so far?'

'One hundred and sixty. And the petition has eighty signatures. It's nowhere near enough.'

'She's had such an interesting life,' Grace said. 'My grandparents are *so* boring.'

'Didn't your grandad serve in the war?'

'Yeah, but he didn't *do* anything. He was stationed in Bournemouth the whole time—'

'That better not be a phone I see, ladies.'

Saffie sheepishly pocketed her phone and tried to turn her attention back to Miss Simmons and the symbolic importance of Desdemona's strawberry-spotted handkerchief, but all she could think about was how there was still so much to do, and how little time there was left. She had posters to make, a speech to write, media contacts to conjure up . . . she made a mental note to borrow Shabz's notes after class and turned to a fresh page in her exercise book. Her grandmother was more important than sixth form she thought, as she began yet another to-do list.

*I won't let you down, Nanny.*

* * *

'Dear Ms Cartland, MP,' Saffie read aloud. She was pacing up and down in the living room, reading from a sheet of paper that had been scribbled on so many times she could barely make out what she'd written.

'Do you need to say "MP"?' Carmen asked.

'It sounds better, don't you think? More formal.'

'It definitely does,' Andy agreed, his head bobbing up and down, like the nodding dog he kept on the dash of his van.

'Since when do you know anything about writing to MPs?' Carmen remarked.

Saffie chewed on her lip. The skin in the corners of her mouth was chapped and sore. Her parents always bickered, but this was different. Her mom was snapping every time her dad opened his mouth lately. She didn't have time to worry about them though. They could figure their own shit out. *She* had to save her nanny.

'I need something to grab this woman's attention,' she said. 'I've been emailing her every day since Nanny was arrested. I haven't had a response yet—'

'We can use that,' Andy said suddenly. 'Name and shame her. Birdie's one of her loyal constituents and she can't be arsed to reply? I'm sure the papers will want to know about *that*.'

'Dad . . .' Saffie's eyes boggled. 'That's fucking *brilliant*!'

'Language,' he said automatically, but an unfamiliar feeling of pride swelled in his chest. He looked over at his wife to gauge her reaction. She looked right through him.

'Carry on Saff,' she said, unsmiling.

'Okay. Dear Ms Cartland, MP, I am writing to invite you to join our protest—'

* * *

'Hello! I'm Rita from number forty-three and this is Saffie and we'd like to invite you to a protest we're having for Birdie Brown—'

Up and down the balconies of Clent House and the surrounding blocks, residents were receiving word of the upcoming 'Free Birdie' block party. Marley had stressed the importance of getting the residents of the estate on board, and so they'd been going door to door, doling out leaflets and the promise of free food. The majority of Birdie's former neighbours were eager to lend their support.

'I had no idea she'd been taken! Last I heard she went to live with family.'

'It's wicked what they'll do to folk. You can count me in, chick.'

'We'll be there. Birdie's such a nice lady. She watched my kids when I had to run my eldest to A&E once. You got a pan stuck on your head, didn't you, Alfie?'

Saffie bit back a giggle as she handed the mother of the unfortunate Alfie a leaflet and moved on to the next door. Only three floors to go . . .

Not everyone, though, was willing to participate.

'My own situation – it is not good,' one older Pakistani man said sympathetically. 'What if they see me on TV? I cannot risk getting in trouble.'

Saffie thanked him anyway and moved on. The next door was opened by an elderly black woman dressed in a sleeveless nightgown, the flesh hanging heavily from her bare arms. Saffie introduced herself and held out a leaflet. The woman didn't take it.

'Birdie shoulda had her papers in order. I had mine in order, and I'm not in jail.'

'It's not her fault, she—'

The woman closed the door. Saffie gritted her teeth and moved on.

* * *

It was the night before the protest and the kitchen was a mess. Rita was at the stove, stirring a vat of vegetable samosa filling, while Angharad diced onions and Carmen crimped the edges of golden-yellow patties, Levi Roots' cookbook propped up in front of her by a tin of tomatoes. Michelle had already dropped off four stainless steel serving trays of school cake. Tegan was washing up, while Lewis dried and Declan put away the clean crockery. Jade, Grace and Shabz were in the conservatory, daubing giant letters onto placards. Jaxon was asleep on the settee and Saffie was upstairs, practising her speech in the bathroom mirror.

'Next batch is ready for the oven,' Carmen said, her face shiny from the heat.

'Carm love?' Andy appeared at her elbow and she felt her neck crinkle with irritation. 'Can I do anything? Do you want another cup of tea?'

'No thank you.'

Andy lowered his voice and dipped his nose towards hers. 'Is everything alright with you?'

She looked past him and tutted. 'Declan, that's the fifth samosa you've eaten. Leave some for tomorrow please.'

'Sorry Mom,' Declan said guiltily, wiping his fingers on a turmeric-stained tea towel. 'I'm starving. Shall I order a takeaway for everyone?'

Carmen mopped her brow with her forearm. 'Could you do me a favour first? Nanny's friend from bingo said she's got some extra urns we could use for tea and coffee, but she can't get them out of the loft by herself. Could you go round and give her a hand?'

'I'll go,' Andy said eagerly.

'I asked Declan.'

'But I want to help.'

'You can't go clambering up someone's loft. You have a bad back. *Apparently*.'

'What's that supposed to mean?'

'Nothing. If you want to go, fine. I don't care either way.'

She pushed past him and left the kitchen. Andy hurried after her.

'Carmen. Wait. What's wrong?'

Carmen, one foot already on the bottom stair, stopped and turned to face her husband. Overhead, Saffie's voice filtered through the open bathroom doorway. *My grandmother was born in Jamaica, a Commonwealth country that was once part of the British Empire . . .*

'I need the loo.'

'That's not what's wrong with you. You've been off for days. Weeks, even. What is it, love?'

He touched her cheek with his hand. *I could tell him*, she thought. She could tell him about Dean and the ridiculous little fantasy she'd built up in her head – she'd searched for flights to Toronto, for Christ's sake – only for it all to disintegrate, like candy floss, into a sickly, shameful mess. He'd ignored nine messages in a row and then yesterday, he'd blocked her on Facebook. She'd cried in the shower, where no one could hear, but she couldn't wash away the humiliation.

Or she could tell him that Craig was threatening to fire her because she'd had one too many 'family emergencies' for his liking, that she was 'letting her personal life affect her job performance'. Or she could tell him, once and for all, that she'd had enough. Of all of it. Of being a daughter, a mother, the breadwinner, his wife. That he was as useful to her as her broken gravy boat. That lately, whenever she looked at him, she felt absolutely nothing at all . . .

'Are you worried about tomorrow?'

She exhaled through her nose. 'Yes Andy. I'm worried about tomorrow.'

He wrapped his arms around her and squeezed her tightly. 'Don't be. This protest will do the trick, you'll see. Saffie's done brilliantly. All the organising and the whatnot. I think she gets it from you.'

She didn't respond.

'Right. I best go get those urns. And I'll go to the chippy on the way home, how does that sound?'

He kissed her and strode confidently out the front door, car keys jingling in his hands. Two seconds later he came back.

'Carm?' he asked sheepishly, poking his head around the door. 'Where does this friend of your mom's live?'

* * *

The morning of the protest dawned bright and cold.

'It's freezing,' Shabz said, tucking the ends of her hijab into her coat. 'Do you think people will show up?'

Saffie looked around the courtyard. Not a single person had come out yet – doors were tightly closed, curtains were drawn, as though they didn't want to see. As though they were shutting her out.

'They'll come,' she said, sounding far more confident than she felt, handing Lewis a stack of placards. They'd made about a hundred – Saffie had spent all her Christmas and birthday money in WHSmith on poster boards and red, white and blue paint.

*Free Birdie!*

*Shame on the Home Office*

*She was invited*

'Are we ready?' Rita asked, peeling tin foil off a tray of samosas. Andy's decorating table had been set up for the refreshments, and Declan was assembling a rudimentary sound system out of the boot of his car.

Saffie nodded. Her eyes were burning from lack of sleep, but her body was thrumming with adrenaline.

*This has to work.*

Grace arrived first, her parents standing awkwardly on the sidelines in their cashmere coats until Grace gave them placards, which they gamely held aloft, followed by Marley, his boyfriend and all their friends, then Michelle, pushing Claudette in a hired wheelchair, and then Miss Simmons and Mr Danks, head of sixth form, and more of Saffie's school friends, and then the Bingo Babs, wearing oversized T-shirts emblazoned with Birdie's face over their coats, and then, as slowly as water dripping from a leaky tap, people began to trickle down from the flats.

'Declan. Turn the music up,' Saffie declared.

She had stayed up until two thirty curating the perfect playlist. Soon the courtyard was humming with energy; despite the chill in the air, the atmosphere was happy, and hopeful. There were more people than she'd expected – among the crowd, Saffie spotted the woman from the top floor who'd refused to participate. She was holding a placard high above her head and whining her waist to "Uptown Top Ranking".

Marley pushed his way through a sea of 'Free Birdie!' posters to the refreshment table. 'This is a great turnout! You should be really proud of yourself – I'm sure Birdie is.'

But Saffie wasn't satisfied.

'The MP didn't show. I was really hoping she'd come.'

'You can't trust politicians,' Andy said sagely, swigging

from a flask of tea. He'd put a little rum in it. Birdie was right, it *did* taste good.

'It's still early, Saff,' Carmen said comfortingly. 'Give her a chance, she might—'

'Saff!' Angharad rushed over, clapping her white mittens in excitement.

'Some people from the news are here – there are cameras and everything!' She beamed, her front teeth protruding slightly over her bottom lip. 'They want to speak to you!'

The protest had not just attracted a news crew. A journalist from the *Daily Smethwick News* came over and introduced himself, expressing surprise that the 'Ms Lloyd' who'd emailed him was a sixth-former.

'I'll be happy to give you an interview,' Saffie said, trying to sound as grown-up as she could. 'But I have to give a speech in a minute. Help yourself to refreshments.'

'You never told me you'd invited the papers!' Carmen hissed out of the corner of her mouth.

'I didn't want to tell anyone in case no one turned up.'

But her fears had been for nothing. As she made her way up to Rita's flat, she was besieged on all sides by people offering their support, or congratulations, or expressing their disgust at Birdie's treatment. The size of the crowd overwhelmed her. The index cards in her coat pocket seemed to burn a hole right through to her chest. She felt sick.

*Nanny's relying on you*, she scolded herself. *You can't back down now.*

Rita was waiting outside her flat, a microphone wire trailing from an extension cord that disappeared into her living room. Saffie accepted it, her hands shaking.

'Testing,' she whispered, feeling silly. No one in the courtyard below paid any attention to her.

'Testing,' she said again, a little louder. Declan cut the music and gave her a thumbs up.

*You can do anything you want to, my girl*, she heard her nanny say in her ear. She reached into her pocket for her cards.

'Hello. Thank you all for coming today.' Her voice sounded funny – high-pitched and girlish. She cleared her throat and gripped the microphone a little harder. 'You all know why we're here. Birdie Brown, my grandmother, used to live here. It was her home, and this was her community. She had to leave because she couldn't pay her rent. She couldn't pay her rent because her pension had been stopped, and her pension was stopped because the government had decided she was an illegal immigrant.'

In the courtyard below, a sea of people looked up at her. There must have been a hundred people – more than a hundred – packed shoulder to shoulder, shifting silently on their feet.

'My grandmother was born in Jamaica, a Commonwealth country that was once part of the British Empire. She moved to England in the 1950s with her parents. They were invited by the government, who called them British citizens and encouraged them to build new lives in the UK. But then something changed. The government decided it had let in too many people, and they didn't want them here anymore.'

A ripple of anger washed over the crowd.

'The government is trying to backtrack. They're removing British citizenship for anyone who wasn't born here – people like my nanny. They want to deport her. She's sitting in a detention centre right now, waiting for them to put her on a flight back to a country she hasn't seen since she was seven years old. She's sixty-eight.'

The ripple grew bigger, like a swell about to burst over the shore.

'My nanny has lived in Birmingham her whole life, practically. Her whole life she was British until someone told her she wasn't. We can't let them deport her because of someone else's mistake. We can't let them deport her because the government says she doesn't belong. She *does* belong. This is her home, and we want her to stay.'

There was a brief moment of silence, and then the crowd erupted in applause. Saffie breathlessly handed the microphone to Marley and fell back against the wall, out of sight from the crowd below. She didn't think her legs would hold her up any longer.

'My name is Marley, and I work for a charity where immigrants can get free advice and support. There's a lot that we can do to raise awareness and help not only Birdie but others in her situation—'

Carmen pulled her in for a tight hug. 'You did brilliantly!'

'I missed out loads. I couldn't concentrate on my notes.'

'That doesn't matter. Your nan will be so proud of you.'

As Marley wrapped up his speech to more applause, Saffie held out her hand for the microphone again.

'Sorry, me again. I forgot to say, you can follow #FreeBirdie on social media for updates and to add your name to the petition.' She felt more confident, this time. 'That's a petition to get the Home Office to release Birdie Brown from the detention centre and to reinstate her British citizenship. Thanks.'

As she made her way back to the refreshments table, the news reporter was waiting for her.

'Can we have a quick interview?'

'Oh, sure.'

Declan had turned the music back up and the atmosphere became even more electric. Saffie leaned in closer to the reporter's microphone.

'And you organised this whole protest by yourself?'

Saffie shook her head. 'I had a lot of help, from family and friends. But this is a *community,* and communities take care of their own. All these people came here today in support of my nanny.'

'And what are the next steps?'

'We want to take this all the way to parliament,' Saffie said boldly, staring straight into the camera. 'We invited the local MP today, but I guess she doesn't care about her constituents.'

'Saffie!' Carmen mouthed from behind the camera, mortified. Saffie flashed an innocent smile.

'And finally, does your grandmother know that so many people have come out to support her today?'

Saffie felt a lump rise in her throat. 'She will. Love you, Nanny.'

After the interview, Saffie spoke to three different journalists and posed for photographs. They made her feel ridiculous – *no don't smile, look angry, that's right, hold the placard up a little higher* – but she was willing to do whatever they wanted to spread the message. Shortly after that, the police arrived. Four uniformed officers stepped out of their vehicles and told them they had to disperse.

'We have every right to be here!' Saffie said. 'We're not causing any trouble.'

'Do you have a permit for this protest?' one of the officers asked.

'It's not a protest,' Andy said quickly, stepping in front of his daughter to shield her from view. 'It's a street party. If this was for the pissing queen you'd have no problem with it, but when it's a bunch of black people you have to shit all over it—'

'You need to calm down.'

Andy puffed out his chest. '*You* calm down, mate. We're not doing anything wrong.'

Carmen tugged on his sleeve. 'Shut up, you'll get yourself arrested!'

'Rather me than Saffie,' he replied valiantly. 'Or *you*, for that matter.'

He turned back to the police officer. 'I'm the one who organised this so if you have a problem, you can blame me. Don't go hassling anyone else, alright? This is all on me. I organised this whole thing by myself.'

'*Andy*!' Carmen gasped.

'It's okay, Dad,' Saffie said, stepping out from behind him. 'Rita, is that mic still in your flat?'

She addressed the crowd again, thanking them for their support and urging them to leave calmly and quietly. There were some boos from the crowd, displeased that a good time had been cut short, but they left good-naturedly and in high spirits.

'You've done a great job,' Marley assured her, later that afternoon. They were cleaning up the courtyard (*we can't leave a single scrap of rubbish behind*, Saffie lectured), stuffing paper cups and discarded napkins into bin bags, with the help of Tyrone Middleton and handful of other residents from the flats.

'I wish Susan Cartland had shown up,' Saffie grumbled again, and Andy gave her arm a squeeze.

'Don't worry, love. You told her off on the evening news. I'd love to see her face when she watches it!'

Saffie scrunched up her nose. '*If* she watches it,' she said. The adrenaline was wearing off and she was left with nothing but a niggle of anxiety in the pit of her stomach. 'I don't know. Have we done enough?'

* * *

On Monday morning, Saffie walked into school feeling like a celebrity, albeit a reluctant one. The attention embarrassed her, especially when Mr Danks called her to the front of the assembly to praise her efforts.

'The whole school is behind you,' he said warmly, shaking her by the hand. 'Does this mean you've decided on a career in politics?'

'Actually . . . I was thinking law. Human rights.'

A week passed, and the online petition gathered steam. She hadn't got the national coverage she'd been hoping for, however, and Saffie was fraught with nerves. She'd posted her final interview with her nanny the night before. The camera zoomed in on her face, worn and shellshocked, staring at a spot on the kitchen wall.

'What does "home" mean to you, Nanny?'

Birdie didn't respond. Saffie tried a different question.

'Is England your home?'

Birdie looked right into the camera. '*Of course it is. Why wouldn't it be?*'

Saffie pulled out her mobile at lunchtime to check how many views it had gotten. The phone lit up with hundreds of notifications – likes, more likes, media requests, racist abuse, more likes – 'Oh my God! Susan Cartland has emailed me!'

Dear Saffron,

My apologies for not getting in touch sooner. I am sorry I was unable to attend the vigil for your grandmother, but I commend your efforts to spare one of my constituents from an unjust punishment. Like you, I think your grandmother's treatment at the hands of the opposition is deplorable and I shall be personally intervening to do everything I can to halt her removal.

'She only cares because you made her look bad,' Grace said, reading over Saffie's shoulder.

'So? She's going to help! I need to call my mom—'

Carmen picked up on the second ring.

'Mom, guess what? I have the *best* news . . .'

She tailed off. Her mom was crying.

'Mom? What's wrong?'

'Oh, *Saffie*. I have something to tell you.'

# Eighteen

## *2010*

The hospice smelled of nutmeg and cinnamon scented potpourri, and it reminded Birdie of spiced buns. Auntie Luce always made a couple of fat buns at Easter, the rich dough bursting with plump raisins, and she would slather each slice with creamy butter and top them with cheese. She wondered if Precious remembered.

Her mumma was dying.

The hospice staff had gone out of their way to make her final weeks more comfortable. They even remembered to call her Precious, not Amaretta, as was written in her notes, because she no longer recognised the name she had been born with.

The warning signs had been easy to ignore. Precious would misplace her keys, she would forget names and faces. Small, insignificant indications she would chalk up to old age, though she was still an active member of her church and a well-known figure in her community. Precious thought she and Leslie would have had more time, time enough to dust off their plans and spend their final days in the warmth of the island's embrace. But in 2007 Leslie died, a sudden heart attack while he pruned his beloved roses. The night before the funeral, Precious tore every last item of clothing out of the wardrobe, flinging coats and dresses and shirts to the floor, a storm of cotton and silk and seething ire. She wouldn't go back to bed, she told Birdie, until she'd found Leslie's good tie.

'The one he wore at our wedding,' she cried, her fingers clawing through his drawers. 'The blue one with the orange stripes. That's the one I want him to be buried in.'

Birdie crossed the room and touched her mother's arm. She was freezing.

'Mumma. He's wearing his favourite tie. We dropped it off at the funeral parlour two days ago.'

Precious made a noise of disbelief in the back of her throat.

'He was wearing it when we went to see him this morning, remember?'

Precious put her hand to her head, as though waking up from a trance.

'Right. Right . . . would you look at this mess? I need to tidy up—'

'We'll do that tomorrow, Mumma. Come on.'

Birdie guided her mother back towards her bed and settled her beneath the Laura Ashley duvet, then climbed in after her, nestling her cheek in the hollow of Precious's back.

'I'm not tired,' Precious said. Birdie hugged her tighter.

'Sleep, Mumma. You need to sleep.'

Birdie put that incident down to stress, but when Precious almost set fire to the kitchen, burning a pot of rice she had no memory of putting on the hob, her daughter insisted they go to the doctor. A swift series of tests and scans followed. Birdie spent her sixtieth birthday in a neurologist's office as he outlined the next steps, Precious's hand clasped in hers. The neurologist handed her a leaflet. *Living with Dementia*.

The same day, Birdie moved in with her mother. She had experience after all, in lifting and cleaning and feeding adults rendered incapable of looking after themselves. It was a stroke of luck really, that Birdie could look after her the way Precious had once looked after her. She knew about *needs assessments* and *care plans* and the small things she could do to alleviate – not cure, there was no cure – the symptoms. Birdie did the best she could, but in the end, no amount of mothering could stop the inevitable. No amount of fighting would keep her mumma alive.

She visited the hospice every day and sat by Precious's bed for hours. It became her second home. It was funny, how time seemed to work in that place. She was running out. She had too much. She sat and she ruminated, because what else was there to do? As she watched Precious sleep, her arms, thin as twigs, resting on top of the crisp white sheets, she thought about all the questions that would go unanswered. The questions she never thought to ask her mumma until it was too late. Had she been a good daughter? Was she a good mother? Had she made the right choices?

Birdie took her mother's limp hand in hers and brought it to her cheek. 'Tell me I did the right thing, Mumma.'

Precious slept on and Birdie was left to her memories. One kept coming back to her, though she tried to ignore it, tried to think of something else, to focus on the rise and fall of her mother's chest . . .

The day Jimmy left her.

Had it really been twelve years ago? She remembered how cold it had been in the run-up to Christmas. How she'd shivered and complained about her old, cold bones (funny, how'd thought of herself as an old woman *then*) and so Jimmy suggested they take a holiday, just the two of them. He went to the travel agent and brought home one of every brochure, and they flipped through the glossy pages together, admiring the sun-drenched possibilities displayed on each page.

'We could learn to flamenco dance in Mallorca,' Jimmy said. 'We could ride a gondola down the Grand Canal. We could hire a tandem and cycle down the Champs-Élysées—'

'Don't be daft. A tandem, at your age?'

'Cheek! I'm not that much older than you. But it doesn't have to be Paris. We can go anywhere you want. I mean it. The garage is finally in good shape, and I can leave Kevin in charge for a week or two.'

'Not Scott?'

Jimmy frowned, but he didn't say anything.

'How can he learn to be responsible if you don't give him any responsibilities?' she probed. He began to flip faster through the pages.

'Because he doesn't want any responsibilities, Birdie. You know that. He's an adult but he acts like he's still a bairn.'

Scott, although in his mid-twenties, lived with his parents, after turning up on their doorstep a few months before and asking if he could 'crash' there for a while. He had no money and no job and Jimmy, after much cajoling from Birdie, had taken him on at the garage. At first, the arrangement worked well, and Birdie had been sure that in time Scott would do them both proud. Perhaps he could even take over the business one day. *Jimmy and Son's Garage and Car Repair* – but then Scott started slacking, showing up late and leaving early with a catalogue of half-baked excuses. Jimmy bemoaned his lack of work ethic. Scott accused Jimmy of giving him the dirtiest, least desirable tasks. Every day there was a new disagreement.

'He just needs a bit of encouragement.'

'Encouragement? What he needs is a kick up the bahookie. I warned you, Birdie, but you didn't want to listen. You coddled him so much the boy can't stand on his own two feet.'

'Better than him being locked up,' was Birdie's usual rebuttal. 'Better than him being dead.'

It had been hard, raising a black boy in Birmingham. They had police brutality to contend with, blatant bigotry to endure – they were told to turn the other cheek, but some had instead had their heads turned by gangs who promised camaraderie and safety in numbers. How many times had Handsworth been set on fire by rioters? How many mothers had lost their sons? Birdie had promised she wouldn't let her boy go down that path. When it came to Scott, she had always insisted that she knew best.

'He's afraid of hard work,' Jimmy continued. 'I don't know where he gets it from.'

Birdie changed the subject.

'How about a river cruise in Germany? You'd look handsome in a pair of lederhosen.'

Jimmy looked at her out of the corner of his eye. 'You think I'm handsome?'

She smirked. 'Jimmy Milne, you're the handsomest man this side of Ballingry. Even if you are too old to ride a tandem. Now come here and give me a kiss.'

'I'll give you more than a kiss, woman,' he cried, and pounced on her. Birdie shrieked and laughed all the way up the stairs.

But they never did go on holiday, did they? No, she'd tidied the brochures away onto the bookshelf, hidden on top of a stack of books by Jeremy Clarkson and a Princess Diana biography. Birdie found them again months after Jimmy had left, corners folded over, swanky resorts circled in biro. Jimmy had written *Birdie's birthday?* next to a Caribbean cruise that had sailed from Southampton in May. She'd crumpled up the brochures in a fit of anger and thrown them away.

He'd left in 1998. Birdie could remember every minute of that day: the garish Christmas songs on the radio; fighting another granny for the last Furby in Woolworths; checking in on Carmen, who had high blood pressure and had been placed on bedrest for the last month of her pregnancy; helping Declan write a letter to Father Christmas (*are you sure you don't want to ask him for a* green *Furby, Dec?*) and worrying about Scott and Jimmy. There was something wrong at home. Some kind of tension between father and son that was simmering beneath the yuletide spirit. Like some horrible advent, it came to its climax that day.

What she remembered most was Jimmy shouting. *That's strange*, she thought, as she turned her key in the lock. *Jimmy never shouts.*

'This is the last straw, Scott!'

'I didn't do it!'

Birdie rushed into the house. Jimmy and Scott were stood nose to nose in the centre of the living room, staring each other down like stray dogs about to fight over table scraps. The lights on the tree twinkled in time to a mechanical-sounding tune, "We Wish You a Merry Christmas" on an endless loop. It would be many Christmases before Birdie could listen to that song again.

'What is going on?'

'Ask your son,' Jimmy spat. The tips of his ears were bright red. 'Ask your son where he got the money for that flashy Mazda parked outside.'

'It's not mine, I told you—'

'What are you talking about, Jimmy?'

'He's been stealing from us.' He sounded as though an invisible hand was crushing his windpipe. 'First it was car parts—'

'That wasn't me! It was Kevin—'

'And then I checked our bank statement today. *Five grand* is missing from our savings account. Five grand, Birdie. He's taken the lot.'

'I said I didn't do it!'

'You're a liar *and* a thief! After everything your mother and I have done for you!'

Birdie wedged herself in between them, forcing Jimmy to take a step backwards. They both towered over her.

'Everybody needs to calm down!' she insisted, placing gentle palms on Jimmy's chest, but he angrily shook her off.

'I won't stand for this Birdie. He's taken all of our savings. Every penny we were saving for that holiday. He's nothing but a lying sack of shit.'

'It wasn't me!' Scott said. It came out like a childish whine.

'Then who was it?'

Scott licked his dry lips. 'Carmen. Or Andy. *He's* never got any money—'

'Oh, Scott.' It sounded ridiculous even to Birdie's ears, and Jimmy shook his head in disbelief.

'Listen to him. He'll blame the milkman next. Why don't you be a man and own up to it, son?'

Scott puffed out his chest and rolled back his shoulders, as though he were winding up to throw a punch.

'Son? I'm not your son. You're not my *real* dad.'

'And that's why you thought it was okay to steal from me?' He grabbed Scott's chin and forced him to look at Birdie. 'She's your mother. What's your excuse for stealing from *her*?'

Scott wrenched himself free from Jimmy's grip.

'Touch me again,' he threatened, and Jimmy laughed.

'Think you're a big man, do you?'

'I'm more of a man than you. You're just some chump who shacked up with my mom and raised someone else's kids. You're a loser. You're a sad old man—'

It all happened so fast. Suddenly Scott was flat on his back, his nose a bloody mess. Birdie dropped to her knees and pressed a tissue to her son's broken nose.

'You're pathetic!' Scott screamed, blood and snot bubbling up in his nose. It gushed out between his fingers. 'You're a pathetic old man! I hate you!'

Birdie wanted him to stop, wanted to put her hand over his mouth, like she used to do when they hid from his father behind the living room curtain. His giggles would always give the game away. Only no one was laughing now. She looked up at Jimmy. His face was white, with two pink spots on his cheeks.

'Get him out of my sight, Birdie.'

'He needs to go to A&E,' she began, but Scott struggled to his feet.

'Don't worry, I'm leaving.' Blood dripped down the front of his jumper. A drop, and then another, splashed on the living room rug.

'Scott, don't—'

The front door slammed. An icy silence fell, like a blanket of snow. Birdie shivered, despite the fact she was still wearing her coat.

'I've never seen you like that before.'

'Can you blame me?' Jimmy's hands still shook. 'He's not welcome back in this house, Birdie. I mean it. The boy is a thief.'

'Do you have proof that it was him? It could have been – I don't know, hackers, or—'

'Hackers? This isn't *Mission* bloody *Impossible.* It was Scott. The car parts too. Come on, you know this. Or are you going to let him manipulate you again?'

'He said he didn't do it,' she said helplessly, and Jimmy ran his fingers through his hair in frustration.

'For the love of God, Birdie. Will you take the blinkers off? The boy's in serious trouble this time.'

'What do you mean?'

'I don't know all of it. I don't think I *want* to know all of it,' he began slowly. He told her about strange cars pulling up outside of the garage, Scott's odd behaviour and his sudden, ostentatious displays of wealth.

'New car, new clothes . . . I was wondering where he'd found the money. Now I know.'

'And you kept all of this from me?'

'I was trying to *protect* you. You were busy with Carmen. I thought I could sort him out myself.'

'Your idea of sorting him out is hitting him?'

Jimmy flexed his hand. His knuckles were flecked with blood.

'That was a mistake. But you heard the things he was saying, Birdie—'

'He didn't mean it. He'll apologise.'

Jimmy looked incensed. 'An *apology*? I don't want a bleeding apology! I want the money he took from us! And if he doesn't have it, I want to know who does. First thing tomorrow I'm calling the police.'

Birdie was horrified. 'Jimmy, you can't. I won't let you.'

'Just like you never let me discipline him,' he snapped. 'What if he goes after your mother's savings next? Or robs a bank?'

'He's not going to rob a bank, don't be so bloody daft—'

'He has to learn there are consequences to his actions—'

'He'll pay us back! He did last time!'

'He took fifty quid from your purse, last time. This time it was *five grand*. How do you think he's going to pay that back?'

'I don't know.' She wrung her hands. 'But I'm not going to hand Scott over to the police. You said he's in trouble, so we need to help him. He's our *son*.'

'He's not my son,' Jimmy said flatly.

'Don't say that.' Birdie rushed to his side and tried to take his hands in hers. 'You don't mean that.'

'Why shouldn't I mean it? It's the truth. You've never really let me be his dad, have you? Not when it mattered. You always kept me at arm's length.'

'Of course you're his dad,' Birdie insisted. 'Of course you are.'

'I always tried to be respectful. I never wanted to overstep my bounds because I knew you'd been through a lot.' He looked at her. 'I did everything I could to show you that you could trust me. But you never really did, did you?'

'Of course I trust you—'

'You always said you knew best. That mother's instinct trumped anything I could offer, that I didn't understand what it was like for him. I might not be black, Birdie, but I know a thing or two about being a man. I could have helped you if you'd let me.'

'Help me now,' she said.

'It's too late for that. The boy doesn't respect me, and he never will. And I might not be his real dad, but I deserve respect in my own home. Scott is no longer welcome under this roof.'

'But where will he go?'

'I don't care. Just as long as it's far from this house.'

'What about me?' Her legs began to tremble. 'Do you expect me to never see him again?'

He folded his arms and looked away. 'You can do what you like. As long as it doesn't involve me. Or my money. What's left of it.'

'And you think I'd be able to come home to you every day, knowing you put my son out? You think I could sleep next to you at night, not knowing where my son is?'

'He has to learn. He can't keep running back to Mommy expecting you to fix it every time,' Jimmy said firmly, but Birdie shook her head, anger rising up in her chest.

'I'll try, though Jimmy. I'll try to fix it, every time. I am *never* going to turn my back on my kids. And if you're asking me to choose between you and my son then . . . then you know my answer.'

He looked at her, his face unreadable. 'Right you are,' he said slowly. 'Right you are.'

She regretted it immediately, the things she said to him. *Fine. Leave. Some father you are. Just like Winston. Just like Tony. I don't need you. I never needed you.* By the time she'd calmed down enough to think straight, it was too late. He'd gone.

She sat at the dining room table for hours. She felt nothing but numbness, a cold, sinking feeling, as his parting words played on a loop in her head. *I won't let that boy make a fool out of me any longer*, he'd said. *Or you.*

*Or you.*

*Or you.*

Sometime around three in the morning, she heard the front door open and she lifted her head from the table.

'Jimmy?'

It was Scott. The swollen flesh of his nose looked shiny and tight, like a pig skin stretched over a drum.

'Why are you still up? You weren't waiting for me, were you?'

'Where have you been?'

'Just . . . out. Is Dad here?'

'He's gone.' Her voice cracked. 'We need to talk.'

'Mom. It's late. You should go to bed.'

'No, Scott. Sit down.'

'Let me just get a glass of milk—'

'I said sit down.'

He obeyed. He looked nervous, like a little boy about to get a telling off, and Birdie's heart broke a little bit more.

'I need to know the truth,' she said.

'I didn't—'

'The truth!' she shouted. Scott bit his lip. He lowered his eyes. 'Did you steal from your father? From me?'

'Yes.' It was barely a whisper.

'Why?'

'I . . . I owed someone some money. But I promise, I'll pay you and Dad back, every single penny—'

'How much did you owe? Five grand?'

He floundered helplessly.

'How much, Scott?'

'Ten,' he whispered, and Birdie reeled.

'Ten thousand pounds?'

'I'm sorry—'

'You could have talked to us. We could have helped you!'

'I'm so sorry, Mom.'

He broke down in tears. Birdie hadn't seen him cry like that since he'd fallen over in the school playground aged twelve and broken his arm. He'd been so stoic in front of his friends, but the minute Birdie swung through the sick bay doors he'd begun to sob in pain, clinging onto her with his good arm.

'I didn't mean for any of this to happen, you have to believe me. I don't know what to do—'

'We'll sort it. I promise,' she said. Scott looked up at her, his eyes full of pathetic hope, and she wrapped her arms around him.

'I'll never do it again,' he cried. 'I'll never do it again.'

Jimmy had called it manipulation, but Birdie knew better. He was just a lost, lonely boy in desperate need of comfort. And she was his mother. She would be the one to comfort him. She wasn't going to walk out on him now.

She was not the sort of parent who left.

* * *

Precious stirred and opened her eyes.

'Winston? Is that you?'

'It's me, Mumma,' Birdie said. She scooted her chair closer to the hospital bed. 'It's Birdie.'

Precious reached out a frail, bony hand. It was hard to imagine those were the same hands that had brushed Birdie's hair, spooned mashed yams into her mouth and slapped her across the back of her legs when she misbehaved.

'My dress was lined with pins. Do you remember?'

Fragments of the past came back to Precious in quick and fleeting flashes, the edges so sharp they cut her to ribbons.

'I remember,' Birdie lied.

'You have some nerve showing up like this. I should never have married you. I should have married Errol.'

'Your sweetheart . . . he died, didn't he? In the war.'

'He didn't die,' Precious half-whispered. 'He was stationed in America and decided he didn't want to come back to me.'

'I'm sorry Mumma.'

'Why do they all run away? Why aren't they content to stay at home, the way God intended? Why don't they want to stay with me?'

'Hush, Mumma. It's okay.'

'Auntie Luce doesn't like you. She told me not to go through with it. But I love you. You can be enough for me and I can be enough for you. Remember what you said?'

Birdie wondered if her mother remembered that Winston had been dead for the last ten years. Perhaps she did. Perhaps she was talking to his duppy, standing at the foot of the bed, unseen to all eyes apart from hers. It was hard to imagine her parents reuniting in the afterlife. Perhaps it was easy to find forgiveness there, if such a place existed. Birdie hoped so, for her mother's sake.

Birdie wished she'd had more opportunities to tell her mumma how much she meant to her. How in awe she was of her. To thank her for everything she had sacrificed. She'd tried her hardest to be a good mother, like Precious had been. Was her mumma proud of her? It was too late to ask now.

Precious sighed and fell back against the pillows, her eyes closed in a fitful slumber. Birdie stroked her hand and wondered what else her mumma might say to her puppa, if she had the chance. *What would you say to Jimmy if you were the one lying there?* the little voice in the back of her head said. She tried to push it aside, but it persisted.

*If it was your last chance, what would you say?*

'I did the right thing,' she said, aloud. And then, 'Come back. I need you.'

* * *

The crematorium was packed. Standing room only, with people jostling for space. The curtains closed around her mumma and Birdie let Carmen lead her, as docile as a lamb, past an extravagant display of bouquets to where the cars were waiting. Their relationship had always been as tempestuous as the seas: they fought, then they made up, then they fought again. Carmen had been so angry about Jimmy that she'd threatened to keep Birdie away from her unborn granddaughter, only changing her mind somewhere between the tenth and eleventh contractions. But Carmen, it had to be said, had been Birdie's rock those past few weeks. Scott was nowhere to be seen. He showed up halfway through the wake, walking into the banqueting hall with a girl on his arm.

'Nice of you to show up,' Carmen hissed.

Scott rolled his eyes. 'Denise, this is my sister. Her gob's so big it's got its own postcode.'

Birdie intervened before Carmen had a chance to retort.

'Scott! There you are. What happened to you? You were supposed to read your nanny's favourite poem.'

Scott kissed her on the cheek. Birdie thought she smelled beer on his breath.

'We had car trouble. I'm sorry.'

'Don't worry, Declan read it in the end. I'm just glad you're here now.'

'Is there any food?' Denise asked, tugging on her mini skirt. At least, Birdie thought to herself, the skirt was black.

'There's curry and rice and plantain. Carmen, will you fix Denise a plate?'

Carmen unenthusiastically complied, leaving Birdie alone with her son. Tension settled between them.

'How's the pub?' she asked. Birdie had done what she had said she would do, and sorted Scott's life out. She'd helped him find a job so he could start paying Jimmy back, seventy-five pounds a month until the debt was cleared. She hadn't talked to Jimmy in years. Last she'd heard, he'd moved back up north – he must have wanted to get as far away from her as he could. Her *and* Scott.

Scott hesitated. 'I'm not working there anymore.'

'Why? What happened?'

'It's not important—'

'Yes, it is. You should have told me.'

'Why? I don't need to tell you about every little detail. I'm not Carmen. I don't need to ring you every time I wipe my arse so you can say "well done".'

'Don't be unkind to your sister.'

Scott rolled his eyes again.

'So what happened with your job? Last time we spoke, you were still enjoying it—'

'I don't want to talk about it,' he said through gritted teeth.

'Why not? Did something happen? You didn't . . .' she lowered her voice. 'You didn't get *fired*, did you?'

'I said I don't want to talk about it—'

'You *did* get fired—'

'Stop it, Mom!' Scott hissed angrily. 'Why are you always interfering? I'm fucking sick of it.'

Someone at one of the tables behind them laughed. All along, Birdie had said that she didn't want the wake to be a bleak affair, that she wanted people laughing and reminiscing, but now she couldn't fathom what could possibly be so funny. Her mother was dead and her son was talking to her like she was a bit of muck stuck to the bottom of his shoe. There was absolutely nothing to laugh about.

'You know what, I'm done. I'm not staying here so you can interrogate me.'

He turned to go, but Birdie grabbed hold of his sleeve.

'You've only just arrived. This is your nanny's wake, you can't leave—'

'Let go, will you?'

Out of her periphery she could see Carmen and Claudette hurrying towards her. She could see the shock on their faces. Was she making a scene? Was everyone craning their necks to see, to gawk at the spectacle? She didn't care. With a forceful wrench, Scott yanked himself free of Birdie's grip. He took two steps backwards and held up his hands. A plea for her not to get any closer. A barrier which she could not cross.

'Let *go* of me Mom, for fuck's sake. Let go of me.'

'You need to leave,' Carmen said, putting one arm around her mother. So did Claudette. *Why*, Birdie thought, *are they trying to shield me from my own son?*

'Go on, you've caused enough trouble today.'

'He doesn't need to leave,' Birdie insisted, but Scott was already walking away. Denise, her paper plate heaped high with curry and rice, scuttled after him. Birdie could hear conversations tentatively resume behind her, and Carmen asking if she was okay, but she didn't respond. All she could think about was what her mother had said to her.

*Why don't they want to stay with me?*

* * *

## *2012*

Birdie knew that loss was a part of living, but it didn't make the loss any easier to bear. There was no one left who'd known Birdie Brown as a pickney of Portmore, and she felt as though some invisible chain to the past had been broken. But hark at her! *The problem with getting older*, she decided, *is that you have too much time to ruminate.* So she kept busy: days out with Claudette (her friend had a ludicrous idea to climb Snowdon, though they could barely manage to get their backsides to the top of the Lickey Hills); doting on her grandchildren; getting to know her new neighbours on the estate (Precious and Leslie's house had been given back to the council, and Birdie had moved into a one-bedroom flat not too far from where she'd grown up) and volunteering at the local community centre. She'd found a flyer for a group of grannies who played bingo once a week and had called the number at the bottom and asked for Nancy. The woman at the other end of the phone gasped when she introduced herself.

'Not *Birdie Brown*? Birdie, it's me! Nancy Bower! Well, it's Nancy Hall now. Do you remember me?'

Of course Birdie remembered her old school friend. They spent over an hour on the phone catching up as the decades fell away between them. Nancy apologised for not staying in touch, but Birdie said an apology wasn't needed.

'You had your own life to lead,' she said.

And Nancy's life had been a rich one. She'd moved to Australia to teach in a remote school but had not been able to adjust to the heat. After five years she'd returned the UK and on her first day back in the country, she'd accidentally hit a cyclist with her car. He survived, and they'd married three months later. She had five children and twelve grandchildren, with the first great-grandchild on the way. She explained to Birdie that the Bingo Babs was just one of the ways she stayed active during retirement.

'I go to Zumba on a Tuesday and I'm doing a beginner's

Spanish course at Birmingham Library. We have to keep busy, don't we? Otherwise we'll just sit around and stew.'

Birdie agreed. She didn't want to spend her days worrying about her son from a distance, or her daughter's feckless husband, or the life she might be leading if she and Jimmy hadn't come to such blows . . . he was married, according to Carmen. He and his wife travelled a lot. Well. Birdie had never wanted to travel much, had she? She was content with what she had at home.

It was a sunny Saturday morning, and Birdie was surrounded by a sea of red, white and blue. The community centre was hosting an Olympics party for the children, and Birdie had volunteered to decorate. She purchased paper plates and plastic hats and metres and metres of bunting, but she was sure she had some miniature Union flags left over from the Jubilee street party somewhere. The kiddies would love waving them about, if only she could find them.

There was the sound of a key in the lock, and Carmen's voice in the hall.

'Mom?'

'In here,' Birdie called back, her head beneath the bed. 'Carm, do you think it would be unpatriotic to cheer for Usain Bolt? He's such a handsome fella. And he's so *fast*. I saw on the news that he's probably going to beat his own world record and while I'm rooting for *our* girls and boys I don't think anyone will mind if I cheer on Jamaica too, will they?'

She emerged, dusty but triumphant, a clutch of tiny flags in her fist.

'Aha! I *knew* these would come in handy again . . . Carm? Where are the kids?'

'I left them with Andy.'

Carmen was stood in the doorway to Birdie's bedroom, her

face crumpled like a piece of notepaper. Unfortunately, Birdie could read every furrow in her brow.

'What's happened?'

Carmen fiddled with her wedding ring.

'Carmen?'

'Scott's in trouble.'

'What kind of trouble?'

'He was arrested,' Carmen said quickly, hoping to get it over with as soon as she could.

'*Arrested*?'

'Jake – Andy's friend – heard about it down the pub. Scott stole from his employer. They caught him on CCTV.'

Birdie sat on the edge of the bed, the quilted duvet cover rustling beneath her weight. After their altercation at the funeral, Birdie had stepped away and given her son the space he'd asked for. It had felt completely unnatural to her, but she thought it was what he needed. All she had ever wanted was for him to be happy, to be settled . . . she remembered holding him in her arms. *I'll never do it again*. He'd promised her. He'd promised. Oh, Scott . . .

She heard Carmen say something about irrefutable proof, and prison time, without really comprehending the words. Carmen said something else too, about a girlfriend.

'What was that?'

'I said his girlfriend is pregnant, apparently.'

Birdie grasped for a name. 'Denise?'

'No. This one's twenty-something. Can you believe it? He's old enough to be her dad.' Carmen grimaced. 'I bet she only wants a mixed-race baby because she thinks they're cute. Jake's girlfriend Cat said she looks like she uses drugs. I bet *they* both do.'

'I'd know if your brother was on drugs,' Birdie said

immediately, and then realised how foolish a statement that was. What did she know of her son, really? 'They won't go too hard on him, will they?'

'He's looking at six to eight years. It's not your job to clean up his mess, Mom,' Carmen added quickly. 'He's brought all this on himself.'

*Let go of me, Mom.*

Carmen was right. It wasn't her job to clean up his messes. But he was having a *baby* . . .

'Can you find a way to get in touch with his girlfriend? Don't look at me like that, Carmen. Like it or not, she's family now. She's carrying my grandchild, and I have to help her.'

* * *

## *2016*

Life was made up of choices, large and small. Right, and wrong. Birdie, rapidly approaching her seventies, had come to accept this. You had to get on with things and, like her father had once said, hope for the best.

She had her growing family around her – *five* grandchildren, she'd tell anyone who'd listen – and she was content with what she had, though Carmen told her she should expand her horizons a bit.

'Don't be silly. Where would I go, at my age? Besides, I'm needed here. Claud's got a long road of recovery ahead of her, and Tegan—'

Carmen rolled her eyes. They were walking arm in arm around the Bullring, shopping for the twins' birthday. Although it was early summer, it was an unseasonably cold day, and Birdie was wearing her warmest cardigan. Sixty-odd years and she still hated the cold.

'You're always doing everything for other people. It's time you put yourself first, don't you think?'

'By going on holiday?'

'Why not? We're thinking of going away for our anniversary, actually. It'll be twenty-five years next year, can you believe it?'

Birdie couldn't. A quarter of a century, married to Andy Lloyd. Carmen deserved a bloody medal, not a holiday.

'I suggested Tenerife. Won't that be lovely? We haven't been abroad in donkey's years.'

'I'm sure it will.'

'You should come.'

'What?' Birdie was taken aback. 'Really?'

'Of course. I know you don't have a passport, but it's easy to apply these days. We can get a form from the Post Office this afternoon—'

Birdie thought about it for a moment. It would be nice to visit warmer climes. And she was sure she could put up with Andy for a week if it meant sunning her old bones.

She smiled. 'Okay. Let's go and pick up a form.'

She posed for a photo in the little kiosk outside Boots and paid the application fee. She bought herself a sarong and a pair of flip-flops down the indoor market. And then she received a letter saying that her passport application had been denied.

'Maybe we filled out the form wrong,' Carmen surmised. 'But it doesn't really matter. We've decided not to go away after all. We can't really afford it on just my salary.'

'Oh. Alright then.'

It was a shame. But then, there was nothing to suggest

that she couldn't pick up a new form and plan a little holiday for herself, was there? Carmen was right, she should expand her horizons a bit. She could dip into her savings, just this once. When was the last time she'd truly done something for herself? She could go to France, or Spain, or Italy, perhaps. Or perhaps, she thought, as she got off the bus and walked down Purcell Close, she could even go to Jamaica. Fancy her sitting on Treasure Beach in her new sarong and flip-flops!

She put her key in her front door and bent down to pick up the pile of post. Most of it was junk, glossy leaflets and takeaway menus, but there was one small, stiff envelope with her name written in bold, black letters. It looked important.

She opened it.

**NOTICE OF UNLAWFUL IMMIGRATION**

# Nineteen

## *2017*

Birdie sat on a metal bunk bed and stared at the cold, blue wall, paying little mind to the familiar feeling of anxiety gnawing away at her stomach, or the ache in her tired heart, or the numbness of her soul. She hadn't gone for breakfast. She didn't know when she'd last felt hungry, or when she'd last smiled, or how many days she had spent locked up. It had been an indefinite number of days. Waiting to be deported.

It felt inevitable now. Her family kept telling her to have hope, but hope hadn't saved Victorine, or Maliha, and it wouldn't save any of the other women in the removal centre. A week ago, Saffie had called to tell her about some sort of protest she had organised on Birdie's behalf. With breathless confidence, she'd told her nanny about the size of the crowd, the media interest, the growing number of signatures the petition had amassed. Her voice sounded so far away. Birdie was proud of her granddaughter. But she worried for her, too. Saffie was too young to experience such a crushing failure. Her granddaughter believed that she could change the world, but Birdie had learned that some worlds were unchangeable.

If she had left when her mumma had wanted to, right after Winston abandoned them, then none of this would have happened. She wouldn't have her family, but it would have saved her so much pain. Would that have been preferable? Would she be the same Birdie Brown if she hadn't lived the life that she had lived? She didn't know. All she knew was that it would have been easier, as a young gyal, to assimilate herself back into the culture she'd left behind. An old woman had no chance.

Her new cellmate – they'd brought her in after Victorine had been taken, a revolving door of the unwanted – told her that she should start 'practising her accent' for when she arrived in Jamaica.

'So you don't stick out so much,' she said. 'If they think you're English they'll take you for a ride.'

She was trying to be kind, but what did it matter what Birdie sounded like? Shedding her Birmingham accent wouldn't soften the blow when the axe finally fell. She remembered Luce once saying that she sounded like an English pickney, and she heard again her disappointed voice echoing around her head. *It's not my fault*, she wanted to say. *None of this is my fault.*

Birdie remembered the day Winston told her they were leaving Jamaica. Puppa's smile, his foot bouncing, like a man forcing himself to be static when all he wanted to do was stride away from the table and never look back. Her mother's face, already etched in grief, already mourning a life she didn't want to leave, but one that she would give up for love. Their choices had set her on a trajectory. Perhaps this holding cell had always been the inevitable outcome.

At night, the faces of those she'd loved came to her, like ghosts, floating through the locked doors. Winston, Precious, Luce. Her children and grandchildren. Jimmy. The people who'd known her at every stage in her life. All the different versions of Birdie she had been. She thought of all the sadness she'd endured in life, and all the happiness too. She traced her hands over her skull, feeling the lines of her face. She ran her hands through her salt and pepper hair. Was it flesh and bone that made a person? Or was it their legacies, those they left behind? Was it their decisions, their choices, their regrets? Was it the communities they built for themselves, and the homes they created? Did a stamp in a missing passport define somebody? Or was it their memories, the stories they told, the things they remembered?

What would people remember about her, when she was gone?

Somewhere, a door clanged. Footsteps paced along the corridor. The door opened, and she slowly turned her head.

They were calling her name.

# Twenty

## *2017*

'They're letting me out.' Birdie could hardly speak. She was sat on the bottom bunk, her cheap mobile phone shaking in her hands.

She heard Carmen gasp.

'What?'

'I said, they're letting me out.'

'Oh my *God*. When? Now? Are you sure? Mom? Mom, are you there?'

Yes, she was sure. Birdie had been called to the warden's office and told she was being released. She'd asked him to repeat himself. She'd asked him to repeat himself three times, and the warden had gotten shirty with her.

'Do you *want* to stay?'

On the walk back to her cell she had pinched herself, hard enough to leave a bruise. She looked at it as Carmen cried in her ear, a welt on her forearm as big as a fifty pence piece. *It's real*, she thought. *I'm going home.*

It had taken her twenty minutes to pack up her belongings in a clear plastic bag. She left the tracksuit she had been given neatly folded at the foot of her bed and sat impatiently in the visitors' room. It took hours for her family to arrive. Her foot jiggled beneath the table. *Hurry up, Carm—*

And then suddenly they were there, with watery eyes and triumphant smiles. Saffie grabbed her left arm and Carmen her right, as though they were worried she might lift off and float away. Lewis and Jade argued over who got to carry her plastic bag. Birdie held her breath as she crossed the threshold, waiting for someone to yank her backwards and haul her back to her cell. But it didn't happen.

She was free.

On the long drive home, she was quiet. Carmen kept reaching over to pat her knee. Saffie livestreamed the journey until her battery died. They passed a sign that said 'Birmingham, 50 miles'.

'We're nearly home, Mom,' Carmen said, and the children cheered from the back seat.

Lewis had painted a sheet to read 'WECLOME HOME NANNY' (Carmen refused to let him ruin a second sheet. *Perhaps Nanny won't notice*, she'd said) and hung it from his bedroom window, and Andy had ordered an Indian. They would have done more, Carmen apologised, but it was so short notice.

'It's fine. I don't want a fuss,' Birdie said.

'No, don't say that. We should celebrate properly – we could have a party with all your friends.'

'No. No party. I just want things to go back to normal.' She glanced around at her family, hoping she was imagining the looks of trepidation on their faces. 'Things *will* go back to normal now, right?'

'That's what we need to ask the MP,' Saffie said pragmatically. 'She wants to come by tomorrow to speak to you. She said she's bringing someone from her PR team.'

'She wants all the glory, I suppose,' Andy scoffed on the way to the kitchen, his hands loaded with dirty plates, though Saffie was more generous.

'She *is* the one who got Nanny out. Although she said my social media campaign was the . . . hang on, what did she call it? The "spark that started a fire".' Saffie couldn't help a tiny, satisfied smile. 'She said she had absolutely no idea what was going on in those removal centres and as soon as she heard she was moved to shine a light on the injustice—'

'That's bullshit,' Andy shouted over the roar of the hot tap. 'She was content to sit on her bum and do nothing until you made her look bad on TV.'

'Your dad's right,' Carmen said. In the kitchen, Andy punched the air like a scoring midfielder.

'It doesn't matter *why* they let you out,' Saffie stressed, turning to her grandmother. 'The real battle is making sure you *stay* out. Marley said that a cycle of arrest and release is quite common—'

'No.' Birdie's hands clenched around her knees. 'I'm not going back in there.'

She would rather die than go back.

'Hey, it's okay. With the MP on our side, it's looking good for us.'

It was better than okay. The next morning, Susan Cartland arrived and, perched self-importantly on Carmen's crushed velvet settee, personally invited Birdie to reapply for Indefinite Leave to Remain. *There won't be a fee*, she said ceremoniously, as the photographer – an intern who found local politics more choked up in tedious red tape than he'd imagined – snapped a few photos on his phone.

Birdie wanted to know why she wouldn't have to pay a

fee, but Susan Cartland said that she shouldn't worry about that.

'Just focus on your wonderful family and move on from this horrid ordeal. It was absolutely my pleasure to intervene on your behalf, Ms Brown. I'll be raising your case at PMQs next week. You have my guarantee that, while I remain your MP, I will continue to fight for the victims of Home Office cruelty—'

Marley had never heard of them waiving the fee before.

'*No one* has. It's unprecedented,' he added, presenting the forms for her to sign.

Whatever the reason, Birdie's third and final application was approved and she was told to visit her nearest UK Visa and Citizenship Application Service Point (*Christ*, Carmen said. *That's a mouthful*) to have her biometric ID card processed. After that, she'd be able to apply for British citizenship, once and for all.

Citizenship would not make her a different person, Birdie knew. And yet with it, she would be able to walk down the street without looking behind her. She could sleep soundly without fear of being dragged from her bed in the middle of the night.

Not unless they changed the rules, again.

Could they?

Would they?

* * *

## *2018*

It had been over a year since Birdie had been freed from the detention centre. In that time, her pension had been reinstated and she'd moved into a place of her own near Carmen's and taken her place back in the community: sticky finger painting at the crèche; bingo with the Babs; a cup of tea and a gossip with Rita once a week; dinner with Tegan and Jaxon every Friday and regular visits with Scott. Carmen and the kids popped in and out as they pleased, bouncing between the two houses like yo-yos. She and Michelle took Claudette to Snowdonia for her seventy-fifth birthday; they caught the train to the top of the mountain and drank champagne from plastic cups.

'Here's to you,' Birdie said warmly, but Claudette corrected her.

'Here's to *you*,' she said, leaning heavily on her walking stick. 'I don't think I could live without you, sis. Thank God it's all over.'

Everyone kept saying that. *It's all over. You can move on.* But although her life had been restored, Birdie feared she would be tied to the Windrush Scandal for the rest of her life.

Her seventieth birthday was approaching. So too was the seventieth anniversary of the sailing of the *Windrush*, a fact which people found fascinating. *Fancy being born on the same day*, they said. *No wonder you were caught up in it.*

'My father went to see the ship at the dock. He nearly missed my birth,' she'd reply, and then she'd tell the story the way Luce used to tell it, because it was funny, and she wanted people to laugh. Because if she thought about the scandal, she might cry.

The day before her birthday, a local journalist called and asked how she was going to celebrate.

'Quietly,' she responded. 'A meal with my family, no fuss.'

'But surely, after the time you had, you'd want to make a big splash? Go wild, fulfil your heart's desires, that sort of thing?'

'I've already got everything I want. I've got my family and my health. I'm happy.'

'And your citizenship ceremony is next week, right? What a treat for the birthday girl.'

It was the last letter Birdie would receive from the Home Office. She'd stuck it to the fridge with a magnet from Dudley Zoo.

**We are pleased to invite you to a ceremony during which you will be bestowed with British Citizenship.**

'I wouldn't call it a treat,' Birdie said. 'Not that I want to sound ungrateful, of course—'

'Of course. But I bet you're excited, aren't you? To finally be British?'

*I was British all along*, she wanted to say, but she had a feeling that wasn't the answer he was after. So she just said yes, she was excited, and then he had one last question for her.

'What would you say to the government about the Windrush Scandal?'

'No comment,' she said firmly. So many people, West-Indian migrants, just like her, had been rounded up and ripped from their homes, and the figure was growing daily. It hadn't been a comfort to learn her experience was not a unique one – if anything, it made her feel even more insignificant, like a careless mistake someone had tried to rub out. What had she done wrong? What had any of them done wrong? She still didn't know. Saffie was pestering her to speak to the journalist who'd blown the lid off the story, but Birdie refused. What if she got in trouble with the Home Office? She wasn't a British citizen *yet*. She didn't want to rock the boat, for fear it might upset the precarious safety she'd found. Saffie said that they couldn't do that, but Birdie wasn't taking any chances. She knew they could do whatever they liked.

'Alright,' said the journalist, disappointed he hadn't gotten a juicy quote. 'Everyone at *Daily Smethwick News* wishes you a happy birthday, Bridget.'

'It's Birdie,' she said, but he'd already hung up. She sighed and caught sight of the letter on the fridge.

Please let it be over soon.

* * *

Birdie woke on her birthday to a brilliant blue sky and a new ache in her hip that demanded she acknowledge the mile-stone. Seventy years old.

*Happy birthday, Birdie Brown.*

She stared at the ceiling, the vestiges of a dream clinging to the edge of her subconscious. She thought she'd dreamed about her parents but before she could pull it back into sharp focus, her mobile phone buzzed on the nightstand, and their smiling faces faded away. She had a flurry of calls and texts from her loved ones and then, as she tucked into a birthday breakfast of ackee and saltfish, her son rang her from prison.

'Happy birthday, Mom.'

'Thanks, Scott.' Birdie set down her fork and smiled. 'Sixty-three days to go.'

'Sixty-three days.'

Her son was being let out on probation. When she'd heard the news, she had wept with joy, but Scott was filled with quiet trepidation.

'I've only ever seen Jaxon across a table,' he'd said. 'What if he doesn't like me in real life? And what if I'm no good at being a dad? I don't know what I'm doing.'

'Then you'll learn. Being a parent is *hard*, Scott,' she'd said with gentle firmness. 'You'll have to work at it, every day, and you'll make mistakes. But it's worth it. I promise you.'

They chatted about Birdie's plans for the day, and then Scott said that his time was nearly up.

'Love you, Mom,' he said before he hung up the phone. 'We'll celebrate together when I'm out, alright?'

Birdie couldn't wait.

* * *

Carmen took her for a birthday lunch in the city centre. They caught the train from Galton Bridge to New Street Station, where Carmen guided her enthusiastically through the throngs of casual midday shoppers.

'We're here!' she cried upon reaching their destination, and Birdie gasped in surprise, her open-mouthed reflection mirrored in the polished glass doors.

'Not The Ivy, Carm! You can't afford this. Honestly, Wetherspoons is good enough for me—'

'Not for your seventieth birthday it's not,' Carmen said, smiling at the maître d' and asking for two glasses of champagne before they'd even sat down.

'Carmen!' Birdie said, overwhelmed by the largesse, but Carmen told her to stop fussing.

'This is on Andy. He's done a lot of overtime this month especially and he said to order whatever you want, no expense spared.'

Birdie's mouth fell open a second time. 'Well,' was all she managed to splutter. 'You two are certainly in a better place.'

'We are,' Carmen beamed. 'And it was all because he stood up to the police.'

'He did what?'

'Didn't I ever tell you that story?' Carmen accepted a slender flute of champagne from a friendly waitress. 'The police came to shut down the protest and he dived right in front of Saffie like some kind of action hero. He looked just like Bruce Willis, only with more hair. It was *really* sexy—'

Birdie pulled a face.

'It was! And then—'

'You made up?' Birdie said quickly. She didn't want the gory details.

'After a long talk, yes. We stayed up all night. I told him he needed to find a job or else I would leave him. And I told him some other things as well. About Dean—'

'Dean?'

'It's not important. What's important is that Andy *listened*.' She lowered her voice reverentially, as though she were recounting a miracle. 'And he's been trying really hard ever since.'

'Well,' Birdie said after a pause. 'I'm glad. You deserve to be happy.'

'So do you, Mom. Cheers.'

After lunch, they wandered arm in arm around the giant John Lewis in Grand Central. Birdie needed a new dress for the ceremony – she'd put back on all the weight she had lost, and a little bit more for good measure – but she couldn't decide between one of a pretty pink and one of a soft, spring green.

'Get both,' Carmen suggested, but Birdie shook her head. 'Go on. Treat yourself! You can wear one tonight.'

'I don't need a new dress for tonight. We're only going for a carvery.'

'It might be nice to get dressed up,' Carmen said ambiguously, so Birdie, after dithering for a few minutes more, purchased both dresses and carried them protectively, in sheaths of shiny plastic, over her arm. She also ordered Declan and Angharad's wedding present, a dinner service with a delicate blue design lapping the circumference of the plates, like waves breaking against the shore. They weren't getting married until July, but she wanted to be organised. It would be no time at all before she needed to start thinking about her Christmas list . . .

Their train was delayed, so Carmen said she'd get them both a cheeky drink from Marks & Spencer for the journey home. As Carmen waited in the queue, Birdie wandered out to the station concourse and gazed up at the dome-like atrium. It all looked so new, so modern and white, with coffee shops and gleaming storefronts and a champagne bar, where three bottle blondes in expensive jackets clinked glasses of fizz and brayed with assertive confidence. The old station, where she and her mother had waited for her father, had been demolished decades ago. She looked around the concourse, passengers swarming about like bees, and tried to picture it – Mumma's growing anxiety, the noise, the smoke, her first glimpse of Puppa after a year apart – but the image in her mind could not be superimposed over the top of reality. It had all been torn down. Or torn away. Ripped out of history. Another piece of evidence that she had been here, that she had arrived in England on the day she said she did, gone . . .

'Mom? Ready to go?'

Before they parted ways at Galton Bridge, Carmen gave her mother a big hug, the plastic sheaths crumpling between them.

'I'll see you in a few hours,' Carmen said. 'And I forgot to say – Saffie said she'll meet us at the restaurant because she'll be coming straight from a seminar.'

'She didn't mention that on the phone this morning.'

'Perhaps they changed her timetable at the last minute,' Carmen said vaguely. 'I don't know how university works. Right. I'll pick you up at six!'

Birdie walked the short distance to her new home in the late afternoon sun. There was a large pile of birthday cards waiting for her on the welcome mat and she arranged them on the mantle, beneath the photo that Saffie had had restored. Her armchair and dresser had been rescued from Andy's shed, though Precious's plates were not on display. After the accident only three remained and Birdie had given one to Carmen, one to Saffie, and one to Jade. A little reminder of where they came from.

The house looked nice, Birdie had said, once she'd straightened out the jumble of furnishings and crockery and bedding that had been donated by friends and family, but it didn't really feel like *home* yet. Perhaps it just hadn't been lived in long enough. It took time for a person to settle into a place, to seep into the walls, to become part of the furniture. She couldn't, after all, think of Auntie Luce without picturing her in front of the stove, or Mumma without seeing the sewing machine. Puppa would always belong on the back veranda, sipping coffee as the sun stretched overhead, beckoning him towards the horizon.

She remembered when Saffie had asked her what 'home' meant to her, and even now she was still pondering the question. It had to be more than just a place to keep your things, didn't it? More than a roof over your head? She thought about it as she got ready, slipping the green dress over her head. The soft material crackled with static as she adjusted her wig. Perhaps one day she'd come up with a good answer.

Carmen beeped her horn from outside. Birdie took one last

look in the mirror then picked up her handbag and left the house. She smiled politely at her next-door neighbour, who returned a suspicious stare. She tried not to be offended. Friendships took time to marinate, she knew. Acceptance took even longer.

'You look beautiful,' Carmen said as Birdie got into the car, eyeing the green dress with approval.

'So do you.'

Carmen was wearing a low-cut top of deep purple and pair of pleather trousers Andy had bought for her, and she felt the most attractive she'd felt in years.

'Where are Andy and the kids?' Birdie asked.

'He had to work late,' Carmen said offhandedly, checking her wing mirror and refusing to meet her mother's gaze. 'They'll meet us there.'

Birdie hadn't been born yesterday. She'd known about the surprise party for weeks – she'd overheard Carmen on the phone to the caterer ('I know mutton is cheaper, but curry goat isn't curry goat if it's mutton instead of goat, is it?'). At first, she had wanted to tell her daughter not to bother, to cancel it, but then she remembered that her family and friends had shared the load of the ordeal too. Maybe it was what *they* needed to move on. God knows they deserved it.

They pulled up outside the community centre, blanketed in darkness, and Birdie feigned surprise.

'What are we doing here?'

'This is the address Saffie gave me,' Carmen said in artificial shock, one hand on the car door. 'I'm just as baffled as you are. We should find out what's going on.'

Birdie carefully arranged her face as Carmen held the front door open for her.

'After you, Mom.'

She took a step into the darkness and waited for someone to turn on the light. Then, she was knocked backwards by a sudden shock of noise. The steel band began a rousing refrain of "For She's a Jolly Good Fellow" and hugs and kisses rained down from all directions, an outpouring of love. She felt her eyes fill with unexpected, grateful tears.

It was a wonderful party, with laughter, music and food. Yellow, green and black streamers hung from the ceiling, and red, white and blue balloons covered the parquet floor. Once every lick of curry goat had been mopped up, and every last grain of glistening rice had been chased from the plate, Carmen got to her feet and clinked on the side of her glass.

'Thank you all for coming tonight,' she smiled, glassy-eyed. 'As you all know, we've had a tough time of it as a family. But Mom finally gets her citizenship next week—' the room erupted with applause, 'which means they can't kick her out, not now, not ever!'

Carmen turned to Birdie, her lipstick smile stretched wide.

'You've always been there for me. We might argue from time to time, but I love you to the moon and back. I couldn't ask for a better mother.'

She threw her arms around Birdie and she squeezed her back, unable to speak around the lump in her throat. Then, the assembled guests began to bang in unison on the tables.

*Speech. Speech. Speech.*

Birdie shook her head no, but the chanting got louder. *They won't stop!* Carmen laughed.

Birdie stood to a chorus of drunken cheers and waited for them to settle down before she began in a wavering voice.

'I just want to say . . .' She tailed off and stared towards the back of the room. Her breath hitched in her throat. It couldn't be . . . A blurry figure dressed in a mauve shirt had slipped through the door and was standing hesitantly in the half shadows. Her stomach swooped as she thought about how much she'd struggled over the damn buttonholes, and the way he'd smiled and declared he would save it for best . . .

'I . . .'

Carmen poked her in the arm and Birdie turned towards her. The look on her daughter's face told her that *she* was the one behind this, and she could also tell that Carmen wasn't sorry at all.

'Say something!' Carmen whispered, and Birdie looked back into the crowd. Her eyes found his again. She took a deep breath.

'I just want to say that I am so grateful for all that I have. It's been a wonderful evening, and I thank you all from the bottom of my heart.'

She looked around the room at the familiar faces. The family and friends she had collected over the years. The people she loved most in the world.

'Like Carmen said, it's been a difficult few years, but it's over now.'

Was it over? Everyone else seemed to think so. They all thought she should be looking to the future again, just like the passengers of the *Windrush* had looked forward, the smell of sea salt lingering in the air as they imagined the better life that waited for them in England. So why was she waiting for something to go wrong?

Someone dimmed the lights, and Saffie strode up to the table, a pink and white cake in her hands, her face illuminated by glow of seventy candles.

'Make a wish, Nanny!'

*Make a wish*. Birdie knew exactly what to wish for. She wanted a life without fear. She wanted a life where she didn't have to question her identity. And she wanted to know, without a shadow of a doubt, that they wouldn't try to take her away again.

Cameras flashed. Birdie inhaled. Then she looked up at her granddaughter's face and she stopped.

She shouldn't be wasting her wish like that. Not when she already knew who she was. She was Birdie Brown. She was a daughter, a mother, a grandmother. She didn't need a piece of paper from the government to confirm that, did she? And as for her fear . . . she'd lived long enough to know that fear and uncertainty were unavoidable in life. What she really wanted was a life filled with *hope*. Hope for Carmen's continued happiness, and the hope that Scott could step up as a father. Hope for her grandchildren, that they would always feel like they belonged.

The crowd began singing an off-key rendition of "Happy Birthday". Even in the semi-darkness, Birdie could feel Jimmy's eyes on her. She hoped, too, that they could have another chance together – after all, this wasn't the first time he'd come back to her, was it? And most of all, she hoped that her remaining years, however many she might have, were happy ones.

Birdie didn't notice Lewis and Jade sneaking up behind her with confetti cannons.

Yellow and green confetti rained down from the ceiling in slow motion.

She made her wish.

# Author's Note

Like many people, I learned about the Windrush Scandal when the news broke in April 2018. Amelia Gentleman, a journalist for the *Guardian*, published an article entitled "The children of Windrush: I'm here legally, but they're asking me to prove I'm British", in which eight Caribbean-born individuals shared their harrowing stories of being asked to prove their British citizenship. If they could not, they would be deported. They were the victims of then-Home Secretary Theresa May's "Hostile Environment", a policy designed to make life in the UK so unbearable for those without Indefinite Leave to Remain that they would voluntarily leave. But these eight were not the only victims. In fact, thousands of Commonwealth citizens, many of whom had spent the majority of their lives in the UK, had been wrongly classified as illegal immigrants and faced the threat of detention and deportation. The article caused public outcry, but it took weeks for the government to admit its mistake. By that point, the damage had already been done – lives had been shattered, and families had been ripped apart.

While Birdie's story is a work of fiction, I have tried to be as accurate as possible regarding what the real victims of the Windrush Scandal went through and the support – or lack thereof – that they had available to them. For example, there exist charities much like the organisation where Marley volunteers that offer assistance to immigrants who cannot afford or access legal aid. Yarl's Wood is a real immigration removal centre that houses adult women and families indefinitely. Birdie Brown could be a very real person in your community. A compensation scheme for victims was launched in 2019 by the Home Office, but not every victim of the scandal has received the justice they deserve. At the time of writing, sixty-six claimants have died while waiting for the government to make good on its word.

In researching this book, alongside the memories of my own family members, I drew upon a number of accounts from the Windrush Generation, as well as critiques of the scandal, including: *Hostile Environment: How Immigrants Became Scapegoats* by Maya Goodfellow (Verso, 2019); *The Windrush Betrayal* by Amelia Gentleman (Faber, 2019); *Homecoming: Voices of the Windrush Generation* by Colin Grant (Vintage, 2019); and *Windrush: The Irresistible Rise of Multi-Racial Britain* by Mike and Trevor Philips (HarperCollins, 1998).

# Acknowledgements

This book is about the power of community. I am so grateful for mine.

Firstly, thanks to Gemma Milne for making an introduction that changed my life. To my agent, Laura Williams: I am beyond grateful for the work you put in to make this book a reality. I've said this before, but I shall go on saying it – I could not have done this without you! Thanks to my editor, Kate Bradley – from the very beginning I have felt like I am in safe hands, and it means so much that Birdie found such a brilliant champion in you. Also thanks to Renée Lewis, Laura Gerrard, Helen Gould and the whole HarperFiction team for your care and dedication. Thank you to Sarah Foster for the incredible cover artwork.

My family is present on every page and in every paragraph. Thanks to my mum and dad for letting me spend my entire childhood with my nose in a book, and to Devina, Demi and Marcus for a lifetime of love and laughter. With them, I know exactly where I belong.

This book is dedicated to my grandparents: Nancy, Bert, Jim and Janice. I hope I've made them proud, but I'd also like to give thanks to Auntie Noreen for sharing her life story with me, particularly her memories of her arrival in England. I wish she'd also shared her chicken, rice and peas recipe with me (seriously, mine never tastes quite as good), but I am grateful for that time we spent together.

Thanks to the staff at the Library of Birmingham and Birmingham and Wolverhampton Archives for their assistance while researching this book. Special thanks to the West Midlands Writers' Club for taking me into their midst – I've learned so much, in such a short space of time, and gained some new friends too.

Thanks to Sarah Robinson for being a friend when I needed one most, and thank you to Alice Lloyd, Amy Drake, Anna Hajilari and Sophie Kilmartin for making the Jewellery Quarter feel like home. Thanks also to Jackie Hall for all the invaluable advice and encouragement.

Finally, thanks to the three people whose support means more than they could ever possibly realise: Rebecca Snell, the wisest of souls and the walking embodiment of 'tough love'; Philip Ellis, the person I can always rely on for writerly advice and constructive criticism (usually followed by a cocktail); and Paul Geary – thank you for being my most ardent and vocal supporter, right from day one. I love you.